"NOW, GARY, NOW!"

Manning made no reply. He didn't need to. The automatic grenade launcher began spewing 40-millimeter death at the already crippled motor launch. The grenades blew the little boat to cinders, biting off great chunks of it, as if the vessel were being devoured from stern to bow. The flaming bodies that were thrown into the sea bore horrible testament to the destruction.

McCarter turned his attention back to the boat that was still moving.

Grimaldi did the same. He was harrying the motor launches to keep them from targeting the Filipino ship again with their handheld rockets.

From what McCarter could see of the men on the decks, they didn't look military. At least, they weren't wearing uniforms. But there was more. Military men had a certain bearing and, from what little he could see through the smoke, the sailors on the motor launch didn't have it. They were casual. Pirates, or maybe civilian contractors. But how would such men get their hands on the latest high-tech weapons from the US, weapons whose export was strictly controlled?

Either RhemCorp was careless or RhemCorp was dirty. But they didn't yet know which.

DON PENDLETON'S

STONY

AMERICA'S ULTRA-COVERT INTELLIGENCE AGENCY

MAN ®

WAR TACTIC

A GOLD EAGLE BOOK FROM

W☉RLDWIDE ®

TORONTO • NEW YORK • LONDON
AMSTERDAM • PARIS • SYDNEY • HAMBURG
STOCKHOLM • ATHENS • TOKYO • MILAN
MADRID • WARSAW • BUDAPEST • AUCKLAND

Recycling programs
for this product may
not exist in your area.

First edition August 2015

ISBN-13: 978-0-373-80452-8

War Tactic

Special thanks and acknowledgment to
Phil Elmore for his contribution to this work.

Printed in U.S.A.

WAR TACTIC

PROLOGUE

The South China Sea

Yanuar Wijeya squinted at the ship in the distance as he stood on the bow of the *Penuh Belut*, a rust-eaten, twenty-five-meter *dhow*, or Arab freighter, that served as the mother-tender to his two fast-attack motor craft. Salt spray flecked his face. In his gnarled fingers he held a pair of binoculars, only one half of which still worked. The other set of lenses was badly cracked and stained. With one eye closed, he could see his first mate, Mhusa, in the lead fast-attack vessel. The deceptively soft popping of gunfire, mild at this distance, told him that his men were already taking fire from the Filipino freighter.

The freighter was a large one, many times the size of his own craft. While it could have outrun the *Penuh Belut*, it had no chance to flee the motor craft. The captain of the Filipino vessel had opted to turn and fight rather than let Mhusa's crew use the freighter for target practice.

Wijeya wore combat boots without laces on otherwise bare, callused feet. His cut-off jeans were bleached yellow-white from dirt, oil and the pitiless sun. The handle of a machete jutted from the MOLLE-equipped scabbard on his back, which also bore a pistol-grip shotgun. In the rhinestone-studded belt that barely held his pants above his hips, Wijeya carried two Indonesian *kerambit* knives. The ring-handled knives with their curved blades were the only reminder of his homeland, which was otherwise a place he was happy to leave behind. Also behind his belt was a pitted Soviet Bloc Makarov pistol. Wijeya had himself pried the pistol from the fingers of a dead man.

From the pouch tied to his belt, Wijeya took a khat leaf, telling himself he would permit himself no more this afternoon. The drug was a pleasant one, a stimulant that sharpened his senses, helped him keep his edge. He had, however, seen too many men fall under the spell of the leaves. He had no desire to hollow himself out, or worse, to become distracted and sick if the supply were to dry up. Khat, like every other luxury aboard the *Penuh Belut*, ebbed and flowed. There were days that they were rich and days that they were poor. Until very recently, the poor days had far outnumbered the rich ones.

But not so much now.

As if his benefactor could read his thoughts, the satellite phone in Wijeya's pocket began to vibrate. Sighing, the pirate captain pulled the device out and pressed the glowing green key. The voice he heard was familiar. Its owner had never wasted time saying hello to him, or asking after the well-being of his crew.

"Are you on schedule?"

"We are doing it now," Wijeya answered. He was not an uneducated man. He spoke English well; he had attended the National University of Singapore, a final gift from his once-affluent parents. His father had been a supremely arrogant man, unable to see the folly of his ways even when a series of reckless investments had left the family destitute. The thought made Wijeya want to laugh. His benefactor reminded him often of his father. It was the haughty way both men spoke. Perhaps, one day, the invisible man on the satellite phone would swallow a gun barrel the way Wijeya's father had.

The thought brought a smile to the pirate's lips.

If only my father could see how far I've come, he thought. There was real bitterness in him, he knew. But a man was what he was. He remained as he had been made.

"We are taking the ship now," Wijeya said. He pressed the working half of the binoculars closer to his eye and recited the registration number of the vessel. "This is the one you specified, yes?"

"Yes," said the voice. "Are you in the correct position? The locations have been calculated for specific impact. It's a pattern. I don't want you to deviate from it."

"This you say to me every time we speak. I waited until we reached the coordinates you specified. I was careful. I am always careful."

"See that it remains that way," the voice warned. "Your success in the region is thanks to the XM-Thorns I've been sending you."

"Yes. This I know," said Wijeya. "Very well. You promised us more. And more rifles. More ammunition for them."

"You will have it," the voice promised. "Put in to your usual port and I'll make sure the provisions are waiting for you. I always do."

"Yes," said Wijeya. "This I know."

"No prisoners this time," said the voice. "Leave none alive."

"But—" Wijeya began.

The line went dead. Wijeya took the phone from his ear and stared at it. Always, it was the owner of the voice who cut off the transmission. Never had the mysterious speaker bothered with parting sentiments. The pirate switched the phone to standby, noting the battery charge percentage, and tucked it back into his pocket.

He told himself that this invisible man, the voice, was a means to an end. He had first encountered emissaries of the voice while in one of the ports of call his crew frequented. Those had been lean days, scratching out a living taking whatever vessels they could, never daring to attack a ship much larger than their own. Controlling the crew, in those days, had likewise been difficult. It was back then that Wijeya had been forced to fall back on his Silat training; the martial art of the blade that, when he had learned it as a child of privilege, had been little more than theory to him.

Again he laughed to himself. When his father had agreed to pay for private lessons from a wizened old man from a nearby village—a man renowned for his Silat prowess—no doubt Wijeya's parents had thought the move one to keep their rebellious son out of trouble. Give him the discipline of a martial art, they had thought. Give him something to fill his idle hours. Yet today Wijeya had killed no less than four men in personal hand-to-hand combat with his *kerambit* knives. Three of those had been crew members who sought to take the title of captain from Wijeya. One had been a drunken fool in a port town, who had been quicker with a switchblade than Wijeya would have thought the old drunk capable. The scar that now curled across Wijeya's abdomen was proof of that.

He told himself to focus on the task at hand, to stop wool-gathering while his face grew slick with droplets of sea foam. Once more he pressed the working lens of the binoculars to his eye. Behind him, he could hear Lemat, the little Frenchman, bearing the walkie-talkie. Lemat's approach was wreathed in static. Wijeya smiled at his own joke.

"Captain," said Lemat. "The launches report they are ready."

"Tell them to begin the attack," Wijeya directed, never taking his eye from the motor craft circling the target freighter. Sporadic gunfire continued from the deck of the target ship. That was a surprise, honestly.

Shipping lines, despite the increased dangers to their freight from pirate crews like Wijeya's, had felt the turn of the global economy just as had everyone else. They were always looking for ways to cut costs. One of the methods they employed was cutting back crews, which left little extra manpower for such things as guards. Wijeya knew that some of the ship captains had taken it on themselves to purchase, quite illegally, arms with which to equip their men. The idea was that in the event of pirate attack, the crew would take up weapons and fight off boarders. Every major shipping company had corporate policies forbidding this practice, but men had a way of ignoring rules that could get them slaughtered.

Still, it would not matter. Not in this case.

"Move us in," Wijeya told Lemat. "Prepare to support our boarding crews."

Lemat gave the order. The *Penuh Belut* began to vibrate beneath him as her diesel engines thrummed to life. Large quantities of black smoke began to spew from the aft section of the old boat. Wijeya knew every inch of the *dhow*'s deck plates, every streak of rust, every weld. He had spent more years aboard her now than he cared to think.

"Sir?" Lemat prompted. He held the walkie-talkie to his ear. "Mhusa asks if he may fire rockets."

"Tell him above the water line only," Wijeya said. He waited while Lemat relayed the order. Moments later streaks of smoke joined the motor launches and the upper decks of their target. The explosions that rang out scattered men from the deck of the larger ship. Soon, automatic gunfire from Wijeya's attack boats carried across the water.

The automatic weapons were nothing special, but they were reasonably new and all in good working order. Kalashnikov rifles were plentiful in this part of the world. A man with enough cash could purchase a warehouse full of them for twenty dollars US each. But Wijeya's benefactor saw to it that the flow of ammunition for the weapons, new and reliable magazines, and parts for repair was steady. The voice knew Wijeya's major ports of call in the area and never failed to arrange for supply drops.

More important than the automatic weapons, however, were the XM-Thorns. The high-tech rocket launchers had given Wijeya the power to take on craft many times his size. The rockets and their launch tubes were made of a high-tech, carbon-fiber and alloy combination that resisted salt corrosion, making the weapons light and easy to store aboard ship. With the XM-Thorns, it was possible for Wijeya's launches to attack even a cruise liner if they so chose.

Large craft had a number of weaponry that could be employed against pirate ships. The bigger the enemy craft, the greater the danger. Some of the weapons employed by captains in the region were approved by their corporate masters and some were not. While cowardly businessmen disapproved of giving crewmembers SKS rifles or handguns, they were happy with anything that was not a gun that could still drive away the likes of Wijeya. One of the most popular options, given the vast quantity of water available, was high-pressure hoses. Another, employed mostly by the affluent cruise liners, was a sound cannon. Wijeya, before his benefactor had found him, had once been on the receiving end of such a sound weapon. It had been…unpleasant.

But everything had changed one day in a seedy bar in Manila. Wijeya and what was left of his crew at the time—Mhusa, Lemat and two or three others—had been drinking away their latest failure, determined to use up the last of their coin. Staring into the bottom of a dirty glass full of rum, not sure what he would do next or how he would survive, Wijeya had thought perhaps he was destined to keep failing at life. Bitter recriminations had rolled through his mind, waves crashing on the breakers of his failed dreams.

But then a stranger had handed him a business card.

Wijeya remembered looking up at the stranger. The man had the look of a go-between, a messenger. Nothing about his features was remarkable. The stranger had nodded once at the card then disappeared into the smoky darkness of the bar.

On the card was written nothing but a phone number. It had taken a few more drinks before Wijeya's curiosity got the better of him. Expecting some sort of scam, some kind of confidence routine, he had dialed the number, prepared to take out his frustrations on whoever answered. It would feel good to shout at someone. Perhaps then he would get into a fight. With the cracked receiver of the bar's pay phone to his lips, he listened to the ringing at the other end while sizing up the other patrons in the bar.

There, he thought. That one. The one with the fat face and the loud mouth. He looks like he might be Samoan. I will enjoy putting my fist through that face.

But then a voice had answered the telephone call.

Over the course of many telephone calls to come, Wijeya would come to know that voice, the voice of his benefactor, very well. The voice had told him that a very special man was being sought, a man who could take instructions exactly. The reward for following such instructions would be wealth and success, more than any pirate could ever want. The means through which this would be done were simple: all a good pirate needed to conquer even the largest vessels was the correct weaponry. Would the latest XM-Thorn rockets, capable of sinking even a cruise ship, not be sufficient to such a task?

Wijeya had told the voice he thought it might be.

And so Wijeya had entered into the service of the mysterious voice. He supposed he would never know how long the voice's agents had spied on him, watched him and evaluated him before Wijeya was finally given the business card. It did not matter. He did not care. All he cared about was money. Thanks to his benefactor, thanks to the voice, there had been plenty of that.

Wijeya had often considered the possibility that his was not the only crew his benefactor had chosen to finance. This simply made sense. Whatever the voice might be trying to accomplish, the pirate attacks were clearly being coordinated across a large area. That explained why the coordinates were so precise, and it also explained the voice's insistence on strict timetables. A single pirate ship that started attacking where it was not supposed to could easily run afoul of other crews funded by the voice, could it not? At least, that was how it seemed to Wijeya. Not for the first time, he pondered what it was his benefactor might be trying to do. And then…what would happen to Wijeya and his crew when the voice achieved its goal?

In the back of his mind Wijeya knew that there was great danger here. It might not be near. It might be many years yet in coming. But he was not stupid. He knew that his benefactor had something more in mind than simply advancing the lifestyles of pirate crews. Wijeya's attacks were very specific, conducted at times and locations of the voice's choosing. Sometimes the targets were also specified, and other times it was enough that he find any vessel within a given range of coordinates. Just what this was accomplishing for the voice, Wijeya did not and could not know. But he knew he was a pawn. He knew that when his usefulness to the voice ended, he would either be cut loose to make his own way or he would be killed.

The former was, fortunately, the more likely. A man of wealth and power who had little time to spare on hellos or goodbyes would hardly occupy himself with the assassination of one such as Wijeya. It was far more possible that one day the calls and the weapons would stop coming. At that point, it would be up to Wijeya to leverage the success they had experienced thus far.

Already, he and his crew were several steps ahead of most typical pirates. They were not scrounging just to eat. They were actually making a profit. Most of his men drank and whored their way through whatever shares they earned. Mhusa, who cared as little for money as he did for the future, gave most of his earnings away. Lemat was investing his and probably had a foreign bank account, as well, but then, Lemat was always overqualified to be a pirate. He had been some kind of accountant or businessman in his previous life, before a disgrace had prompted him to leave. How a man like that managed to adapt to life at sea, Wijeya did not know. But Lemat had already managed to serve with distinction aboard a cruise ship, acting as purser, before he'd been caught embezzling and thrown in prison. Wijeya had caught wind of it in yet another portside bar. Sailors talked. He had needed someone who could help him with the financial aspects of his business. So he had bribed Lemat's way out of jail and spread around enough money to ensure the Frenchman's freedom that Lemat was beholden to Wijeya from that point on.

Wijeya had also explained to Lemat that, should the Frenchman ever steal from Wijeya as he had stolen from previous employers, Wijeya would flay him alive. The warning seemed to have had its desired effect.

The *Penuh Belut* passed through a pall of black smoke

wafting from the deck of the target freighter. Wijeya waited while his men moored the tenders alongside the motor craft, which were secured to the sides of the target vessel with grappling hook lines. Each launch had one man with an AK-47 in it, to stand as guards. Wijeya's other crewmen, led by his first mate, the one-eyed Liberian, Mhusa, would already be aboard. He could hear sporadic gunfire, but it was all the hollow metallic clatter of Kalashnikovs. That meant his men had control of the target ship.

Lemat threw a grapple, the line to which was also connected to a rope ladder. Crewmen already aboard the target freighter hauled the line up and pulled the rope ladder with it. Wijeya used this to ascend, planting his feet on the deck of his prize. His attack crews were already rounding up the enemy sailors. A cluster of prisoners stood on the deck. Mhusa, with his AK-47, glowered at them. A nearby pile of captured rifles showed that most were bolt-action Mausers. There were a few ancient Russian rifles mixed in, and one or two M-1 carbines. A few clips of ammunition were scattered among the pile. The poor sailors had not had much with which to work. They had been no match for Wijeya's men.

Mhusa separated an older man from the group of prisoners and shoved him forward. "This is their captain," he said. "His name is Gable."

"Take your hands off me!" said Captain Gable. "This is a violation of maritime law!"

Wijeya stood in front of Captain Gable. He reached behind his back and withdrew the machete from its scabbard. "There is no law here," he said. "There is only strength." He motioned to Mhusa, who forced Gable to kneel. To the Liberian, Wijeya said, "Lean him forward. I want a clear shot at his neck."

"What?" Gable protested. "You can't be serious."

"Kill the others," Wijeya ordered. There was a sudden thunderous report as two of Wijeya's men opened up with their automatic Kalashnikovs, murdering the survivors among Gable's crew. The dead prisoners fell to the deck on top of one another. The spreading pool of blood quickly reached Wijeya's boots.

"Wait," Gable said. "Wait!"

Wijeya raised the machete. "No survivors," he repeated.

"There's no need for that!" pleaded Gable. "You don't… I mean, we can work something out! Ransom, yes? My company would probably pay a ransom. You don't have to—"

"Yes," said Wijeya. "I do."

The razor-sharp blade of the machete sang downward.

CHAPTER ONE

Stony Man Farm, Virginia

Barbara Price, Stony Man Farm's mission controller, pushed a lock of honey-blond hair from her eyes as she climbed out from under the briefing-room conference table. Examining her tight slacks for dust, she brushed her hands across her thighs and looked to Aaron "the Bear" Kurtzman. Kurtzman was sitting in his wheelchair, looking at her expectantly.

"Well?" he said.

"Let 'er rip," Price stated.

Kurtzman nodded and pressed a button on the control box in the surface of the table. He had spent the past few days wiring up new, higher-resolution, flat-screen monitors for the walls of the briefing room. Tasks such as these were among the hundreds of behind-the-scenes undertakings that Kurtzman and his cybernetics team fulfilled in support of the Farm's missions. While Kurtzman's upper body was massive and he could easily have pulled himself under the table to make the necessary connections, Price had offered to do it for him, if only to save him time.

At Kurtzman's touch, the wall screens switched on, displaying a test pattern.

"Well, that looks good," said Price. "We should be ready when Hal calls for the briefing."

"Yeah," Kurtzman agreed. "I just want to—" He stopped.

One by one, the wall screens switched from the test pattern to the image of a rounded, purple cartoon monster eating a lollipop. As Price watched, amazed, the monster began to find its way through a series of mazes bearing math problems. At the end of each passageway, it devoured another piece of candy.

"What in the world?" Price asked.

"Gadgets." Kurtzman spit the name as if cursing.

"Gadgets?" Price asked. "What does he have to do with it?" Hermann "Gadgets" Schwarz was the technical expert on Able Team, one of the Farm's two counterterror teams. He was as skilled with electronics and hardware as Kurtzman, the Farm's computer expert and support team leader, was with software.

"Our network runs in several shells," said Kurtzman. "I keep the loosest security on the outer shell, the one that runs the office hardware. Encryption for our transmissions is handled on a deeper level of the network. But the outer layer, the one that handles just general connectivity among the hardware, can be adjusted internally."

"I don't follow," said Price. "What's the connection?" She pointed at the cartoon monster. "What *is* that, Bear?"

"That," Kurtzman explained, "is Candy Monster Maze Farm online, one of the most popular smartphone apps on the market. It's one of those addictive puzzle games. I keep deleting it from the outer network shell. Gadgets keeps hacking his way in to put it back on, no matter how many times I revoke his admin privileges."

Price hid her mouth behind her hand so Kurtzman would not see her smile. Schwarz was a notorious practical joker whose antics often helped the Farm's personnel blow off steam. Given the extreme stress under which they all operated, Price was secretly grateful for Schwarz's effect on morale. It might explain why, even though Able

Team's leader, Carl Lyons, was an irascible grump, unit cohesion in Able Team was as high as it had ever been.

That was also true of Phoenix Force, Stony Man's other counterterror team. Before David McCarter had become the leader of Phoenix Force, he was noted for his sharp tongue and glib nature. Yet the Briton had been awfully serious in the years since assuming leadership of the team, following the death of veteran Farm commando Yakov Katzenelenbogen.

It was true what they said about the mantle of leadership. Price spent all her time worrying about the personnel of both teams, not to mention the support personnel who held them all together and made their missions possible.

Kurtzman had produced a wireless compact keyboard and was now typing furiously at it. The purple, spherical monster was replaced on the wall screens with lines of code. As the monitors returned to the test pattern and then to a live feed of Hal Brognola sitting at his desk, a voice shouted from the corridor outside the briefing room.

"No!" said Schwarz as he walked through the doorway. He was holding his secure satellite smartphone and watching the screen as he walked, tapping away with both thumbs. "I was almost to level ten. Now I'm going to forfeit my bonus lollipops."

"Gadgets—" Kurtzman snarled.

"Uh," Brognola interrupted from the wall screen. "If we could begin? I have an appropriations committee meeting in half an hour." Brognola was speaking from his office on the Potomac. As Director of the Sensitive Operations Group and one of the few men alive who understood the extent and scope of the Stony Man Farm Operation, Brognola had his fingers in a lot of pies in Washington.

Not for the first time, Price looked at the big Fed, wondering about his health. Over the years Brognola had cut back on a number of bad habits as stress, work load and time had conspired against him. How he managed on a day-to-day basis was a testament to his mental and physical strength. Nobody was shooting at Hal—although, over the years, that had happened a time or two—but he shouldered a load that was as great or greater than any of the fighting personnel on the Farm's black-ops staff.

Schwarz put his phone on the table. Kurtzman glared at the slim, nerdy-looking counterterrorist. Schwarz offered a sheepish grin before turning to greet his fellow Able Team members.

Drinking from a disposable coffee cup that was probably full of Kurtzman's own nuclear-strength brew, which Kurtzman fermented in an industrial coffeemaker in the Farm's office annex, Carl "Ironman" Lyons strode into the briefing room. He nodded at Schwarz before settling his big frame into a chair of his own. The former LAPD detective was a big, imposing man…with a temper to match. Nonetheless, he was an extremely effective leader. Being able to tolerate Schwarz's sense of humor on a daily basis was probably a big point in his favor.

Behind Lyons was Rosario Blancanales, who had been nicknamed "Politician" for as long as Price had known him. Blancanales, a soft-spoken Hispanic man with gray hair, was an expert at "role camouflage" and a former Black Beret. As Lyons and Blancanales exchanged knowing looks first with Schwarz and then with Kurtzman—who was still doing his best to look angry at Schwarz—Price signaled Kurtzman to bring up the satellite feed for Phoenix Force. The Phoenix Force team was preparing to embark from an air base in Manila and had set up a portable satellite transmission unit in one of the outbuildings. It looked as if the five members of Phoenix Force were sharing space with several stacks of wooden crates and other supplies, including a leaning tower of oil cans.

While they barely fit within the field of view of their field camera, the members of Phoenix Force were all present. There was David McCarter, the fox-faced Briton who was their team leader. Beside him crouched Rafael Encizo. The stocky, Cuban-born guerilla fighter was much shorter than square-jawed giant Gary Manning, a demolitions expert who had once served with the Royal Canadian Mounted Police. Kneeling in front of them was Calvin James, a lanky black man and former Navy SEAL from Chicago's South Side. Also kneeling to fit within the camera frame was T. J. Hawkins, the youngest member of the team. The Georgia-born former Ranger had also earned himself a set of para wings along the way. His easygoing manner belied just how experienced he was at what all the Phoenix Force commandos excelled—the dealing out of fast, efficient, overwhelming force.

"Okay, Hal," Price confirmed. "We're go."

Brognola cleared his throat. He pressed a button on the keyboard at his end. The display of his office was replaced by a graphic representation of the South China Sea, with several blinking target points indicated.

"Beijing has laid claim to most of the South China Sea," he said without preamble. "This isn't the abrupt territory grab it might seem. They've been rattling their saber in the area for quite some time. It wasn't that long ago that they started sending oil rigs into the region, stepping up their resource exploration in waters claimed by nations like Vietnam. Sovereignty over all kinds of islands, and the waters around them, is in dispute. Most of Asia is getting nervous because China has gotten more and more aggressive over the past few years. They're the new military power on the block and they know it."

"Like their new stealth fighter, which uses stolen American Raptor technology," Schwarz put in.

"Just so," said Brognola. "China also has a pretty spotty record of conducting 'military exercises' in the area that have proved dangerous to anyone who gets in the way. They've consistently expanded the budget for the People's Liberation Army. Throughout Asia, world leaders are concerned that China is getting ready to just take what it wants, and the rest of the world can like it."

"Given how badly stretched our own military is," David McCarter said, "it makes sense. The Chinese are starting to feel like they can do what they want and nobody's going to stand up to them."

"There's that," said Brognola. "But, potentially, it's already gotten to a shooting war, albeit a poorly publicized one. These red target indicators all designate locations for raids. Several Filipino ports and a number of cargo vessels and naval craft have been attacked. Some of the survivors of these raids are claiming the attackers were running Chinese colors, although so far, there's no proof of that."

"So they're, what, trying to back up their claim to the area through force?" Lyons asked.

"Possibly," said Brognola. "Beijing swears it isn't behind the armed aggression, although the Filipinos are screaming bloody murder and asking for NATO intervention. It isn't just the Philippines that have seen their ships attacked, either, although so far they've taken a good portion of the damage. And it isn't uncommon for China to say one thing while doing another. The tensions are high. The entire region has become very volatile."

"What's our stake, Hal?" Lyons asked.

"The Man wants us to get to the bottom of the attacks," Brognola replied. "Obviously there are very sensitive politics at play."

"You mean the Chinese hold our markers," said Mc-Carter. "And they're not shy about letting us know we owe them money."

"The global economy is more complicated than that," Brognola said. "If things go south between the US and China, it will have far-reaching effects throughout the world, not just for us or for them. And, frankly, if China is getting more aggressive, we may need to step in and put them down."

"Except we can't look like we're doing that," said Mc-Carter.

"Correct," said Brognola. "That's why it's us and not a more overt military action. The White House considered sending a carrier into the region, and still might, but that's symbolism only. What we need is real problem solving…but the problem solvers can't be linked to the United States government. That's where Phoenix Force comes in."

"Bloody hell," McCarter said quietly.

Brognola pretended not to hear. "The world cannot afford war with China. But first, we've got to neutralize the immediate threat while getting to the bottom of what's going on. We have tasked several of our newer satellites to tracking the comings and goings of the marauder ships. Using advanced imaging technology similar to methods we've employed before, we have produced a list of potential target sites, as well as probabilities for future raids. There is definitely a calculated pattern to the attacks. They are not random. Your job, Phoenix, will be to neutralize the raids while determining, if you can, who the players are. You will be supported by Jack Grimaldi, who'll act as your pilot for both transportation and air support."

"We saw G-Force outside," Calvin James said. "He's got a pimped-out Sikorsky waiting for us."

"And Able, Hal?" Lyons asked.

"That's where the other shoe falls," said Brognola. "What evidence the Filipinos have recovered points a strange finger away from China and toward the United States. Several fragments and discarded pieces of weaponry have been recovered from the raids. They're the latest high-tech hardware from RhemCorp, a United States contractor."

Schwarz made an exaggerated face-palm. "Not again."

"Gadgets is right," Blancanales said. "This wouldn't be the first time we've encountered an American businessman selling high-tech weaponry to foreign powers. I'm starting to think the security clearance process our military employs for vendors may be seriously flawed."

"Regardless," Brognola continued, "Able will investigate RhemCorp's facilities here in the United States. Export of the weapons concerned is strictly controlled by US law and security regulations. The only way these weapons are getting out is if they're doing so illegally."

"Let's just go arrest the guy," muttered Lyons. "I guarantee you it's the suit in charge."

"RhemCorp's CEO is this man," Price said. She reached across Kurtzman and tapped a key on his keyboard. The photo of a middle-aged man with oddly smooth features appeared on the wall screens.

"Whoa." Schwarz whistled. "Somebody's been at the Botox."

"That guy's doctor left him with just the one expression, I guess," Lyons said.

"Harold Rhemsen," said Price. "He's forty-five years old. No known political ties. He's a registered independent. No affiliations to any group more controversial than the local rotary. We've been through his business records."

"I searched pretty thoroughly," Kurtzman advised.

"Obviously we can always go deeper. He could be hiding things using shell corporations we've not yet discovered. But so far, no smoking guns. Whatever he's doing, if he is dirty, is pretty well concealed, and probably goes back a long way."

"How so?" Brognola asked.

"I can answer that," Schwarz offered. He was quietly typing with his thumbs on his smartphone again, but he did not even look down as he spoke. "Financial fraud is like trolling the internet. The longer you have to set up your dummy accounts, the older they'll be when somebody looks at them, and the more legitimate they'll appear."

"Spoken like a man who has done his fair share of online trolling," Kurtzman commented, spearing his colleague with a disapproving eye.

Schwarz flushed slightly. Kurtzman picked up for him. "The point is," said Kurtzman, "everything about Rhemsen could be made up, but if it was established long enough ago, it's going to take a while for us to find evidence of that."

"I still say we just roll in there and arrest him," Lyons said. "He's going to lie. And then we're going to leave. And when we come back he's going to try to kill us. Let's just cut to the end."

"Five bucks says he tries to kill us right way," Schwarz said.

"You're on," said Lyons. He turned away from the electronics expert as the monitors switched from the picture of Rhemsen to the feed from Brognola's office.

"If I could continue…" Brognola cleared his throat again. "Obviously, I need you to use some discretion. Able Team will be operating under the auspices of Justice on this, since the origin of the US-made weaponry has nothing to do with China itself. But of course the two are connected, if only because the raids are being conducted using these illegally obtained rocket systems."

"XM-Thorns," Schwarz declared, apparently scrolling through data that had been uploaded to his phone. "Nasty stuff. Very compact. Very light and very powerful."

"Yes," Brognola agreed. "That's part of what makes this so urgent, separate from the greater political concerns where China is involved. Bear has transmitted complete mission dossiers to all of your secure smartphones, including the specifications for the recovered weaponry, the target lists and real-time updates as our satellite imaging provides new data for Phoenix." He looked down at his watch. "Now, if you'll excuse me, I've got to get to that meeting."

"We're on it," McCarter stated. "Wheels up in five."

"Thanks, Hal," Price said. "Stay safe."

"This is Wonderland," Brognola responded. "Nobody's safe. Good hunting, all of you."

The screens went blank and then returned to the test pattern. Lyons stood and gestured to his Able Team colleagues.

"Let's move, ladies," Lyons grumbled. "I'll draw an SUV from the motor pool and have Cowboy fill it with things that explode." He was referring to John "Cowboy" Kissinger, the Farm's armorer.

"Catch you later," Schwarz said to Price and Kurtzman. Blancanales nodded. The two men followed their team leader into the corridor, leaving Price and Kurtzman alone in the briefing room.

Kurtzman pushed his chair away from the table. Just as Price, too, started to rise, the image on the conference room screens once again became that of the purple, spherical monster chasing candy through its puzzle maze. Kurtzman sighed heavily and put his head in his hands.

Price hurried out, hoping she could make the control room before she started to laugh.

CHAPTER TWO

Fayetteville, North Carolina

"Level twenty-one," Schwarz announced triumphantly. He went through the motions of a little victory dance in the passenger seat of the old Chevrolet Suburban, something he had been developing for the past several levels. Or at least, that was what he had been telling Blancanales and Lyons. From the driver's seat, Lyons shot him a sidelong glance.

"You can quit that anytime," he growled.

"No, I really can't," Schwarz said. He had his secure satellite smartphone in his hands and was once again playing the candy monster game. He did not look up as he spoke. Blancanales, as he often did, pretended not to hear the exchange, instead watching out the window of the SUV.

The old Suburban was one that had been in the Farm's motor pool rotation for a while. It had steel running boards, which you hardly ever saw on big SUVs these days. It even had a few patched bullet holes that Blancanales had noticed when Lyons had first brought the vehicle around. He knew that, regardless of its appearance, the old truck would be well maintained by the mechanics at Stony Man Farm. Not for the first time it occurred to him how fortunate they all were to be able to take the maintenance of their vehicles and weapons for granted.

The resources of the Farm were extensive, but they were not limitless. Brognola went through a number of different legal and political gymnastics in Washington to divert the funds from various black bag project budgets to pay for the Farm. It helped that the President of the United States was in on the Sensitive Operations Group's existence, of course. The Man always saw to it that budget expenditures manipulated by Brognola were signed off as they came up. But it was still an ongoing battle, not just coordinating a venture as elaborate and as dangerous as the Farm's counterterrorism efforts, but also making sure the budget money flowed where it needed to flow. Blancanales understood very well the politicking and people wrangling that must come with the job. He was glad the tasks did not fall to him.

"Level twenty-two!" Schwarz whooped and moved his arms in a tight circle like a sorority drunk at a nightclub.

"I am going to throw that thing out the window," Lyons threatened. "You've been doing that for the past two hundred miles."

"I could go back to 'I spy with my little eye,'" Schwarz said. "I spy—" he began.

"Pol," Lyons said without turning to look back at Blancanales. "I want you to take out your Beretta, put it to the back of my head and put me out of my misery."

"You can make it, Ironman," Blancanales said encouragingly. "Maybe focus on the mission. Count to ten and think of England."

"One," Lyons muttered. "Two. Three…"

They were outfitted with their usual complement of personal weapons, as well as some of the latest goodies from Stony Man Farm's armorer. Lyons was carrying his customary Colt Python in a shoulder holster under his bomber jacket, while Blancanales and Schwarz had opted for light windbreakers to conceal their pistols. Blancanales had long ago become very comfortable with the Beretta M-9, while Schwarz often opted for the Beretta 93-R machine pistol. His slightly oversize, select-fire pistol also rode in a shoulder holster. His twenty-round magazines were also compatible with Blancanales's weapon, should it come to that.

In a large duffel bag in the back was Lyons's tremendous automatic shotgun, a drum-fed Daewoo USAS-12. There was also a cut-down Colt 9 mm SMG for Schwarz and a short-barreled M-4 carbine for Blancanales. Plenty of loaded magazines, grenades, explosive charges and other hardware had been provided—Blancanales wondered, sometimes, how many blacksuits spent their days just thumbing ammunition into magazines for the Farm's counterterror teams—as had been an M-32 six-round 40 mm grenade launcher. The modified Milkor MGL-140 with a fore-grip, collapsible modular buttstock, recoil pad, and quad-rail Picatinny fore-end could empty a half dozen grenades on target in less than three seconds. Their grab bag of firepower from the Farm also included plenty of Hellhound breaching/antipersonnel rounds and DRACO thermobaric grenades. Blancanales would have to check to be sure, but he thought their load-out also included some buckshot rounds—each grenade boasting twenty-seven 00 buckshot spheres that could blow a cone almost a hundred feet across at almost 900 feet per second.

It was a pretty typical bag of tricks for Able Team.

Each man also carried a tactical one-hand-opening folding knife with an integral guard, sizable chunks of steel that had been honed to razor edges. Blancanales had been resisting the urge to play with the one issued to him. It was clipped inside his right front pocket.

"Level twenty-three," Schwarz announced. He turned

to regard Lyons smugly. Lyons kept his eyes on the road, but Blancanales thought he could see the big former cop's shoulders tense. Lyons might not really snatch the phone and pitch it out the window, but he seemed to be giving it some serious thought.

"Here's what we're going to do," Lyons said, still staring straight ahead. His knuckles grew less white on the steering wheel as he spoke. "We hit the parking lot and break out the heavy hardware. Gadgets, you break left, cover the left side of the lobby as we head in. Pol, you break right. Watch the flanks while I drive up the center. You'll lay down covering fire as I—"

"Wait," Blancanales said. "What?"

"Uh," Schwarz said. "Ironman?"

"What?" Lyons said, sounding annoyed.

"Are you…are you planning to just roll in and shoot everybody?"

"Well, what else?" Lyons said. "Obviously he's the bad guy. He's going to try to kill us as soon as he figures we have enough evidence to take him down. So, like I said at the briefing, we just cut to the end. It will save a lot of time and hassle."

"You're not serious," Schwarz argued.

Lyons sighed. "No. I'm not. But it got you to put down that damned game for thirty seconds, didn't it?"

Blancanales looked at Schwarz, who looked at Lyons. Lyons looked at both of them before turning his attention back to the road. Then Carl "Ironman" Lyons began laughing. It was a deep, hearty laugh.

"You had me going," Blancanales admitted.

Schwarz blew air through his mouth. "Yeesh," he said. "Remind me not to get on your bad side, Ironman."

"You're already on it," Lyons said. "You and that candy monster whatchamacallit."

"Level—" Schwarz started.

"You announce what level you're on one more time," Lyons warned, "and I'm going to throw you out of this truck at seventy miles per hour." Schwarz wisely chose not to comment further. "Twenty bucks says this Rhemsen character tries to punch our tickets the moment he thinks he can't get away with his lies."

"You're on," Schwarz said. "We've seen too many corrupt captains of industry. Sooner or later one of them's bound to be a patsy." He looked back at Blancanales. "You want in on this action, Pol?"

"I know better than to get in the middle of you two when you're bickering," Blancanales said.

"This isn't bickering," Lyons said. "I'm not bickering."

"I might be," Schwarz said.

"Might?" Lyons shot him another side-eye.

Blancanales could not help but grin. It was not too much longer before the windshield-mounted GPS announced the turn for their destination. Lyons pulled onto the RhemCorp property and rolled up to the guest parking spots near the front. He was careful to back the old Suburban in for a fast getaway, should it come to that. While he was doing that, Blancanales sent a scrambled text to the Farm from his satellite smartphone, alerting Barbara Price and mission control that they were on-site and preparing to make contact with Harold Rhemsen.

"Check it," Schwarz said as they exited the vehicle. He jerked his chin toward the guards at the front door. There were two outside the building, one on either side of the ornate double doors. Both had Brugger and Thomet MP-9 submachine guns with extended barrels and skeletonized stocks. The weapons had red-dot optics and fore-grips with built-in weapon lights.

"That's a lot of hardware for civilian contractors on American soil," Blancanales noted.

"There's still time to break out the bigger guns," Lyons said. "I'm game."

"Now you're just teasing," Schwarz put in.

"Come on," Lyons said. "Let's go through the motions." He reached under his bomber jacket and adjusted his shoulder holster. As they neared the security guards, the insignia on the two operatives' uniforms became visible.

"Blackstar," Schwarz mumbled under his breath.

"Well, that's just great," muttered Lyons. "How many legit businessmen would sign on with those ghouls? Want to give me that money now, Gadgets?"

"I'll pay as I go," Schwarz quipped.

Blancanales frowned. Blackstar was a notoriously discredited military contractor and mercenary supply outfit. Government oversight committees were even now investigating Blackstar's parent company for war crimes in both Iraq and Afghanistan. If RhemCorp was employing armed mercenaries for security, that did not bode well. Blancanales was tempted to think Lyons's plan to just knock the place over might be a good idea.

Lyons eyed the two Blackstar men hard as Able Team passed between them. The trio of counterterror operatives emerged in the lobby of RhemCorp. It was an unremarkable space, not overlarge. The building itself was similarly nondescript. Able Team had seen some pretty lavish and indulgent office structures in their time working on United States soil. Whatever sort of power-broker Rhemsen was, he wasn't the kind of man given to ostentatious displays of wealth.

Lyons, with his teammates close behind, strode up to the reception desk. The receptionist was an older woman, her face lined and haggard. Blancanales watched as Lyons tried and did not quite succeed in hiding his reaction when she looked up from paperwork in front of her.

"Yes? May I help you?" she asked. Her voice was piercing and nasal. It was the kind of voice television comedians put on for a laugh. Evidently this was the one she'd been born with.

"Agents Perry, Tyler and Hamilton," said Lyons. "We're with the Justice Department." He flashed her the Justice credentials Brognola's office had issued to Able Team. Lyons had no idea what names were actually written on the credentials. In situations such as this he just offered the first three names that came to mind. He could always disclaim these as cover identities if someone started to ask questions and demanded to closely examine the identification cards. The badge contained in the ID holder was completely legitimate. Able Team's operatives were, for all legal purposes, fully authorized operatives of the United States Justice Department. Brognola would back them up on that, no matter what.

"Do you have an appointment?" asked the receptionist.

"No," Lyons answered. "It's a matter of national security. Have Mr. Rhemsen greet us in the lobby. We need to speak to him privately."

"I'll see if he's in," she said, reaching for the telephone on her desk. The big former cop reached out and laid a heavy paw on the handset in its cradle.

"He's in," Lyons said. "No runarounds. No excuses. No meetings that can't be interrupted. Get him down here. Now."

Something in Lyons's expression caused the receptionist's already pale face to turn gray. She looked at the handset, waited for Lyons to release it and picked up the phone. She pushed only a single button, waited a moment and then said, "Sir. You had better come down. Right away."

Moments later the single elevator in the lobby chimed. When the doors slid open, the man who slithered out was wearing a suit that was probably worth as much as Able Team's SUV. Blancanales was momentarily taken aback. Rhemsen's face was a ghastly mask of too-smooth flesh stretched across his skull in a way that made him look like a snake. His eyes, under hooded lids, were very blue— too blue to be natural. He was obviously wearing colored contacts.

"Gentlemen," Rhemsen said, showing a thousand-watt smile full of capped and brilliantly white teeth. "I understand there's a rather urgent matter that demands my attention."

"You might say that," Lyons said. "Justice Department. We need to talk to you about some weapons systems RhemCorp manufactures."

"I can't imagine you would have anything else to talk to me about," said Rhemsen. "Come with me, gentlemen. We'll go straight to my office." He gestured for them to follow him to the elevator.

Able Team stepped in with Rhemsen in the lead. There were several security guards milling around in the lobby, and as Rhemsen put his hand in front of the electric eye of the elevator, two of the goons started to walk over.

"Nope," Lyons said. "Your Blackstar Bunnies can wait in the lobby."

The shadow of something unpleasant passed across Rhemsen's plastic face, but he managed to hide it right away. "Of course, gentlemen," he said smoothly. At a hand motion from him, the guards suddenly discovered very interesting and invisible things to occupy them on either side of the elevator doors.

Rhemsen took his hand away and looked at Schwarz, who was standing closest to the control panel.

"Uh...floor?" Schwarz asked, looking glib.

"The one labeled 'P' for 'Penthouse,'" said Rhemsen.

Schwarz pushed the button. The elevator began to move, silently and swiftly. Quiet saxophone music began to filter in through the elevator speakers.

"I've never heard an elevator version of 'Soul Finger' before," Schwarz commented.

"You still haven't. I think that's 'Girl from Ipanema,'" Blancanales said.

Lyons glared daggers at them both. The elevator reached its destination.

"I assume this has something to do with my Thorn missile systems," said Rhemsen. "I assure you, gentlemen, I am the victim of a smuggling ring. I'm very aware of export controls and other regulations that the government puts on restricted hardware."

The doors opened. Blancanales was amazed to see that Rhemsen's office was oval in shape. It was, in fact, a reasonably accurate replica of the office of the President of the United States. Framed on the wall were, not the paintings of the President and the Vice President, or even the President and the First Lady, but Harold Rhemsen dressed as some kind of Napoleonic general. On the desk, which was itself a replica of the President's, was a gold placard. It read, The Buck Stops At My Bank Account. To say it was all a little megalomaniacal would be an understatement.

Rhemsen seated himself at his desk and opened a desktop humidor. "Cuban cigar, gentlemen?" He grinned that electric smile again. "Apologies. A bad joke. Cuban cigars are, of course, illegal to import. These are, somewhat regrettably, Honduran, but I assure you they are of fine quality."

The members of Able Team looked at each other.

"Will you have a seat, gentlemen?" Rhemsen gestured

to the quartet of leather-upholstered chairs arrayed in front
of his desk. Apparently he was accustomed to entertain-
ing visitors.

The Stony Man operatives sat. Lyons produced a sheaf
of papers from inside his bomber jacket. "These are the
particulars," he said. "They detail the items recovered and
what we've been able to determine about the provenance
of the missile systems. They're not counterfeit, before you
suggest it," Lyons said. "We've run into that excuse before.
These are verifiably your gear, Rhemsen."

"You don't look like government agents," Rhemsen
said, still smiling. Something in his body language shifted.
Blancanales didn't like it. He saw Lyons tense and, next
to him, Schwarz sat straighter.

"What makes you say that?" Lyons said. His hand began
to inch toward his chest.

"Government agents wear suits," Rhemsen said. "They
also understand how to be polite. How to follow the rules.
Obey the forms. You gentlemen…well. You're not gentlemen at all, are you? You're…thugs."

"Now just a minute, pal," Lyons said. He started to rise
in his chair. Blancanales knew the action was intended to
cover the draw from his shoulder holster.

"I wouldn't," Rhemsen warned. He pointed to the mirror on the wall behind them. When he spoke next, his
voice was raised. "Lower it," he said.

The pane of glass slid down on electric motors. Four
of Rhemsen's Blackstar guards were standing there, their
tricked-out submachine guns pointed at Able Team. The
green dots of laser targeting systems danced across Able
Team's foreheads.

"I'm going to have to owe you that twenty," Schwarz
said quietly to Lyons.

"Son of a bitch," Carl Lyons said.

CHAPTER THREE

At The Edge of Puerto Galera, South China Sea

The retrofitted Sikorsky S-61R, mounting 7.62 mm belt-fed M-240 machine guns and a Mark 19 automatic belt-fed 40mm grenade launcher, had extra fuel pods, giving it longer range. At the stick, Stony Man ace pilot Jack Grimaldi held the combat-ready troop helicopter low over the waves. Through the open door of the fuselage, the members of Phoenix Force watched their target.

David McCarter held a high-tech monocular to one eye and adjusted the magnification. "Bloody hell. I hate waiting," he muttered.

That drew some muffled snickers from the other members of the team. McCarter shot Calvin James a squint-eyed glare before returning to the monocular.

"Why do I get the stink eye?" James asked.

"You were closest," McCarter replied without looking back at him.

"Figures," James said.

Through the monocular, McCarter watched the Filipino naval vessel. It was relatively small as patrol craft went, but still more than large enough that a marauder would have to be insane to try to take it down. Yet the Filipino navy had lost two ships just like it to what was either pirate activity or, frankly, the covert action of the Chinese military, which of course was the source of all the tensions in the region. It was Phoenix Force's job to figure out which…while putting a stop to all the fun and games in the South China Sea. At least, that's what the Phoenix Force leader had taken away from the briefing. Sometimes the nuances were lost on him…mostly because he chose to ignore stupid nuances in favor of getting the mission done.

That was all part of leadership. Nobody had told him that; he'd had to figure it out on his own, ever since taking over for Katz. It wasn't about the orders you executed. Any idiot could follow orders to the letter. Leading Phoenix Force was about knowing when judgment calls were needed in the field. Things changed and the best-laid plans of mice and morons went awry, or some such tripe. He didn't dwell on it too much. He had too much work to do to be dwelling on such things. And then, too, there were the men whose lives he was ultimately responsible for.

"You think they know we're out here?" T. J. Hawkins asked. His drawl made the question seem more casual than it really was. "If I was the captain of that boat I'd want to know what we were doing, shadowing them all day."

"Hal has squared it with the Filipino authorities," Grimaldi put in from the cockpit. Given the noise of the helicopter, none of them would be able to hear each other under normal circumstances. Grimaldi had patched in to the wireless frequency connected to the team's earbud transceivers, tiny radios that sat in their ears like hearing aids. Through these, the team members could hear each other and also Grimaldi as clear as day. The transceivers were "smart," too; they had noise-canceling software built into them that cut the noise from gunfire and other ambient sounds.

"Squared it how?" Manning asked. The big Canadian rarely took things at face value. He frequently acted as McCarter's sounding board.

"You know," Grimaldi said. "Did that thing he does."

"That thing?" Hawkins asked.

"Vague promises of assistance and threats of reprisal," James answered. "Followed by assurances that the government of the United States will remain within their territory for no longer than it takes to get the job done. And, of course, the implied threat that if they don't cooperate, things might get a hell of a lot worse when whatever big bad force we've come to deal with gets out of hand."

McCarter looked at James. He opened his mouth to say something.

"I mean I've heard," James added.

In the distance, a pair of fast motor launches hove into view. They were swift enough, their engines powerful enough, that they threw up great sprays of seawater as they punched through the waves.

"That's it, lads," McCarter said. "Those are our targets."

"Those dinky things?" Hawkins said. "That Filipino navy ship will tear them apart—"

Plumes of smoke erupted from the launches. The shoulder-fired missiles surged from the smaller craft to level the deck of the Filipino ship, tearing holes in whatever structures they encountered.

"Bloody hell," McCarter muttered. "Jack! Get us in there, now!"

"Roger." The Sikorsky roared as Grimaldi squeezed all available speed from the mighty craft, sending the nose dipping as the chopper threw itself toward the ship.

"T.J., Rafe, on the guns!" McCarter ordered. "Gary, get on that grenade launcher and stand by. Calvin, with me!"

There were grunts of assent from the others. McCarter rushed to connect his drop harness and made sure James had done the same. As the chopper picked up speed, the

Briton could hear the pop of automatic gunfire from the targets below.

"In range," Grimaldi announced.

"Hit them, lads!" McCarter shouted.

Vibration traveled from the deck up through McCarter's boots as the M-240 machine guns opened up. Manning looked at McCarter expectantly.

"Wait for it, Gary," McCarter promised.

The Sikorsky swooped low, like a hawk plucking a field mouse from the ground. The first of the two motor launches erupted in fire as the machine guns touched off something on the deck. McCarter waited for the arc of the chopper's travel to take them over the smoking, flaming deck of the Filipino ship. Then he pushed off, signaling James to follow.

The line caught him and jerked him up a few feet short of the deck. The Briton hit his quick-release lever and landed on the deck, hard, rolling out and bringing up the Tavor rifle attached to his single-point harness. Every member of Phoenix Force had been equipped with one of the high-tech Israeli assault weapons. The bullpup-configured rifle fired NATO-standard 5.56 mm ammunition and was modular, configurable for different missions. Manning's Tavor had a 4.0mm grenade launcher affixed, while all the rifles had close-quarters red-dot optics.

Each man also carried a 9 mm Glock handgun. At least, that was the plan John Kissinger, the Stony Man armorer, had had when he'd outfitted Phoenix Force for the mission. Kissinger had also seen to it that each man had a full-size, drop-point combat, fixed-blade knife to mount on his gear. But McCarter, as he usually did, had insisted on his beloved Browning Hi-Power. Kissinger had known better than to argue the point.

Outfitting the team with foreign weapons was part of

the drill. In the shadowy world of politics and plausible deniability, everybody knew what was going on, but everybody pretended they didn't. That was one of the reasons even allies routinely spied on each other. There would be no doubt, if Phoenix Force was captured or killed, that they were likely a Western commando team. But as long as there was no concrete proof, they could operate outside established international laws. The very notion was ridiculous to McCarter. There were no international laws that were not enforced behind the barrels of guns. Like the one he held now.

The deck of the Filipino ship was on fire. The crew was doing what they could to douse the flames. McCarter threw them a salute, hoping they would understand he was on their side. They regarded him suspiciously if they noticed him at all; for the most part, they were too worried about survival to spare him much time. He immediately went to a section of the railing that was clear of debris, braced his Tavor and started tracking the second motor launch.

The first of the two fast-attack boats was trailing a thick plume of black smoke. As McCarter watched, the Sikorsky flew past, turned and lined up the grenade launcher.

"Now, Gary! Now!" McCarter said.

Manning made no reply. He did not need to. The automatic grenade launcher began spewing 40 mm death at the already crippled motor launch. The grenades blew the little boat to cinders, biting off great chunks of it, as if the vessel were being devoured from stern to bow. The flaming bodies that were thrown into the sea bore horrible testament to the destruction being wrought. McCarter turned his attention back to the boat that was still moving.

Grimaldi did the same. While the second boat, the moving boat, was out of position, he had pursued the wounded first vessel, but his strategy was a sound one. He was harrying the motor launches to keep them from targeting the Filipino ship again with their handheld rockets. From what McCarter could see of the men on the decks, they did not look military. At least, they did not wear uniforms. But there was something more to it. Military men had a certain bearing and, from what little he could see through the smoke of the carnage on the water, the sailors on the motor launch didn't have it. They were casual. That meant they were pirates, or at least, civilian contractors. But how would such men get their hands on the latest high-tech weapons from America, weapons that were strictly controlled when it came to export to foreign powers? Either RhemCorp was careless or RhemCorp was dirty. But they did not yet know which.

McCarter let the red dot of his Tavor optics fall on the moving motor launch. It continued to fly through the water, making widening circles around the Filipino ship. The crew, around McCarter, was starting to bring the fire under control. James took up a protective position at McCarter's back, looking in toward the deck, and started shooing sailors away from his position with a collection of hand gestures and dirty looks. The sailors seemed content to give the two Phoenix Force members plenty of room, especially when McCarter started firing on the pirate launch still rolling through the waves.

"David, this is G-Force," said Grimaldi over the transceiver frequency. Phoenix Force typically used first names as code names for missions like this. Surnames could be tracked, but first names and nicknames would yield little if overheard.

"Go ahead," said McCarter. He did his best to lead the speeding motor launch and started squeezing off short bursts with the Tavor, knowing he had little chance of hitting any of the men on the deck of the small, fast-moving craft from this distance.

"From up here," said Grimaldi, "it looks like their circuits are getting wider. They're going to try to break off at some point, once they think they've got enough range not to get cut apart when they give us their backside."

"You're right about that," McCarter said. "Keep them moving. Our friends here have had enough Thorn rockets for one day."

"Roger that," Grimaldi said. "What do you want me to do once they start running?"

"Let's follow them back to wherever they're going," McCarter said. "Small ships like that, they're going to have another, bigger craft somewhere around here. Plenty of ships in these waters. It will make it easier if we know precisely which one we're looking for. Have the Farm do some serious real-time imaging of what's moving, too. If we lose them, maybe they can sleuth out what we're hoping to find."

It was the Farm's satellite imaging technology that had given them the priority target list they now had. Kurtzman and his team of computer jockeys had found a crazy kind of pattern to the pirate strikes, or whatever they were, and had accurately predicted the assault on the Filipino ship. McCarter wondered what other wizardry the Farm's personnel might come up with once they had some actual combat data to work with.

"David?" Grimaldi's voice sounded again in McCarter's ear. "Something's up. I've got unusual activity on the deck of that ship. They're dumping something into the water."

Something white under the churning waves caught McCarter's eye.

"Calvin!" McCarter called over his shoulder. "What do you make of that?" He pointed.

"Oh, hell, no," James said. He looked at McCarter.

The Briton swore, grabbed James and threw them both to the deck. The action came none too soon. Whatever was in the water struck the side of the Filipino ship and exploded, shaking the vessel and throwing shrapnel up over the railing. McCarter flinched as something burned his cheek.

Some kind of klaxon began to sound belowdecks on the Filipino ship. The sailors trying to put out the fire on the deck became even more agitated, several of them disappearing below.

"What the hell was that?" James asked. "Some kind of torpedo?"

"We'll figure that out later," said McCarter. "Right now we've got to keep them off us. G-Force, did you copy that explosion? They're using some kind of submerged hardware to target us. We may be going down. Do what you can to keep them off us."

"On it," Grimaldi said. "G-Force, out!" The Sikorsky immediately took a more aggressive posture, driving the motor launch farther and farther out.

McCarter didn't know what kind of range the submersible weapons had, or whether the enemy had more of them, but when no more came spinning through the waves, he figured they were doing okay.

Grimaldi finally reported that the motor launch was heading off and asked for orders. "Should I follow as planned?" the pilot asked.

"Negative," McCarter answered. He and James were making their way below now. Their weapons hung on their slings. The Filipino sailors looked at them strangely but seemed to understand that these men in combat fatigues without insignia were somehow on their side. If nothing else, the fact that McCarter had fired on the pirates had established that. Eventually, the two men encountered a man directing a work crew. Water was rushing in through a rupture in the hull, but the crew was moving fast to patch it. The man overseeing the action wore the uniform of a captain in the Filipino navy.

"Captain!" McCarter called. "English?"

The captain whirled and fixed them with a wide-eyed look. "I speak," he said. "Who are you?"

"Friends, Captain," McCarter said. "I'm with a regional counter-piracy force. Your government was told we would be in the area."

"Chopper?" the captain asked. He pointed above his head, as if Grimaldi's bird could be seen through the bulkheads.

"Yes," McCarter said. "That was us. We're here to help. Tell us what to do."

The sailors were struggling to manhandle metal plates into position, which the other members of the work crew were bolting down. The captain gave up on finding the words and simply pointed. McCarter and James joined the Filipinos and began heaving metal plates from one side of the compartment to the other, fighting against the rising waters already swamping their boots.

"This is G-Force," announced Grimaldi's voice in McCarter's ear. "The pirate craft has withdrawn. Repeat. The enemy vessel has withdrawn. I am flying standby cover to make sure nothing else creeps up on us. I've also alerted Filipino naval command that one of their ships is in distress, although I suspect the folks aboard her have already done that. I'm told help is on the way."

"Good," McCarter said. "Get ready to touch down on the deck if it looks like we can't keep this thing afloat. We didn't see any wounded, but if they've got them, we need to be prepared to evac."

"Roger," Grimaldi acknowledged. "Wait. Wait, I have contact again. The launch—"

A burst of static made McCarter grab his ear in pain. He tapped the transceiver as suddenly there was nothing on the line.

James looked at McCarter and pointed to his ear. "Do you have anything?" he asked before going back to helping the Filipinos mount another metal plate.

"Nothing," McCarter said. "G-Force? Come in, G-Force!"

The klaxon, which had been quiet, started up again. Red lights mounted in protective steel cages began to blink above the compartment hatchway.

"Captain?" James asked. "What is it?"

"Pirates!" the Filipino shouted. "Pirates come back!"

Another explosion, somewhere under the water and near the hull, caused the entire beleaguered ship to tremble beneath their feet.

"Oh, man," said James. "I do not like the sound of that."

"Captain!" McCarter called.

"We die now," the captain said.

CHAPTER FOUR

"You owe me twenty bucks, Gadgets," Lyons growled.

"I'm pretty sure," Blancanales said, "that you two established that."

The members of Able Team were zip-tied by wrist and ankle to straight-backed wooden chairs. They sat in a storage room on the basement level of Rhemsen's headquarters. There was no other furniture in the locked room. The walls were bare cinder block. The only light was a bare energy-saver compact fluorescent bulb plugged into a light socket hanging by its wire from the ceiling.

"It's good to know that RhemCorp is committed to keeping the world a greener place," Schwarz said, looking up at the bulb.

"Shut up, Gadgets," Lyons and Blancanales said in unison.

"Not for nothing," Schwarz continued, ignoring them both, "but I really enjoy these pre-interrogation banter sessions."

"If I had a dollar for every time we've been captured and worked over by some goon squad," Lyons began.

"I do," Blancanales said. "I've been investing my captured-by-goons dollars. I'm going to leave Able and retire early. Now seems like a good time."

"Don't you start, Pol," Lyons warned. He opened his mouth to say more but the door to the storage room was thrown open. In it, framed by the scant light from the overhead bulb, stood a man in a gray Blackstar Corporation T-shirt and a pair of tiger-striped fatigues. The pants were bloused into polished combat boots, probably steel-toed. Lyons took special note of the chromed .45-caliber automatic in a drop-holster on the man's thigh. The man was big, as big as Carl Lyons, with swollen biceps and sinewy forearms to match. He cracked his knuckles through the half-fingered leather gloves he wore.

"Well, well, well," the newcomer said. His head was shaved smooth, his features craggy and thick. His jaw was square enough to cut diamonds. "Three little pigs, trussed up as nice as you like. Feel flattered, little piglets. I'm a commander in the Blackstar Corporation, which means you rate the big guns."

"You got the wrong room, Tinkerbell," Lyons said. "Stripper-gram delivery is down the hall."

That brought a frown to the Blackstar man's face. "The name," he said, his tone low and menacing, "is Fitzpatrick, Jason J. 'Jay' to my friends and the lovely ladies I always leave wanting more. And to you, I answer to 'God.' Because that, my little pigs, is what I am—God of your universe, until you beg me to kill you."

"Oh, no," Schwarz said. "He's going to douche us to death."

Fitzpatrick quietly closed the door. He turned and fixed Schwarz with a stare Lyons could only describe as bloodthirsty. That was bad. Lyons had seen that type before. Fitzpatrick was probably a vet, but one of those who had done his tour or tours just at the edge of crazy. There were always men who took a war zone to mean that there were no rules…and that meant there was no need for humanity. Fitzpatrick had the look of a man who enjoyed killing… and who knew he did because he'd indulged the urge. As the big Blackstar man came closer, Lyons noted the clip of a folding knife in his left-hand front pocket.

"Say that again," Fitzpatrick said to Schwarz.

"Are those weight-lifting gloves?" Schwarz said, looking up at the Blackstar man. "Please tell me those aren't weight-lifting gloves. Nobody is that gigantic a douche nozzle."

Lyons winced despite himself. He saw Fitzpatrick draw back his hand; saw the motion telegraphed from a mile away. Then the big Blackstar mercenary pimp-slapped Schwarz so hard that, for a moment, Lyons feared his partner's jaw might be dislocated. The Stony Man Farm electronics expert did his best to ride the momentum of the strike, but there was only so much he could do strapped to a chair. Blood sprayed from Schwarz's lower lip.

"You're going to find," Fitzpatrick said, "that I've got no sense of humor. No sense of humor at all."

"That explains the dude-bro body spray," Schwarz said.

"Stop it, damn you!" Lyons barked. Schwarz turned to Lyons and managed a bloody grin. Fitzpatrick did the same then slapped Schwarz across the face again. This time, the electronics whiz did not manage a witty retort. Lyons felt fire begin to smolder deep in his stomach.

"Now," Fitzpatrick said, "this is relatively simple. You came onto this property representing yourself as federal agents. You claim knowledge of Mr. Rhemsen's export activities. Obviously you have connections. I want to know what those connections are. I want to know exactly what government agency is looking into Mr. Rhemsen, and I don't for a second believe it's the Justice Department. Who are you with? Intelligence? CIA? Homeland Security? NSA?"

"NSA," Schwarz said, spitting blood. "And we need

to talk to you about all the porn you're downloading on your wireless phone."

This time Fitzpatrick cuffed Schwarz on the side of the head. It was a casual blow, almost contemptuous, but there was a lot of muscle behind Fitzpatrick's strikes. Schwarz could not take that kind of punishment for long.

"You're a coward," Lyons heard himself say.

"What's that?" Fitzpatrick said. He sounded genuinely curious. Fixing his attention on Lyons, he took a step closer. "Let me guess," he said. "You're the leader of this little band of heroes, aren't you? You have the look."

"You want to beat on somebody, Tinkerbell," Lyons said, "you beat on me. Only a coward picks the skinniest guy in the room."

Fitzpatrick looked at Blancanales, then back to Lyons. "I don't know," he said. "The gray-haired fellow there doesn't look much more substantial. But I have this thing about beating up senior citizens."

"I doubt it," Lyons said.

"Okay, you got me," Fitzpatrick replied. "I don't care who I beat up. But you're missing the point, hero. This isn't a fight. It isn't even schoolyard bullying. This is an interrogation. You're going to tell me who you work for. You're going to tell me what the government knows. And when you've finished telling me, I'm going to kill you quickly, and you're going to be grateful."

"Fat chance," Lyons said.

"I'm sorry," Fitzpatrick said. He flexed his fingers together, cracking all his knuckles at once. "I might have given you the idea that we were debating that. We aren't. I'm telling you exactly what's going to happen. I like to skip to the end."

"Funny," Schwarz said. "We were just talking about that."

"Enough," Lyons growled. He admired his partner's

courage, but now was not the time. Provoking this psychopath was just going to make things worse.

"Still," Fitzpatrick said, "I get your point. And, yeah, this is hardly sporting." He drew his folding knife from his pocket. Lyons realized it was one of Able Team's knives, taken by the Blackstar guards when Lyons and his team were searched and then tied up. Fitzpatrick snapped open the blade with a flick of his wrist, ignoring the thumb stud that would have let him snap it open more securely and with less grandstanding. The Blackstar man examined the edge against the tip of his finger. "Nice and sharp," he said. He went for Schwarz again.

"Over here!" Lyons shouted, straining against his zip ties hard enough to make his chair shift beneath him. The wood of the chair creaked in protest. "Over here, you son of a bitch! Try me!"

"Cool your jets, Captain Ham-hands," Fitzpatrick taunted. "See? I can make funny jokes, too. You like jokes, little man?" He was talking to Schwarz now. "You're going to love this one."

Lyons braced himself for what was to come. The men of Stony Man Farm were no stranger to the types of horrors that could be visited on an imprisoned man. In years past, when the Mafia had held sway, it was nothing to their torturers to carve up victims so badly that a mercy killing was the only option. It was an art with some of those jackals. Fitzpatrick didn't have that kind of finesse, but he was probably no stranger to stabbing helpless victims. Able Team's leader told himself that he just might have to watch Schwarz die in front of him.

"You do this," Lyons said, "and you're going to die with your neck under my boot."

"I'll do what I can to live with the fear of that," Fitzpatrick said. He reached out and, in one smooth slash, cut the zip tie securing Schwarz's left wrist.

Lyons's jaw dropped.

Fitzpatrick wasn't finished. He cut the tie securing Schwarz's other wrist, then the ones at the Stony Man commando's ankles. Stepping back, he struck a martial arts pose and beckoned with one hand. "Come and get it, little man."

"Perry," Lyons cautioned, using his cover name. "Don't."

"Sorry, boss," Schwarz said. "But I couldn't live with myself if I didn't kick this jackass in the—"

Fitzpatrick danced close as Schwarz was rising from the chair, lashing out with something concealed in his left hand. The tick-tick-tick of the electric transformer was unmistakable. The Blackstar man had just lit up Schwarz with a stun gun that he had concealed on his person. The effect was immediate: Schwarz's muscles clenched and he went weak in the knees. Fitzpatrick grinned and threw down the little black plastic box.

To his credit, Schwarz did not fall, but Fitzpatrick followed the jolt with a knee to the Able Team operative's groin. As the electronics expert doubled over, the Blackstar commander drove both his massive elbows down onto Schwarz's back, knocking the much slimmer man into the floor.

"Stop this!" Blancanales called out.

"You'll get your turn," Fitzpatrick said. He threw a savage kick to Schwarz's ribs. Schwarz grunted in pain and tried to roll out. Then he was up, on his feet, shaking but game, his hands raised and ready. "Hey, we've got a player!" Fitzpatrick said. "Come on, boy. Show Uncle Jay what you've got. I promise, I won't cripple you so badly that you'll have to have somebody feed you for the rest of your life. But then again, my promises usually don't mean jack."

"You are such a dick," Schwarz said, and kicked Fitzpatrick in the face.

It was a good kick, and Schwarz might have laid low a smaller man with it, but he was weakened from the stun gun and had already had his brain knocked around inside his head for a few rounds. Fitzpatrick absorbed it, shook it off and slammed a Muay Thai round kick into Schwarz's flank that dropped him to the floor again.

"Tell me what I want to know," Fitzpatrick said to Lyons. He stood with his foot on Schwarz's chest as Schwarz gasped for air. "If you don't, I'm going to beat this man to death in front of you. I'm guessing that the idea of that bothers you a lot, big man. You hero types, you live and breathe for this kind of thing. Seeing your buddy get his guts stomped out…well, I'm betting that's more than you can handle."

"You'd be surprised," Schwarz started to say, trying to form another verbal jab. Fitzpatrick cut him off, raising his boot and slamming it down, driving out what little air Schwarz had in his lungs. Schwarz wheezed in pain.

"He's cute, in a stupid sort of way," Fitzpatrick said. "Every squad's got one of this guy. The guy who's always cracking jokes. The guy who never takes anything seriously. And you know what happens to that guy, big man? One day he gets fragged, and nobody much cares, because everybody is sick and damned tired of hearing him talk all the time."

"I'm pretty sick and tired of hearing *you* talk," Lyons said. He kept his voice low. It was a struggle to maintain his self-control. He wanted to punch this Fitzpatrick into a bloody bag of meat.

Schwarz was still stirring on the floor, so Fitzpatrick

kicked him in the head. Schwarz grew still, his limbs slack. He was still breathing—Lyons could tell that much—but he was clearly out cold. Well, that was probably for the best. Unconsciousness was Schwarz's best friend right now, especially because it meant he couldn't run his mouth and take any more punishment.

"I think we've exhausted the entertainment value of that one," Fitzpatrick said. He went to Blancanales, whose eyes followed the knife carefully before landing on the stun gun still on the floor. "Oh, you're thinking about that, aren't you, Gramps?" the Blackstar commander said. "You think that little battery-powered toy is going to put me down? You're going to have to do that on your own. And you're going to have to do it while your team leader watches you get your—"

Blancanales slammed the heel of his palm up under Fitzpatrick's jaw before raking his fingers back down the man's face. In World War II jargon, the maneuver was called a chin jab, and if Blancanales hadn't been trying to do it while rising from the chair in which he'd been held, it might have done some serious damage. As it was, Blancanales's full body weight was not supporting the strike. Fitzpatrick hissed in displeasure and slammed an elbow into the side of his opponent's head. Blancanales went down but, thanks to his training, managed to perform a shoulder roll and come up again.

Fitzpatrick was ready for it. As Blancanales rolled through the fall, Fitzpatrick stuck to him like a shadow and when Blancanales started to rise again, the bigger man slammed the butt of his chromed pistol into the back of Blancanales's skull. The Able Team warrior made no sound as he dropped to his hands and knees, stunned. Fitzpatrick stopped long enough to grin smugly at Lyons.

"Pretty proud of yourself, aren't you, Tinkerbell?"

Lyons said. "Beating up a couple of guys who can barely stand because the circulation to their hands and feet has been cut off for an hour. Yeah, you're a real macho guy."

Fitzpatrick kicked Blancanales, but it wasn't a rib-cracker this time. Blancanales was able to roll away from the kick. The Blackstar man dropped on top of Blancanales anyway, wrapping one thick arm around his captive's throat. Dazed as he was, Blancanales didn't appear to have much of a chance, not the way this "fight" had been set up against him from the start. Fitzpatrick tucked his arm into the crook of his other limb and wrapped one hand around the back of Blancanales's head in a classic rear naked choke. It wasn't long before Blancanales was unconscious. Fitzpatrick dropped the commando and stood, once more facing Lyons.

"Just you and me now, champ," he said.

"I'm game for a main event," Lyons said. "Cut me loose and I'll show you a few things."

"You keep calling me Tinkerbell," Fitzpatrick said. "You saying what I think you're saying?"

"Tinkerbell's a fantasy," said Lyons. "That's what you are. A fantasy. A legend in your own mind. I'm going to break you, Tinkerbell. I'm going to show you that the real life ain't nothing like the badass fantasy you've built for yourself."

"I gotta admit," Fitzpatrick said, "that I did not see that coming. It was about the last thing I'd thought you'd say. And now I'm going to leave you alone in here with your buddies."

"Come on!" Lyons shouted. "What are you afraid of, you coward?"

Fitzpatrick laughed. "You probably think you've got me figured out, big man," he said. "But, news flash. You don't. Much as I'd like to kick your behind all around this room, that's not the game. Making you watch me beat up these two, now *that's* the game. I'm going to come back every half hour, give or take. Just long enough for your guys to shake it off each time I clean their clocks. Of course, it's going to get worse as I go. Pretty soon they'll be lucky if they still remember math. Some teeth are going to come out. And before we're done I may start cutting off fingers, just for the fun of it."

"Keep talking," Lyons warned. "Just keep talking."

"I want you to think about that," Fitzpatrick said. "I want you to think about what I just did, and what I'm going to do. Wait for twenty minutes. A guy like you probably can do it in his head. I don't care if you count it off. Just wait for it. And when I come back, know that I'm going to keep taking your little boys apart until you give me the information. It's not a lot to ask. It won't even get anybody else killed. Are their lives—" he gestured to Blancanales and Schwarz "—worth what you're withholding?"

The big Blackstar man took the time to strap the two Able Team operatives back into their chairs. Then he left, closing the door behind him.

Lyons blew out a sigh of relief.

Schwarz opened one eye. "Is he gone?"

Blancanales opened both of his. "I thought that guy would never shut up."

"He talks almost as much as Gadgets," Lyons said.

"Hey," Schwarz complained. "That's not fair. I think he cracked my ribs."

"First good news I've heard all day," Lyons teased.

"Then get ready for the second good news," Blancanales said. There was a click. Blancanales shifted in his chair and, suddenly, his hands were in front of him, unrestrained. Using the folding knife he had lifted from Fitzpatrick's pocket during the fight, he cut the fresh zip ties securing his feet. Then he cut Schwarz's bonds and went to free Lyons.

"Gadgets," Lyons said, "you still owe me twenty bucks."

"Pol, can I borrow twenty bucks?" Schwarz said.

"Depends," Blancanales answered. He held up the brown leather billfold he had also picked from the Blackstar commander's pocket. "How much cash you figure a guy like that carries on him?"

CHAPTER FIVE

"Captain!" shouted McCarter over the klaxon. "Keep your people working on the repairs. We'll handle the threat out there!"

The Filipino captain seemed unconvinced, but stopping his ship from sinking was foremost on his mind. He said something that McCarter either couldn't understand or could not hear—it was indecipherable to the Briton—and turned back to his repair team. McCarter, meanwhile, held his Tavor tighter to his body and rushed back up the gangway to take the ladder to the deck. James hurried close behind.

Once on the deck, McCarter immediately started taking fire. He ducked back, using the metal shell around the gangway for cover. "Look out! Contact forward!"

James scooted up around his team leader and managed to make the deck before sparks caught on the metal. Bullets rang like angry bees around both men. James was fast, though, faster than the enemy gunfire. He dodged in and around the structural outcroppings on the deck, using them for cover, working his way to the left. McCarter took the cue and started working toward his own right. The gunfire was coming from the bow, whereas they were currently amidships.

Abruptly a storm of wind and sea spray caught him in the face. He looked up, following the noise. The Sikorsky shot past, flying laterally, as Grimaldi lined up the nose. Then the great chopper's guns and grenade launcher opened up, targeting a section of the water itself. McCarter watched, amazed, until the gunfire from forward of his position drove him back behind the cover of the next "step" in the deck layout.

"G-Force!" he called, pressing his transceiver against his ear. "Come in! What are you doing?"

There was still no reply. McCarter had thought perhaps something about the structure of the ship had interfered with their signal, perhaps depending on where Grimaldi was positioned relative to McCarter and James. But now, on the deck, with line of sight to the chopper, he still could not raise a signal. What the bloody hell was going on?

"David," said James in his earbud, "I've got eyes on them. They're hiding behind a railing about five meters from the bow. The area just to the left of the gray tarp. I'm seeing some grappling hooks, too. Looks like not all the pirates were blown up when we took out that first launch."

"Makes sense," McCarter responded. "The rats found the nearest sinking ship."

Just then, another set of explosions rocked the damaged Filipino vessel. McCarter was drenched once more with spray. What he saw, when he looked to the sea once more, was bewildering for a moment. Grimaldi was still strafing the water and sowing the waves with 40 mm grenades. Then there was yet another explosion, bigger than what a grenade or even a series of grenades going off could create.

That cheeky bastard, McCarter thought. He's detonating whatever those submersible torpedo weapons are. He's keeping them off us.

There was no way to explain what was interfering with his communications with the chopper, but Grimaldi was obviously alive and doing fine…or as fine as a man could do while taking fire in a combat zone. There was small-arms fire coming from the second motor launch, the one that survived, and that boat was now making fast circles well wide of the Filipino ship. The idea, McCarter imagined, was to keep the launch out of range of the Filipino ship's guns and to avoid becoming a target for the Sikorsky.

McCarter tried to gauge just how many men might be aboard that launch. It couldn't be that many, given the boat's size. If the fast-attack boat had carried a limited payload of Thorn rockets, that might explain why the crew had turned to whatever those torpedo-like devices were. He made a note to scan back through his dossier in the Farm's mission brief to look for other technical specs on RhemCorp weaponry. So far, the Thorns were the only ones that had been used in previous attacks, and thus those were the only ones McCarter had bothered to familiarize himself with.

A shipment of rockets was one thing; weapons could go missing, and frequently did, when they were shipped overseas. But if the pirates were equipped with a full array of RhemCorp's catalog, that looked very bad for Harold Rhemsen and his company.

None of which made a damned bit of difference right now, McCarter considered as the ship on which he was currently taking fire might sink out from underneath all of them at any minute.

"How many shooters do you have?" McCarter asked James. He did his best to work his way up toward the bow. The deck of the Filipino ship descended from the bridge area to the bow in graduated steps, each step bordered by a metal railing and whatever structural reinforcement was required for the equipment built into that area. This translated into plenty of cover, but it also meant the shooters near the bow could keep laying down bullets relatively unhindered from farther down the deck.

"I've got eyes on two," James said. "No, scratch that. Three. One looks half scorched, but he's mobile. They've all got Kalashnikovs and they look plenty mean."

"They've got nowhere to go unless they take down this ship," McCarter said. "If they can't make it safe for the other launch to swing back and pick them up, they're out of luck. I think the penalty for piracy, even internationally, is still hanging around these parts, mate. Can't say I blame them."

"Yeah." James said nothing more for several moments, giving McCarter time to get into position.

Finally the Briton judged he was as close as he was going to get to the pirate boarders. Around them on the deck, fires still continued to burn, although the Filipinos had all disappeared. They were below, trying to keep the ship afloat. Hopefully none of the fires up here would get bad enough to seriously endanger the boat before they could be attended to.

From where he was now positioned, McCarter could see the tops of the three pirates' heads. One of those heads was shaved bald and looked very red, then very black. Those were nasty burns. Shock and exposure might kill that man before somebody could put a round through his dome. For now, though, the pirate was mobile and fighting.

"I've got them, too, now," McCarter advised James. "On my mark, I want you to lay down enough fire on the left to drive them over to the right. There's a gap in the railing there. Just crowd them, mate. Drive them toward the gap. I'll do the rest."

"Affirmative," James said.

"Now!" McCarter ordered.

James's Tavor started belching 5.56 mm death. The

Stony Man commando squeezed measured bursts from the weapon, which Phoenix Force had used many times before. The compact design and modular ergonomics made the rifle a favorite among combat troops. It was comfortable and accurate. The red-dot optics offered good, fast, target acquisition, and the rate of fire was quick enough to be truly fearsome.

From his position, McCarter was basically guessing. In combat, you took what you could get. Much like a hunter who ascertains his target then fires at the shadow where his target will be, McCarter simply waited for what light he could see through the gap to disappear. He did not need much. A single moment was all it would take.

There it was.

McCarter fired, just once, then once again for good measure. The shadow disappeared from the gap. That would be his pirate target falling away from the section of railing that had betrayed him.

"Lather, rinse, repeat," James said through the transceiver. Once more he drove the pirates back toward the gap where McCarter could see them, and once more McCarter took the shot that was offered. The trick would not work a third time, however. No matter how hard James tried to light up one section of the railing, the third and final pirate simply would not move from his spot.

"I think he might be down," James said. "I can't get him to budge."

A shot rang out from where the pirate was sheltered. There was a pause, then two more shots, one of which ricocheted close to McCarter.

"No such luck," McCarter stated. "He's still with us, mate."

"Cover me," James directed. "I'm going over there and have a talk with that man."

McCarter allowed himself a tight, grim smile. When

Calvin James had a heart-to-heart talk with someone, it usually involved the business end of a combat knife. The Stony Man commando was one of the most experienced knife fighters McCarter had known in his professional career.

The Sikorsky continued to make arcs overhead, its guns blazing, chasing and harrying the motor launch. Finally, though, the pirate craft stopped making circuits closer to the Filipino ship and started to recede instead. McCarter reached for his earpiece, intending to give Grimaldi orders. If they could make sure the ship was going to stay above the water line, the Briton would feel comfortable tasking the Sikorsky once more with pursuing the pirates back to their tender. No sooner had he touched the earbud than he realized, of course, that he could not.

The Sikorsky turned to present the cockpit to the deck of the Filipino ship. McCarter checked for enemy fire. There was none. The gunfire had all ceased. The only sounds now were the distant whine of the motor launch as it retreated, the crackling of flames aboard the Filipino ship and the ringing of the alarms belowdecks. McCarter stood and signaled Grimaldi to come closer.

As the chopper turned, McCarter could see that there was damage to the fuselage. Wisps of smoke trailed from a scorched hole in the helicopter. There was some connection between the damage and the radio failure, but McCarter had no idea what that could be.

T. J. Hawkins began to descend on a drop line. The youngest member of Phoenix Force hit his quick-release when he was still a couple feet from the deck. He dropped and absorbed the fall with his knees.

"Hawk," said McCarter when he joined him, "what's the condition of the chopper?"

"They hit us with something," Hawkins said.

"One of the Thorn rockets?" McCarter asked, knowing as he said it that it could not be true. If the Sikorsky had taken a Thorn it would have been damaged much worse than it had been.

"No. Some kind of nonexplosive warhead that crippled our electrical systems," Hawkins elaborated. "Jack is keeping the chopper up there, but there's a whole lot that's not working. He says he needs time to set her down and get her properly repaired."

"Then following the pirates is out of the question," McCarter said.

"Jack says we're lucky he hasn't taken up swimming, so I'd say yes, that's about the size of it," Hawkins drawled. "He says if you want anything, flash him with Morse where he can see you."

"Bloody hell," McCarter swore. "My Morse code is as rusty as my…well. Actually, it does seem to come up now and again, doesn't it?"

The Briton worked his way around to where James had gone to have his "talk" with the third boarder. He found James going through the pockets of the dead man, who was slumped against the railing on the deck in a spreading pool of his own blood.

"Ghastly," McCarter commented. "Did you put him down?"

"No," James said. "Found him like this. I guess those last few shots were his way of saying goodbye. He's got a nick in his femoral artery. Bled out fast."

"I'm sure no one will mourn his passing," McCarter said. "Not much, anyway." The man was gray from blood loss. As it turned out, this was the scorched pirate, who had evidently gotten the worst of the explosion that had obliterated the first of the pirate launches.

There was a sudden bustle of activity from below. The

Filipino captain and several of his men emerged. Four of the sailors carried M-16 A-1 rifles, one of the standard infantry weapons of the armed forces of the Philippines. The soldiers took up formation, two kneeling, two standing, and aimed their weapons at McCarter, James and Hawkins. The captain looked more than a little annoyed.

"We no sink," he said.

"Now see here, mate," McCarter said. "I realize perhaps now that things are under control, you're feeling like asking just what we're doing on your ship. But as you can see—" he pointed to the helicopter hovering overhead "—we're the reason you didn't get blown out of the water."

"I check with my government," the captain said. "You no move."

"That's fair enough, mate," McCarter said. "We no move. But I'd like to signal my chopper to put in to port. He's got electrical problems."

The captain's eyes narrowed and his hand drifted to the M-9 automatic now holstered on his belt. Evidently the captain had decided, after seeing to the damage to his vessel, that a trip to the armory had been in order. McCarter couldn't say he blamed the man. Under the circumstances, it seemed unlikely that McCarter would himself just ignore boarders who claimed to be on the right side.

More crew members were moving around the deck now, using portable extinguishers to put out the fires still burning. The captain watched them, probably to make sure everything was under control. In the distance across the water, several vessels were now approaching.

James pointed, but the captain shook his head.

"You called for help?" McCarter asked the captain.

"Navy coming," the captain announced. "Hope you three check out."

"We will, mate," McCarter said. "We will." He took his

signal mirror from a pouch on his web gear and angled it at the chopper. Hoping he was getting the message across, he did what he could to flash "port" a couple of times. Grimaldi got the hint, dipped the nose of the helicopter then turned and limped away.

"There goes our ride," James said.

"I'm sure the captain here could be convinced to help us put in to port," McCarter said. "Once he's determined to his satisfaction that we're not his enemies. Which I think he already understands, for the most part."

"I can feel his understanding through those four assault rifles," Hawkins said.

"People have different ways of expressing trust," James said.

McCarter wasn't sure, but he thought he saw the Filipino captain crack a smile.

"Trust issues," the captain noted.

"What's that, mate?" McCarter asked.

"I have," the captain said, grinning.

The troops lowered their weapons. James and Hawkins exchanged glances.

"Don't we all," James said. He blew out the breath he had been holding. "Don't we all."

CHAPTER SIX

Fitzpatrick entered Rhemsen's office and helped himself to a chair without being asked. As he always did, Rhemsen glared through that frozen plastic face of his, but there wasn't much he could do about Fitzpatrick's liberties. After all, Rhemsen knew as well as Fitzpatrick did that without Blackstar men to provide muscle for RhemCorp's operations, there would be nothing between Rhemsen and a half dozen major enemies the man had already made.

Some of those enemies, like the Mob, wouldn't hesitate to start knocking over RhemCorp holdings if they thought they could do so without provoking a war. But with Blackstar guarding Rhemsen's assets, and given just how many men with guns Blackstar could put on the street, even the mafia knew better than to poke that hornets' nest with a stick.

"You look nervous, boss," Fitzpatrick said. "More nervous than usual. Nervous even for you, I mean."

"What do you think, Jason?" Rhemsen said. He was drinking something with a lot of ice in it. The glass clinked when Rhemsen snatched it and gulped the contents down. His eyes were wide when he looked up again. "There are powerful forces that know what we're doing."

"Which powerful forces are those, Harry?" Fitzpatrick said, grinning. He knew that Rhemsen hated being called "Harry."

"Don't be a fool," Rhemsen said. "Government involvement was inevitable. But it's too soon. It throws off my timetable considerably."

"Wait a minute," Fitzpatrick said. "I thought you said you had this all figured out. That's why we grabbed those guys. That's why you said it was okay to disappear them. How deep are you digging this hole? I don't want to end up in prison for the rest of my life."

"I'm the reason you aren't already there," Rhemsen argued. "Don't forget that, Jason. Without me, without my lawyers, without my financing, Blackstar wouldn't even exist in its current form. The corporation that now bears the name isn't the first to hold the moniker, nor will it be the last before we're finished. If you want to stay one step ahead of Uncle Sam and his investigators, you need me as much as I need you."

"Would you calm down already?" Fitzpatrick said. "You're worse than my mother. Or you would be if she was still alive, that miserable broad. Look, I know that, all right? I just want to know what you think this means for the operation."

"What do you *think* it means?" Rhemsen shot back. "We're going to have to suspend our sales pipelines outside the country until we're sure we aren't compromised. And I need you to mobilize elements of Blackstar in the Philippines. If the government is sending agents to my doorstep, it means they're certain RhemCorp hardware is involved. They just don't know what they can prove yet as far as I am concerned. So they'll be investigating both ends, and that means there will be government agents sniffing around the ports in the South China Sea. Set a trap, if you can. Lure whomever the government has sent and make them disappear. That should stall things, at the very least, as they try to figure out where they went wrong. Make sure your men coordinate with my pirates."

"Listen to you," Fitzpatrick said. "*Your* pirates. You're paying a bunch of broken-down, sea-going thieves and you're hoping for loyalty. That's not going to end well. They're not professional soldiers. Not like me. Not like my men."

"They're vicious and, for a price, they take orders," Rhemsen said. "That is precisely what I require them to be. Isn't that what you call it? 'Pay to play.' Isn't that how Americans refer to trade with China? America hates China, paints it as the aggressor, disrespects the nation with the largest standing military force on Earth...but then, for a price, sells its manufacturing to this nation it so reviles."

"You talk like you're not part of that," Fitzpatrick said. "Last I knew you were part of the American capitalist machine, Harry."

"So I am," Rhemsen replied. "Fortunately for both of us I've spread enough of the proceeds around that capitalist machine in Washington, in the form of bribe money. It will serve to slow the process of any investigation that will arise. Or at least, I thought I would do so. These men...it worries me, not knowing exactly who or what they represent. Money will only take us so far if forces inside Washington have decided to take direct action against us. This is unusual. Direct action is usually last on a long list of delaying tactics in the government."

"It doesn't matter," Fitzpatrick said. "I'll break those agents. If their leader doesn't crack, one of his two subordinates will. I'll kill one of them if I have to. That ought to shake the other one up. And if it doesn't, watching them both die will soften up the big one. It should only take a few days of sleep deprivation and torture to get him to spill."

"I'm not sure we *have* a few days," Rhemsen said. "And I wish you wouldn't talk that way."

"Don't be a weakling," Fitzpatrick said. "What do you

want me to say—'enhanced interrogation'? We both know what I've got to do to get them to talk. But you need to consider something, boss."

"And that is?"

"What are you gonna do if they come clean? Let's say laughing boy and his two friends turn out to be NSA operatives. Are you prepared for the fallout from killing agents of the most secretive intelligence agency in the country?"

"Intelligence is a dangerous business," Rhemsen declared. "People employed in it disappear all the time."

"If I didn't know better, boss," Fitzpatrick said, "I'd think you spoke from experience." He dragged his boots from where he had propped them on Rhemsen's desk and planted them on the floor. "I'll get what they know. And then we can assess just how badly your revenue streams are impinged. But I gotta ask, Harry…"

Rhemsen sighed. "What is it you 'gotta ask'?" The last two words were full of contempt.

"What's your exit strategy?" Fitzpatrick pushed up from the chair. "I know mine. Blackstar can't keep reorganizing under new management forever. Sooner or later, some of those investigative hearings, or the Infernal Revenue bastards, are going to catch up to us. When that happens, I've got enough money and guns tucked away to keep me happy for a good long while, sitting on a beach with a drink in my hand in a country with no extradition treaty."

"I've never heard of such a plan," Rhemsen said dryly. "Truly, you possess a unique mind."

"So it's not the most original of plans," Fitzpatrick said. "But it will work and it's enough. What happens to you and your company, Rhemsen? The US government might forget about one guy, but they're not going to forget an entire corporation running high-tech weapons to enemies of the homeland. What are you going to do when this all comes out and they freeze your assets, Rhemsen? You ready to spend your nights on television, maybe on one of those webcam things, talking about how the American government is going to ice you? It's only a matter of time after that happens, you know, when they find somebody to cry 'rape' and then bring you up on charges. It happened to what's-his-name, the internet guy."

Rhemsen started to say something when the phone on his desk rang. Glaring at Fitzpatrick, he picked up the receiver and put it to his ear. There was a pause. "Yes," he finally said. "Yes, Mr. Lao. I'd like to meet to discuss with you those matters that have…occupied us previously… Yes…Yes, of course…All right. My secretary will apprise you of the time and location." He hung up the phone.

"You doing online dating now?" Fitzpatrick quipped.

"Shut up, Jason." Rhemsen sounded tired. "Just do your job."

"When have I not?"

"Just… Fine. Let me worry about my 'exit strategy,' Jason," Rhemsen said. "What I need from you is to find out just which branch of the government I need to throw money at next. Get those field agents to talk. Once they do, make sure nobody finds the bodies. That should be simple enough, even for you."

"Man, you are grumpy today." Fitzpatrick sneered. "You stay up here in your ivory tower for as long as you like, Harry. I'll go do the dirty work."

"See that you do."

Choking back another retort, Fitzpatrick figured he had needled the King of Plastic Surgery enough for one day. He left Rhemsen's office and sauntered down the hall, taking the elevator down to the subbasement level. He was now on the east end of the substructure. All the way on the opposite wall, the west end, was the interrogation section.

Rhemsen didn't like it when Fitzpatrick called it "the dungeon," but that's what it really was, and for the first time in a long time, it was being put to its intended use. The "storage closet" had never really been used for storage. Rhemsen's manufacturing facilities were all elsewhere. This building was nothing but offices full of engineers and bureaucrats, operatives and con artists. That's how all the suits looked to Fitzpatrick. He took a dim view of any profession he did not really understand, figuring that if he couldn't tell what a man did after ten seconds of explanation, then what that man did was probably bull.

Fitzpatrick liked to keep things simple.

At the thought, he cracked his knuckles again. He was really going to enjoy this. Growing up, he'd always been "hyperaggressive" or so the counselors had called it. With few prospects for college and a dismal high school record marred with disciplinary problems, it was only a matter of time before he'd ended up charged with assault and battery as an adult. He just liked fighting too much. So he'd joined the Marines.

That had lasted only as long as boot camp, where a savage fight with another recruit had ended in his washing out. He'd tried to join the Army after that, but whatever black mark was on his record had kept him out. He was actually marching out of that Army recruiting center, mad as he'd ever been, when one of Blackstar's recruiters had appeared out of nowhere to chat him up.

So he wanted to fight for his country, did he? Well, there was a way he could still do that. All he had to do was sign on with Blackstar. The pay was good and the questions were few. All he had to be able to do was follow orders.

Well, Fitzpatrick didn't give a damn about fighting for his country. He just wanted to fight, and he wanted to be paid for doing it. Blackstar or, more correctly, the company that would become Blackstar several name changes later, was happy to have him. Fitzpatrick rose quickly through the ranks. It helped that, eventually, he'd learned to channel his urge to smash people and things. Being able to hold that impulse in check, most of the time, allowed him to advance in the company's ranks and assume even greater positions of authority.

Now, he had a reasonable amount of autonomy. Blackstar didn't care what he did as long as he got things done. The company's management was busy for the most part just fielding and evading various congressional investigations, so they didn't care what was happening with him as long as the money flowed. Rhemsen paid well and he needed a lot of manpower. And so the cash came in, Fitzpatrick stayed employed, Blackstar's management left him alone and everybody was happy.

But it looked as if that all might come thundering to a close, if they couldn't get a handle on what was really going on. Rhemsen's weapons sales were the only thing keeping the company going, keeping it profitable. Rhemsen had slipped up and admitted that much to him before. The money spent in research and development on the Thorns, the GGX drop charges, the EM pulse taggers, the portable torpedoes…it was a lot. And apparently government contracts, combined with all the controls and regulations the government expected RhemCorp to follow, meant that the company couldn't manage a decent profit level. At least, that's what Rhemsen said. Who knew what that margin was supposed to be? Harry had expensive tastes, from what Fitzpatrick could see. No dude who was addicted to plastic surgery could be trusted around money, if you asked Jay Fitzpatrick. There was something just… wrong…about that guy's face. He was probably skimming profits from the company.

Either way, for the cash to keep flowing to Blackstar and thus into Fitzpatrick's pocket, RhemCorp's illegal arms sales, and the shipping pipelines that sustained them, had to stay open. Fitzpatrick wasn't privy to all the details in the South China Sea, but Rhemsen had alluded to big markets over there. Whatever his hired pirate crews were doing had something to do with all that. That was why Rhemsen had risked arming the pirates with Rhem-Corp's own hardware. It wasn't just an expedient means of accomplishing his goals in that part of the world. It was also some of the only leverage Rhemsen had, with the rest of his cash tied up in hiring muscle like Blackstar and the pirates themselves.

What a tangled web. That was what people said, right? The thought brought Fitzpatrick back to what Rhemsen had said about China and its government. What the hell had that been all about? And who was Lao? Could be Rhemsen was reaching out to the money men in China to back some of his losses. That didn't seem like a smart strategy to Fitzpatrick, using China to debt-roll Rhem-Corp's operations, but Fitzpatrick only cared so much. His interest in RhemCorp's financial health extended only as far as how much of Rhemsen's money was going into Blackstar's coffers. Even that was a relative thing. Jason Fitzpatrick wasn't really the loyalty type. He just knew not to crap where he ate.

He would do the job Blackstar needed him to do, and even enjoy it, as long as they kept paying him. If anything changed he'd find another outfit to take him. Private contracting was all the rage these days. Wars were expensive and outsourcing was economical. The business world had discovered that a long time ago. For that matter, hiring mercenaries to do the dirty work was a long-standing tradition in the history of war. He wasn't exactly a student of history, but he knew that much.

As he made his way through the darkened corridors of the sublevel, he reached the first high-security door, where a pair of Blackstar guards stood, subguns at the ready. Normally there was no need to keep anybody down here, but with high-speed, low-drag spooks like his three prisoners cooped up down there, he figured he had better post the men. Better safe than sorry. Although, if he was honest with himself, he really wasn't very impressed with what he'd seen so far from the captives.

"Jerry," Fitzpatrick said, nodding to the guard on the left. He threw a half salute to the man on the right. "Ryan."

"Sir," the two men said. "All quiet, sir."

Fitzpatrick looked at the men's equipment belts. "Who the holy hell authorized you guys to draw grenades? Are those…are those frags? Are you nuts?"

"But you said they were dangerous," Jerry said.

"Paurich and Witkowski have grenades, too," Ryan said, sounding defensive.

"The guys stationed inside?" Fitzpatrick said, incredulous. "I can see we need to have a serious talk about things that go boom and the dangers of enclosed spaces."

He reached into his back pocket for his wallet, where he carried his RFID security card. The card could simply be held in proximity to the electronic locks securing the double set of security doors. It formed an airlock, of sorts, with two guards out here and two more in the space between here and the room holding the prisoners.

His wallet was gone. "Shit."

Jerry and Ryan exchanged glances. "Sir?" Ryan asked.

"Hey," Jerry said. "Did you hear that? Like somebody

dropped a soda can on the floor. Something heavy and metal." He turned to put his ear to the security door.

Jason Fitzpatrick turned and ran for his life. He was almost to the stairwell, down the corridor from the security doors, when a tremendous explosion—like what you'd get if you detonated several stolen grenades all at once to breach a security door, for example—made his ears pop and threw him to the floor. He tasted blood from where his face had made contact with the steps. His vision threatened to gray out.

In less time than it took to think of it, Fitzpatrick was running through his actions in the dungeon. Yes, there could have been time during the fight for them to lift his wallet. But taking that wouldn't help unless... No. Damn it, they had the knife he'd taken off of one of them, too. And that meant that the spooks were on the loose, probably with the B&T subguns the guards in the airlock space had been carrying. They might also acquire additional weapons from Jerry and Ryan, if either of those guys still had equipment intact after the close-range blast.

Fitzpatrick wasn't sticking around to find out.

He took the steps two at a time, bounding up until he reached the ground-floor office level. Racing through the lobby, he told the miserable old bag at the front desk, "Security breach! Go to condition alpha! Condition alpha!"

He didn't wait to hear if the old battle-ax actually did what he said. He was already running out the front door for the parking lot. By the time he had the high-powered Dodge Charger running and had pulled to a tire-burning stop in front of the building, Rhemsen was rushing out with a briefcase in his hand.

The sound of automatic gunfire could be heard inside the building.

"Get in, damn you!" Fitzpatrick ordered.

Rhemsen practically fell into the Charger and slammed the door. He clutched his briefcase to his chest as though it could stop a bullet—which, actually, it could, because Fitzpatrick had seen to it that Rhemsen added a ballistic plate to the inside of the case. It was commercial security stuff, the kind of thing any nervous business executive could buy, but that didn't mean it wouldn't work.

"What is happening?" Rhemsen demanded. "Why did you use the evacuation code?"

"Because your spies or agents or whatever they are, are armed and loose," Fitzpatrick snapped. "And now that they know we're dirty and what's in store for them if we catch them, they're going to shoot first and ask questions later. That's what I'd do, in their position. So we're getting out of Dodge, boss. We're going to the factory."

"What good will holing up there do?" Rhemsen said. He sounded almost hysterical. "This is exactly what we were not supposed to let happen! If those agents do not disappear, everything will start to fall apart at once!"

"Keep your shirt on," Fitzpatrick said. "We've still got this." He reached across Rhemsen, popped the glove compartment and removed the remote detonator that was housed inside.

"You're going to blow the building?" Rhemsen asked.

"It's the only way to make sure they don't walk out of there. We've got to do it now, before they clear the place."

"It is…it is a very final move," said Rhemsen, hesitating. "I am not sure we are ready to cross that line."

Fitzpatrick swore under his breath. He poured on the speed, making the Charger's powerful engine scream. Putting the pedal to the floor, he focused on the road, making sure they didn't do something as stupid as cracking up trying to escape. When they reached the main highway, he throttled it back a bit, so as not to get the attention of the cops. But the detonator had limited range. Even if they'd had all the time in the world, which they did not, Rhemsen needed to push the button.

"Push it, boss," Fitzpatrick said. "Push the button."

"I am not sure…"

Exasperated, Fitzpatrick reached out and clamped his hand over Rhemsen's, forcing the businessman to close his fingers over the remote. The detonator beeped. Rhemsen bowed his head.

Fitzpatrick smiled, waiting for the sound of the building being flattened—the deep, rumbling explosion that would kill everyone still inside.

"Three," he said.

"Damn you, Jason!" Rhemsen said. "What have you done?"

"Two," Fitzpatrick continued. "One…"

CHAPTER SEVEN

Calapan, Mindoro Island

It was easy to think of Puerto Galera, the northwestern-most municipality of the Philippines's Oriental Mindoro province, as nothing but resorts, colorful umbrellas and girls in bikinis. But as was usually the case with resort towns, there was much of Puerto Galera that tourists never saw...and for good reason. Venturing too far out of the tourist areas was never advisable for young, pretty people who lacked life experience. Some of the area around Puerto Galera, namely Calapan, the only city in the province, could be pretty rough.

Oriental Mindoro, for its part, was roughly 140 kilometers southwest of Manila, bordered by Batangas Province on one side and the Verde Island Passage on the other. Calapan City, the provincial capital, boasted a population of 125,000 people. It was the busiest seaport on Mindoro Island and the hub of the province's industry and commerce. Much of Calapan was colorful and bustling as one would expect...but as in any city, there were seedier areas, and it was in these that Phoenix Force would find what they were looking for.

What appeared to be concrete or stone buildings, many of them painted bright colors, predominated. Many of the streets were absolute riots of overhead wires, shop signs and other obstacles. The streets were crowded with a number of vehicles, many of them motor scooters and bicycles. Pedicabs and motor-trike carts and conveyances were also abundant. The general mood, at least in the main part of the city, seemed positive enough.

Phoenix Force, dressed in combat gear, drew more than a few stares, but the presence of their Calapan City police escort helped discourage too much gawking. The provincial government had insisted on sending "protection" into the city with Phoenix Force, most likely to keep an eye on these foreign interlopers whom their government seemed inclined to indulge.

As for what had brought them to Calapan, well…that was something altogether different. McCarter was very suspicious of the timing. No sooner had they concluded their little adventure aboard the Filipino naval vessel than the Farm had received word through channels that a local informant, somewhere in Calapan, wanted to turn traitor for pay. The informant claimed to be part of a pirate crew operating in the area; a crew that took its orders from somewhere else. Just where that was, or from who, the informant wouldn't reveal…not until he was paid handsomely. An address in Calapan was provided, but it was a street only, not a specific location. The Farm had decided that, with Grimaldi temporarily grounded in Puerta Galera, this was a great time for Phoenix Force to stretch their land legs and check out the tip.

Bloody convenient, wasn't it? McCarter had been in a lousy mood all morning, considering the implications.

As for the Sikorsky, repairs were under way. Grimaldi had a pair of somewhat bewildered Filipino naval techs assisting him. Once all the dust had cleared, a few phone calls back and forth to Washington—with Hal Brognola involved—had been made, and the brass had satisfied itself that Phoenix Force was trying to help the locals, the

Filipino government had fallen over itself to render assistance. Something about McCarter and his men helping to prevent the sinking of a Filipino naval ship. Go figure.

An analysis of the damage to the Filipino ship, as well as Grimaldi's firsthand account of what had happened to his chopper while it was in the air, had been cross-referenced with the Farm's database. It was not a surprise that RhemCorp-manufactured weapons were being used. Now they could add several more examples to the list of contraindicated hardware known to have been employed by unauthorized, hostile forces in the South China Sea region. That list now included the XM-Thorn rocket, a portable torpedo system called the Mariner 21 and something called an EM Pulse Tagging Projectile, which was fired from the barrel of a conventional assault rifle like a rocket-propelled grenade. It was the pulse tagger that had damaged Grimaldi's whirlybird.

The rocket-propelled projectile was essentially a battery with a propellant behind it. On contact with its target, it discharged its payload, creating electrical disruptions. Originally, according to the annotations in the files, the weapon was contracted by the Department of Defense as a means of neutralizing vehicles. In field tests, it seldom completely incapacitated an enemy target, particularly armored vehicles. Despite these limitations, RhemCorp marketed the weapon for crowd control and traffic enforcement in the United States, as a means of partially disabling runaway vehicles. Kurtzman had added a note in the dossier that said sales of this particular weapon were abysmal. Apparently, Rhemsen had taken a bath on the thing. Interesting.

Their liaison from the Filipino military was a competent-looking character named Ocampo. As they neared the target street, McCarter turned to Lieutenant Ocampo and gestured left and right.

"Can your men take up positions at either end of the

street—cordon it off?" the Briton asked. "I don't want civilians caught in the crossfire if things get ugly."

"You expect that this will be...ugly?" Ocampo asked. His English was good, his tone sour. He seemed to know his business, but he also seemed less than thrilled with the presence of an armed, foreign contingent on his streets.

"I always expect it will be ugly," McCarter answered. "That way I'm never surprised."

"Very well," Ocampo said. "Use caution, American."

"I'm British," McCarter said. "But I'll try not to take it personal, mate." Turning to James and Encizo, he said, "Take the left side of the street," then directed Manning and Hawkins to take the right. "I'll go up the middle, see if I can't tempt somebody into taking a shot at me. We'll check house to house until we either find our informant or come up empty."

"I don't like this, boss," Manning said. "Something's off about it."

"Timing seem a little fishy to you, too?" McCarter asked. "Can't say I blame you. Come on, lads. Let's trip the trap if there's one to be found."

With the Filipinos standing guard at either end of the street, Phoenix Force began working their way down the killing funnel. That's what it was, after all. A well-armed enemy fire team could use the barriers of the houses on either side to channel an opposing force and wipe it out. McCarter hoped that whatever they were facing, it wasn't a machine gun team at the end of the street.

But if it was, they'd find a way. They always did.

The first few houses yielded nothing. Either nobody was home or the folks who were refused to answer. That was fine. They were looking for a willing informant, not trying to drag local citizens from their homes to interrogate them. They had gotten about two-thirds down the row of small homes when Rafael Encizo held up his hand.

"Hold on," Encizo warned. "This door's unlocked." He splayed his fingers and the wood-slatted door creaked open.

The smell of death hit them hard.

"On me," Encizo said. The other members of the team backed him up, two high, two watching the street. McCarter and James joined Encizo inside the dwelling.

"Bloody hell," McCarter cursed.

"I think we've got the right joint," James said.

Emblazoned in black spray paint on the wall was a huge skull-and-crossbones, the pirate symbol known the world over. The graffiti was obviously meant as a warning. The predominant color of the walls was not the paint, but great, gory whorls of dried human blood.

A dead man lay on the floor. He had been stabbed dozens of times. He had also been disemboweled; his entrails had been wrapped around his throat. A pair of coins, unremarkable local denominations, had been placed over his eyes.

"Get Ocampo up here," McCarter called to Manning and Hawkins outside. "He's going to want to see this."

When the Filipino squad leader entered the home, he had his hand on the pistol at his belt. Beyond a slight wrinkling of his nose, he did not flinch despite the abattoir smell of the place. The dead man on the floor was not the only corpse. In an adjoining room, there were two more corpses, both of them female.

Ocampo squatted near the dead man, careful not to kneel in the puddle of congealed blood.

"He anybody to you?" McCarter asked.

"No," Ocampo answered. "He could be street trash or he could be a resident of Calapan. This house is registered to a local landlord who rents his dwellings to work crews and sailors. It is a common practice here."

"What's with all the business?" James asked, moving his hand to encompass the desecrated body.

"That I can tell you," said Ocampo. "It is a message. Your pirates are telling all in the neighborhood that to speak of their business is to earn a bad death. It is a way of discouraging others who might try to sell them out." Ocampo's radio flared to life. He held up a hand and unclipped the unit from his belt. "Ocampo," he said. The static-laced reply made little sense to McCarter, but Ocampo's expression changed. "Vehicles," he said to McCarter. "Approaching quickly from both ends of the street."

"Pull your men out!" McCarter shouted.

Explosions sounded at the end of the street. These were followed by gunfire.

"Contact east, contact west," Manning reported from outside. "Repeat. We have enemy action on both sides of the street."

"Go, go, go," McCarter said. He followed Ocampo to the front door. "Two by two, lads. Let's—"

A Jeep, its hood trailing dwindling flames, rolled through the cordon at the east end of the street. There was gunfire coming from inside it. As McCarter watched, the vehicle accelerated, hurtling straight for Phoenix Force. But the Jeep was not alone. Another vehicle, an old four-wheel-drive of a make McCarter did not recognize, plowed through the cordon at the opposite end. The Filipino soldiers fired at it. Return fire from the truck drove them back under cover.

And then the shooting was directed toward Phoenix Force.

"Down!" McCarter ordered. He tackled Ocampo and covered the man with his body as bullets ripped into the front of the house. Warmth touched his cheek; he reached up and realized he was covered in blood. It was not his. Ocampo had been shot and now lay, unconscious, beneath him.

The two vehicles circled and met, nose to nose, in the center of the street, forming a wedge to give the shooters inside cover. The men within piled out and used the engine blocks to shield themselves. Smoke was now gathering at both ends of the street. Whatever explosives the gunners had used to make their way past the locals' cordon had been heavy enough to start serious fires, which explained why one of the two trucks had caught on the way.

The shooters themselves were a surprise.

As McCarter dragged Ocampo back through the doorway with the rest of Phoenix Force covering them, he got a good look at the gunmen. They were running the very latest in AR-pattern assault rifles, full automatic, with all the bells and whistles: red dot sights, low-profile hand guards and fore-grips, rails everywhere. They were also kitted out in black combat BDUs with modern web gear. They also wore black helmets with night-vision goggles pushed up. These were professionals; there was no doubt about that.

What were they doing here? What was their tie to the pirates?

Phoenix Force was now inside the bloody home of the would-be informant, using the dubious cover of the front walls to fire around the edges of the doorway. Bullets punched through the plaster and sprayed the men with gray-white dust.

"We can't stay here," McCarter said. "Ocampo needs a medic and we're sitting ducks as long as we're stationary. Find us a back door!"

Manning disappeared through the doorway to the small

kitchen. Once there, he reported through his transceiver. "No back door."

"Then make one!" McCarter directed.

"Roger," Manning said. The big Canadian retreated to the front room and aimed his Tavor with its underslung 40mm grenade launcher. "Fire in the hole!"

The members of Phoenix Force ducked and covered their heads. Manning triggered his launcher.

The back of the house was blown apart. Chased by gunfire from the street outside, McCarter tasked Manning, the biggest of them, to carry Ocampo. Then he led his team out through the hole Manning had created.

The street outside was deserted. There was an ancient Volkswagen bus parked in the alley. McCarter looked left, then right. He saw no civilians, but the enemy gunfire was growing closer. They were going to come pouring through that empty house any minute now.

McCarter looked at James.

"You thinking what I'm thinking?" James asked.

"Too right, mate. Start 'er up!"

The van was unlocked. Manning secured Ocampo in the back and the other members of Phoenix piled in. McCarter took the passenger side while James got to work hotwiring the engine.

"I love these old buckets," James said.

"Hurry," McCarter urged.

"Know why I love these old buckets?" James said, bent under the dash.

"They're coming," McCarter said.

"Because they're so easy to wire," James said as the engine coughed to life.

"Go, go, go," McCarter urged again. "Put some distance between us and them. And avoid any civilians on the street!"

"Nag, nag, nag," James muttered under his breath. He guided the VW away, putting the old bus through its gears as swiftly as the machine would allow. They were a hundred yards down the street when the first of the enemy gunmen burst through the grenade hole at the back of the dead informant's place.

"Contact rear!" McCarter shouted. Twisting in his seat, he leveled his Tavor and started squeezing off rounds. "We need as much space between us and them as we can get." He braced himself against the frame of the open passenger-side window as the bus slewed sideways. James managed to get them through the turn, but only barely, and the old VW nearly came up on two wheels as he did it.

"We're overloaded!" James said. "They're going to catch up."

"Then let's give them something to catch up to," McCarter huffed. Looking at Hawkins and Encizo, he directed, "Cover Ocampo. Shield him with your bodies if you have to." He then directed Manning to break out the rear window.

"Copy," Manning said. He positioned himself at the back of the van and smashed out the glass with the butt of his Tavor. Shucking open his weapon's grenade launcher, he loaded a fresh 40 mm grenade from his bandolier.

"Where are we going?" James asked from the driver's seat.

"Find us a small, tight alleyway," McCarter ordered.

"That's what she said," muttered James.

"We'll funnel them the way they wanted to funnel us," McCarter proposed, pretending he had not heard. "Listen up, lads. We're facing a numerically superior force of combat professionals, provenance unknown, motivations unknown. Chances are very good this trap was set for us specifically."

"You think they killed some guy just to make it more realistic?" Hawkins asked.

"It's possible," James interjected. "Life's cheap hereabouts. Or maybe they knew they had some loose lips in their crew, so they figured they'd kill him and us at the same time. Send their message. You know, efficient."

"That actually makes a lot of sense," McCarter mused. "Here. Turn left here."

Once more James nearly had their stolen vehicle up onto two wheels. Ocampo groaned as he shifted in the back. That was a good sign. It meant the man was alive to groan at all. He was bleeding badly, though. They needed to get him patched up.

"Hawk," McCarter said, once more positioning himself in the passenger-side window. "Get a field dressing and some fast-clot on that man's wound. Keep him as comfortable as you can. It's going to get worse before it gets better."

"What I wouldn't give for some air support right now," Encizo said.

Bullets began to ricochet off the old Volkswagen. The enemy shooters had successfully tracked them down and were closing the distance in their own vehicles.

"You and me both, lad," McCarter responded. "You and me both."

CHAPTER EIGHT

Charleston, South Carolina

Lyons drove the Suburban past the sign proclaiming the city's limits. The vehicle had come through its time in the RhemCorp headquarters parking lot relatively unscathed. There was a bullet hole in the upper corner of the windshield that would require replacement glass when they could manage it. To stop the wind whistling through the hole, Blancanales had patched it on both sides with rigging tape. Lyons would have felt bad about retiring one of the Farm's most faithful old trucks, if it came to that. It still might, for that matter.

"I have never seen a woman scarier than that receptionist," Schwarz said. He shouted in pain. "Ow! Come on, man. Be careful, Pol."

"I'm doing my best," Blancanales muttered. He was perched on the edge of the rear bench seat, doing his best, in the limited room available, to finish re-taping Schwarz's ribs. The Stony Man electronics expert had complained so much about how tight the wrap was the first time that Blancanales had offered to do it over again.

"Wussy," Lyons said from the driver's seat.

"That's easy for you to say," Schwarz protested. "I can't remember the last time one of my plans involved you getting beat up."

"You're blaming me for this?" Lyons said. "I thought

it was your idea to distract him so Pol could play Artful Dodger. Isn't that why you went out of your way to poke Laughing Boy with a stick?"

"I'm still blaming you," Schwarz said. "Ow! Okay, okay, Pol. That's good enough."

"He's right. You are a wussy," Blancanales said.

"Don't you start, Pol," Schwarz warned. "And you didn't get your face all bashed in, either." Schwarz was, in fact, sporting several small bandages on his face. His lip was badly cut and swollen.

"Let's hope that he's there with Rhemsen," Lyons said. "I want another crack at that ape."

"You suppose he knows by now that his building didn't blow up?" Blancanales asked.

"I almost had a heart attack when we walked in there and found that old biddy waving the wires around. There was enough C-4 packed underneath the reception desk to blow that place sky high."

"Let that be a lesson to you, I guess," Lyons said. "When you've got one of those ornery old ladies who knows where all the bodies are buried, chances are good she knows which wires to pull out so you don't blow up both her and her collection of desktop family photos."

"You figure they'll put her in jail?"

"Probably not," Lyons said. "No crime against answering phones for a criminal. At least, not that I know of. She can always claim she knew the bomb was there, but thought it was some kind of government security policy. You know, to protect from having foreign agents steal military-contracted designs."

"You should be a lawyer, Ironman," Schwarz teased. "You'd be good at it."

"You insult me like that again and I'll make your upper lip match the bottom one," Lyons said.

"You used to be fun," Schwarz muttered.

"Wrong," Lyons said. "I was never fun."

"He's got you there," Blancanales noted.

Lyons focused on the road, reading the GPS coordinates for the RhemCorp factory they were trying to find. According to the Farm, this manufacturing facility was the closest Rhemsen-held asset to the headquarters they had just visited—and which Rhemsen himself had just fled. It was the logical fallback location.

Unfortunately, Barbara Price had explained that politicking, once again, was holding up action that should be taken right away. Specifically, Lyons had informed the Farm that Rhemsen was actively working against the United States—based on his immediate kidnapping and torture of agents of the US government—and that this meant he should be declared an enemy of the state by the Department of Homeland Security. Rhemsen, though, was lawyered up to hell and gone, apparently, and while they could conceivably come after him for the kidnapping, declaring him persona non grata on American soil was going to take more time. Wheels in Washington had to be greased; reluctant politicians whose pockets Rhemsen had lined had to be persuaded; some of the officials that RhemCorp money had outright bought and paid for would have to be pushed out of the way. Brognola was on the case in Wonderland, Price had explained, but it was going to take a while before they had all the obstacles cleared. And of course RhemCorp was a big military contractor, so there were plenty of people, from the Hill to the Pentagon, who stood to have egg on their faces as word of Rhemsen's treason spread.

Add to all that the fact that they still didn't know the exact dimensions of what Rhemsen's treason meant, and it was a formula for delay, hesitation and more delay. This was why Lyons hated politics. Right now, blacksuits and Feds and Department of Homeland Security leg-breakers should be busting down the doors of every asset, every property, that Rhemsen held. The man should, as far as Lyons was concerned, be shot on sight…but then, he'd suggested that at the beginning, hadn't he? Lyons could feel his hands tightening on the steering wheel again.

The one thing the government had been able to do was to put Rhemsen on a no-fly list and suspend his passport pending an investigation. That investigation was never going to happen. The man wouldn't live long enough, as far as Lyons was concerned. But it meant that Rhemsen couldn't just get on a plane and fly out of the country. He couldn't charter a private jet, either; his company's air assets were being monitored. Any guy smart enough to have built a corporation on military-grade weapons and defense contracts had to understand that these were just a few of the steps that would be taken against him if he turned up dirty.

So what did Rhemsen think he was going to get out of all this? Was he just so arrogant that he thought he could never be caught? It didn't make a whole lot of sense. But then, neither did it make sense for him to tip his hand right away by trying to take Able Team out as soon as they'd walked on the property. Why wouldn't the guy try to buy himself some more breathing space by putting Able Team off, telling them a convincing lie? It had happened plenty of times before on similar missions. But, no; he had tried to go right for the throat, kind of the way Lyons had wanted to do, and now Blancanales was banged up and Schwarz had been downright abused.

He had teased Schwarz because that's what the men of Able Team did, but deep down, he was also really angry. Fitzpatrick was a bastard and then some, and Lyons was going to get some payback before this mission was over. He'd made a promise to that big son of a whore, and he meant to keep it.

It was going to feel good to knock over Rhemsen's factory.

"Pol," Lyons said, "make sure that M-32 is ready back there. Gimme the DRACO thermobarics. I want to make an impression."

"There will be Blackstar troops there, I'm betting," Schwarz said.

"You're already into me for twenty bucks," Lyons argued. "You let me do the betting. But, yeah. They'll be there. And as far as I'm concerned, these Blackstar guys are shoot-on-sight if they don't lie down and comply right away. We're going to announce our intention to arrest Rhemsen and any other members of senior management we choose. The goon squad can either comply or they can fall down dead. Those are going to be the choices."

"I love it when you talk tough, Ironman."

"Play your candy monster game or something, Gadgets," Lyons said. Something in the distance caught his eye. "There. Look there. That's the entrance to the industrial park, and there's a RhemCorp logo. And unless I'm mistaken, those two silver SUVs have Blackstar's corporate insignia on the doors. Which means the goons inside are probably trigger-happy."

"Let's go say hello," Schwarz said. He racked the slide on his Beretta 93-R. "I feel like I want to introduce myself to some Blackstar guys."

"I hear that," Lyons said.

The two SUVs were parked on either side of the road, clearly meant to challenge anyone who might choose to pass. That squared with what Lyons would expect of RhemCorp's heightened security. Batten down the hatches, gents, because the US gub'mint is coming to get us. Yeah, that was how they would think. And they were just arrogant enough to think they could sit out there in front of God and anybody and not face any consequences.

Was he mad about what had happened to his teammates? Hell yes he was. But what he was about to do would set it all right in his mind. He drew the Colt Python from its shoulder holster and let his hand fall to his lap, below the level of the window. Schwarz climbed up front, into the passenger seat, and held his Beretta out of view. Lyons hit the buttons on his console and made sure both panes of glass were rolled all the way down.

They drew abreast of the two Blackstar trucks. One man was standing outside. There was another pair of men in one vehicle, and a single passenger in the other. The man on foot walked up to Lyons's side of the truck and held out his hand.

"This is restricted private property," the guard said. "Nobody comes through without an appointment. Do you have an appointment?"

"No," Lyons answered. "I have a 'hands-up.'"

"A what?" the guard asked. "What do you mean?"

"I mean get your hands up, pal, because I'm with the United States Justice Department and I'm here to arrest you."

The guard's hand twitched toward the pistol in the highride belt holster at his side. Lyons snapped up the Python and punched a single .357 Magnum hollowpoint round through the center of the man's face.

Schwarz started spraying 3-round bursts into the cab of the opposite truck. The two men inside were spread throughout the interior before they could bring up their own weapons. Lyons, climbing out of the Suburban, watched the remaining Blackstar guard shift to the driver's seat, fire up the engine and practically burn rubber pulling away. He fled in the direction of the RhemCorp property.

Lyons took a half step to the right and widened his stance. He bent his knees, dropping lower, and extended both his arms. Thumbing back the hammer of the Python, he took a deep breath, let out half of it and held the rest. His finger took up slack on the trigger. A little more. A little more...

The shot, when it rang out, surprised him, as it was meant to do. The bullet took the driver in the head. His SUV heeled to the right and struck one of the trees lining the road.

Lyons holstered his Python and went to the rear of the Suburban. From the big duffel in the back, he took his Daewoo 12-gauge shotgun and loaded a drum magazine. "Pol," he said. "Get on that Milkor M-32. I want to make an impression. Gadgets, take the wheel. You're going to drive."

Schwarz did as Lyons instructed. He looked up as Lyons climbed onto the running board on the driver's side. Blancanales took the one opposite. As Lyons jacked a round into the chamber of his massive automatic shotgun, Schwarz said, "I know what's missing." He poked at the radio for a moment before finding a station he found acceptable, then jacked up the volume. The pounding strains of a Southern-rock song vibrated the Suburban's speakers.

"Let's take care of business," Schwarz said. He stomped the accelerator.

The Suburban surged forward. Schwarz did his best to keep the ride stable, with his team members hanging off the sides, but safety wasn't the primary goal here. It was rapidity of target acquisition. The private drive leading to the RhemCorp factory twisted and turned a bit up

again. There were two more patrol SUVs parked close to
the main lot by the structure.

"Get ready to get down," Schwarz cautioned.

Lyons shot Schwarz a quizzical glance.

"Sorry," the Able Team electronics whiz said. "Got a
little excited."

"Justice Department!" Lyons bellowed, his voice carrying across the parking lot. "Put down your weapons and
put your hands on your heads!" He turned to Blancanales
and said, "Pol, if they shoot—"

Gunfire crackled from the two trucks.

"Got it," Blancanales said. He triggered four rounds
from the Milkor. The revolving grenade launcher *chunk-
chunk-chunk-chunked* toward the enemy, ripping apart
the trucks fore and aft, blowing apart the men inside. A
great pall of black smoke drifted across the parking lot as
the vehicles blazed bright, burning and throwing sparks.
Schwarz narrowly avoided the two blazing wrecks as he
guided them toward the main building.

"Pull us up alongside the front door," Lyons ordered.
"Put my side to them. I haven't emptied a drum in a while."

"Oh, man," Schwarz said. "That thing is so damned
loud."

"What?" Lyons said.

"I said that thing is so… Oh. Okay. Ha-ha," Schwarz
said.

"And you thought you had all the jokes," said Lyons. As
Schwarz brought the driver's side in line with the front of
the building, Blackstar troops were scrambling to mount
a defense. There was a quartet of men taking up position in front of the big, mirrored-glass doors fronting the
building.

"Good thing I've already got bad luck," Lyons declared,
holding back the trigger of his Daewoo.

The USAS-12 jumped and bucked in Lyons's big fists. The weapon disgorged its payload of mixed 00 Buck and rifled slugs, a deadly combination that gave Lyons both crowd-clearing firepower and reasonable accuracy at greater distances. He had individual magazines tucked away in the duffel bag that were either one or the other, but right now he was feeling that Kissinger's "party mix" was called for.

Mirrored glass fell like rain. Blood flowed. The men in front of the doors were torn apart, their shots going wide or high, their lives ended in less time than it took to consider the finality of their foolhardy stand.

Lyons reached into the truck through the open window and took his canvas war bag, which was full of ammunition and explosives. He slung it across his chest. Then he stepped over the corpses and walked through the shattered front doors. Blancanales and Schwarz fell in at his flanks, walking a few paces behind, covering him from the side and also the back. They, too, had retrieved their heavier weapons from the truck. Schwarz had his Colt SMG and Blancanales had his M-4.

"Can I do the yell?" Schwarz asked.

"Knock yourself out," Lyons said as Blackstar men piled out of an elevator into the factory's shabby lobby. He loaded a fresh drum into his shotgun.

"Justice Department!" Schwarz hollered. Already, the Blackstar guards were pointing guns, raising barrels and preparing to fire.

"Duck," said Blancanales.

Schwarz and Lyons hit the deck. Blancanales fired out the remaining grenades in the Milkor, but this time, he wasn't using DRACO rounds or even conventional high explosives. This time he had loaded shotgun rounds. The massive cone of metal pellets shredded the men piling out of the elevator, turning the lobby and the elevator shaft beyond into a heaping pile of bloody meat. The elevator doors tried to close, opened again, tried to close again. A warning bell began to chime.

There were too many broken, dead men blocking the doors' electric eye.

"I, uh, guess we'll take the stairs," Schwarz suggested.

"The building specs include two floors," Blancanales pointed out, looking at his smartphone. "Heavy manufacturing on the ground floor, offices above."

"Then we go from low ground to high," said Lyons, "while making sure nobody skips out. Gadgets, cover the stairs. Pol, watch my back. I'm going to take the manufacturing area and clean it out."

"We don't know how many Blackstars are in here," Blancanales cautioned.

"Well, it's a lot fewer now," Lyons growled. "I'll count while I shoot if it makes you feel better."

Blancanales shook his head. "Just sayin', Ironman."

"Got it. All right, let's move out."

"Not once," Schwarz said, sounding disappointed.

"What?" Lyons asked. "Not once what?"

"Not once has telling them to give up, we're the Justice Department, actually worked."

"Let's go," said Lyons. "We've got people to meet and stuff to shoot."

"The stuff is usually people," Schwarz argued.

"Shut up, Gadgets," Lyons said.

CHAPTER NINE

"Fire!" McCarter shouted.

Garry Manning sent a 40 mm grenade hurtling toward the closest of the pursuing trucks. The round blew apart the grille and front bumper, shredding the flimsy sheet metal and sending portions of the engine through the passenger compartment. Unfortunately, the alleyway widened at that point, allowing the second vehicle to come around and take up the chase. Now the pursuit vehicle was weaving left and right, moving perilously close to the houses on either side of the street.

"I can't take another shot," Manning said. "Not if they're going to keep doing that. I might hit one of the houses."

"Small arms!" McCarter directed. Manning started firing short bursts from his Tavor. McCarter, from the passenger-side window, did the same. "T.J., how is Ocampo?"

"It's not real bad," Hawkins said. "He's starting to come around."

Well, that much was a relief. As for the rest, it wasn't good. McCarter cursed under his breath. While it could be much worse, they were still very much on the defensive. No battle could be won this way. They needed to find a way to seize the initiative, put their pursuers on the defensive.

"Gary," McCarter said. "Get out."

Manning looked back at McCarter. Then recognition flashed across his face. He nodded, once. "Got it," he said.

Throwing open the rear doors of the Volkswagen bus, he jumped out and hit the road, managing to stay on his feet. A smaller man wouldn't have been able to manage it. Encizo, meanwhile, moved up to cover the rear with his rifle at the ready.

"I'm circling," Manning reported through his transceiver. "Getting around behind them."

"Too right," McCarter said. "Calvin, slow it down. Make us a tempting target. Let them get in close. They'll be too focused on us to notice Gary lurking back there."

"Hang on," James said. "This is going to get nasty." He braked and the bus squealed in protest. The vehicle was in very poor repair, its engine rattling away as if the hamsters were getting tired on their giant wheel.

The pursuing truck full of gunmen loomed closer. Muzzle-flashes blossomed at either side as shooters leaning out the windows took aim at the Volkswagen. Bullets ricocheted off the old metal bus, shattering the mirror on McCarter's side and forcing him to duck back inside for a moment.

"Anytime, Gary," McCarter said.

"Roger," came Manning's voice through the transceiver link.

The sound of the grenade launcher was lost in the din of the combat outside. Its effects were anything but unnoticed. The rear of the chase vehicle exploded in a bright yellow-orange fireball, throwing the truck up off its rear axle, knocking it aside. Manning wasn't finished, however. He reloaded and fired another grenade, blowing apart the front of the truck and scattering the gunmen inside across the alleyway.

Manning reappeared not long after. James slowed and let the big Canadian climb back aboard the bus. They drove another couple of blocks.

"There." McCarter pointed again. "That garage. Pull in there."

"Hope nobody's home," James said.

"We'll do what we can for them," McCarter said. "But right now we need to get off the street."

The rickety garage door was open, so James just pulled the van right inside. Manning leaned out of the rear doors and stretched to pull the door down. When it was closed, James cut the engine, as much to keep them from choking on fumes as to kill the noise from the wheezing, underpowered engine.

"You two check the house," McCarter directed Encizo and Manning. "The rest of us will stay here with Ocampo until you clear it."

The two Phoenix Force commandos nodded and left the vehicle.

The door to the house was locked, but Manning easily snapped it open by placing the blade of his knife between the doorjamb and the lock plate.

"What is happening?" Ocampo asked quietly.

McCarter turned to the wounded Filipino. "I'm afraid we've run into a spot of trouble," he explained. "The hostile force that attacked us was clearly gunning for us specifically. The guy with information about the pirate activity in this area was either a complete dupe or unwitting bait in the trap. A force of heavily armed men, professional soldiers, has targeted us. We've eliminated several of them, but I suspect there are more—an unknown quantity of hostiles hunting us through this neighborhood."

"My men?" Ocampo asked.

"I'm sorry, mate," McCarter said. "I don't know their status. I do know I saw some of them fall when the hostiles broke through the cordon."

It was a delicate thing. Ocampo could choose to blame

Phoenix Force for bringing this battle to his turf, or he could channel that anger into a desire to get the shooters who had attacked his men. It would be a hell of a lot easier for Phoenix Force if he blamed the gunmen and not McCarter's men.

Ocampo eased the pistol from his belt. He checked to make sure a round was chambered. "We will…we will make sure these men pay for their crimes."

"Too right," McCarter said. "Hawk, bind that wound again. We don't want it coming loose."

"Got it," Hawkins said.

Ocampo groaned as Hawkins tended to him.

"It's a through-and-through," he said. "If we can keep him from bleeding out or going into shock, we're doing pretty good." He took his portable med kit from the thigh pocket of his fatigues and began looking for single-use ampoules. Selecting the ones he wanted, he pointed toward McCarter. Ocampo looked away and Hawkins jabbed him with the needle.

Ocampo laughed. He looked back at Hawkins. "I am not so weak that I must be distracted like a little boy."

"I wasn't trying to offend anybody," Hawkins drawled.

"Rest easy, American," Ocampo said. "I am not offended. And I have been shot before."

"You have?"

"This is, as they say, not my first Rodeo Drive."

"Rodeo," Hawkins corrected.

"Yes," Ocampo said. "Some years ago I was part of the force of medics, engineers and their security personnel sent into Central South Iraq under Polish command. A 'humanitarian contingent,' we were called. We suffered wounded during that time, but lost no one. Not officially. It was bad business. And I was one of the wounded."

"I remember that affair," McCarter said. "The insurgents took a hostage, didn't they? A truck driver named Angelo de la Cruz. They demanded that Filipino troops withdraw from Iraq."

"And to our national shame, we did that very thing," said Ocampo. "He was the father of eight children, and I do not begrudge him his freedom. But this giving in to terrorist demands…it is a very bad signal to send, is it not?"

"Yeah," Hawkins said. "That's true."

"House is clear," Encizo said through his transceiver. "Nobody's home, David."

"All right, lads," McCarter said. "Let's set up shop. Stay away from the windows. Let's make as little noise as possible. Come on, Lieutenant. Let's see if we can't find you someplace better than the back of an ancient hippie bus."

Hawkins and McCarter helped Ocampo into the house. Once inside the modest dwelling, they found the bedroom and propped Ocampo up on the bed. From there he had a reasonably good view of the street from the bedroom window. He held his pistol at the ready, obviously determined to do what he could.

"Watch the back and the garage," McCarter told Manning. "You two—" he nodded at Hawkins and James "—take up station at either end of the bedroom hallway and we'll watch the front from the living area." Motioning to James, he added as they moved, "Lock that front door."

James threw the bolt on the door. The living room was as shabbily furnished as everything else in the house. There were a few framed family photos on the wall: a man, his wife, their two kids. Wherever the family was right now, McCarter was glad it was not here. He hated the thought of damaging their home, of occupying it, but it was necessary for the team's survival and the success of the mission. There was a glass jar sitting on a crate being used for an end-table next to a threadbare sofa. The jar had change in it. McCarter smiled.

From his pocket he took the money clip he had been issued. It was full of a thick roll of local currency. Phoenix Force was always issued cash before foreign and "plausibly deniable" missions, given they never knew when they might need to buy some cooperation, pay off some corrupt official or otherwise meet field expenses. McCarter did some quick math, peeled off a wad of bills and dropped it into the jar. It was probably more money than this family would see in a good long while. Hopefully it would make up for Phoenix Force's presence here.

"I've got movement across the street and up four houses," James stated. "Confirmed, contact. Enemy shooters. Black BDUs, assault rifles. AR-pattern. These have to be our boys." He paused. "All right, they're kicking in doors, sweeping from house to house. It's just a matter of time before they get to us."

"Get ready," McCarter said, peering out his own window. "Can you give me a count? I can't see from this angle."

"There are an awful damned lot of them," James said. "I count at least twenty, and there are more beyond that. I'm seeing more vehicles. Four-wheel-drives, local make. Those little runabouts that everybody likes so much in these parts."

"I can feel the odds against us climbing, mate," McCarter said. "Everybody hold fast. We need to take them by surprise if we're going to have a chance to break through. Don't engage until they're on top of us."

There was a chorus of assent. McCarter flexed his fingers on the grip of his Tavor. They still had plenty of ammunition for their weapons, but that was going to change fast if the firefight became protracted.

"They're two houses down," James warned.

"Steady, lads," McCarter said. "Everyone get your smoke grenades ready. Find a window. Get ready to smash it out if you have to."

"Here they come," James said. "Wait. They've rousted someone from the neighboring house. Repeat, we've got civilians on the field. Civilians on the field."

The civilians moved past McCarter's point of view. "They're on their way out of the combat zone," the Briton said. There were two elderly Filipinos, a man and a woman. McCarter did not intend to let them get hurt. "Let them get clear."

There was a pounding at the door. Someone outside said, in English, "Open up! We're coming in if you don't open up!"

"David?" James asked through his transceiver.

"Wait for it," McCarter said. The pounding at the door grew more intense. From where he crouched, McCarter actually heard the sound of a pump-action shotgun being racked.

"They're going to breach!" James whispered.

"Steady," McCarter cautioned.

The old couple disappeared into a cross-alley on the opposite side of the street. There was a thundering report as the gunmen outside blew the lock on the front door.

"Now!" McCarter ordered. He opened fire through his window at the few armed men he could see.

Calvin James brought his Tavor up and fired several rapid bursts directly through the front door. There was a brief scream, cut short, as the man on the other end of the breaching gun discovered that some doorways fired back. Then James was diving out of the way as return fire from the gunmen began to stitch the bare floor and the wall beyond. James rolled to the side of the entrance, using the wall for cover, knowing that this was not worth much. Bullets were passing through the exterior walls of the house with ease.

"Calvin, get clear," McCarter urged. James did so, scooting across the floor like a crab, staying out of the worst of it as bullets blew plaster dust through the air above his head. There was little left of the front door, which had been blown to splinters by the concentrated fire of armed men reacting to the loss of one of their own.

"Smoke now!" McCarter ordered. He pulled the pin on the smoke canister he had palmed, let the gren arm itself and dumped it out the window. James was not positioned by a window, so he could not do the same, but Manning, Encizo and Hawkins acknowledged the order via their transceivers. Thick, dense, artificially black smoke began to fill the street outside.

The gunmen responded by firing blindly into the smoke cloud. McCarter motioned to James then smashed out what little glass was left in his window. He climbed out with James covering him and then took up a crouch near the corner of the house. Through the smoke, he could see the black-clad shooters running, confused, trying to acquire their targets.

"Gary," McCarter said quietly. "Work your way around the back, to the side of the house. Take up position with your launcher. Wait for the pretty lights."

"Copy," Manning said.

In combat, motion was life. But motion without a purpose, movement just to move, was seldom helpful. And in this case, it was going to get the enemy shooters killed.

In the smoke, McCarter's red-dot sight was not useful. He fired from the hip, aiming with his barrel, shooting in brief, controlled bursts for maximum effect. There was more screaming, and more men fell. The muzzle-flashes that followed were visible through the smoke. As was predictable, the gunmen had grouped together in the pall, making one clustered target, believing that if they moved in so they could see each other, they would not be disoriented by the cloud.

"Gary," McCarter said. "Hit them."

The *chunk* of Manning's launcher was the kind of sound a man either ignored or learned to fear. He ignored it if he had never heard it before; it was not all that impressive, a vaguely pneumatic thump from which the Vietnam-era M-79 "Thumper" and handheld launcher took its name. "Blooper" was another name applied to that particular weapon. Nothing about the sound, the first time a man heard it, was menacing. It was merely curious.

A man who had been on the receiving end of a Thumper learned to fear that sound to his very core, however. In the smoke, McCarter could hear the rhythmic *thump-thump-thump* as Manning loaded, fired, ejected the shell and loaded to fire again. The gunmen in the smoke were too close to each other. They never stood a chance.

By the time the smoke cleared, there were only a few stragglers who were now fleeing down the street. McCarter and James took aim with their Tavors and shot them down with well-placed and patiently timed head-shots. The bodies hit the street just as a new sound reached McCarter's ears. It was the sound of multiple engines approaching.

"Contact west!" Manning shouted.

The trucks that broke through the smoke were olive-drab in color and bore the insignia of the Filipino military. McCarter held his Tavor over his head. "Hold fire! Hold fire!" he announced. "These are Ocampo's people."

There were a few tense minutes as armed infantry piled out of the troop trucks. The hard looks on the soldiers' faces were replaced with relief when Ocampo managed to limp outside with Hawkins helping him. The lieutenant explained the situation to his men. He then, with the assistance of one of his own men, walked slowly to McCarter.

"My government is very angry," Ocampo began.

"How do you know?" McCarter asked. "Not that I doubt it."

Ocampo held up a wireless phone. "I called them. That is how my troops knew to come here. I thought we would be saving your lives." He looked at the crater in the street and the dead bodies scattered around it. "I can see that I was wrong. But our intelligence agents report that there are more armed men in the city. We do not know who they are. We are hunting them, but we have not found them. They may find you first, and I have been forbidden to offer you further support. Your government and I will have to have a…heart-on-heart chat, yes?"

"Heart-to-heart," McCarter said. "But, yeah, I can see how they might need to do that."

"Just so," Ocampo agreed. "American?"

"I told you, mate. I'm British."

"A Western power is a Western power," said Ocampo, smiling. "But I thank you for saving my life."

"You're welcome," McCarter said. He turned to go but, before he did, he ducked back inside the bullet-riddled house. Once more he withdrew his money clip, shrugged and dumped the remainder of his cash into the jar in the living room, which had somehow escaped all the gunfire without taking a bullet. Then he left. He did not look back. As he hit the street again, Ocampo and his troops were pulling out.

"They're still hunting us," Encizo said. "And now we've got no local support."

"Fair enough," said McCarter. He hefted his Tavor, checking the magazine. "Let's go, lads. Our work here isn't done. Not by a good bit yet."

CHAPTER TEN

Lyons stalked through the factory floor. There was a lot of machinery here, most of it devoted to manufacturing casings of some kind or another. He saw plenty of stuff that looked like rocket warheads without any guts in them, and he saw electronics. What he didn't see was explosives. From what little he knew about the process to make warheads of this type, the explosives to arm them wouldn't be added until a final stage at a different facility. That enabled a factory such as this to sit in a relatively "normal" industrial neighborhood, without the additional security and controls that would be needed for explosives and other munitions. It also meant he didn't have to worry about accidentally blowing the place up with his team inside it.

Movement at the corner of his eye caught his attention. He ducked behind the nearest piece of machinery, some kind of pipe-fitting gadget used to bend lengths of cylindrical metal.

Lyons was in no mood for pretending, playing political games or dragging this out any longer than was absolutely necessary. From his vantage behind the pipe-fitting machine, Lyons pulled a frag grenade from his war bag and popped the pin. Holding down the spoon, he called out, "Hey, you! Yeah, I'm talking to you. Justice Department. You're under arrest."

Bullets immediately swarmed his position, blowing pieces from the machine and showering him with fragments of metal. The ricochets flew in every direction, knocking out overhead lights, digging furrows in the floor and generally wreaking havoc. Lyons waited for the shooter or shooters on the other end to burn through an entire magazine, which was what they seemed inclined to do. When the anticipated lull in the shooting came, he called out, "You have until the count of ten to surrender, or I'm going to kill you!"

"Up yours!" one of the gunmen shouted.

That seemed pretty unambiguous to Lyons. He was going to stick to his original impulse on this mission. That meant cutting to the end whenever he could, slicing through the red tape that always seemed to characterize these operations.

"Okay, ten!" Lyons called out, and threw his grenade.

Ducking back again, he counted in his head. He heard the grenade land on the concrete floor, heard it skitter across the hard surface and heard it come to a stop.

Then he took three more grenades from his bag. As the first explosion ripped through the manufacturing floor, he was pulling pins and readying more bombs. He kept tossing them, staggering them for effect. The explosions that rolled through the room ripped apart workstations and hand tools…and the men hiding behind them. Lyons risked a look from behind his cover and counted three— no, four bodies hitting the floor in pieces.

Time to go to work.

Lyons was up with the USAS-12 in his fists, a fully loaded drum of mixed 00 Buck and rifled slugs ready to go. In a combat crouch, he glided through the manufacturing area, sidestepping the circle of destruction his grenades had made. The smoke was clearing. An alarm began to ring somewhere in the building. He looked up, wondering if sprinkler heads were going to drench him, but there was no such system in place.

Just as well. He hated working in the rain.

There was more movement at the far end of the manufacturing space.

"Hey!" Lyons shouted. "Justice Department!"

One of the figures raised an AR-15 rifle and squeezed off a shot. Lyons dodged to the right and triggered a triple blast from his USAS-12.

A slug preceded and followed by cones of buckshot, each of the pellets as big around as a 9 mm bullet, ripped into the gunman and dropped him, disemboweled, to the floor. The dead man's buddies ducked behind the obstacles nearest them. The machines and workstations formed a maze of hard cover that could easily stop bullets, which was why Lyons had resorted to grenades in the first place.

"Not so fast," the Able Team leader said. He lifted the barrel of his shotgun and held back the trigger once more, moving the weapon left and right, spraying slugs and shot like a fireman with a hose. The ceiling tiles and the metal light fixtures hanging from them wrenched from their moorings, split and cracked and scattered. This debris, much of it sharp-edged, began falling on the hiding gunmen. At least one man was impaled through the neck by a spar from the overhead lights, which had ripped apart at a sharp angle and formed a spear driven by gravity.

"Lights out," Lyons declared, realizing as he said it that he sounded like a certain famous action-movie star. He looked around, hoping there was no one to overhear him ham it up like that. For crying out loud. He had been hanging around Schwarz for too long.

The big former cop finished his circuit through the manufacturing floor. He put a finger to the transceiver in his ear. "Gadgets, Pol, what's the story up there?"

"We're encountering heavy resistance in the north stairwell," Schwarz explained. "Can you work your away around to the south?"

"Will do," Lyons said. "Let me know if you punch through on that side. If we can, we'll meet in the middle."

"Roger," Schwarz said.

Lyons hit the fire door at a good clip, only to rebound from it with a deafening boom. He rubbed his shoulder and stared at the door for a split second. Well, hell. So much for taking anybody on the other side by surprise.

From his war bag he produced one of the little plastic-explosive door poppers Kissinger had cooked up—a button of C-4 with an adhesive backing and a pre-timed detonator that bore only a single switch. Lyons peeled the adhesive backing, slapped the bomb on the fire door near the crash bar and flicked the switch. Then he backed away several paces and flattened himself against the wall.

The door blew, shooting the crash bar three feet to the floor and leaving a smoking crater in the door's metal surface. Lyons let his USAS-12 fall to the length of its sling, which he had draped over his shoulder, and pulled his Python from its shoulder holster.

"Three," Lyons said. "Two. One."

The door flew open and a man in a Blackstar uniform practically fell out of it. He was carrying a mini-Uzi submachine gun and, when he recovered his bearings, looking shaken from the explosion, he turned to bracket Lyons. The poor bastard never had a chance. He was moving so slowly that a good street caricature artist would have had time to draw a picture of him. Lyons almost casually extended his Python and pulled the trigger, double-action punching a .357 round through the man's throat. The guard dropped his weapon and clutched at his throat before collapsing to the now bloody floor.

Lyons counted again, this time silently. He was right to do so. He had guessed that the first man, probably standing just inside the door and lying in wait for anyone who tried to enter the stairwell, had been a little shell-shocked by the explosion. But it also stood to reason that there would be a second man. These Blackstar thugs always seemed to roam in pairs or groups. The second guy, seeing his partner rush in like the fool that he was, had waited, hoping that whatever hostile force was on the other side of that door might reveal itself—or even get shot—before he had to put his own bacon on the line. Now the Blackstar man was peeking out the half-open door, maybe thinking the dead guy and the dead guy's killer had managed to off each other in the brief firefight.

"Hey, dipwad," Lyons called. "Over here."

The look on the Blackstar thug's face was priceless. He turned, locked eyes with Lyons and then actually squeezed his eyes shut, as if not being able to see it coming might mean it wasn't. Lyons didn't waste any time telling him to put down his weapon. The mercenary was already reaching for the pistol holstered at his side. The Able Team leader simply shot him in the chest, center-mass, and watched him fall.

"Not…not…" the man struggled to say.

Lyons walked over to stand above him. "How many more of your people in the stairwell?" he asked.

"Get me…get me a doctor…"

Lyons closed his eyes and pinched the bridge of his nose. When he opened them again, he said, "You guys, you make me laugh. You shoot at anybody who looks at you funny. You don't care how many people get hurt. You'll kill a cop, you'll kill a Fed… It's all the same to you. But when you screw up and get tagged, it's all, 'Get me a doctor.' You'll get a medical examiner, pal. That's a coroner, if you're not up on the current lingo. That's what you get."

"Only…following…orders…" the man struggled to say. His eyes started to roll back into his head.

"Isn't it funny," Lyons said, lining up a mercy shot over the man's forehead, "just how many murderers hide behind a line like that."

He pulled the trigger.

Bounding up the stairwell, taking the steps two at a time, he made his way into the office area.

What greeted him was the usual cube farm. Gray, fabric-colored half walls separated the desks from each other. There was no one around that he could see, but from here, the shooting from the stairwell at the opposite end of the building was loud enough to put his combat senses on high alert. The Blackstar men were guarding the stairwells and doing everything they could to prevent enemies from coming up. But they'd gotten distracted. Schwarz and Blancanales were apparently giving them a hard enough time that they'd forgotten to cover Lyons's end of the building.

The barest of pressures against his shin stopped him.

Lyons froze. He looked down, realizing what was happening. The Blackstar men weren't terribly experienced, from what he'd seen of them in combat, but they had known enough to reduce the variables they were facing. The guards posted in Lyons's stairwell had been perfunctory. What the Blackstar goons were counting on was that this end of the building was wired. As he crouched, examining the tripwire he almost hadn't noticed, he could see light glistening along several other wires. A forest of trip lines had been laced through the office area, each connected to a black satchel that he assumed contained a heavy payload in explosives.

Just how high were they planning to blow this place?

"We've got a problem," Lyons said through his transceiver. "I can't get any farther from this side of the building, not without blowing the whole thing. We've got enough high explosive packing this floor to drop the building on our heads."

"We're still trying to get through the stairwell on our side," Blancanales said. "Something weird is definitely going on. They keep throwing men at us."

"Rhemsen!" Lyons growled. "They're covering Rhemsen's escape! If he's here, if he's in this building, that's his way out. I'm betting there's a helicopter on the roof. No other reason they'd fight so hard to keep us from going up there."

"We can hold them in the stairwell," Schwarz suggested. "Thanks to the bottleneck, it wouldn't even take both of us."

"All right," Lyons said. "Pol, hold that exit, bottle them up down there. Gadgets, break off, meet me out front. We've got to find a way to target the roof. Maybe there's a fire escape or something."

"Affirmative," Schwarz said, all business now that a mission objective was at stake.

Lyons backed away from the wired offices, raced back through the wreckage on the manufacturing floor, crossed into the front lobby and ran back out the front. Once there, he could hear the rotors of a chopper spinning up. He could also hear the distant gunfire from inside the structure as Blancanales kept the Blackstar thugs contained in the stairwell.

"We've got to move fast," Schwarz urged. "They're going to get the idea to circle back through the offices, down and around, and flank Pol, if there's any way to get past the trip wires. The explosives might be remote-detonated. No way to know."

"They're green," Lyons said, "given the degree of training mercs like these usually have. But, yeah, that's going to be obvious even to them. Do we have anything that can take down a chopper?"

"Nothing air-to-air," Schwarz said. "We could try the grenade launcher."

Lyons looked at the truck, then at the parking lot, then back at the angle to the roof of the building. "Will grenades blow the charges on the second floor?"

"Not if it's C-4 or Semtex," Schwarz answered. "Without the detonator signal, an indirect impact won't do it."

"Trip wires," Lyons said. "A piece of wreckage hits those and they might blow." He went to the Suburban and grabbed the grenade launcher from the back. "Gadgets, back us up." He then stepped on the running board. "Pol," he said through the transceiver, "lay down some fire and get the hell out of there. We might need to knock the building down"

"Fair enough," Blancanales returned. As Schwarz fired up the truck and Lyons climbed onto the running board again, Blancanales came barreling out of the building.

"Hurry!" he shouted. "They're right behind me!"

Blancanales had time to hop on the opposite running board. Schwarz stomped the accelerator and sent the big truck rolling backward through the parking lot. As the helicopter started to rise from the roof, Lyons began firing off grenades at a forty-five-degree angle, trying to punch them up and over and into the roof. The first of the grenades had yet to land when the hammer of God flattened the roof of the building.

"Holy—" Schwarz started. Whatever he was about to say was lost in the shockwave as the building was obliterated from the top down. Smoking wreckage flew through the air, pocking the lot with fragments of mortar and cracking the paving. Schwarz managed to steer the truck in and around the biggest of the falling chunks, avoiding major damage to the Suburban. Smaller pieces of the building dented the hood and roof and left another crack in the windshield.

"Damn it," Lyons said.

"Dead guy!" Schwarz shouted as he pulled to a stop.

"What?"

Schwarz pointed to a smoking human body as it finished its arc through the air and landed wetly on the pavement in front of them.

Lyons walked over to the dead man and nudged the corpse with the toe of his boot. His teammates joined him. High above the building, they could now see a helicopter receding into the distance.

"There goes Rhemsen," Blancanales said.

"We'll get him," Lyons promised. He took out his secure satellite smartphone and stabbed at it a few times with his thumb. "How do you make the camera work on this thing?"

"You're bad at phone," Schwarz said.

"'Bad at phone'?" Blancanales repeated. "Is that what the kids say these days? It's not even really a sentence."

"Just…whatever. Somebody take the guy's picture and send it to the Farm," Lyons grumbled. "He's wearing what's left of a suit. That means he wasn't Blackstar or, if he was, he was somebody in charge." The dead man was Asian. The expression on his face was one of utter horror. His eyes were still open, staring at nothing.

Schwarz stepped in and snapped the shot. "We're going to want to let Barb and Hal know that we just blew up a building on American soil."

"That was *not* my fault," Lyons said. "Rhemsen blew the building. The first of the grenades didn't have a chance to set anything off before it went up."

"You think this guy was still alive when they blew up the building around him?" Blancanales asked. "Couldn't have liked him too much."

"No honor among treasonous scumbags, I guess," Lyons said. He hit the quick-dial for the scrambled line to the Farm. It did not take long for Barbara Price to answer.

"I'm here, Ironman," she said. "What have you got?"

"Trouble," Lyons replied. "Lots and lots of trouble."

CHAPTER ELEVEN

"What have we got?" McCarter asked. He was crouched in an alley in Calapan, the passageway formed by two strips of shops in a run-down commercial area of the city. The overhead wires were very thick here, a dizzying array of telephone and power cables that could not have been more chaotic if they had been deliberately laid out for maximum chaos. From where he was watching, the Phoenix Force leader could see what was either a shoe store or a cobbler—he was a little rusty on the local lingo—a discount electronics place, three or four little bodega-type eateries and what he took to be a Laundromat.

Calvin James and Rafael Encizo were across the street, using the stripped frame of an old Citroën for cover. Gary Manning and T. J. Hawkins were behind McCarter, covering the way they had come, making sure nothing snuck up behind them. It had been a very difficult afternoon, moving from house to house and steering clear of the civilian population while dodging patrols of professional gunmen in black battle-dress utilities. Several times they had been engaged by the hostile force, and several times they had inflicted heavy casualties on the enemy to facilitate a withdrawal. But they were running out of new area to cover. The black-ops group, whatever and whoever they might be, were clearly herding their quarry into gradually smaller areas. McCarter didn't like that at all. He was starting to see some of the same shops and landmarks as the enemy drove them into the smaller piece of real estate.

As for the Filipinos, they were clearly very angry. McCarter would put money on the notion that somebody higher up in the government had decided to divert all military and police presence. The locals had been instructed, by officials higher up in their body politic, to cooperate with McCarter's team, to accommodate Phoenix Force's presence. But of course they wouldn't like it, and now that Filipino troops had been killed in a battle the Filipinos would see as imported by foreign interests, they were looking to see some justice done.

Specifically, they were probably figuring that both sides of whatever private war this was—the black-clad shooters and the smaller squad that McCarter knew as Phoenix Force—would winnow each other's numbers, making them more manageable once Filipino security forces decided to step back in. Hell, odds were good that the black-uniformed men would wipe out Phoenix, leaving only one group of hostiles to be dealt with. That wasn't what McCarter thought of the situation, of course. But it would be how the local powers would see things.

Normally, withdrawing support and allowing two hostile forces to go at each other in a residential neighborhood would seem reckless, even depraved. But somehow the word had spread through this and the adjacent neighborhoods, by whatever means the locals had of communicating with each other, and warned them to clear out. Perhaps a word to someone on the street from someone in the military or police was enough to get that signal out and through the neighborhoods.

The city had that feel to it, as though a web of street people and personalities held it together. However it had happened, McCarter was grateful. It meant that they would not be tripping over civilians and endangering innocent lives while fighting for their own. But it did not bode well for the political pressure that would be brought to bear on Hal Brognola. Just one more burden for the man who held them all together. How the big Fed took that weight, day after day, McCarter honestly didn't know.

"It looks like a two-man advance patrol," James reported from across the street. He was watching through a monocular, keeping close tabs on the black-uniformed gunmen. "They're headed this way. I just saw one of them use his radio. Didn't look like he spoke long enough to be giving the main force this position. Probably just an all-clear while they fan out to look for us, try to prod us in whatever direction they're making us go."

"You caught that, eh?" McCarter asked.

"Hard to miss," James said. "I don't like feeling like cattle being led to slaughter."

"I heard that," Encizo said.

"I tell you what I'm tired of, mate," McCarter added. "And that's not knowing who it is that's hunting us. Fair bet to say these aren't pirates. Not a peg leg or a parrot among them."

"You thinking what I'm thinking you're thinking?" James asked.

"I'd like to take some prisoners, mate," McCarter said. "Think you and Rafe can oblige?"

"Let me confer with my partner here and see if I can get him to go along," James said.

"Me being so difficult and all," said Encizo.

They didn't have long to make arrangements, as the two enemy gunmen were already approaching. They didn't need much time. Phoenix Force had worked together for so long that they hardly needed to speak. Each man on the team knew his role and understood how to get his job done.

Encizo and James flattened themselves against the dusty road. The automobile frame was up on blocks, giving them enough room to scoot under it. Once underneath, both men positioned themselves on either side of the wreck. Now it was a question of timing…and luck.

The men in the black BDUs carried M-4 carbines with the latest high-tech accessories. Their web gear was also very modern. Whoever these men were, they were well equipped. The patrol was coming very close to the stripped car now. At the last moment, the two men both broke to the right side of the car, which was closer to where James was hiding compared to Encizo's vantage.

The men were staggered slightly, and as they passed what was left of the Citroën, two black hands shot out from underneath it, quick as rattlers. James grabbed one ankle and yanked for all he was worth. The abrupt motion ripped the legs out from under the two men, forcing their limbs to bend out in a way that few men—save for those flexible enough or trained sufficiently to perform splits— could comfortably sustain. They toppled. One of the men was wearing a helmet that wasn't strapped down and he lost it as he fell; he also cracked his skull very badly on what little there was of the pavement.

"Go, lads, go!" McCarter said. The rest of Phoenix Force fell in behind him as they crossed the street, quickly, to avoid being seen if any more of the hostiles were moving at the end of the street. Together, the five men of Phoenix Force grabbed the two prisoners and moved to the opposite alley mouth, then past it, and finally into the empty storage room of a vacant bodega. Hawkins had scouted the location earlier and reported the front of the business boarded up, the windows painted over. It was a perfect temporary hiding spot, although it wasn't a place they could stay for long. The more time they spent in the city, the greater the chances they would be caught and incur casualties. McCarter intended to make sure that did not happen.

Once they were inside the storage room, Hawkins took up station at the door, his rifle ready. There were some dusty old folding chairs piled in one corner. Encizo went to the pile, taking out the top one and setting it up. Manning placed the first man, the one who had retained his helmet, in the chair and held him there with viselike grips on the man's shoulders. James, for his part, eased the second prisoner to the floor.

"I think I broke this one," he said.

"Come again?" McCarter asked.

"I think he's got a concussion," James said. "Or worse. He hit his head pretty hard. Not looking so good."

"Go through his pockets," McCarter ordered. He turned to the other man, whose eyes were wide with fear. On the man's load-bearing vest was a logo that, now that he could read it while he wasn't being shot at, McCarter recognized. "Bloody Blackstar," he said. "That's who you're with?"

"You can't do this to me," the prisoner protested. His name was sewn to his uniform: Alan. McCarter assumed that was a surname and not that Blackstar had decided to treat its employees with easy familiarity.

"You're an American?" James said, looking up from the unconscious man.

"You're damned right I am," the prisoner said. "Alan, Michael K. I demand to speak to someone from the United States Embassy. I have rights!"

"You're adorable, mate," McCarter said. He let his Tavor hang by its single-point sling, took his Browning Hi-Power from its holster and made a show of press-checking it to make sure a round was in the chamber. Then he jacked back the hammer and put the barrel of the pistol under the man's chin. "Now, let's look at the realities of this situation, Alan, Michael K. We're both foreign nationals on Filipino soil. The locals aren't very happy with us, thanks to the mess your boys made. And, well, there's the little problem that you lot are a bunch of cowardly murderers who don't care who you kill. I mean, that's what you do, right? Pull triggers for money. Cash for kills. Isn't that the Blackstar way?"

"You got nothing on me," Alan said.

"I think you're not quite getting it, friend," McCarter said. "I don't need to 'have something' on you. The only thing I need to have on you is this weapon. And if I choose to put a bullet through your head, well, nobody is going to miss you, least of all me."

"I'd listen to him," James added. "I've seen him murder helpless victims before."

McCarter had to force himself to keep a straight face. To Alan, he said, "Oh, right. That reminds me." He pointed the Browning and fired a shot at the body of the fallen man.

James flinched, put two fingers against the man's neck and shook his head. "You finished him, man. He's dead."

The Briton turned back to his prisoner, who was now staring in open-mouthed terror. This Alan character didn't realize that, from where he sat pinned by Manning, he couldn't really see the body of his friend. McCarter had fired into the floor, not into the unconscious man. These Blackstar characters might all be first-rate bastards, but that didn't mean McCarter was just going to go around murdering people in cold blood. Of course, that was exactly what James was trying to make Alan think was going to happen. McCarter almost chuckled. He could not remember the last time he'd played "good cop, bad cop."

James muttered something about dragging the body out of the room. He very carefully lifted the unconscious man, keeping his body between Alan and Alan's partner, and moved the "body" into the main area of the shop. McCarter, meanwhile, holstered his gun and took out his knife. It was time to ramp up the tension.

"What are you going to do with that?" Alan demanded. He had started to sweat profusely. McCarter allowed himself to feel sad for the men of Blackstar. It certainly hadn't taken long for this particular employee to crack.

"You didn't actually think I was going to let you go that easily, did you?" McCarter said. "A bullet is quick, mate. A flash of light, some pain you don't really have time to register, and suddenly you're looking at your uncle Steve in the fires of hell, comparing notes on all the sins you committed in life. Or maybe there's just nothing ever again. Either way, it's like throwing a switch. You don't get that."

"What do you want? What do you want? Tell me! I'll talk!"

"Oh, I know you'll talk, friend. But I don't want you to talk. I want you to *scream*."

"Just tell me what you want to know!"

McCarter smiled. The poor lad was ready to spill it. "Tell me everything you know about what happened here. Your mission. The circumstances that led to it. Hold back nothing." He waved the combat knife under Alan's nose. "If you tell me everything, maybe I'll even let you keep most of your skin."

Alan's shoulder slumped. Manning pressed harder, keeping the pressure on both figuratively and literally. The prisoner winced. "I just work for Blackstar. They said there was a squad of half a dozen men, tops, operating here in the city, and that it was our job to bait them and eliminate them."

"They?" McCarter prompted.

"My bosses at Blackstar. Jay Fitzpatrick, for one. A few men who report to him. It's what we do."

"How were we to be baited?"

"Management has some kind of arrangement with the pirates who operate locally. I guess word was handed down to one of those crews that we were setting a trap, and that one of their number should put out the word he was looking to sell intel on the pirate operations here. Once that guy was in position, we were sent in to take him out and make it look like his fellow pirates were sending a message about squealing. Code of silence among pirates, all that crap. So we eliminated everyone in the house and painted the place to make it look like his buddies had done it."

"Then you just had to wait for us to blunder into your little trap," said McCarter.

"Yeah," said Alan. "They told us the squad we were supposed to take out would respond to the bait. Whoever did it, whether it was the Filipinos or somebody else, was our target. That's all I know. There's nothing else I can tell you."

"Good to know you're particular about who you murder," said McCarter.

"I was just doing my job, man."

"So you were present when the fake informant was murdered?"

"I… Yeah. Yeah, I was."

"And you killed others in the house, too."

Alan realized his mistake then. He opened his mouth, tried to speak and stopped. Finally he said, "I was just doing my job."

"And I'm just doing mine," McCarter said. "The only difference is, I'm not a murderer." He holstered his knife, drew his pistol again and waved Manning out of the way. Manning frowned but nodded and then stepped aside.

"I have rights!" Alan said again.

"So did the people you killed," McCarter retorted.

Desperate, Alan lunged forward and tried to knock the pistol from McCarter's hand.

Calmly, McCarter avoided the frantic attempt to disarm him. He pistol-whipped him and then turned. "Come on, lads. Let's get out of here. Leave them. They'll live or die. If they live, it's more than that murdering bastard deserves, and then the Filipino authorities will pick him up."

"I'll phone it in anonymously," said Gary, putting his secure phone to his ear.

"Good man," said McCarter.

Phoenix Force hit the street again, crouched and ready. They were not, however, prepared for what greeted them. A massive force of Blackstar troops was marching down the end of the road. The Phoenix Force leader had no way to be sure, but he was pretty certain that might be the total number of troops Blackstar had in the area. They were going for broke.

There was no way Phoenix Force could fight them all. There were far too many.

"Those two must have emergency transponders, some kid of panic switch we didn't notice when we took them n," Encizo said.

"Could be in the helmets," James ventured. "Some kind of 'I've fallen and I can't get up' transmitter. They're coming right for us."

"Lads," McCarter warned. "We had better try to make a run for it."

"We'll never make it," Manning noted.

Static broke through the transceiver link and McCarter cocked his head. "What was that?"

"Did you hear…Jack?" Encizo asked him.

"I said," Grimaldi repeated, "you guys realize you can track each other through your sat phones, right?"

"Uh, yeah?" James said.

"Well, so can I," Grimaldi said.

The massive Sikorsky roared overhead, putting its mass between where Phoenix Force was crouched and the knot of Blackstar shooters. As the Sikorsky passed by, McCarter recognized Filipino military officers manning the guns and grenade launcher. One of those was Lieutenant Ocampo, his left arm in a sling, his right arm manning the launcher.

"Lieutenant Ocampo," Grimaldi continued, "wants you to know that he and his men don't share his government's anxiety about our presence. He would like to further inform you that he is grateful for the chance to pay you back for saving his life."

McCarter started to reply. Whatever he might have said was cut off in the din as the Sikorsky's weapons opened up. The machine guns blazed, the grenade launcher puffed smoking death and the street full of Blackstar men became a bloody scene out of a horror movie. It took several minutes for the shooting and the screaming to stop. At least one of the Blackstar men tried to throw a grenade, only to have the weapon explode in the midst of his fellows.

the time the dust and debris from that explosion cleared, the Blackstar forces were so many corpses in the middle of the bullet-scarred street.

"When this is over," James said, "I'm buying Lieutenant Ocampo a beer."

"Get in line, mate," McCarter said.

CHAPTER TWELVE

Atlanta, Georgia

"Would you mind telling me what the hell is going on?" Fitzpatrick demanded, throwing open the door to Rhemsen's office. This plant in Atlanta was one the largest and the most secure of RhemCorp's holdings, hidden behind multiple layers of security. For one thing, the property bore no RhemCorp branding. It was instead tucked away in an industrial park area and labeled with the names of half a dozen nondescript holding companies. This helped disguise the true size of the facility while discouraging potential onlookers.

The Atlanta plant was also the site Rhemsen used to hide all of his most-off-the-book projects. Whether it was the true size of the weapons inventories he was producing, or the production of other black-ops munitions that he was not authorized to build, the laundry list of incriminating evidence here was enough to make even Fitzpatrick nervous. Rhemsen had explained, for his benefit, the many safeguards, legal and financial, that protected the facility from discovery, both with regard to ownership and relative to the arms manufactured here. These reassurances, however, meant little to him right now.

"You have a lot of nerve barging in here right now," said Rhemsen. He was sitting behind his desk. There was a hand mirror on the desk, and Fitzpatrick knew what that meant. The son of a bitch had been sitting there staring at himself close up, examining every pore and wrinkle, probably obsessing about his next facelift. How any man could be so vain and not magically become a woman was a question Fitzpatrick would never be able to answer.

"I know you didn't just give me attitude," Fitzpatrick said. He felt his face grow hot. Not for the first time, he considered wrapping his big hands around Rhemsen's neck and seeing just how much pressure it would take to make the man's eyes bulge out of their sockets. "Maybe you'd like to explain just why you think that's okay, with this company falling down around our ears and my men dying like it's free!"

"You've never struck me as particularly solicitous of the health of your troops," Rhemsen commented.

"Stop evading my damned question, Harold!" Fitzpatrick took a step forward and put his big hands on top of Rhemsen's desk. He was going to do it this time. He was going to reach across that desk, grab Harold Rhemsen by the neck and beat him unconscious.

Rhemsen glared back. "You triggered the charges prematurely," he said. He pointed at Fitzpatrick as he did, punctuating each word with a jab of his finger. "The explosion killed Lao. We were lucky to get away."

"Why should I give a damn about Lao?" Fitzpatrick countered. "You said yourself he was just a Chinese bag man. We don't owe him anything and, honestly, I would think you, of all people, would understand that we're better off with him dead. He *knew* things, Harold. Lao was on the inside of our operations here, thanks to the information you had to share with him to get him to invest. He obviously wasn't going to make the chopper, not with armed government agents breathing down our necks. Hell, we were lucky to make it aboard ourselves. If I hadn't triggered those charges to cover our escape, there might not have been an escape at all. Or do you want to spend your life in some white-collar prison, doing other people's laundry in a bright orange 'trustee' vest?"

"Lao was a very important person," said Rhemsen.

"That's not what you told me."

"Certain details are mine to keep," Rhemsen insisted. He slumped back into his chair.

Something about the action made Fitzpatrick feel silly, looming over him as he was. He raised his hands from the desk and stood there, unsure what to do with his arms. Finally he crossed them over his chest. "I get that," he said. "I really do. But I can't prioritize things like collateral damage if you don't tell me what I need to know. Just how bad is it?"

Rhemsen sighed. "No, you're right. I should have been more forthcoming. It's just that Lao… He was so highly placed with the Chinese government and its military that I could not see him falling. His death can be blamed on the Americans easily enough. The Chinese need not ever know the exact circumstances. I have made them aware that the United States government is investigating."

"I never liked relying on their money, Harold," said Fitzpatrick. "Dangerous business, getting in bed with Communist dictators."

"We have more pressing concerns," said Rhemsen, sitting forward. "With the obliteration of the factory in Charleston, the United States will waste no time investigating. For the time being, we are safe at this location. There are enough layers of disguise to prevent even their intelligence community from finding us. That factory, with the exception of a few outlying holdings, was the major center of production for RhemCorp, as far as they know. Maintaining this secret factory in parallel was always essential to our strategy, given how frequently the Department of Defense insisted on conducting inspections. Now the ruse will shield us long enough for us to get out of the country."

"I'm not ready to do that."

"You had better become ready," Rhemsen said. "Jason, I realize that the timetable has been significantly accelerated. But did you not just speak to me about your exit strategy? I know you have this thought out."

"I understand what you're trying to do even less now," Fitzpatrick complained. "How does what you've done so far help us? My men in Mindoro were ground up and spat out, Harold. Do you have any idea how many troops I lost? I might as well have lined them up and shot them all myself!"

"That is regrettable," Rhemsen said. "I had no way of knowing that the assets the United States would employ to the South China Sea would be so effective. I genuinely believed your men were up to the task. I still believe it. We simply have to find the right way."

"Your operation is blown," Fitzpatrick stated. "Whatever you think you're accomplishing out there…it doesn't matter. I'm pulling my men out."

"No," Rhemsen said. "Don't do that. I need Blackstar's support. I still have multiple pirate crews working to my directions in the area. I'm going to need Blackstar's support for the next leg of the operation."

"Maybe it's time you explained to me exactly what you're doing, then, Harold."

Rhemsen took a deep breath. "Very well. Very well, I will do so. Jason, the United States is a nation in decline. It is deep in debt. Its military is foundering. Its sway on the world stage is diminishing. You understand this, yes? You see it, too?"

"So what if I do?"

"Men of vision, men who can see what is coming and respond to it beforehand, are men who succeed. They are the men who become rich. The biggest arms market in the world is the nation with the largest conventional fighting force. That nation is China, and I intend to see to it they are well supplied. But an open war with China is years away. Some say a few, some say many. I wish to make money right now."

"What are you getting at?" Fitzpatrick asked.

Rhemsen steepled his fingers as he leaned back in his chair. "The world must fear China, Jason. I am using the pirate crews to create the impression that China is expanding its territory in the South China Sea by force. The plan has been carefully crafted for maximum effect. It is based on everything from the stock market to major trade routes to the cable news cycle. I have devised a method for achieving maximum impact from the minimum required number of raids and strikes."

"To do what?" Fitzpatrick demanded. "So far all I can see is you bringing down the ceiling on our heads. We're blown in the US."

"I thought I said as much," Rhemsen said. "We will have to leave the United States, yes. But I have been arranging with Lao to establish manufacturing sites in China. It was for that reason that I met with him so often. He was more than just an investor. He had the political clout to get the factories approved, the workers detailed, the funds allocated. He has served his purpose. The factories have already been started."

"But what is the point, Harold? Why make the world 'fear China' if what you want is to get into bed with them?"

"I am building the market, Jason," Rhemsen said. "A world that fears China's territorial designs will react accordingly by deploying more military might against her. As tensions rise, the world's governments may even begin to discuss sanctions. This will, in turn, prompt the Chinese to invest even more heavily in their military…and in an armed space program, something Lao and I were discussing at length. RhemCorp products will make all that possible. We will arm China for defense against these nations, even as we establish to those antagonists that China is a threat and must be menaced. Thus the market will feed on itself, and we will profit."

"Do the Chinese know?"

"Of course not," said Rhemsen. "They would have me killed immediately if they had any idea. But they don't. That is why I used the pirates to accomplish the necessary physical tasks. The pirate crews not only give me the means, but shield me from discovery. None of them knows directly about the other. Not a single one of those men knows who has hired him, either. I have conducted all of the operations through paid intermediaries. When I speak to them directly, I do so by satellite phone. It is a foolproof plan."

"But we're killing ourselves in the States," Fitzpatrick said. "We can't come back here. Once the Feds start looking into our operations, we'd be *lucky* if they just put us in prison. This is death-penalty stuff, Harold. Treason."

"Of course it is," Rhemsen agreed. "But as I've said, the United States is not where the money is. It is a calculated burning of a bridge we won't need."

"I don't like it," Fitzpatrick said.

"I anticipated this," Rhemsen said. "And now, Jason, I am going to reward you for all your hard work."

Rhemsen rose and went to the gold-framed oil painting on the wall behind his desk. The painting was of Rhemsen himself, of course, but it was a younger Rhemsen, with a face not contorted into a plastic death mask. As Fitzpatrick watched, Rhemsen slid the painting aside to reveal an electronic wall safe. He placed his palm against the reader and waited while the safe door popped open. Then he reached in and removed a briefcase. This he placed on his desk. From the upper right drawer of his desk, he took out a leather-bound journal.

"What's all that?" asked Fitzpatrick.

"This," said Rhemsen, opening the briefcase to face him, "is one million dollars." He spun the briefcase so that Fitzpatrick could see its contents. The Blackstar commander's jaw dropped. "This is your payment, Jason. This will help finance your new life somewhere other than the United States, and reward you for all the work you have done making RhemCorp's foreign empire possible. You understand now, yes?"

"China," Fitzpatrick said. "It was either that or Russia, wasn't it?"

"Exactly," Rhemsen said. "The only two industrial nations with enough military might that our operations would be shielded from United States' reprisals. But Russia, for all its rumblings of once again becoming a major military power, thanks to their leadership's saber-rattling, still clings to too much baggage from its Soviet days. The Russian *mafiya* controls a great deal of the commerce there. They are a...cooperative entity, responsive to bribes and other pressures, but very unpredictable. Prone to violence. Their involvement in the *krokodil* drug trade alone is enough to give me pause."

"The Chinese are just as corrupt. It's just political."

"So it is," Rhemsen said. "But that means there is a single, strong, controlling entity whose favor we must court. Having secured this, we are well prepared to move forward. So I selected China because it is where the money is…and it has the power to protect us from the Americans' wrath. Once established in China, I will not require the use of Blackstar's troops any longer. I will have the Chinese military to protect my holdings, and they will be grateful to have me."

"So you're cutting me loose?" Fitzpatrick asked.

"I am setting you free," Rhemsen said. "I know you, Jason. You would not be happy in China. You will want to find a country more suited to your…recreational tastes, yes? And now I shall see to it you have the finances to do so. With this and the money I know you already possess, you should be well equipped for a comfortable retirement. That sandy beach full of pretty, willing women, perhaps?"

"But…why?" Fitzpatrick asked.

"Why treat you with such kindness?" Rhemsen almost managed a smile through that paralyzed plastic face of his. "Do you think me so incapable of appreciation? Of loyalty? But…no, I must be honest. I have one request, one condition." He handed Fitzpatrick the journal.

"What's this?"

"That is my personal journal, Jason," Rhemsen said. "Where you are going, you will be beyond the reach of the Chinese. I will be, as you've said, in bed with them. While I believe the relationship will be a mutually beneficial one, I did not get where I am today by being stupid. That journal details everything I've done and, if the information were ever released, it would shame the Chinese. It would make them look very foolish indeed. That is information they will not want floating around the internet or spoken of in government meetings and political rallies. I therefore give it to you. Keep the journal somewhere safe, tucked away in some safe-deposit box somewhere with your cash. All I ask is that if China ever decides I have outlived my usefulness and 'disappears' me, you send the journal to the press."

"An insurance policy," Fitzpatrick said.

"An insurance policy," Rhemsen echoed. "Should I sense that they mean me ill, I will make sure they know the information exists and that it will be released if something happens to me. You are the last person they would expect me to trust. In their minds, you are hired help. They do not understand that when a man works with another man for as long as we have, loyalty is inevitable."

Fitzpatrick would have argued that under any normal circumstances. He'd never had any particular loyalty for Rhemsen. But with a briefcase full of cash and a bona fide political hot potato staring him in the face, he wasn't going to do anything to queer the deal.

"You got it," he said. "I can do that."

"I knew I could count on you, Jason."

"So now what? It's going to take time for us to make arrangements to pull up stakes. Just arranging for transportation out of the country is going to be difficult. We are well and truly screwed right now, Harold."

"We will give them something else on which to focus," Rhemsen said. "Do you remember the manufacturing facility on Hilton Head Island?"

"Yeah," Fitzpatrick said. "We shut it down because the overhead costs of maintenance on the building were too high."

"I have already arranged for a chain of events to take place in the South China Sea," Rhemsen told him. "Those events will keep these federal forces, whoever they may be, occupied there while we complete our plans. In the meantime, I want you take the helicopter and arrange for an assault force of your men to go with you. As many men as you can afford to take. The Special Interests division here will have the equipment you need. The advanced interrogation unit and other man-trapping devices we've been working on? You should take these, as well. Use them to arrange an elaborate trap in Hilton Head. Then return here. I want you at this facility, by my side, for as long as possible until we both leave the country and go our separate ways. And if your men can successfully kill those government agents, whoever they are, so much the better."

"How do you know they'll go to Hilton Head?" asked Fitzpatrick.

Rhemsen indicated the laptop computer on his desk. "When we shut down Hilton Head, I made sure there was a data trail leading from our holding companies to that site. All I must do, to reveal the location to the authorities— without making it too obvious, of course—is remove the blocks on those connections, the firewalls holding the data secure. Once I have done that, American intelligence will easily ferret it out. The best part is that they will believe they have found it on their own, which is why our trap will work. All it requires is for you to apply your considerable imagination to the problem and commit enough men to secure it. Make sure, however, to leave a substantial security force for us here."

"You think they'll be able to find this place?"

"Nothing is impossible," Rhemsen said. "But it should take them long enough that we will be gone. If we aren't, I want our forces here at full strength. If nothing else, your men can battle the meddlers long enough to allow us to escape. My private jet will be fueled and ready at the airport. I've bribed the appropriate personnel. No one will interfere with us when we finally leave the United States."

"I've got to hand it to you, Harold," Fitzpatrick said. "You've got it all figured out."

"So you feel a little better about our endeavor?"

"Let's just say," Fitzpatrick said, closing the briefcase and picking it up, "that a million dollars in cash helps take the sting out of whatever else I might be feeling."

CHAPTER THIRTEEN

Off the Coast of Puerto Galera, South China Sea

"It's bad, David," Barbara Price explained through the secured connection from the Farm. "The attackers have never been this brazen before, but the Filipino government has gone apoplectic."

"I can't say as I blame them, given the mess they think we brought to their shores," McCarter said into his phone. "Any chance we're going to be able to square that?"

"Hal is already running interference," Price said. "He's said it's not as bad as they made it sound."

"Well, that's a relief," McCarter replied, "because they made it *sound* like they were willing to leave their streets to a pair of foreign paramilitary forces in the distant hopes that these two groups would kill off enough of each other to make it easier to mop up whatever was left."

"Yes," Price said. "Hal explains that was a very extreme overreaction. Elements within the Filipino government are going to see what he calls 'political and social ramifications' as a result."

"In other words, somebody's going to pay with their career."

"That's about it," Price admitted. "We're still a little ways away from having cooperation from the Filipino government again, but it's coming."

"I hope Lieutenant Ocampo isn't going to suffer for helping us."

"Not that I can tell," Price said. "Hal was very specific about that. He assures me that things will be smoothed over soon. He just needs to finish separating the good from the bad while making judicious use of the hammer at his disposal."

"Nobody likes to get knocked with the influence hammer." McCarter chuckled. "All right. Please extend to him my regards. I know it isn't easy."

"How are *you* holding up?" Price asked. "I know a lot falls on your shoulders, David."

"I'm fine, Ms. Price," said McCarter, "but I do thank you immensely for your consideration."

That brought one of the throaty laughs that made Price so damned sexy. McCarter noticed it, of course; he always did when she was in the room. You couldn't be human and *not* understand that the honey-blond mission controller could have been a fashion model if she'd chosen. But he admitted to feeling more paternal toward her than anything else. He suspected most of them felt that way. Price was, after all, already spoken for: she was married to her job at Stony Man Farm, although she did occasionally entertain a certain gentleman caller who had been part of the Farm from the start. McCarter allowed himself to wonder, for a moment, how that particular gentleman was faring in his endless war for justice.

"So what is our new target?" McCarter asked. Grimaldi had the coordinates and was flying them, in the Sikorsky, to their destination. The chopper was fully repaired from its previous battles and also fully restocked with ammunition and grenades. Apparently, as Jack had described it, there had been a few near moments at the heliport near the docks, when it looked as though his Filipino military escorts were going to try to take him into custody.

Ocampo had showed up not long after, looking surprisingly well for a man who had been shot earlier. The lieutenant had explained that, while his wound was not terribly serious, the attitudes expressed by his government were much more turbulent. That was why the plucky lieutenant had taken the initiative to make sure Phoenix Force was taken care of. Apparently he was confident that his superiors would sort things out, but worried that this process might take longer than Phoenix Force had. So he had endangered his own career to see to it.

"The target," Price explained, "is a Filipino freighter, the *Bapor na Pangkargada*, which left Puerto Galera this morning. It didn't get very far. It was set upon by pirate vessels, fast-attack launches like the ones you faced earlier…only these weren't pirates at all. They're flying the Chinese flag."

"Bloody hell," McCarter said. "Do the Chinese have anything to say about that?"

"The Man has been in touch with Beijing," Price said. "They vehemently deny any involvement in the attacks. They say they have no assets in the area that are not tied up with their drilling platforms or otherwise recognizable as regular Chinese navy."

"So why aren't they here?" McCarter asked. "Any other time, if their interests were threatened, the Chinese would be all over this location."

"You're right about that," Price conceded. "Under normal conditions, a hostile force falsely flying the Chinese flag would be reason enough for the PLAN to steam the *Liaoning* in there. Or one of the new 60,000-ton Type 089 carriers they built based on the *Varyag*, the retired Soviet carrier they acquired for 'study.'"

McCarter nodded, although he knew she couldn't see him. The *Liaoning,* the first aircraft carrier produced by China for the People's Liberation Army Navy, a name that always made him half chuckle. Ostensibly, the *Liaoning* was a "training ship," meaning it was meant to give the Chinese experience with running carriers. The reality was nothing so mundane, as the Chinese had been growing increasingly belligerent on the world stage.

The *Liaoning* and the Type 089 carriers were intended for Beijing's new Shenyang J-15, the Chinese "Flying Shark." The J-15 was a carrier-based fighter aircraft highly derivative of the Soviet Sukhoi Su-33, bearing Chinese-produced technology and weapons systems. This was, in turn, derived from the fourth-generation Shenyang J-11, a copy of the Soviet Flanker air-superiority fighter intended to compete with F-15s and similar tech.

McCarter took the phone from his ear for a moment. "Jack, ETA to target?"

"We're five minutes out," Grimaldi said. "I've been trying to raise the *Bapor na Pangkargada*, but I'm getting no response."

"No response from the target," McCarter told Price. "Do you really think the Chinese would be so bold? If they did it, denying they did it is a delaying tactic only."

"I agree it doesn't make a lot of sense," Price said. "The Filipinos are ready to go to war over it."

"No offense to them," said McCarter, "but there's no scenario where that works out in their favor."

"Nor ours," said Price. "If they write a check we have to end up cashing, it's going to set that whole part of the world on fire."

"Right," said McCarter. "We'll do what we can to stop the world from catching aflame, Barb."

"Good hunting, David."

"I'll be in touch. Phoenix, out."

As the Sikorsky came within range of the freighter, Mc-Carter took out his monocular and surveyed the deck. He saw men in what definitely appeared to be Chinese military uniforms moving around. They carried what looked like AK-pattern rifles, too, which was consistent with Chinese military forces. That, in itself, though, meant nothing. Neither did the fact that the ship was now running the Chinese flag. Anybody could run a flag up a flagpole.

Anybody could get a Chinese flag, too, although he wasn't sure where a man bought such a thing on short notice. For that matter, he had never understood where foreign protestors obtained the American flags they burned at protests. He suspected there was a thriving mail-order business, or whatever people did these days. Maybe you could buy flags on the internet. Bloody hell, but he was starting to show his age. He didn't do a lot of online shopping. He didn't do a lot of shopping, period.

Enough wool-gathering. It was time to get to work. "T.J., Rafe, on the guns," McCarter directed. "Gary, take the launcher."

"I miss out on all the fun, man," James complained.

"Don't worry, Calvin," McCarter said. "I think there'll be enough action to go around." He stowed his monocular and grabbed one of the hand straps overhead. "Ready, lads. Jack? Take us in. Let's hose those decks down!"

The nose of the Sikorsky dipped as the chopper picked up speed. Grimaldi guided the helicopter past the freighter, stern to bow, moving just fast enough to make it difficult for the gunmen on the deck to hit them.

"Fire!" shouted McCarter.

Encizo, whose side of the chopper faced the boat, leaned into his machine gun and started firing. His rounds scattered men to either side of the deck, blowing out chunks of the railing and digging furrows into the decking. Several of the uniformed men fell, screaming, overboard, to disappear under the waves. Still more fired back with their

Kalashnikovs, filling the air with the hollow metal clatter of the Russian-pattern assault rifles.

"Coming around for another pass," Grimaldi said.

"Do you see any crew members?" James asked McCarter. "Anybody at all that isn't in one of these Chinese uniforms?"

"No," said McCarter. "And that has me bloody worried. This hostile force controls the ship. They could have massacred the crew to do it."

"And if they didn't," James said, "they could be holding them hostage."

"I'm hoping it won't get to that," McCarter said. "Let's go, lads. Once more unto the breach and all that. Get us closer, Jack. Put the other side to them so Gary can bring the launcher into play if he has to. I want a good look at these bastards."

"You got it," Grimaldi said.

They started slow, gathering speed as the Sikorsky built up momentum after the Stony Man ace pilot swung it around. As wind began to whistle through the open doors, Manning prepared to lay down a devastating rain of grenades. McCarter hoped to avoid that if he could. It was entirely possible for the Phoenix Force men to lay down enough firepower to sink the freighter, but that was not their goal. Their aim was to surgically remove the enemy while freeing the crew of the ship. Keeping that freighter intact was part of keeping the crew alive…if they weren't already dead.

Bullets ricocheted from the chopper's fuselage as they closed on the ship. Now it was Hawkins's turn to fire on the deck. He did so with precision, riding through medium-length bursts, careful not to simply wash the deck in death in a spray-and-pray overreaction to the fire they were taking. A lot of less-experienced soldiers might be tempted to give in to that urge. It was one of the reasons that combat engineers were forever designing burst modes into automatic weapons, rather than simply trusting the operator's trigger control to get the job done. Under stress, a man who panicked tended to simply hold down the trigger and empty the weapon. It was the reason that later versions of the M-16 rifle employed a 3-round burst setting compared to the earlier versions' simpler full-automatic.

A sharp, metallic snap sounded somewhere near the rear of the chopper. Smoke started to flow from the back.

"Jack!" McCarter shouted. "We've got smoke!"

"White or black?" Grimaldi yelled back.

"White!" McCarter said.

"We're okay," Grimaldi said. He risked a glance back while guiding the chopper up and over the freighter, out of the direct line of sight of the gunmen on the deck.

"You sure?" said McCarter. "You don't want to check?"

"I'm pretty sure we're mostly okay," Grimaldi answered.

"Mostly?" James said.

"Pretty sure?" Encizo said.

"I've got a bad feeling about this," Hawkins drawled.

"Are you quoting…?" Manning started to ask. Hawkins shook his head. Manning shrugged.

"Hang on, hang on," Grimaldi said. "I'm getting something on the radio."

"From the Farm?" McCarter asked.

"No," Grimaldi said. "This is a local RF transmission. It's garbled. Let me work on it for a minute." He adjusted the dials. "Almost got it… There!" He flipped a switch on the control panel. The sound of the transmission played over all their transceivers, audible despite the noise of the chopper itself.

"This is *Bapor na Pangkargada*," said a voice in accented English. "I repeat. This is *Bapor na Pangkargada*. We are speaking to you from this vessel. You will immediately withdraw your helicopter."

"Fat chance of that," McCarter said under his breath. He knew, though, that this was not the end of the transmission. There was going to be more, and it was going to be worse.

"We have wired the boat with explosives," warned the voice on the radio. "We are holding the crew of this ship hostage. There are twenty-two men here—twenty-two members of the crew. We will kill them one at a time if you do not remove yourself from this airspace. You have sixty seconds to withdraw."

The transmission went dead.

"Jack," McCarter said. "Mark that!"

"Got it."

The Stony Man pilot pulled up, moving the chopper back, putting it out of range of small-arms fire from the deck of the freighter. He began to work the chopper in a slow oval around the ship. They could see the motor launches moored to either side of the freighter, and these were similar to the pirate craft they had seen before.

"It doesn't make sense," Manning said. "They're wearing Chinese uniforms and running the Chinese flag…but their boats are the same craft you'd expect pirates to use. Why not use Chinese attack craft if they want the world to know China is responsible?"

"I hate feeling like I've been played," McCarter said.

"Thirty seconds," called Grimaldi.

"I don't like it," the Briton said. "I don't like it all, mates. We're deep in the weeds here."

"Could it be Blackstar?" Encizo suggested. "Masquerading as the Chinese?"

"To what end?" McCarter said.

"They're mercenaries," James answered. "War is good for business."

"But picking a fight with China is a good way to end a war before you begin," Encizo said. "Blackstar is a big company, but they can't match China's conventional army. Like it or not, the Dragon is a superpower, or an emerging one, and the folks in Beijing have a lot to prove. They're not going to back down if they think they'll lose face... and people masquerading as Chinese troops to hijack a ship are the kind of thing that ought to bring down the red hammer."

"Fifty-five seconds," Grimaldi said. "I'm pulling us out."

"Right," McCarter said. "Take us back to port, Jack. We need a new plan, and we need it quickly."

The radio crackled to life once more. "Do not return here," the voice said. "This ship belongs to the People's Republic of China. This territory for many kilometers belongs to the People's Republic of China."

"Many kilometers?" James repeated.

"He sounds like he's reading off cue cards," Grimaldi put in.

"I'm calling the Farm again," McCarter said. "Something's damn fishy here, and we're going to get to the bottom of it if we have to swim back out there."

McCarter clenched his fists. This wasn't over. Not even slightly. He checked his chronometer. "Get the Filipino navy on the horn, Jack," he said. "Like it or not, we're going to need their cooperation. We need radar fix on that ship to verify they don't leave. And we're going to need more naval support to get out there and do what we've got to do the hard way."

The Sikorsky thundered on toward Puerto Galera.

"It's going to be tight, David," James said.

"We don't have much daylight left," McCarter agreed,

nodding, "but maybe we can use that to our advantage. A lot is going to depend on what the locals can help us do."

"You think they'll bite?" James asked.

"Let's say I'm hoping Hal is as persuasive as I think he is," McCarter said.

CHAPTER FOURTEEN

Hilton Head Island

Hilton Head Island was a resort town named for one William Hilton, who in 1663 was modest enough to name after himself the headland adjacent to Port Royal Sound's entrance. With twelve miles of beach fronting the Atlantic, the island saw millions of visitors and well more than a billion dollars in tourist money. While it was easy to dismiss the entire area as one big resort, home to a handful of wealthy residents and the seasonal tourist glut, the city did have a small industrial area not far from the Hilton Head airport.

It was this complex to which Able Team was headed. The island, fortunately, was accessible using Route 278, which followed a series of bridges connecting the island to South Carolina. Schwarz looked up from his candy monster game long enough to acknowledge the Pinckney Island National Wildlife Refuge, which their bridge carried them through at the fringes before they entered Hilton Head itself.

They passed several gated communities on their way to their destination. The season was on and the tourist trade was brisk. Lyons wasn't happy about that. He would have preferred they roll through this town when it was the least popular place on the planet. There would be fewer innocent people to get in the way of a bullet, that way.

Fortunately, though, the property the Farm had sleuthed

out and identified as one of Rhemsen's holdings looked largely deserted. With luck, that would mean there wouldn't be any civilian employees wandering around. The fact that they hadn't encountered many of these in their previous raids on Rhemsen's properties just proved that Rhemsen was making some kind of move, some kind of transition from legitimate business—if his business had ever been truly legitimate—to whatever he was doing that made it okay, in his mind, to start killing federal agents.

As business plans went, it didn't make a whole lot of sense to Lyons. They had seen enough of these nut jobs over the years that nothing truly surprised him, of course, but he liked to think that on some level he understood why a man went bad. Every one of these bastards, all the villains and terrorists and crazed, power-mad lunatics they came up against, had some plan, something they were trying to accomplish. Sure, sometimes that made about as much sense as a screen door in a submarine, like that death cult operating out of Germany a few years back. Terrorists he understood. Rich guys like Rhemsen trying to make a buck, even through treason and reckless arms sales to foreign powers, he could at least grasp. Money was a powerful motivator. But killing just because you wanted the world to die? That was nutty stuff.

So where did Rhemsen fall on that spectrum? As Lyons drove, he considered what they knew. The guy's background checked out. He'd grown up a privileged orphan after his parents died young. Educated in Oxford. There was something in his file about an accident during his college years that might explain why his face looked so odd. It wasn't detailed in his file, but the Farm had dug up some records relating to a hospital stay during that period.

That might explain why Rhemsen's face looked like twenty miles of bad gravel road that had been smoothed over with cold patch. Lyons's first assumption had been just vanity. You saw enough of those Hollywood guys who went under the knife too many times and ended up looking like old English ladies with missing eyebrows.

Driving here, Blancanales had raised the question of whether they should call in the cavalry, have the National Guard roust the joint. The problem was no longer one of having sufficient legal recourse to bring in Rhemsen. Lyons had even placed a call to the Farm to make sure, checking with Price to see if maybe there was a flaw in his logic. She had confirmed what he already expected, though.

Already, an entire building on American soil had been blown up. While civilian casualties had been zero domestically over the course of Able Teams' operations against RhemCorp—the only dead men had been members of the Blackstar goon squad, who had all been engaged in trying to murder federal agents—this was the sort of thing that made the Feds nervous. Brognola hadn't mentioned it during their initial briefing, concerned as he was about the South China Sea angle, but Lyons had been a cop for most of his life in one form or another. Arguably, he still was, even though he had traded his job in law enforcement for one in counterterrorism.

People were all up in arms these days about the militarization of police. He got that. The tactics in which Able Team and Phoenix Force traded were by definition extralegal. It wouldn't do for too many people to discover just how the Farm got things done, because working outside the law made lots of people, from civilians to politicians, nervous. That was why it was necessary for the Special Operations Group to work covertly, as it did.

The RhemCorp site was separated from the main road by a winding drive lined with carefully landscaped trees.

Lyons was careful, as he guided the truck along that drive, to watch for Blackstar men in hiding. He scanned the roadside with a practiced eye. A lot of American soldiers had returned from Iraq and Afghanistan with a healthy fear of debris by the roadside. Lyons, veteran at counterterrorism that he was, had started his career as a cop, but the idea was the same...and the dangers were also the same.

The Blackstar security forces had showed absolutely no hesitation when it came to trying to murder federal agents. They would not be above rigging roadside explosives to take out intruders. He wondered if they might have gone so far as to line the drive with mines, or anything exotic like that, but it seemed unlikely, as vehicles would pass in and out of the property on a regular basis if that property was active. Still, there was no guarantee.

That was the thing about power-mad, greedy, reckless murderers. They were a little on the unpredictable side.

The whole thing struck him as weird, for an arms-manufacturing facility to be hidden away in such a posh resort area as Hilton Head. He was pretty sure they had passed some gated communities along the way that housed some fairly well-known celebrities. It wasn't something he would mention in front of Schwarz, though. He didn't feel like enduring the near-endless enjoyment Schwarz would get from making fun of Lyons's unexpected pop-culture knowledge. That was the electronics expert's territory, after all.

"What are you grinning about, Ironman?" Schwarz asked.

"Nothing," said Lyons.

"It's never nothing when you say it that way," Schwarz said.

"Shut up, Gadgets," Lyons said pleasantly.

"Okay, now I know something's up."

"How does that work?" Blancanales put in. "All he said was 'shut up.' He's always telling you to shut up."

"And he never listens," Lyons said.

Schwarz raised a finger. "Over the years I have become something of a connoisseur of Carl's 'shut ups,'" he said. "Like a fine wine, each one has a subtle bouquet, multiple layers of meaning suspended in—"

"No, seriously, Gadgets," Lyons interrupted. "Shut up." He pointed. "Something feels wrong."

The nose of the Suburban was now at the edge of a small parking area around the Hilton Head RhemCorp building. There was no external signage, nothing to indicate what this building was or to whom it belonged. If it had taken so long for the Farm to sleuth out this particular location, that probably meant there was juicy stuff hidden here. Or that there had been. You never knew, with these joints.

Schwarz paused, his jovial demeanor evaporating. "Yeah," he said.

"You feeling it?" Lyons asked.

"Yeah," Schwarz answered.

"Me, too," Blancanales said.

"Grab the duffel," Lyons directed as he surveyed the lot. There were plenty of cars here. The facility wasn't empty. There were bound to be people working here and they would have to sift through these to determine who were civilians and who were shooters. Anybody in a Blackstar uniform had better lie down the moment Able Team hit those front doors, though, or Lyons was going to consider them fair game. He had been shot at enough by these goons. And he was really, really hoping to get his hands on Jason Fitzpatrick.

That big bastard had a beat-down coming. That much, Lyons was sure of. Something about the whole setup here, though, was eating at him. It was ticking at the back of his mind, making him question everything. The nagging itch continued as he took his shotgun from the duffel, slung his war bag over his shoulder and made sure that he had enough loaded drum magazines for the weapon. His partners armed up, too.

"No guards," Schwarz said.

"No guards!" Lyons said. "That's what it is. Every other facility we've come up against has been guarded to hell and gone, full of Blackstars with itchy trigger fingers." He swept the parking lot with his big hand. "There are just as many cars parked here. There should be just as big a presence."

"Maybe they're watching us from inside," Blancanales ventured.

"I don't see any cameras," Schwarz said. "Nothing moving at the windows, either."

"I don't like it," said Lyons. "We should see something. There should be more activity."

Lyons marked the path they would have to walk, through the thickest of the parked cars, to the front door of the building. That's when he saw it. He cursed himself for a fool. It should have been obvious from the moment they'd pulled up.

"Every one of these cars is a beater," Schwarz noted, apparently hitting the conclusion the same moment Lyons froze in his tracks. "Not a brand-new car among them. Not one."

Lyons's eyes went to the wheels of the nearest cars and then to the space between them. The cable snaking underneath the vehicles, connecting each one to the next, was the same color as the asphalt beneath. He very nearly missed it.

"Ironman—" Schwarz started to say.

"Run!" Lyons roared. He grabbed Schwarz by the collar and Blancanales by the shoulder, shoving them both ahead of him, propelling them forward. The men of Able Team managed to clear the parking lot kill zone just in time.

Lyons felt it before he heard it. There was a rush of air, almost as though the space around him was being sucked past through a giant vacuum. His ears popped. A wave of heat, pressing against him like the palm of an angry war god, shoved him toward Schwarz and Blancanales, dumping him on top of both men, toppling all three. They landed just short of the steps to the front door of the building.

The explosion was powerful enough to blow out the glass on the ground floor of the building. It shattered the panes of the front doors and dropped countless pebbles of safety glass on Able Team. Lyons could feel his exposed skin burning. He expressed himself as loudly and with as much profanity as he could manage.

"That's telling them, Ironman," Blancanales muttered from underneath him.

"Carl…" Schwarz said. "You're crushing my spine."

Lyons rolled off and into a kneeling stance. He brought the shotgun up just in time. Uniformed Blackstar security personnel were now appearing at the shattered front doors, their AR-pattern rifles swinging Able Team's way.

"Oh, hell, no," Lyons said, holding back the trigger of the USAS-12.

He rode out the recoil, spraying 00 shot and slugs in combination, feeling the mighty shotgun buck and tremble in his fists. The men at the doorway, standing elevated as they were compared to his position, were blown apart at the shins, their legs ripped into bloody stumps. The screaming was inhuman. Lyons kept firing, empty-ing his drum, making sure that if anyone was coming behind that first wave, they, too, would be knocked down for the count.

The sharp reports of Blancanales's M-4 were punctuated by the lighter chatter of Schwarz's Colt SMG. The Colt subgun had a tremendously high rate of fire. Schwarz stitched his way through the ranks of the enemy wounded, giving them mercy shots to end their suffering.

Lyons could hear ringing in his ears and smell the discharge from their weapons. He paused, shucking the last drum and slamming home a replacement from his war bag. Jacking in the first round, he looked at Schwarz and Blancanales. "Come on," he said. "Let's clean house."

They strode up the steps with Lyons at the tip of a wedge formation. Schwarz and Blancanales covered his flanks. Each man was responsible for his side of guarding their six o'clock. Ready for any amount of firepower—at least, that was how Carl Lyons felt—the three counterterrorists entered the previously masked RhemCorp building.

The foyer was pocked with holes from their weapons fire. That wasn't what caught Lyons's practiced eye, though. The very first thing he noticed was how terrible the walls had looked before they were covered in bullet holes.

"This place was deserted," Schwarz said. "Look at how much dust is still in the corners of the window frames on either side of the door."

"Could they have reactivated the place by coincidence?" Blancanales offered. "Put it back into service for some purpose?"

"Just before we find it?" Lyons said. "Not likely. And those rigged junkers in the parking lot…? That's not a security measure. That's a trap. They were laying for us."

"Us specifically?" Schwarz asked.

"I'd put money on it," Lyons said. "Watch your backs. And keep a sharp eye out for more explosives. We know Rhemsen has a thing for rigging his buildings. I don't want to go up with this joint."

"Split up?" Schwarz asked.

"Not this time," Lyons said. "I'm not making it that much easier for them. We stay in formation. Cover each other's backs. Be ready for anything."

"Left or right?" Schwarz said. There were exit fire doors on either end of the foyer.

"Left," said Lyons. He very carefully tried the door handle. It was locked. There was no way to check to see if the door itself was wired. He backed up and brought up his leg.

"Wait," Schwarz said. "Let me." He took out one of the plastic-explosive poppers still in the duffel Blancanales had thrown over his shoulder. This he affixed to the door. All three men backed up once the button was pushed.

The door exploded. There was nothing larger to indicate an explosive surprise on the other side.

Lyons went forward, low, while his partners covered the sides of the door. Over the iron sights of the USAS-12, Lyons crept across the threshold, waiting for bullets that might come at any moment.

The adjoining room was some kind of office area. The cubicles were permanent parts of the structure, faced with drywall and most likely framed with wood beneath. The desks were covered in dust. There was computer equipment on some of them, but the units were ancient.

"This is a 286 with dual three-and-a-half and five-and-a-quarter drives," Schwarz said, pointing to one. "I haven't seen one of those in years."

"We're not collecting souvenirs," Lyons said.

"This is a piece of IT history, Carl," Schwarz argued.

"I've got five bucks that says we just blow everything up before we leave," Blancanales said.

"I'm not taking that bet," Schwarz said, now sounding somewhat gloomy.

"You're not taking any bets until you pay me what you owe me," Lyons said as he reached the exit door. This, too, was a fire door with no window. He placed his ear to the door and listened.

"Anything?" Schwarz whispered.

Lyons shook his head. He put his hand on the door handle and, this time, the exit was unlocked. He started to ease the door open.

"Stop!" Schwarz hissed. "I heard a click. I definitely heard a click. I mean I think I did."

Lyons looked up. The door was open perhaps an inch. He glanced at Schwarz in irritation. "Did you or didn't you? Pol, you hear anything?"

"I don't think I heard anything," said Blancanales.

"Am I about to trigger a bomb or aren't I?" Lyons demanded. "Gadgets, get over here and check it out."

Schwarz knelt by the crack in the door and peered through with one eye. He held up a hand. "There's a wire. Hang on." He took his folding knife from his pocket, opened it and placed the blade in the gap between the door and the door frame.

"If the bomb has been triggered," Blancanales said, "won't cutting the wire release the pressure and set it off?"

"Fifty, fifty," Schwarz said. "Gimme a sec."

"Wait, what?" Lyons said.

Blancanales dragged in a breath and held it.

Schwarz cut the wire.

CHAPTER FIFTEEN

The members of Phoenix Force paddled their rubber launch through the cover of darkness. Twilight had only recently transitioned to full darkness. The stars overhead, the sound of the waves…it would have been a beautiful night, if not for the grim business that awaited them on the captured freighter. The *Bapor na Pangkargada* looked deceptively quiet as they made their way silently toward it.

The Glock pistols the men carried—as well as McCarter's Browning—had threaded barrels. The team had affixed sound suppressors to their pistols to facilitate quiet takedowns once they got on board. To do that, though, they would first have to create an opening. At the front of the boat, Hawkins and Encizo took the lead in steering the rubber landing craft, which had been borrowed from the Filipino navy.

They did their best to avoid any obvious light sources on the deck of the ship. These included brief flares they had been tracking as they made their way from a Filipino patrol boat that had paused far enough away not to tip their quarry that they were approaching. So far the cooperation they were getting from the Filipinos was a testament to Brognola's ability to cajole, persuade and smooth over potential international incidents.

"There it is again," James whispered. His voice was so quiet he almost wasn't making any sound at all. You had to be extremely careful when maintaining noise discipline on open water. The water carried sound incredible distances. Something as innocent as a muffled cough could give them away if the soldiers on the deck of the freighter were alert.

McCarter nodded. One of the men on the deck was chain smoking, and every so often he would light up a new one with a lighter that might as well have been an acetylene torch. The thing gave off a bright yellow beacon that was easily visible from across the water. If these blokes were Chinese military, McCarter couldn't believe it was the kind of behavior troops weren't taught to avoid.

The Chinese uniforms worried McCarter. None of it fit, and he couldn't see the Chinese making a mistake like that. There was no denying the Chinese flag the attackers had run up on the *Bapor na Pangkargada*, but that in itself was suspicious simply because there was no denying it.

It didn't make sense for the Chinese to tip their hand like that. They weren't above muscling into the region, of course. They had already planted oil rigs in territory claimed by other nations, pretty much daring anybody who wanted to make an issue of it to come and try. But always, with the Chinese, was the idea of flexing their might. They had an awful lot to prove. Essentially, everything they did was geared toward saying to the world, "We are a superpower," and they conducted their affairs accordingly. Capturing hostages on a Filipino freighter was the kind of thing that drove the Filipinos crazy and created diplomatic tension with the Chinese, especially among NATO nations who were looking on in anxiety over the South China Sea and China's expansion into it. But it didn't project strength. Strength would have been sending off their new aircraft carriers here to flex China's might, daring any other nation to risk taking on the largest conventional army in the world.

So who gained from this? And why?

They aimed for a section of the freighter as far as possible from the enthusiastic smoker. Once they were as close as they could get, it was time to break out some of their specialized gear. While it was not always possible for the Farm to supply or relay equipment for the teams to points around the world, the SOG had access to assets around the globe. Some savory, some not, the teams could usually call a courier for specialized weapons and equipment when time was critical. It was one of these couriers who had brought the men of Phoenix Force a TAIL system.

The Tactical Air Initiated Launch unit was one used by the American Navy SEAL teams. Actually, McCarter knew, the Navy had since moved on to a somewhat more sophisticated system, the RAIL, which was intended for rescue operations as well as for the tasks the TAIL system was used to perform. Beggars couldn't be choosers in this situation. McCarter doubted the pirates, whether Chinese soldiers or not, would know or care about whether the most advanced, latest version of counterterror equipment was being used to facilitate their deaths.

Technically, what Phoenix Force did had nothing to do with death. They were not a death squad and their goal was not to kill the invaders who had seized the *Bapor na Pangkargada*. Their task was to neutralize those enemies by whatever means necessary. If there was a way to do that without killing the pirates, so be it…but McCarter did not think that likely. Nor was he going to invest a great deal of time trying to find a solution that preserved the lives of men who had taken the boat's sailors hostage. The fastest way to neutralize those attackers and preserve the lives of the ship's crew was to put bullets in the attackers' brains as quickly and efficiently as possible.

With his Tavor slung across his back, McCarter press-checked his Hi-Power and made sure the suppressor was screwed on tightly. He also made sure it was straight. You could cross-thread a suppressor and get it out of alignment with the barrel, which would end up fouling your shot or jamming the gun…or worse. He didn't fancy having a finger or two blown off because he couldn't be bothered to check the little things.

When he thought about it…that was what combat was. It was a lot of planning, a lot of attention to detail, including logistics, your plan and its backups, contingencies, and equipment. You did everything you could to stack the odds in your favor and to reduce uncontrolled variables. You planned things down to the tiniest detail and you tried to make provision for even the things you could not anticipate.

And then you made contact with the enemy and your whole plan would be shot to hell, so you did what you could with what you had, and trusted that your preparations would enable you to cope with the fluidity of a combat operation while accounting for and protecting the lives of your men.

James took the magnetic clamp and its attached cable, fixed one end to the plastic cleat built into the rubber attack boat and wound the cable around it a couple of times. Then he affixed the magnetic clamp to the hull of the freighter, drawing the lines snug so the rubber boat would stay close to the target ship. Then it was time to deploy the TAIL.

"All set," James announced.

McCarter nodded. It was time to tell their Filipino friends to make the distraction they needed.

The patrol boat that had ferried them in was only supposed to wait long enough for them to launch. It had started moving away as soon as they cleared it. Now it was waiting some distance away, close enough to be able to provide a distraction, but not so close that the pirates would think an attack was imminent.

McCarter took the walkie-talkie from his gear that one of the navy honchos had given him. He keyed it. "Now," he said.

He would have to hand it to the Filipinos. Their response was almost immediate. Only fractions of a second after McCarter sent the signal, the patrol boat's warning siren began to wail. Then emergency flares cut through the sky and illuminated the scant clouds.

James triggered the TAIL. The grappling hook fired out and cleared the railing on the freighter. It did not take long for the Phoenix Force man to secure the line and make it ready for the climb up.

While this was happening, there were shouts on the deck. The little display had caught the attention of the armed pirates aboard. None of the shouts were in Chinese, at least not that McCarter could tell from this distance. That was an interesting data point.

"Up the line, lads," McCarter instructed. "Let's get moving."

One after another, the Phoenix Force commandos hauled themselves up the line. McCarter did it easily, but he could feel the strain on his muscles, could feel the exertion that it took to haul an entire adult male decked out in web gear and carrying combat weaponry up the side of a freighter. He thanked whatever merciless gods of combat there were for small favors, however. The seas were relatively calm tonight, which meant they weren't fighting a pitching, roiling surface as they tried to make their way up to the target.

McCarter was the last one up the line. He joined the rest of Phoenix Force on deck and took cover with his teammates behind a formation of metal shipping crates lashed to a pallet on the deck. Now they would need to work their way across the ship, first to seize control of the deck, then to make their way below. The attack had to take place in stages, for with the hostages being held below somewhere, they would need to search belowdecks. That meant precision, which required time.

"Fan out," McCarter said. "Take targets of opportunity. Our priority is to get below and get to those hostages." The considerable size of the force on the freighter meant that Phoenix Force was wildly outnumbered and outgunned. "Neutralize as many as you can," he added. "Leave no one operational if you can put them down."

There was a chorus of assent, amplified through his earbud transceiver. "Calvin," McCarter said, "you're with me."

Encizo, Hawkins and Manning peeled off to the left while McCarter and James went right. The two groups of Phoenix Force soldiers would circuit the ship and, once they had completed their ring, would be ready to make the transition to belowdecks.

McCarter and James half crouched, half walked, gliding along in the combat step that allowed them to make stable firing platforms of their upper bodies while continuing their forward motion. The grip of the Hi-Power in his fist felt very familiar. He wondered, for a moment, just how many thousands on thousands of rounds he had put through weapons like this. How many times had men stood between him and his goals—evil men, predators, who would be eliminated, had to be eliminated, because they were willing to hurt others to get what they wanted?

These ideas floated through the back of his mind even though his principal consciousness was on the mission at hand. Every muscle was primed. Every nerve was live. He saw everything at once as he scanned the deck ahead of him. In the distance, the fireworks continued to go off, and the majority of the pirate invaders, whoever they were, seemed to have clustered near the bow of the ship. There were, however, still sentries patrolling further aft.

A man in a Chinese uniform, who was clearly of African descent, rounded a corner of the superstructure and nearly walked straight into McCarter while gazing back over his shoulder. He had time to open his mouth to register his surprise. So close were they that McCarter could smell the man's body odor and hear the intake of breath as the dark-skinned man made ready to shout the alarm.

McCarter shoved the nose of the suppressor up under the man's chin, turned his head and pulled the trigger.

The warm, wet spray brushed his cheek and the front of his combat fatigues. There was nothing to be done for it. They were going to get a lot bloodier before this was all over. The Briton eased the body to the deck and stepped over it. Fortunately, the proximity of the body to the weapon had muffled the shot. A suppressor and subsonic ammunition could reduce the noise of a gunshot to a dull clap, rather than a sound-barrier-breaking bang, but no suppressed weapon was truly silent.

James saw another sentry. This one was smoking, too. Whether he was the man they had seen lighting up on the deck, or a different man, there was no way to know. This man, too, was about as far from ethnic Chinese as it was possible to get. He was Caucasian, with a nasty knife scar that wound from above his right eye and across his face. His nose was a cleft ruin. His teeth were mostly rotten. If these weren't actual pirates, disguised as Chinese operatives, McCarter would eat his watch cap.

The ugly man was that much uglier when James was done with him. The smoker was leaning casually on the railing, oblivious to anything but the fireworks in the distance, when James crept up behind him and put the blade of his combat knife into the scarred man's neck. That was when the dying man turned to fix McCarter with a death stare. James finished his bloody work and then wiped his knife on the sentry's uniform shirt.

"David, this is Rafe," Encizo said through the transceiver link.

"Go," McCarter said.

"We've taken out three men here," Encizo said. "Moving forward to the bow."

"Looks like we're slipping, partner," James commented quietly. "Three to our two."

"Anything noteworthy?" McCarter whispered.

"None of them are Asian," Encizo noted. "They're in poor health, scrawny, and two of our three looked like they had substance abuse problems. These are hired help. Mercenaries, maybe. Or pirates."

"That was my thought, as well, mate," McCarter agreed. "Continue your sweep. McCarter, out."

"Got it," Encizo said. "Out."

James led the way as he and McCarter continued their circuit. Soon they were within earshot of the men clustered at the bow. It was terrible discipline, but these men were not Chinese military by any stretch. The implications were staggering: A false-flag operation that targeted the Chinese and tried to start a war in the South China Sea? He could not imagine what anyone, not even the Chinese, would want with that.

"This is Gary. I'm in position," Manning said. "We have eyes on the bow."

"So do we," McCarter said. "Get ready."

"Rafe, standing by," Encizo said.

"T.J., ready," the Texan said.

The Briton eased his pistol back into its holster. The suppressor hung low beyond the drop-leg rig itself. He eased his Tavor into position on its sling, disengaging the safety. James, next to him, was doing the same. The time to be covert was over. It was time to take this ship back from the men who had stolen it…and show them what happened to those who preyed on those who had done them no harm.

From his gear, McCarter took a smoke canister. "Smoke, ready," he reported.

"Smoke, ready," Encizo echoed from the other side of the ship.

"Now!" McCarter barked. He pulled the pin on his smoke grenade and let it fly, tossing it into the middle of the group of uniformed men. The canister was joined by Encizo's grenade. When they blew, they filled the area with thick, purple smoke. "Fire!" the Briton ordered.

The men of Phoenix Force triggered their Tavors in short, accurate bursts. The pall of smoke that filled the bow, combined with the gunfire and the scant return fire the uniformed gunman managed, turned the area of the bow into complete bedlam. An explosion ripped a hole in the railing and left a splintered crater in that section of the decking.

"Somebody's playing with high-explosive grenades," James said.

"Must have gotten tagged before he could throw it," McCarter said, still firing from his Tavor. "Or he dropped it. Poor lad. Embarrassing. We should make his shame worse."

"I'm down with that," James said.

"Move in, lads. Move in. Calvin, Rafe, hang back, watch the rear and make sure nobody skirts around and tries to come up behind us."

McCarter, joined by Manning and Hawkins, moved in on the targets. The Phoenix Force men fired as they walked, still employing short, aimed bursts, tightening the noose around the disorganized knot of men battling the smoke and the shadows as much as the counterterrorist squad. Finally the last man was down. The three men knelt, keeping their profiles low and their silhouettes small, and waited to make sure they were clear.

"David," Enciso warned, "we've got activity belowdecks. They're coming up the man-way on this side."

The transmission cut out briefly. McCarter could hear automatic gunfire from Enciso's position. The earbud was filtering the sudden decibel increase from the gun battle.

"This is Calvin," James said. "Here, too, although they're not as brave as on Rafe's side."

"Hold them there," McCarter said. "I'll join you on that side. Gary, T.J., back up Rafe. Let's get down there and assess the hostage situation. Move quickly, lads."

"David, something's—" James began.

Whatever else he might have said was cut off in a massive explosion.

CHAPTER SIXTEEN

Lyons had been holding his breath. He let it out when cutting the wire didn't set off anything that went boom. Leaning against the door for a moment in relief, he shot a look at Schwarz, who returned it with a wide grin.

"See?" Schwarz said. "I told you."

"You did not tell me," Lyons replied. "You said fifty, fifty."

"But those are great odds!" Schwarz insisted.

"We're not done talking about this," Lyons growled. He threw the door open the rest of the way and gestured for his two teammates to follow him.

"Wait," Schwarz said. "If the wire wasn't to a bomb..." He knelt to take a look at the doorjamb.

Lyons, meanwhile, took in the lay of the land in this new section of the building. It was a large storage area. There were wooden crates piled high, some all the way to the ceiling. A path, of sorts, stretched out ahead of them. Something about it immediately set off Lyons's instincts.

"It's a maze," he said. "And we're the rats. No way. No way we're going through there. Head back the way we came. We'll try to the other side."

"Wait!" Schwarz called out. As Lyons took a step forward, Schwarz threw his smaller body at the big, former L.A. cop. Lyons looked at him as if he'd lost his mind.

"The wire," Schwarz said. "It's connected to a solenoid of some kind."

Lyons nodded. He reached into his war bag, took out one of his empty shotgun drums, hefted it and tossed it at the door hard enough to make the door move.

A pneumatic hiss accompanied the movement of a sheet of metal. It whistled into place, effectively blocking the door back to the office space, striking the floor hard enough to crack it.

"Holy crap," Schwarz said.

"Yeah," Lyons agreed. "Holy crap."

"Some kind of pneumatic guillotine?" Blancanales ventured.

"Designed to stop us from going back the way we came," Lyons said. "Not cool. We're blowing this door."

"No good," Schwarz said. "This is a solid sheet of tempered steel." He rapped his knuckles against it. "The door poppers we've got won't take it out, and anything large enough could collapse this part of the building."

"Defeating the purpose of blowing the door," Lyons concluded. "All right. Fine. We go forward. But everybody stay on the lookout. Check for wires. Check for pressure plates in the floor. And make sure you don't line yourself up with a hole or gap in the crates that could be a fire lane. I don't want any of us taking a bullet like that."

"Have I mentioned I'm allergic to bullets?" Schwarz said.

"Aren't we all," Blancanales added.

"Let's go," Lyons said. "I'll take point. Pol, you watch the rear. Gadgets, keep an eye on our flanks."

"Got it," the electronics expert said.

Lyons slung his shotgun and took out his Colt Python. With his tactical flashlight in his support hand, he led the way, checking every shadow, every corner. The crates had very obviously been stacked to create a winding pathway through the storage area. The ceiling tiles had been spray-painted black to absorb light. He didn't like that, either. There could be pinhole cameras up there watching their every move through the maze, and they would have no way of knowing.

The path began to widen. The crates had been stacked in a pattern that formed a kind of canyon in front of them. The upper edges of the formation were very close to the ceiling, but there was a gap. Lyons looked up and saw something move.

"Down!" he shouted. "Contact high, contact high, at the edges above!"

Schwarz and Blancanales pressed themselves against opposite edges of the "canyon" walls, aiming up at the top tier of crates. They both began firing; Schwarz with his SMG, Blancanales with his M-4. Shells began to bounce and jingle on the concrete warehouse floor. The return fire from the enemy, shrouded by that top tier of crates, rained down on them.

Fortunately the angle was bad for the ambushers as long as Able Team stayed pressed up against the crate walls. Whoever had designed this ambush had tried to be too clever for his own good. The layout kept Able Team pinned, but made it impossible for them to be shot down as long as they stayed where they were.

That meant, though, that their forward progress was arrested. They couldn't keep going, couldn't either escape this maze or clear the building, if they were pinned into position. The enemy had all the time in the world, because as long as Able Team was pinned down under fire, no effective action was being taken against RhemCorp.

"Fitzpatrick!" Lyons yelled. He had taken up a position next to Blancanales, still holding his Python ready. He would need to take long-distance shots, not lay down a cloud of fire with the USAS-12. Picking off enemies one at a time at distance, that was what the long-barreled revolver was good for. He gritted his teeth. "I want Jason Fitzpatrick! Show yourself, you son of a—"

A single grenade bounced down the steps of the crate walls until it landed on the floor near Lyons.

"I'd call that a 'no,'" Blancanales said.

"You're getting," Lyons said, scooping up the grenade and throwing it back with all his might, "just as bad as Gadgets."

The grenade exploded about halfway up the wooden canyon wall. Pieces of crate burned through the air, wooden shrapnel that embedded itself in Lyons's forearm as he covered his face. He allowed himself a brief, angry roar. It stung like a mother.

Twice more, the men above them tried to throw grenades, and twice more, the men of Able Team managed to toss them back. Lyons got the second one and Schwarz got the third one. Finally, one of the shooters up above tried to get tricky and wait out a count before throwing his grenade. He waited too long and the grenade exploded a fraction of a second after leaving his hand, shredding another section of crates and spraying them with the blood of whatever hapless enemy had thrown the bomb.

"That probably ends the high-explosive portion of tonight's program," Schwarz said. "If they're smart, that is. I wouldn't want any more of that."

"We're still pinned down," Blancanales noted.

"I have a plan," Lyons said. "Get ready to pour your fire into the opposite tier."

"You're not… You're not thinking of doing what I think you're thinking of doing, are you?"

Lyons grinned. "Maybe."

"Uh-oh." Blancanales switched magazines in his M-4. Schwarz did the same with his Colt SMG.

"On my three," said Lyons. "One, two… Three!"

As Schwarz and Blancanales opened fire, leveling a withering stream of fire at the top of the opposite crate wall, Lyons began to slither his way up the wall closest to him. He had to stay low, hugging the crates, so that the angle of fire was simply too tight for the men at the top to effectively target him. The higher he got, the easier it would be for the shooters on the opposite tier to see him. That was why the covering fire provided by Blancanales and Schwarz was so critical to the maneuver…and why it was so risky.

Enemy fire ripped furrows into the wooden surfaces around him. A nearby shot drove splinters into his face, causing Lyons to flinch back and swear. He was able to brush the worst of them out with his arm, but it was a near thing. A few inches to the right and those fragments might have blinded him.

He kept climbing, staying low, making progress as quickly as he dared. Once or twice the men on the opposite wall tried to shoot at him, but his teammates were doing a good job of keeping the bad guys off him. He was maybe two-thirds of the way up the "wall" when he saw one of the shooters on his side stick his head out.

"So long, buttercup," grumbled Lyons. In a single, fluid motion, he cocked back the Python's hammer, extended his arm, lined up the sights on the enemy gunner's forehead and squeezed the trigger. The shot broke free and the hand cannon bucked in his fist, sending a .357 Magnum hollowpoint rocketing away and through the doomed man's skull. He fell as if pole-axed.

Wait for it, Lyons thought.

Sure enough, the man next to the dead shooter got curious and broke cover to check on his friend. The moment Lyons saw the man's face in profile, he squeezed off a shot double-action, working the trigger through its paces as the cylinder rotated, the weapon cocked and the hammer fell. The side of the enemy gunner's face exploded and he, too, dropped. For the slightest fraction of a second Lyons had time to consider the closed-casket funeral that dumb bastard was going to require.

He kept going.

Terrified now, the gunmen began panic-firing in all directions. As Lyons watched in disbelief, they managed a few panic shots into the ceiling. Below him, his teammates were sniping away a few shots every few seconds, conserving ammo while keeping the opposite number of enemy pinned.

Lyons shoved his Python back into its holster, pushed the USAS-12 forward on its sling and pumped his big legs for all he was worth. He had to suppress the urge to let out a war cry as he reached the top of the crate wall and threw himself over the ridge formed by the crate pile.

He landed on top of one of the gunmen.

The poor bastard underneath him was wearing a Blackstar uniform, as were all of the other shooters who had been hiding at the top of the crate canyon. Lyons drove an elbow, hard, into the back of the man's neck. Whether the blow killed him or only knocked him unconscious wasn't important. The man beneath Lyons became very still and all the tension went out of him. That was all the big ex-cop needed. The other Blackstar gunners stared at Lyons in disbelief, suddenly very aware that their guns were pointing up and over the crate wall protecting them from below…while Lyons's weapon was pointed directly at them. The big automatic shotgun was very intimidating at close range.

The Blackstar shooter closest to Lyons looked as if he wanted to say something. His jaw was hanging open.

"Seriously?" Lyons said. "What is this, frigging amateur night?"

"Don't shoot!" said one of three men. The trio was looking down at the man Lyons was still crouching on.

"Throw your guns down," Lyons ordered. "Do it slowly." He heard a sudden flurry of activity. There was more gunfire down below. He didn't dare turn to look, but he was pretty sure he understood what was happening. Now that he had the shooters on this side occupied, Schwarz and Blancanales were climbing up the opposite side and taking on the men over there. It made perfect sense.

"We're civilians," said the most nervous of the trio, the one who had asked Lyons not to shoot. "We have rights. We demand a lawyer."

"Buddy," Lyons said, "I'm having kind of a bad day. My face hurts. My arm hurts. And, honestly, I'm really sick and tired of you jerks. Unless one of you can tell me where Jason Fitzpatrick is, I'm really not interested in having anything else come outta your pie holes."

"He's not here," said the Blackstar shooter. "He helped us set everything up, but then he took the chopper back."

"Back where?" said Lyons.

"Back to headquarters," said the man. "The RhemCorp facility in Atlanta."

"Atlanta," said Lyons. "All right. Now all three of you lay down on the ground so I can tie your wrists. And don't think I don't see you fidgeting there, Shifty Eyes," Lyons said, directing his comment to the man on the talker's right. The nervous spokesman's fellow Blackstar operative had been reaching for something behind his back, very slowly, hoping that Lyons was too slow or too stupid to catch the action.

"Don't shoot," said the spokesman again. "Don't shoot. I swear we don't want any trouble."

The shifty-eyed man went for the gun he was hiding. Lyons squeezed the trigger of the USAS-12. Shifty Eyes turned into so much shredded meat as the buckshot and slug rounds tore through him. The other two were reaching for weapons of their own, but they never had time to manage it. Lyons swung the barrel of his weapon left, then right, before their pistols ever cleared their concealment holsters.

Lyons, from long habit, ducked back, aware that all the racket he had just made might attract enemy fire.

"Ironman? Ironman," came Blancanales's voice in his transceiver. "Ironman, are you all right? Can you hear me?"

Lying on his back, holding the shotgun against his chest, Lyons, looked up at the blacked-out ceiling tiles. "Yeah," he said. "I'm good. What's the sit rep over there?"

"We took out the opposition on this side," Blancanales said. "All Blackstar men, in company uniform. No sign of Fitzpatrick."

"I had one joker claim the guy was here and then left," Lyons said. "Said the fallback was a RhemCorp headquarters in Atlanta."

"Noted," Blancanales said.

"Gadgets," Lyons directed, "get on the satellite phone to Barb and let her know about Atlanta. I'm coming down. Be careful when you head back down. There are way too many places to be hiding booby traps here."

"You didn't seem that worried when you were charging up the wall like a Viking," Schwarz said.

"I was excited about the idea I might never have to hear about your stupid candy monster game again," said Lyons. "Now watch yourself."

The Able Team leader picked his way down the crate wall, avoiding the areas of destruction where the grenades had torn everything to pieces. They had effectively neutralized opposition in this part of the maze, but they weren't nearly through it yet. Not by a long shot.

This whole deal was a deliberate attempt to trap and kill Able Team. Fitzpatrick, Blackstar and RhemCorp had taken note of what Able Team was doing to their assets and had apparently decided to counter it. Chances were that the men behind RhemCorp had seen to it that this facility was discovered just when it was. That was only logical. It was what Lyons might do in the same situation.

Well, they were going to regret trapping Able Team.

The first rule of trapping was that you didn't want to catch anything nastier than the trap. It was like trapping a groundhog then finding out you didn't have a groundhog at all but a badger in your box. Badgers were nasty when they were cornered. They were nothing to mess with.

"Badger, badger, badger," Lyons called quietly.

"What's that, Ironman?" Blancanales said.

"Mushroom, mushroom," Schwarz said, completing the joke. "Ironman...I didn't know you had it in you."

"Don't tell anybody," Lyons said.

All three members of Able Team converged at the bottom of the crate canyon and moved out, still covering each other. Schwarz was reloading again. There was smoke rising from the truncated barrel of his Colt SMG. The weapon had a built-in suppressor that managed some of the furious muzzle-blast from so short a barrel and the drive of such a high rate of fire.

"What did Barb have to say?" Lyons asked.

"She said the Farm would have the coordinates for us as soon as we were clear of Hilton Head," Schwarz reported. "Now that Bear knows where to look, he'll be able to give us that guy's address, phone records and internet browsing history before you know it."

"I don't want to know what kind of pornography he downloads," Blancanales said.

Schwarz looked at Blancanales. "Don't steal my lines," he said.

At the other end of the crate canyon, the path began to narrow. The ceiling seemed lower, too. Sheets of plywood had been erected and braced with metal support struts. From the looks of it, everything had been hastily nail-gunned into place. It looked very heavy, very sturdy, and was also getting smaller by the foot.

"A fatal funnel," Lyons growled. He looked at the panels facing them and the sheets of hinged plywood. He was sure of it. Rapping on the plywood with his fist, he said, "If we can get on the other side of this, we can open it up. This is probably how the work crews got out. Whatever group of guys put this together didn't exit through that little tunnel." He pointed to the entrance of the funnel, which looked small enough to be a laundry chute. It extended forward instead of down.

"Those wires…" Blancanales pointed to the leads attached to the hinges. "If we try to blow this, it might set off a bigger explosion."

"Or they could just be guy wires," Schwarz said. "All this wood is heavy. It's bound to be braced for weight. This was put together very quickly, in time to have it ready for us, I'd bet."

"I like none of these options," Lyons commented.

"I'm skinny enough," Schwarz said. "I'll crawl through." He handed his SMG to Blancanales, drew his Beretta 93-R and took his tactical flashlight from his gear. "I'll play tunnel rat. Once I get to the other side, I can unlock this."

"Be careful," Lyons warned. "You know that's what they want us to do. Go through there."

"Lucky us," Schwarz said. "Get ready, boys. I'm going in."

CHAPTER SEVENTEEN

"Must have been some kind of satchel charge," Calvin James speculated. He had narrowly avoided the worst of the explosion. The blast had sealed the entrance on that side of the boat, though, so the members of Phoenix Force had worked their way around the deck to the other side. They were now contemplating the one remaining hatchway that would take them belowdecks to where the hostages were being held.

"Well," McCarter said, "they may not be Chinese military, but they're smart enough to know that one entrance is easier to defend than two." They probably also grasped that the very hostages whose lives they had threatened were now the only leverage they had while they were being boarded. That would not save the hostages if their captors started to get nervous, but it was a start.

"Gary, post up here with T.J. Rafe, you take the bow, and keep an eye out for any stragglers. Calvin and I will form a two-man team to take this party downstairs. Quarters will be narrow and the five of us will just get in each other's way."

There was a chorus of assent from the men of Phoenix Force. McCarter took the lead, with James behind, as the pair made their way below. The manway was clear, and the chamber they found themselves in below had hatches leading fore and aft. James tried them both. The aft hatch was dogged shut somehow from the other side, but the forward hatch spun when he turned it.

"Forward it is, then," McCarter said. "If we can circle back around we can try to go aft, as well."

"Wish we had Jack on overwatch," James said.

"You and me both, mate," McCarter said. Grimaldi was back at the airfield the Filipinos had designated for him, making sure the chopper was properly repaired after its brush with small-arms fire.

They entered the forward hatchway. The corridor that extended ahead bore several hatches on either side. The hostages, and the remainder of the invaders, could be anywhere here.

"You want left or right, man?" James asked.

"Take the left," McCarter directed. "I'll take the right. Eyes open, Cal. Eyes open."

James nodded and threw open the first of the hatches. He was almost immediately rewarded with gunfire. Several shots ricocheted through the corridor, narrowly avoiding McCarter and James both, before James managed to shut the hatch again.

"Three…" James said. "Two…"

"You toss a gren in there?" McCarter asked.

James had time to nod before the sound of a detonation rang inside the closed quarters beyond the hatch. This was followed by horrific screaming. "Willy Pete," said James, as if that explained everything…because it did. Willy Pete, or white phosphorous, could burn a man down to the bone. It was an ugly way to die…but here, aboard ship, that was the best alternative to a high explosive or fragmentation grenade. There was much less risk of putting a hole in the boat.

McCarter nodded, feeling grim. He threw open his hatch, but the quarters within were empty.

The pair kept going. They quickly realized that this section of the freighter was devoted to living quarters. Each hatch revealed a compartment that boasted anywhere from two to six bunks, depending on the size of the individual compartment. The smell was, at times, very strong.

Twice more, James used WP grenades to eliminate gunmen in Chinese uniforms. The invaders had Kalash-nikov-patterned rifles, which in and of itself was not remarkable. The weapon was the most copied assault rifle in the world, available on the international arms market for the equivalent of a twenty-dollar bill per rifle if you were buying in quantity. A detailed examination of the proof marks on the rifles might tell them if the weapons were made in China or not, but even that wouldn't really tell them anything. The Chinese exported a great number of small arms, including to the civilian market in the United States. Among the more unusual weapons they sold were reproductions for the Cowboy Action Shooting market, like period pump-guns, double-barreled coach guns.

It was a weird world, no doubt about it.

The corridor widened and soon the two Phoenix Force men found themselves in the ship's galley. The tables were stainless steel, bolted down to keep them from moving in rough seas. The cooking and food-prep area was in an alcove beyond, with plenty of enclosed racks for stores and other foodstuffs. There was blood here, but no bodies. What there was of the blood was not extensive, just a few spatters here or there. If McCarter had to guess, he would imagine that the pirate boarders had roughed up the crew as they made their way through here. There was still no sign of the hostages, if in fact there were hostages.

The Briton began to worry. What if the crew had been executed and thrown overboard? Their presence might simply be a bluff to stop the Filipino navy from sinking the freighter in retribution for this act of hostility.

"Have you got anything over there, Calvin?" McCarter asked.

From the other side of the galley, amid the tables, James shook his head. "Nothing. All clear so far."

"Then let's head through that hatch to the other side," said McCarter. He consulted his smartphone, which contained the deck plan for the ship as provided by the Filipino navy. The freighter was not a navy vessel, of course, and there was no reason to think the deck plan was up to date. Some functionary could very well have downloaded this business from the internet, and in fact probably had, likely finding the web site for the manufacturer of the boat or for the freight company whose name the ship sailed under.

Damn, but he was getting old, worrying about every little detail. He held the Tavor tighter, grateful for the bullpup assault rifle's compact profile in the close quarters below decks.

But where were the hostages?

He gamed it out in his mind. If he were holding the vessel, he'd want any high-value assets, such as the hostages, somewhere far below the upper deck, where it would be most difficult to get to them. And he would want a lot of room in which to fight, preferably with lots of cover. That meant the ship's cargo hold. Vessels like this had large holds. After all; that's what they were designed to do. The metal cargo crates, like the ones he had seen lashed to the deck, would be perfect for cover and concealment.

He checked the deck plan once more and nodded to himself. There it was, then. That was where they had to go.

"Through this hatch," McCarter told James, "is an anteroom compartment of some kind. Beyond that is another compartment with a manway to the lower level, where we'll find the entrance to the hold proper."

Somewhere, back in the direction from which they had come, a woman screamed.

James looked at McCarter. "Did you…?"

"Yes, mate, I heard that," the Briton acknowledged. "Could you have missed a compartment when we swept the living quarters?"

"Don't think so," James said. "But it's possible."

"Come on." McCarter led the way as the two men threaded the path back through the galley and into the corridor with the bunk compartments. Once more, both men checked each compartment in turn on his side of the corridor. There was one door, however, that was dogged shut, positioned in roughly the middle of the passageway.

"This wasn't locked before," James said. "I remember checking it. Couple of bunks inside, plenty of clutter. Nothing much else."

"Pop it," McCarter said.

James nodded and produced an adhesive charge from one of his gear pouches. He placed it near the center of the hatch wheel, pressed the button and then backed down the corridor with McCarter.

The explosion echoed through the corridor, making their ears ring. The hatch, however, swung slowly open on creaking hinges. Its lock mechanism had been gutted by the blast. Metal shrapnel had embedded itself in the bulkhead opposite the hatchway.

The Briton tensed, waiting for the gunfire he was sure had to come. There was nothing. He risked a glance with just one eye around the corner, through the open hatch. Still nothing. He did, however, see a clump of blankets beneath the bottommost bunk. It was the sort of thing you would miss while looking for armed terrorists, as it presented not threat, but closer examination made him think there might be a man hidden there.

The woman's scream came again, and it was there, in that room. It was very loud. This time the scream was accompanied by a loud buzzing and clattering. James moved up to watch the Briton's back as McCarter stepped into the compartment and located the source of the noise.

It was a wireless phone.

McCarter held it up. A call was coming in, prompting the phone to emit the scream they had heard. The volume on the device was all the way up, which was why they had been able to hear it.

"Who the bloody hell would have a ringtone like that?" said McCarter.

"That's sick," James declared. He took the phone from the Phoenix Force leader and found the setting to switch the phone to silent. Then he thumbed through the device a few times. McCarter, meanwhile, shoved one boot into the clump of blankets beneath the bunk. There was nothing there. James looked up from the phone. "Jump scare," he said.

"What's that?" said McCarter.

"In a horror movie," said James. "A jump scare is when, like, a cat comes leaping out at our heroes, so the audience jumps, but there's nothing really there."

"Too right," McCarter said. "That's more or less what this was, I suppose. That isn't one of the pirate's phones, is it?"

"We don't know they're pirates," James said. "Could be a mercenary team."

"Pirates in the functional sense," McCarter said. "They invaded and captured the vessel."

"Fair enough," James agreed. "But, no. I'm looking through the photos on here. Whoever belongs to this phone has plenty of pictures from the deck of this very ship. Weather, sunsets, that kind of thing. Obviously one of the crew. I don't speak the lingo, but I recognize enough words in context in these text messages. This is a sailor's phone."

"You're sure?"

"David, there's enough porn saved to this phone's image gallery that I could not be more sure," said James.

"Ah, well," McCarter said. "Gets lonely out to sea, I imagine."

"Right," James said.

"Let's head through the galley, then," McCarter directed. "Time's wasting. Check, check," he added. "How are things up on deck, lads? Anything moving?"

"All clear up here," Manning reported. "Any sign of the hostages below?"

"Nothing yet," McCarter said. "We're on it."

"Good hunting, David," the Canadian said.

In the anteroom, James took the lead and slid down the ladder to the lower deck. McCarter followed. There was nothing remarkable here, but when they hit the next hatchway, the door felt strangely heavy. When James eased it open, they came face-to-face with a man handcuffed to the wheel on the opposite side.

"English?" asked James. "Do you speak English, friend?" The man was Filipino and was dressed in worn canvas pants, boat shoes and a faded T-shirt advertising a science-fiction movie franchise.

"I speak English," the sailor said.

McCarter took up a position guarding the corridor beyond, which led to the hold, at least according to his smartphone's deck plan. James, meanwhile, started patting the man down. He found a standard ink pen with a plastic cap, smiled and took the cap from the pen. Using his belt knife, he sliced the pen cap in two.

"Hold still, bud," James said. "I'm going to pick these cuffs and get you out of there." He set to work with the halved pen cap. "I must be…rusty at this," he muttered, working the lock. "What's your name? You're part of the crew, right?"

"Boyet," the sailor said. "I am part of the crew of this vessel, yes."

"Where are the others?" McCarter asked. "Did you see them? Are they alive?"

"There was a guard," Boyet explained. "When the fighting started to happen above, he became very afraid. He brought me from the hold and chained me here. I think he was going to use me to protect him."

"Human shields," James said under his breath.

"He ran back to the hold," Boyet said. "He left me here to die. I have waited for a couple of hours, chained to this door."

"Open, says me," James said. The handcuff popped, freeing one of Boyet's arms. He massaged it gratefully, extracting himself from the hatch wheel as James popped open the other side. "Like riding a bike," James added.

"The other members of the crew are in the hold," said Boyet. "The pirates have explosives. They have put explosive vests on my crewmates. They did not have enough vests for everyone. I was lucky not to have been given such a thing."

"You are that, friend," McCarter said. "What can you tell me about the invaders?"

"Pirate trash—" Boyet spat "—wearing Chinese uniforms. I have seen the type in many local ports. I do not know where they got their weapons and their uniforms, but they are not men of China. They are cowards. They have locked themselves in the hold because they do not know what to do. Their leader is a black man with but one eye. He is called Mhusa. He holds the detonator for the explosive vests."

"How many pirates?" McCarter asked.

"The ones on the upper deck were many," Boyet replied. "But if you are here…"

"They're not a problem," James said.

"Mhusa has a dozen men," Boyet said. "There are half a dozen crewmen wearing the bomb vests and another ten or twelve merely held prisoner."

"All right," McCarter said. "Boyet, get above. Announce yourself loudly as you approach. My men are waiting, guarding the entrance to the lower decks. They'll see to it you're taken care of. My friend and I are going to go rescue your crewmates."

"Go with God," Boyet said. He did not need further prompting. He hurried off.

The two Phoenix Force commandos made their way silently to the hatchway that led to the cargo hold. The wheel moved easily to the touch. That was actually a bad sign. If the pirates were feeling secure in their hostage measures, they would not feel the need to brace the door. And this Mhusa, if his finger was on the detonator, might be a little quick to start blowing things up if he thought was being threatened.

"Slowly, slowly," McCarter urged. "Go silent, Calvin."

James nodded. He finished easing the door open and the pair stepped through. The cargo hold loomed ahead of them, only dimly lighted by a few electric cells set high in the walls behind metal cages. The lamps buzzed loudly.

There metal shipping crates were piled high, giving the enemy plenty of places to hide. A kind of clearing had been made toward the center of the hold, where crates small enough to move had been shoved aside. Collapsible chairs, dragged from elsewhere on the ship, had been set up here. A stereo was playing music.

"I don't believe it," James said.

"Bugger all," said McCarter. "Now I've seen everything."

The hostages were seated in a ring near the edge of the "clearing" in the hold. They looked tense and nervous, as half a dozen of their number wore explosive vests and were more than close enough to kill the others if they went off. But the pirates themselves, their Chinese uniforms disheveled and, in some cases, partially discarded, were carousing in the center of the cargo hold, drinking from whiskey bottles and singing in broken English.

The English was the least surprising part of it all. A pirate crew of mixed nationality would need a common language. English was one of the more prevalent languages in the world, useful for conducting business. It was also relatively easy to learn compared to, say, Chinese, and more used than French or German.

The idea that, during a hostage op, these men would simply repair down here and start partying…it blew the mind. They were pirates, according to Boyet, and one did not expect a high degree of sophistication from such scum, but this… All the high-tech weapons in the world could not help you if you could not simply stay on the job long enough to complete your mission.

McCarter brought his Tavor to his shoulder. Through its optics, he scanned the group of pirates until he found a large black man with a rag tied across his head to cover one eye.

"Mhusa, I presume," McCarter said to James.

"Shall we?" James asked.

"We shall," McCarter declared.

Driven by some sixth sense, Mhusa looked up and locked eyes with David McCarter.

The Briton pulled his rifle's trigger.

CHAPTER EIGHTEEN

Schwarz was crawling through the tunnel, his Beretta machine pistol and his flashlight leading the way, when his secure sat phone began to vibrate in his pocket. The combined sensations only made his ribs hurt more and he was reminded of the beating he had taken at the hands of Fitzpatrick.

He touched his earbud transceiver, tapping it three times in rapid succession. Schwarz himself was one of the people who had helped design the communications equipment. The three taps would open the line from the Farm but also patch the transmission in to all three Able Team members.

"You have reached Able Team," Schwarz said in a sing-song voice. "We can't come to the phone right now, probably because we're busy fighting evil in another dimension. I've always said that, sooner or later, we would transcend these earthly states and become interdimensional heroes who—"

"Gadgets," Lyons said. "You're overindulging."

"I'm stuck in a death tunnel," Schwarz said. "It lends itself to whimsy."

"I'm not going to ask," Price said. "We have an identification on that dead Asian man whose image you forwarded."

"Go ahead, Barb," Lyons said.

"Your corpse is dead," Price explained.

"Uh," Schwarz said. He kept crawling through the plywood tunnel, feeling like he was crawling his way into a coffin. "Wasn't that what we knew already?"

"No, you're not following me," Price continued. "Your stiff is a known Chinese black-ops agent. His file tags him as 'Simon Lao,' although only Lao is his given name. His history is so shady, his file back-filled with so many false identities, that we're not sure where the real Lao starts and the cover identities end. He's officially died three times that we can verify, and possibly in a couple of other instances."

"Sounds like a bad dude," Lyons said.

"Bad enough that the Chinese disavow any knowledge of him," Price said. "They got real defensive when we made inquiries, and that tells us something. Normally, when they don't want to acknowledge an intelligence breach, they just don't. They get all nonchalant. But this time they issued through channels an emphatic denial, stating they had no knowledge of the man we call Simon Lao, that he most definitely did not work for Chinese intelligence and under no circumstances whatsoever would he be conducting operations on American soil on behalf of the Chinese government."

"Which pretty much means that's exactly what he was doing," Blancanales said. "We've repeatedly dealt with Chinese operations on American soil."

"Call it part of our ongoing mostly cold war with China," Price said. "But, yes, we think there's a pretty good chance that whatever Lao was doing here, he was running an operation of some kind or involving Rhemsen in that operation."

"So we've got a go to take down RhemCorp and Rhemsen himself," Lyons said. "Tell me don't."

"Hal will have to pay some visits to a few folks on the Hill," Price said. "We don't want to look like we're in the business of interfering with American businesses, and we absolutely do not want to disrespect due process. But I think everything we've uncovered while sifting through RhemCorp's computer records, plus the violence already perpetrated by men hired by Rhemsen, gives us cause to take him into custody. If he resists, there's nothing you can do but take him down."

"That's music to my ears," Lyons said. "Do you have the location of his Atlanta property?"

"It wasn't as easy to find as the Hilton Head parcel," Price said, "but Bear has it. I'm transmitting the data to your smartphones."

"Yeah, about Hilton Head," Lyons said. "We're stuck in some kind of horror-movie trap here."

"Say that again, Carl?" Price said.

"He's absolutely right," Schwarz said. "Death tunnel, remember?"

"How long until you can extract?" Price said.

"We're going to finish up here," Lyons said, "and make sure all the loose ends are tied up. There's a nest of Black-star goons here that I want to make sure don't get to go play any more reindeer games."

"We *really* need to work on your action-hero expressions, Carl," Schwarz said. "I'm not following that at all. And I'm stuck in a death tunnel. We've talked about the death tunnel, haven't we?"

"At least in there," Lyons commented, "he can't play that game he likes." He paused. "Barb, what are the implications of Lao's involvement with Rhemsen? Is China behind the attacks in the South China Sea?"

"Not according to the intel we're being fed by Phoenix," Price answered. "That's what doesn't make any sense to me. It's got Hal stumped, too, and he's got a meeting set with the President this afternoon."

"Then we'd better stop messing around and get back to it," Lyons said. "Let us know if anything else pops up."

"And we'll let you know if any more dead guys fall out of the sky on us," Schwarz said.

"Shut up, Gadgets," Lyons said.

"Good luck, boys," Price said. "Farm, out."

"Gadgets," Lyons said, "what is your progress?"

"Give me a minute," Schwarz answered. The tunnel through which he was crawling was starting to become narrower. He was worried that if it got much smaller he would never be able to come out the other side of it. Of course, that was probably the whole "trap" part of the plan.

The surface beneath him changed. He had been crawling on plywood this whole time, but suddenly he felt the coolness of metal ribs beneath the wooden floor. The way ahead was blocked by strips of hanging plastic, like something you might see in an industrial meat-packing plant to separate one area from another. Or a beaded curtain, the way folks used to do it in the 1970s. Honestly, he had never understood the purpose of beaded curtains.

He pushed through the plastic barrier and was almost blinded by the sudden increase in light. The room beyond was open, with ordinary painted walls and the remnant of wall-to-wall carpeting. A metal fire door marked Stairwell waited on this side of things, and the wooden barrier to either side angled back to a pair of hinged wooden flats that could be the door panels Lyons had been looking for. He just had to get past the last part of the tunnel, which had a kind of metal framework to make it smaller.

Something went clunk.

"Uh-oh," Schwarz murmured.

"Uh-oh?" Lyons echoed. "Did you just say 'uh-oh'? Gadgets? What is it? What happened?"

"Uh-oh," Schwarz said again. He felt the metal clamps snap into place as he crawled on his stomach out of the tunnel and onto the floor of the area beyond. Suddenly his head was very heavy. A mechanism clicked. He reached up and discovered that the metal framework that had been attached to the end of the tunnel was now fixed over his head and clamped around his neck.

He tried to rise and couldn't. The contraption was too heavy. He grabbed on to it with both hands and shook. There was a clockwork sound, almost like ticking, but not quite. It was the sound of a mechanism that was driven by kinetic energy. He could recognize that much. Something about his struggling had set it in motion.

The metal collar around his neck tightened.

"Uh," he said. "Guys? I can't move. And I'm in big trouble."

"Pol, step aside." That was Lyons's voice. Schwarz could hear, through the transceiver connection, the sound of the bolt on Lyons's USAS-12 being pulled back.

"Don't!" Schwarz said. "It could be wired to blow!"

"Guy wires," Lyons stated. "It's guy wires, not detonator wires."

"You don't know that!" Schwarz argued. "Guys, don't—"

"Shut up, Gadgets," Lyons said. The transmission cut out, but Schwarz could hear the big shotgun laying waste to the wood of the barrier. It took what was probably an entire drum, but Lyons himself came crashing through the barrier next. From his vantage lying sideways on the floor, Schwarz could only see Lyons's feet. Lyons's boots were followed by Blancanales's footwear.

"Hi, guys," Schwarz said.

"Oh, crap," Lyons swore.

"Please tell me you didn't say 'oh, crap,'" Schwarz said. "That's not good. It's never good when you say that."

"This is bad, Ironman," Blancanales said.

"It's moving. What's that mechanism?" Lyons asked.

"It's like a wind-up toy," Blancanales noted. "If we don't get this thing off him… Hell, Carl, I think this is plastic explosive."

"Oh, crap," Lyons said again.

"You guys know I can hear you talking, right?" Schwarz said. "Can someone please explain to me what's going on?"

"That tunnel was a funnel," Lyons said. "You had to stick your head in this to get out, right?"

"Pretty much," Schwarz said. "But what exactly is this thing? Why is it so heavy?"

"It's made of heavy-gauge steel," Lyons explained. "Like something out of a horror movie. It's tightening a steel cable inside that collar around your neck. I can see the cable being wound up into the mechanism. And there are two racks of plastic explosive in metal cages up top. It's wired to hell and gone."

"Carl," Schwarz warned, "I need you and Pol to listen to me very carefully. This mantrap is designed to kill us all. It traps one person, and then while you're trying to save me before it chokes me to death or beheads me, it blows up and takes you with me. It's designed to play on your sympathies for me. Like a sniper wounding a man and then killing the men who come to save him."

"Quiet, Gadgets," Lyons growled. To Blancanales, he said, "The man most qualified to disarm this thing is the man trapped inside it. We're going to need help."

"Relay?" Blancanales suggested.

"Yeah," Lyons said. "Relay. Get through that fire door and get the hell away from us. Put enough distance between us and you so that if this blows, it doesn't take you out."

"I'm staying, Ironman," Blancanales said. "I'm not letting you two face this alone."

"I need you to do this for me, Pol," Lyons said. "I can't risk firing up my phone next to this thing. The earbuds are low-powered RF, and if they haven't already set it off, they're not going to. But I use my satellite gear next to it and it might blow. If you don't relay to the Farm what's happening, they'll never be able to help us. And if this thing goes off and doesn't kill us, we need someone who can guide in a medical evac team. You get yourself killed over nothing and there's no one left to do that. Now take a photo of this damn thing and send it to the Farm."

Blancanales obviously didn't like it, but he did as he was told. Schwarz heard the man activate his smartphone then walk slowly to the fire door.

"Carl," Schwarz said, "go with him."

"You shut up," Lyons said. "Don't make me tell you again."

"I've got Barb on the line," Blancanales said as he exited into the hallway beyond. "Patching you through now."

"Ironman?" Price said. "What's happening?"

"Pol has just transmitted a picture of a bomb to you," Lyons stated. "That bomb is strapped to Gadgets's face. There's some kind of horror-movie shenanigans happening here and the thing is slowly choking Gadgets to death."

"Possibly beheading," Schwarz put it in. "You're glaring at me right now, aren't you? I can hear you glaring at me."

"I need to know how to disarm it," Lyons told Price. "And I need to know fast."

"All right," Price said. "Give me a minute to talk to Bear."

"Go fast, Barb," Lyons said.

Neither of them spoke for a moment. "Ironman," Schwarz said. His breathing was labored now. The cable around his neck was digging into his skin and starting to affect his ability to breathe.

"What is it, Hermann?"

"Don't," Schwarz said. "Don't call me that. You make me think I'm going to die like this."

"You're not going to die," Lyons promised. He snapped open his knife. "I'm going to disarm this bomb as soon as Barb comes back on."

"Carl," Schwarz said. "Listen to me. I'm not taking you with me. Please, man. Just go. Go behind the fire door, take Pol and get out of this death-trap building."

"If you weren't wearing an explosive bear trap on your head, I would slap you for suggesting that," Lyons said. "Wait for Barb."

"I'm dead in a couple of minutes anyway," Schwarz said. He was fighting the urge to swallow, knowing it would make everything worse if he tried. "Please, Carl. I need you to go."

"You die," Lyons said, "then I die, too."

"We've helped a lot of people," Schwarz said. "I've had a good run. I don't need company for this, Carl. Please. Don't make me responsible for your death."

"We're not done," Lyons stated.

"It can't go on forever," Schwarz said. "Sooner or later, time was going to catch up with us. How many missions have we gone on, Carl? How many ops? Sooner or later, time has got to catch up to us all. I'm okay with it, brother. I really am. Please. Just leave me here. Let me die knowing you and Pol got out."

"Shut up, damn you," Lyons said.

"Ironman... Are you...are you crying?"

"The hell I am," Lyons said.

"Carl," Price said. "Cut the wires in this order. Red, green, yellow, gray. Do not cut the brown wire. Repeat, do not cut the brown wire."

"Avoid the bad brown acid," the Able Team leader muttered. "Got it. What happens if that order is wrong?"

"Bear says the device will explode," Price told him.

"Well, that's not all bad," Schwarz said.

"But not before it cuts off Gadgets's head," Price added.

"Okay, it's all bad," Schwarz said.

"Get ready," Lyons warned.

Suddenly the sound of gunfire in the stairwell reached their ears. Blancanales's M-4 chattered away, rattling the fire door like a drum. Empty shells pelted the metal with musical rhythm.

"I have contacts in the stairway!" Blancanales shouted. "Blackstar men coming down!"

"Keep them off me!" Lyons said. "I need enough time to get this thing off. Barb! Barb! What about the lock? What about the collar around Gadgets's neck?"

"Cut the wires," Price said. "Once you've stopped the bomb, you can wedge something between the cable and the lock to disengage it. Bear says the plans for this thing were in RhemCorp's computer."

"That guy is messed up." Schwarz choked on his words. He could feel his vision starting to fade to orange. Spots began to float in front of his eyes.

"Really, Gadgets?" Lyons said. He began cutting wires. Schwarz couldn't see which ones. "Those are your last words?"

"I…love you…guys," Schwarz said.

"Last wire!" Lyons announced. "Explosive disarmed. I'm going for the collar."

Schwarz couldn't make words anymore. His vision tunneled then turned to nothing. He began to hear everything as if from the bottom of a well.

And then he couldn't hear anything at all.

It was a good run, he thought, before the nothingness took him.

CHAPTER NINETEEN

Mhusa was fast—faster than McCarter would have thought possible in so large a man. Somehow he anticipated what was coming, and when McCarter's burst of 5.56 mm fire ripped through the air above his head, he was not there to be hit. McCarter moved forward, pressing his advantage. The pirates around Mhusa were a disorganized lot. Some had left their rifles on the floor nearby or misplaced them altogether. The heavy firepower these men had used to take the freighter was nowhere to be seen, and might even have been discarded above-decks somewhere. As McCarter advanced on Mhusa, the one-eyed giant fled in and around his own men, allowing the Briton to take down one after the next.

A few of the false-uniformed pirates managed to get off return fire, but James, hidden somewhere in the hold, started sniping them while on the move. He had disappeared from McCarter's side as soon as the Briton started firing, using mobility and the plentiful cover to become a vengeful wraith hunting the pirates. McCarter watched for incoming bullets, but three times out of every five, when he went to neutralize one of the opposition, a bullet from the unseen James and his Tavor took the gunman first.

Mhusa finally ran out of crew members, but not before he had managed to get to the crowd of hostages. Grabbing one of the men wearing an explosive vest, he pushed the hapless Filipino in front of him, shielding his body. The black man was armed with a machete on his belt and a pistol in his waistband. The pistol was an old Hi-Power copy, its finish worn off to bare metal. The pirate leader showed rotten teeth when he smiled, holding the barrel of his pistol to his prisoner's head.

McCarter stopped firing. Crouching on one knee, he surveyed the hold. James was invisible, concealed somewhere, probably drawing a bead on Mhusa at that very moment. The variable was the vests. If Mhusa was willing to negotiate, maybe they could end this.

The sound of a gunshot rang out. James, through the transceiver link, reported, "Found a straggler. Neutralized. There are a few sentries scattered around the hold. I stabbed one and now stalking a third. Will report."

"You do that, mate," McCarter said softly. He stepped into the cleared area at the center of the hold, keeping his rifle out and away from his body with one hand. Carefully, he lowered the Tavor to the deck.

"I will blow them all up!" Mhusa shouted. "I have the remote trigger. It is stuck to my chest. It reads my heartbeat. Kill me and the bombs blow!" With his free hand he ripped open his shirt, showing an electronic device of some kind taped to his chest with medical tape.

"More of RhemCorp's handiwork, no doubt," said James's voice in McCarter's ear.

"Stand by, mate," McCarter muttered so that only his transceiver could pick up his words. "Line up a shot right on that thing, if you can."

"Affirmative," James acknowledged.

McCarter moved closer to where the African and his hostages waited. The crew members wore a resigned look. McCarter had seen that look before, on both prisoners of war and condemned men awaiting execution. It was all too common among those who had resigned themselves to the inevitability of the end. That was something the Briton struggled to accept: the inevitability of his own end. Who could say how long any of them had? That was why it was so important to fight for what was right while you still had the time to do it.

"I am Mhusa," the black man said. "These crew are my prisoners. You will leave now or I will kill them all."

"Blow those vests," McCarter countered, "and you die, too. I don't know as you strike me as the self-immolating type, mate. But then, you don't come over all Chinese, either, do you?"

Mhusa laughed. His uniform was ill-fitting, far too small for his big frame. The boots he wore were obviously his own, not Chinese issue. They, too, were worn, scuffed, and even open at the toes where the seams had split. These pirates didn't live all that well. It was a fact of life as a predator. You could prey on others to make your way, but it would never be a life of ease.

"I am ready to die," Mhusa said. "Can you say the same, little man?"

"Little?" McCarter said, bristling. "Here now, big man, there's no call to be insulting."

Mhusa's grin split his face even wider. "I tell you what, little man," he said. "I can be sporting. For every time you best me, I will release one of the men. Six chances. I give you six chances. If you can free them all, I let you have them. You may take them and leave this place."

"David," said James's voice in the Briton's ear, "he's setting you up. Don't do it."

"I can handle it," McCarter said quietly.

"What is that?" Mhusa said. "What is it you wish to say to me?"

"I said, I can handle you," said McCarter more loudly. "Let's dance."

"No, no," Mhusa said. "It is, as you might say, not good. Not good. Here." He went to one of the bodies on the deck. "I think you have killed all my men—"

There was gunfire from somewhere in the cargo hold. That would be James, eliminating stragglers. There were two more bursts and then a single shot.

"All clear, David," said James. "I've swept the hold. He's got nobody left down here."

"Rafe, T.J., Gary," McCarter said in his transceiver. "Check in."

"Upper deck secure," Manning said. "We are clear. I repeat, we are clear."

"Looks like you really are all alone," McCarter said to Mhusa. The big black man's expression crumpled. Obviously he had been feeling tricky. McCarter doubted the party here belowdecks had been a trap. It simply wasn't effective enough. Much more likely, the pirates had decided to retreat to what they thought was relative safety, then booze it up while things somehow magically worked themselves out above-decks. Mhusa, not being a complete idiot, had posted guards to rove the hold. And he had probably thought these guards would take out James and McCarter when the Phoenix Force men least expected it. Now, he was realizing he would have to make good on his deal.

Mhusa managed to approximate his former smile. He would tough it out, now, all bravado. He released his prisoner, pushing the terrified sailor toward the knot of prisoners, and walked over to one of the dead, uniformed corpses. From the dead man's belt he took a machete that was as long as his own. Then he took his Hi-Power and placed it on the dead man's chest.

"I will come back for that," he said. He turned and, almost casually, tossed the dead man's machete to McCarter. The Briton snatched the blade out of the air. Examining it in his fist, he looked at the maker's mark. The weapon had come all the way from South America. It bore the name of a famous South American manufacturer, known for its low prices and high quality. Well, if he was going to die fighting a pirate duel with a machete as his weapon, at least he wouldn't die for want of a decent blade.

"Can you take him?" McCarter whispered.

"Negative," said James. "I can't get an angle on his chest. If I don't hit him right in that transmitter, it's no dice."

"Stand by," McCarter said.

"Who do you talk to, little man?" said Mhusa. "Do you pray to your god to deliver you from death at my hands?" The giant African slid the machete from its sheath at his waist. He hefted his own blade and took a few practice swings. "Do you know the old African proverb that says, 'Only a fool hones his machete to a razor'? I am such a fool. My blade is sharp enough to shave the hair from your face…and the face from your body."

"Then let's do this, mate."

"That is correct," Mhusa said, laughing. His laugh came from deep in his massive chest. It was throaty and resonant. "I am the first mate of Yanuar Wijeya, my captain for these many years now. It is for him that I am here. And it is in his name that I will kill you."

"Why be loyal to a man like that?" McCarter said. He began to circle, slowly, to his left, holding the machete in front of him, low and at the ready. He tested its weight, its balance, as he did so. It was an unfamiliar weapon, but he was no stranger to blades. "What has he done for you? I can't imagine there's a whole lot of honor among pirates and thieves."

"What would one such as you know of honor?" quipped Mhusa. "Captain Wijeya picked me up out of squalor. I was a man without purpose when he found me in a bar in Manila. I was at the end of myself. I was ready to die. In fact, I am dead. I died in Sierra Leone."

McCarter kept circling. He was hoping that if he just kept moving, kept Mhusa moving with him, it would give James the shot he needed. "What does Sierra Leone have to do with it?" he asked.

"Do you know I was once a professor?" said Mhusa. "I taught English literature. I traveled. I studied. I have written a book. It is not a book one such as you would ever read. But I am an educated man."

"And yet you're a pirate," the Briton said.

"A fitting enough job for a man who has died," Mhusa said. He began to take experimental steps toward McCarter, whipping the blade of his machete ever closer to his opponent. "For a man who has killed his entire family."

"I'm sure there's plenty of murderers to go around among you lot," McCarter said.

"No." Mhusa swung once, very close now, cleaving the air where McCarter's head had been a moment earlier. "You are fast, British. You are very fast. I have fought many men in my time as a pirate. You are one of the better ones, I think."

"I try," McCarter said. He was tempted to take a committed swing, to plant the edge of his blade in Mhusa's face, but if he moved too quickly he would risk mortally wounding the man in a way that didn't take out the heart monitor. That would set off the bombs. He risked a glance at the hostages. They were watching with rapt attention, frozen in place, probably wondering at which moment the signal would be sent to blow them all to bloody hunks of meat in the middle of this cargo hold.

"You do not understand," Mhusa said. "I murdered my family, yes. But it was not because I wanted to. I brought them death. I brought them this death because of my work studying and teaching in other lands. From Sierra Leone I brought them Ebola. The disease is merciless. It kills almost all who catch it."

"Almost all," said McCarter. Keep him talking, he thought. Give Calvin time to work.

"I caught it," said Mhusa. "I was very sick. But my doctors, they knew the secret. It is not the disease that kills a man with Ebola. It is the dehydration. The vomiting, the diarrhea. It dries out the body. When the blood begins to flow, there is nothing left. A man dies a dried-out husk."

"That's pretty awful, all right," McCarter said. He advanced a step, jabbed with his blade. Mhusa slapped the weapon away with the flat of his own machete. The action was casual, almost contemptuous. Mhusa knew his way around a machete.

"They forced me to drink," Mhusa said. "Water, water, water. Gallons of it. They gave me so much water I thought I would drown in it. I was exhausted. I could not throw it up fast enough. And still they drowned me in it."

Despite himself, McCarter understood the man's pain. He had read accounts of the disease—how it ravaged those it took. He did not wish that on any man. "Give me the hostages," he tried suggesting. "Stop this and we can all live."

"You don't understand," Mhusa said. "I told you. I am dead already. I was told I had survived Ebola. The disease did not take me. I grew well again. And when they judged that there was no more of it in me, I went home.

I went home to my wife and child. But there was something that was not known then. Something that I learned only too late."

"The virus lives on," McCarter stated. He leaned back as Mhusa slashed at his neck then withdrew.

"Yes," Mhusa said. "A man who is healthy can have Ebola in his semen for many days after he grows well. Ignorant of this, I came home to my wife's bed. And it was because of me that she became sick. She gave this sickness to my child. And when Ebola began to spread, when the outbreak became pronounced, medical care was not so easy to come by.

"There were riots. People became afraid. In their desperation, they blamed the doctors who traveled from border to border. They began attacking medical professionals in the streets. Then they raided the Ebola clinics, stealing whatever they could find. This included sheets and towels bearing contaminated blood. And everything grew worse."

Mhusa attacked in earnest this time. He advanced, slashing and chopping as he lunged. It was all McCarter could do to block the attacks, to keep the bigger man off him. As the two battled furiously, their machetes scraped and banged together, ringing out through the cargo hold. Mhusa began to sweat, great beads of it streaming down the sides of his black face. McCarter, too, was feeling the exertion. He was very aware that he was now fighting for his life.

"There was no one to treat my wife, no one to treat my only child," Mhusa said as he fought. "I cannot even bring myself…to say their names!" As he spoke these last words he drove the blade of the machete down with all his might. It struck the deck of the ship, drawing sparks. The big African recovered quickly, but not before McCarter managed to slash his weapon arm. Blood flowed freely.

"Give up!" McCarter said. "Give me the hostages! Get on your launch and get out of here."

"There is no going back," Mhusa said. "There is nothing for me to go back to. I traveled the world after I watched my family die. I was hoping for someone, something, to give me meaning before I found the strength to kill myself. Always, when I thought of taking my own life, I saw my wife. And she urged me not to do it. She said it was a sin. It was Wijeya who found me, hired me, gave me a reason to fight on. He promised me much danger. He promised me a way to fill my days with work, so that at night I would sleep the dreamless sleep of a man who is exhausted. And so I devote myself to him because there is nothing else, and no other reason."

McCarter went for broke. He pressed his attack, slashing and jabbing, trying to work his blade up and past Mhusa's formidable guard. "Why are your men impersonating the Chinese?" he demanded. "Where did you get the weapons?"

"The weapons were given to us by Wijeya," Mhusa said, as if that explained everything. "We pretended to be Chinese because Wijeya asked it. His reasons are his own. What do I care? I have told you. I am dead. I seek only the courage of one man who can make this so. One man who can give me back my family."

"You could…save a lot of trouble," McCarter said, breathing heavily now, "if you would just…kill yourself…"

"But I cannot," Mhusa said.

He was in incredible shape for a globe-trotting pirate, McCarter thought. He barely seemed winded, even with all the talking he was doing.

"I told you. Every time I take my pistol and put it under

my own chin, I see my wife's face. She cannot abide the sin of suicide. She tells me I cannot. That this way is too easy. That I am a fighter."

"Bloody hell," McCarter said. Under his breath, he said, "Calvin, if you're going to do it, you've got to do it now. I don't have much left."

"David, I can't," James reported. "There's simply no shot."

Well, that was that, then. McCarter was just going to have to do it himself. He scanned the battleground, looking for something he could use to his advantage. There was only the nearby dead man, the man on whose chest Mhusa had placed his pistol, the man whose machete McCarter even now wielded.

"I can feel it coming," said Mhusa. "Can you feel it, British? I am going to choke you to death. I am going to feel the life leave you as I crush your neck."

McCarter lunged. With a furious burst of energy, he hammered away at Mhusa's machete, driving the man back, focusing on the blade and not the man.

Mhusa was taken off balance by his approach, which was designed simply to shove him back, not to kill him. He did not realize, until it was too late, what McCarter was trying to do.

Mhusa tripped over the dead man.

He fell back and hit the deck. McCarter dove on top of him, slamming the blade of his machete down with both hands, one on the handle and one on the back of the blade. The edge of the machete cleaved the electronic device taped to Mhusa's chest and buried itself half an inch in the African's torso.

Mhusa screamed.

McCarter didn't try to dislodge the machete. Instead he let go of it, scooping up Mhusa's pistol from atop the corpse beneath them. In the same motion, he jacked the hammer back, made sure the safety was off, and shoved the pistol under Mhusa's chin.

"Thank you," Mhusa said. "Thank you, British." He reached up and wrapped his big hands around the Briton's throat.

McCarter pulled the trigger. "Say hello to your family, then."

CHAPTER TWENTY

Atlanta, Georgia

The man known in America as "Harold Rhemsen" signed his name at the end of the entry in his personal journal: Cheung Yeong. As it always did, that simple act of rebellion, that tiny piece of defiance, made him smile.

Over the years of his charade it was this journal, his *real* journal, that had kept him sane. To have kept this journal, in addition to the faked one in which he had also written dutifully every week for years, was a tremendous breach of security. If his superiors in Beijing knew what he had done, they would have him punished for it, maybe even executed him. The existence of the journal, had anyone discovered it through the years, would have endangered his mission and everything for which he had worked since he was a teenager.

He did not care. Without the journal, he would have gone mad long ago. He needed the affirmation, each time he lied, each time he wrote in the journal he had given Fitzpatrick. He needed to know, each time he concluded those lies, that he was himself. That he was Cheung Yeong. That he was born to prominent members of the Communist Party in China, a child of the ruling elite, a man who would live and die a Chinese national. Yes, he was half European by birth, but that had never been held against him. His parents were Party faithful. He was Chinese, despite his unusually pale complexion, his slightly European features. He was Chinese. He was Cheung Yeong.

Without his secret second journal to periodically remind him of whom he truly was, what his mission was supposed to be, he would either have lost himself in the identity they had chosen for him…or he would have put the barrel of a gun in his mouth and ended his own life. Certainly there were guns aplenty in this lawlessness. How anyone survived to adulthood and beyond in this place of individualism and chaos, this place of unfettered me-first childishness, awash in crime and gangs and drugs, with the weight of weak leadership and even weaker foreign policy hanging around their collective necks…it was a mystery to him.

It was supposed to be an honor, and in his heart, he knew that it was. To be chosen as one of China's most highly placed assets, one of her most deeply positioned sleeper agents, with access to funding and resources that were, for all practical purposes, completely unlimited… this was a prize beyond prizes, an honor that most members of the party went their whole life and never realized.

The day his parents had come to him, told him that he had been selected to perform this service to the People's Republic of China, he had been overjoyed. But that had been many long years ago now. Much had happened. There were days that he woke up realizing that he had lived his entire life as another man, a false man, a man he had himself murdered. To realize that most of his life had been spent devoted to a lie…it was humbling. It was also maddening. He had devoted many pages in his journal to this fact, and ripped just as many out. Some thoughts were not meant for posterity, no matter how true. It would not do for someone in Beijing to discover his records and decide that, even long after his death, the least patriotic of his thoughts was worthy of punishment visited on any who descended from him.

But would any descend from him? Would he ever have a son to carry on his line? Over the years he had indulged in sex, usually with vapid American women who could be impressed with money and power. Certainly his looks would not earn him the favors of women. He would find no one worthy of him in such company. The physical act brought with it some small amount of gratification, but he was alone, living in complete isolation, carrying a secret that only he and one other man, now, shared.

That man had been Lao, his handler. Lao alone knew what Harold Rhemsen was and, working together, Lao and Cheung Yeong had formulated the plan they were now executing. That plan had been approved at the highest levels of government in Beijing, but if Cheung Yeong failed, if anything went wrong, he and Lao knew they would be disavowed. That was the way of it. He understood it. He accepted it.

Now Lao was dead, blown to bits by an ignorant fool who would never know the secret that Lao and Cheung Yeong had shared. It bothered him to know that Fitzgerald had so casually ended the life of the one person alive— excepting their superiors in Beijing—who knew that he was not really Harold Rhemsen. He and Lao had not been friends. They had not been close. But when speaking to Lao, he could let down fully the barriers that normally came second nature to him. He could speak as he might speak if he were home, on Chinese soil, and not pretend to be this man whose life he had stolen.

When his parents had informed him of his mission, to infiltrate the United States and to place himself in a position of a power, he had thought little of it. These were just words, vague concepts. He was very intelligent, he was driven and he was capable and adaptable. He had been chosen over many of his fellow students, they'd told him, because his aptitude scores ranked him as most likely to be able to sustain the commitment, the concentration, the focus that would be required to endure such a long and arduous mission.

He had no idea, then, what he was doing to himself. He had no clue what his life would become. Over the months that he was trained in Beijing, at a special facility in which everything was furnished with American goods, with American literature, where all the handlers and Cheung Yeong himself spoke nothing but English, he began to understand the enormity of what faced him. He was given rudimentary courses in espionage. He was trained to pick locks. He was taught how to take photographs using conventional cameras and microfilm. He was instructed in hand-to-hand combat—this last, relatively familiar and even easy, for he had long been a student of Kung Fu under his own father—and then in how to kill a man quickly and efficiently. The two, martial arts and killing, were not the same thing, as he'd quickly learned. He'd embraced his training first from duty, then from necessity, and finally from destination. As the day approached for him to leave Beijing and begin his undercover life, he knew a mounting anticipation, almost a dread, that drove him to learn whatever he possibly could that might keep him alive.

The man who knew, in his heart, that his name was Cheung Yeong took a moment to examine the cramped handwriting filling the pages of his journal. Over the years he had filled many such volumes, of course. Each time he filled one, he burned it, destroying it utterly—but not before summarizing the accounts that it held, so that each journal was a complete account, with necessary and important dates and facts, of his mission on American soil.

The mission had not started in America. It had started with his education. Beijing had arranged for him to be educated at Oxford. His identity was completely fake, of course; he had a convincingly vague lineage and an elaborate cover story that explained where his family money was supposed to come from. In reality, Beijing itself was backing him. Over the years he had become adept at routing money through holding companies and other means of concealing where it came from. Avoiding discovery, especially in the modern era of interlocked data networks, was the watchword. It had become more difficult as the years wore on, but he had become smarter, too.

His first task was to select a suitable identity. His cover identity was good, yes, but it was not good enough. If tested, it would unravel. He needed to become someone who was unquestionably American. There were many American students at Oxford. Their isolation from their home country, their distance from their families, was one of the reasons Beijing had selected Oxford as the site for his infiltration. He got to know his fellow students, ingratiated himself to them, and made sure he was known to be affable and cooperative. This required, at every turn, pretending a joviality he did not truly feel. He hated these foolish, insipid children. He hated their empty lives of wealth and privilege. He hated that he, along among them, was saddled with a burden that far outweighed their world.

Harold Rhemsen was at that time a young man from the southern United States whose family was quite wealthy. The child of aging parents, he had experienced the double blow of losing both his mother and his father to natural ailments while away at school. He had no extended family. Alone to inherit the family fortune, he spoke often of the loneliness that confronted him. Cheung Yeong was quick to capitalize on that, to become Harold Rhemsen's best friend. They became inseparable, bonding in their loneliness, for Cheung Yeong had no family that was not hundreds of miles distant.

Soon, when time and their class schedules allowed, the pair began to take trips into the surrounding countryside. There, frequenting the pubs in which they were barely old enough to be welcome, they established a wider circle of friends. These locals were, of course, merely using their newfound foreign friends for the money that Rhemsen and Cheung Yeong spread around, but that was all right. Rhemsen enjoyed drinking, and Cheung Yeong was content that his plan was moving accordingly. When he judged that the time was right, he alerted his handlers in Beijing. It was Lao himself who met Cheung Yeong for the first time, late at night in yet another English pub, and explained to him how the plan to murder Harold Rhemsen would proceed.

Their circle of pub friends invited Cheung and Rhemsen to a party in the country. It was the usual late-night affair around a blazing fire. The liquor flowed. Cheung made sure to lace the bottle with a drug given him by Lao. He had never known the sedative's name, but it worked quickly and made those affected sleep heavily.

Cheung feigned imbibing all night, secretly tossing his drinks when no one was looking, staying completely sober. When the party started to wind down and the rest of the partygoers began to drift off to drugged slumber, Cheung continued to stoke the fire.

It was easy to drag Harold Rhemsen into the fire.

He would never forget the smell. At his signal, the Chinese intelligence troops concealed in the surrounding woods came forward, secured the burned body, and accompanied both the corpse and Cheung Yeong back into the city. There, thanks to the switching of medical records and the corpse's regrettably incinerated condition, Cheung Yeong's fake identity was retired. He was officially listed as dead, the victim of a terrible drunken accident that would be written off to a bad case of alcohol poisoning that affected all present.

As for Harold Rhemsen, stories were circulated about the poor young man's terrible injury. So badly had the fire burned him that he would be several months recovering. His graduation would be delayed. This was very sad but, apart from that poor dead Chinese boy, whom did Harold Rhemsen truly call friend? Not many on campus.

Thus, when young Harold Rhemsen returned to campus, his face swaddled in bandages while he recovered from reconstructive surgery, few talked to him. No one held his silence against him for how could anyone be expected to cope with so hideous and thorough an injury? It was rumored that the burning was so bad that Harold would be practically unrecognizable when the bandages came off. His speech, too, had been affected by inhaling fire. But he was still Harold Rhemsen. He was still a student of Oxford, and he was accorded concomitant respect.

Seated in his office in Atlanta, Cheung Yeong picked up the hand mirror from his desk and looked at himself again. He spent many long minutes every day staring at that alien face. It had come to horrify him as much as it fascinated him, that plastic mask, that face that made him able to pass for a white Anglo-Saxon male named Harold Rhemsen.

How he hated that frozen face.

Returning "home" to Harold Rhemsen's ancestral property in North Carolina, the man now wearing an approximation of Rhemsen's face had wasted no time asserting ownership. The formation of RhemCorp followed not long after. Between the family fortune and the secret backing of Beijing, supported by industrial espionage carried out by Chinese intelligence agents, RhemCorp built itself up quickly in the field of armament. All that was needed, to secure Department of Defense patronage, was to offer ordnance that was cheaper, that killed more and killed faster. This was easy enough to accomplish. For many years RhemCorp's operations were completely legal, apart from the methods through which its designs were achieved. It was only when the company was established that Rhemsen began to branch out, to serve illegal foreign markets.

Through it all, he had met periodically with Lao, always in secret, determining how his position in the American arms industry could best be used to help China. They had mulled over many possibilities. For some time they had considered sabotaging the weapons themselves, so that American troops in combat would be dealt serious losses. This plan they discarded. Not only had it been tried before by other intelligence operatives, with limited success, but it would not be sustainable. A single batch of bad weaponry would start tongues wagging. While the American military was notoriously slow to respond to reports of defective equipment, respond it eventually would. Then the power and influence RhemCorp had built would be lost, with little to show for it but a few dead American grunts.

No, what they needed was something far more sweeping. It was in discussing this that Lao and Rhemsen—for that was who Cheung Yeong had to pretend to be—hit on the idea of using RhemCorp, first to implicate China, then to reveal the plot as a ruse on the part of a corrupt American capitalist. They had proceeded accordingly with Beijing's blessing and its resources at their disposal.

Only in recent months had Fitzpatrick, that fool who headed the mercenary forces Rhemsen had hired to secure his properties, learned of Lao's existence. It had taken all of Rhemsen's self-control not to murder Fitzpatrick when the explosion killed Lao. But Fitzpatrick was necessary to his plan. After all, if the man known as Harold Rhemsen simply disappeared, there would be nothing to indicate exactly what had happened. Yes, he would be safe in China, but China itself would not be cleared in the scandal involving RhemCorp's weaponry. He was not out simply to destroy the reputation of RhemCorp with the Americans. That was a bonus, implicating corrupt capitalism, but it was not the main thrust of the scheme.

No, for the plan truly to work, it had to appear that Rhemsen, a corrupt American fat cat, had first sold his weapons abroad to illegal interests, then used those interests to fund attacks in the South China Sea that were only made to look as if the Chinese were responsible. This plot would be exposed and, when it was, further criticism of China's territorial expansion would look like more conspiracy to frame Beijing for actions it did not commit.

Westerners were cowards. They hated to appear prejudiced or biased. They would shrink back in their cowardice. The great injustice perpetrated against China by a corrupt American would make the Americans look even more dishonest than they already were, while shielding China from the rabble who sought to deny her the territory that was hers. In the transition, RhemCorp would become a Chinese holding, just as Rhemsen had described to Fitzpatrick. And Rhemsen himself could return to China and live under his own name once more; enjoying the fruits of his labor at the helm of the company he had built.

That idiot Fitzpatrick was key to the plan. The journal Rhemsen had given him was faked. It told only the story that Beijing wanted told. It was filled with Harold Rhemsen's greedy fantasies, his pathological hatred for all Asians—especially the "dirty Chinese"—and an outline of the plot to frame China for aggressions it had not committed, using pirates hired in the South China Sea for muscle. It was also filled with various derisive statements about Fitzpatrick and about Blackstar in general, including Rhemsen's joy at the wanton killing of Blackstar's men.

Sooner or later, Fitzpatrick would read through the journal. It was the type of man he was. He had no honor. He had no respect. He would read the journal, out of curiosity to see just what weapon he possessed. And when he did, he would realize that he had been betrayed—for the journal also contained the admission that the briefcase full of money with which Rhemsen had paid Fitzpatrick was counterfeit. Those provocations should be enough to send Fitzpatrick to the nearest American authorities to plead for immunity from prosecution in exchange for what he knew. Fitzpatrick, craven as he was, would also go to the press. He would see it as the way to cash in on what he knew. The fact that the money was not real would burn him. The big oaf would have been making plans for that money, picturing how he would spend it, feeling rich and powerful. To have that taken away would burn him, would gall him, would make him feel the lack of something he had scarcely possessed before it was stolen back. He would want to find a way to enrich himself, and the press would do that for him.

Should that plan fail, should Fitzpatrick turn out to be less useful than even Rhemsen thought him to be, there would be other ways of releasing the information. But Rhemsen knew Fitzpatrick well. He was confident that the brute would not let him down. Jason Fitzpatrick was, in the grand scheme of things, entirely predictable…and entirely a fool.

Fitzpatrick would be occupied, in the near term, with the tasks Rhemsen had given him. That should see to it he did not begin to thumb through the journal until he had sufficient leisure. The oaf would probably do something like hide the briefcase and journal under his bed at home while he embarked on his current mission. It was how someone like that thought. That was, if you could call it thinking at all.

In the meantime Fitzpatrick's Blackstar men would prove useful. He did not care how many of them died, here or in Hilton Head, as long as the government investigators were eliminated. Why, they need not even be killed, as long as they were delayed sufficiently. There were files here that had to be collected, files that could only be properly destroyed if they were decrypted and deleted using a special algorithm Lao had developed for the purpose. The process was a lengthy one. Only when it was complete could Rhemsen leave this place behind. He would go to the airport, board the jet of which he had spoken to Fitzpatrick, and leave the American dullard to his pile of fake money and his betrayal. Cheung Yeong would finally be free to resume his normal life back in China.

His only regret was that he would have to do that…*with this alien face Beijing had given him.*

Harold Rhemsen hurled his hand mirror across the room and watched it shatter into glistening fragments.

CHAPTER TWENTY-ONE

The chopper that flew Phoenix Force over the South China Sea had been patched, repaired and re-armed. It was heavily laden with both fuel and ammunition, and rightly so. The target to which they now traveled was the hardest target yet: an entire Filipino oil rig that had just been captured by officially "unknown" forces.

If the rig were lost, it would be a heavy blow to the Filipino economy. Discovery of an oil deposit off Cebu Island had given the nation hope of becoming a viable oil producer for the first time in a long time, giving the nation a much-needed financial boost and bolstering its energy security while reducing its dependence on foreign imports. Foreign contractors had been drilling exploratory wells in the islands since the 1960s. The work was finally paying off, and a deposit of natural gas had allowed the rig to be used as an offshore electricity producer, as well. The whole thing was one giant gem of a target for anyone seeking to hurt the Philippines. That made protecting it that much more important. Data, including the schematics and plans for the rig, were uploading to Phoenix Force's smartphones as they flew. McCarter himself was still on the satellite phone with Barbara Price as the team neared its target.

"They're flying the Chinese flag," Price said. "Transmissions from the rig, which have been in broken English, have proclaimed the rig property of the Chinese government. They're claiming that the People's Republic of China has extended its territory to cover that entire area of the South China Sea."

"Is anybody buying that?" McCarter asked. "Before I took him out, this Mhusa character claimed he was first mate to a pirate captain named Wijeya. If he was telling the truth, then this Wijeya, perhaps in conjunction with other pirates, is behind the attacks here in the South China Sea. Our man couldn't tell us where Wijeya got the weapons and the uniforms."

"Able Team is running down Rhemsen," Price advised. "We've located what we believe is his last facility in the United States. It was concealed by several layers of data encryption and cut-outs, holding companies and other concealing methods. That's part of why Bear believes this is the last one. What's more, Rhemsen and his forces, including this corporation Blackstar, have repeatedly attacked both you and Able Team while nominally in Rhemsen's employ."

"Just to play devil's advocate, Barb," McCarter interjected, "how do we know it isn't some other company pulling the strings?"

"In-depth analysis of RhemCorp's financial data, including the records they didn't want anybody to know about, led us to the holding companies that employ Blackstar. That prompted us to sift through Blackstar with a fine-toothed comb. The company, at this point, has just one client. RhemCorp funds Blackstar through a number of different dummy companies, but all roads lead back to Rhemsen and his money. In fact, we don't think Blackstar knows that they're completely in Rhemsen's pocket. Bear has uncovered emails that show Blackstar was under the impression that it answered to more than one client. Rhemsen and his people actively worked to give them that impression. Not that Blackstar's management was particular about breaking the law. It's just bad business to have all your eggs in one client's basket."

"So Rhemsen is a control freak," said McCarter. "He wanted a private army at his beck and call, and he didn't want that army potentially distracted by other buyers. So he made sure there were never any conflicts, and Blackstar, criminals they may be, were never any wiser."

"What a tangled web, indeed," Price said. "What we don't know is why Rhemsen is mixed up in stirring up trouble in the South China Sea. Blackstar is obviously working for him there as well as domestically. They're mixed up with the pirates somehow. And thanks to your good work, Phoenix, we know that it's pirates, not the Chinese, who are sponsoring these terror attacks. Beijing denies that they are involved in the oil rig attack. What's more—this is significant, David—they're offering to provide air support and combat troops. That's never happened before."

"How bloody convenient," McCarter stated.

"That was Hal's thought, too," Price noted. "Which makes me wonder if there isn't some sneaky way that the Chinese government is involved in this. Beijing is getting better at public relations, especially after some nasty missteps."

"You mean that whole thing where they tried to show off their latest air-superiority fighter using footage stolen from an American fighter-pilot movie?"

Price said, "Yes. Yes, very much so. The Chinese hate to lose face when this kind of thing happens. They're eager to prove that they're a superpower. Imagine the public relations coup that they could spin out of sending troops to help us regain an oil rig controlled by pirates…and one that is falsely running their flag to make them look bad. We need more data, but Hal smells a rat, and so do I."

"All right, Barb," said McCarter. "We'll stay on it. Something about this feels like a grandstand final play. This oil rig is the biggest target they've hit yet. And I can't help but feel that the hostage drama with the freighter was designed to keep us busy while they set this up. Tell me, are there news crews on site?"

"The Filipino government is enforcing an air space perimeter," said Price. "Designed to keep the news choppers at bay. They're also maintaining a naval cordon to stop any reporters from blundering into the whole affair by boat. That should keep any innocent casualties to a minimum. And I have some other good news that's just coming over the wire," she added.

"What's that?"

"The Filipinos are reporting that the rig was shut down for some kind of maintenance cycle," said Price. "They were running a skeleton crew, and when the pirates attacked, that crew took a launch and got out of there fast. That's why the rig went down so easily. But it also means that there are no civilians aboard. The only people on that oil rig are the invaders, which, if your intel is correct, are either pirates or Blackstar personnel. Possibly both, given that it was Blackstar who tried to take you down."

"Something that bothers me," McCarter revealed, "is the fact that, from what you've told me, Able has been targeted by Rhemsen's forces, just as we have. That means that Rhemsen knows someone in our government is on to him and actively working against him. For most people, for most corrupt businessmen, anyway, that would be the bloody signal to get out of the country. So why's Rhemsen still trying to duke it out with forces he knows are far more powerful than he is? There isn't a private business alive that can stand up to the power of the federal government once it trains its full resources against someone. What does Rhemsen hope to gain except his complete destruction?"

"You're asking the same questions Hal asked me," said Price. "And I'm afraid I don't have a good answer for you. Everything Rhemsen is doing is absolutely self-destructive. There's no way either he or his company come out of this intact. Not if he hopes ever to do business again. It's suicidal. It's worse than suicidal, actually, because it isn't just his life and livelihood he's affecting. We just don't know."

"We are almost within range," Grimaldi interrupted over the transceiver. "Everybody strap in and gun up."

"That's my cue, Barb," McCarter said. "I'll give the boys the good news."

"Good news?" Price echoed.

"Weapons free, Barb," McCarter advised. "Weapons free."

"Good luck, David—again. Farm, out."

McCarter moved up toward the front of the chopper. "Everyone take your stations," he said, repeating Grimaldi's instructions unnecessarily. "Gary, on the launcher. Rafe, T.J., take the guns. Barb has cleared us to go in hot. There are no civilians aboard the oil rig. Just bad guys. And you know what that means."

"Finally, we get to clean house the way the gods of war intended," Hawkins said.

Everybody but Grimaldi turned to stare at Hawkins. There was an awkward moment of silence.

"Starting to worry about you, T.J.," James said.

"I, uh, heard it in a movie," Hawkins said.

"Right," McCarter intoned. "Well, then, let's get this done, shall we? Jack, take us in."

"Gladly," said Grimaldi. "Hang on to your hats, boys. We're about to put a dent in the price of oil."

"Uh," James began, "you do know we want to liberate the oil rig and not just blow it up, right?"

"Barb might have said something about that," Grimaldi said. He ran a cable from the MP3 player in his pocket to a jack in the control panel. "But I think this is appropriate nonetheless."

"I love it when he gets like this," Encizo said.

Manning shook his head. He hadn't said much in the past few days, and didn't seem inclined to share much now.

Wagner's "Ride of the Valkyries" began to play over the cockpit speakers. Grimaldi let out a war whoop and dropped the nose of the chopper, sending them hurtling toward the oil rig as they picked up speed.

The oil rig was a massive L-shape built on a structure that put it well up above the water. There was a landing pad, a large loading crane and several multistory structures that housed everything from living quarters to supplies to the equipment used in drilling. There was also a very large setup devoted to piping the drilled oil and natural gas, and a pod, or secondary platform, that comprised the natural-gas power-generation facility.

Armed men were all over the rigs. None of them wore Chinese uniforms, even though the Chinese flag was flying from a post on the power station. Some looked to be wearing what McCarter thought of as "paramilitary casual"—castoff BDUs, denim, ragged vests, that kind of thing. The others were wearing the dark uniforms McCarter recognized as belonging to Blackstar security. He took his monocular from his eye and pointed. "Multiple hostiles, confirmed. Looks like pirates and Blackstar goons."

"Even if they're Chinese military in disguise," said Grimaldi, "the Chinese have disclaimed them. No worries about an international incident."

"Right-oh," McCarter said. "Let's light them up, boys! Fire!"

Encizo and Hawkins opened up with the machine guns as the chopper made one low pass over the oil rig. The bullets scattered the enemy below. A few of the gunners on the rig returned fire with Kalashnikovs as the chopper cleared the rig and began to wheel around. The turn brought the grenade launcher side of the chopper into play.

"Target the outlying structural points, Gary," McCarter instructed. "We don't want to bring the rig down. We just want to make things inhospitable for the personnel aboard her."

"Inhospitality, coming right up," Manning said. That brought a glance from his teammates, to which Manning responded with the first broad grin any of them had seen him offer. "Oh, come on," he said. "I can't be the big, strong, quiet one forever, can I?"

"Fair enough," McCarter said.

The 40 mm grenade launcher unleashed hell.

Explosions rocked the outer edges of the oil rig, scattering the gunmen on its decks and pelting them with molten shrapnel. Once more, Grimaldi brought the chopper in low and slow, giving Hawkins and Encizo time to work their guns over the deck. Shells rained down from beneath the weapons as 7.62 mm bullets raked the deck plates over and over. From their vantage in the chopper, they could hear the deck men screaming. More gunfire from below began to burn through the air, some of the rounds tagging the skin of the already abused fuselage.

Grimaldi kept them moving, pitching and sliding in a stomach-churning, yawing motion that made them a harder target to hit. For a second time he brought the grenade-launcher side to bear on the target, and Manning did his terrible work once more, choosing his targets with care and blasting enemies to pieces below. Several craters were blown into the deck of the oil rig, but Manning was cautious and hit nothing that was structurally important. He was also careful to avoid the power-generation pod, as damage to that unit would affect those who depended on power service from the platform.

"Oil Platform 227," Grimaldi said into his radio. "Oil Platform 227, come in. This is Security One. Repeat, this is Security One. You are ordered to surrender immediately or we will recommence attack." He brought the chopper up, flying a lazy circle around the perimeter of the rig, careful to stay well out of range of the types of anti-air weapons they had encountered thus far. He had complained about all the rewiring that had been necessary to shield the chopper's systems from electrical interference and to repair the damage done previously. McCarter imagined he was not eager to go through that again.

"This is Captain Yanuar Wijeya," said the voice that came back to them over the static-filled transmission. "I am in command of Platform 227. Break off your attack or there will be…consequences."

"Jack," said McCarter. "Patch me in."

Grimaldi pressed a pair of buttons on his control console. He nodded to McCarter. "You're live."

"Captain Wijeya," McCarter said. "My name is David. I am the leader of a squad of men whose job it is to clear you lot off that platform. We are going to circle around and deprive quite a few of your number of their lives. Will that be all right with you?"

"We shall see about that," Wijeya said. The line went dead.

"Now, Jack," McCarter said. "Calvin, get ready on those countermeasures!"

James sat in the seat next to Grimaldi and wired to the

console in front of him was a piece of equipment not standard issue on a helicopter. The countermeasures pod they had mounted beneath the big chopper was a tight fit on the belly of the bird, but now James was ready to activate it.

"Ready," James said.

"Tempt them good, Jack," McCarter directed. "I think I'll get him warmed up for you. Jack, push me live on the transmitter again."

"Go again," Grimaldi said.

"Captain Wijeya," said the Briton. "I believe I met a mate of yours on a Filipino freighter not far from here. Chap by the name of Mhusa. Big black fellow. One eye. How did he lose that eye, I'm wondering?"

There was no response.

"Maybe he's not listening," James offered.

"Oh, he's listening, all right," McCarter said quietly. More loudly, so the microphone would pick him up, he said, "It was a shame he had to die like he did. Seemed like an educated man. From the sound of your English, you're not uneducated yourself. Were the two of you friends? My guess is, you were. He was very loyal to you, Captain. Right up until the moment I put a bullet through his brain." McCarter drew his hand across his throat, signaling Grimaldi to cut the transmission.

Grimaldi did so and then pushed the chopper even closer to the platform, making sure their pass was fast enough. Just as McCarter suspected, it was then that the men on the rig broke out all their antiair weapons. They had been saving them, holding them back so they would have the element of surprise. It's what McCarter would have done in their position. But now, enraged, Wijeya would be directing his troops to throw everything they had at the helicopter.

Plumes of smoke rose from the oil rig. Whether they

were high-explosive Thorn rockets or the electromagnetic pulse devices didn't matter. James triggered the counter-measures pod. A blanket of explosive flares fanned out from the belly of the chopper, forming a barrier that deto-nated the missile rounds.

"Now, Gary!" McCarter shouted. "Fire at will! Guns, fire! Fire!"

The fusillade that Phoenix Force laid out cut down countless enemy shooters on the deck of the oil rig. Gre-nades and shrapnel from their explosions sowed even more confusion among the enemy's ranks. The gunners fell in droves, forming a swath of corpses that radiated from the landing platform. Using this gap, this no-man's land of death and destruction, Grimaldi brought the chopper down hard, landing as quickly as he dared. The bone-jar-ring impact shook Phoenix Force in their seats.

The moment the skids were on the platform, Phoenix Force was moving, their weapons ready. The five com-mandos disembarked and hit the deck. Grimaldi took off again, pushing for the sky with all possible speed, creat-ing a downdraft that nearly blew the Phoenix Force men off their feet. He was aloft and putting distance between him and the rig before the Blackstar men and pirates still alive could manage another salvo of antiair ordnance.

Fires were blazing now. They were minor; they would not threaten the structural viability of the rig. McCarter brought his Tavor to his shoulder, picked a target in his red-dot sight and put the man on the deck.

"Let's move, lads," he said. "Drop anything that moves."

Phoenix Force had landed.

CHAPTER TWENTY-TWO

Atlanta, Georgia

"You cried," Schwarz said. "You actually teared up."

"I did *not*," Lyons said emphatically. "You were deprived of oxygen. You were hallucinating."

Schwarz sat in the passenger seat of the Suburban, tapping away at his phone, once more playing his candy monster game. He had been gleefully announcing his level progress again, but this time, Lyons had let it go. There was a red ring around his neck, created by the steel cable of the man-trap device. It had choked him unconscious, but Lyons and Blancanales had freed him before it could kill him, and he seemed no worse for wear. He actually seemed, to put it mildly, quite aware that his teammates were grateful he was still alive, and he was determined to mine that fact for amusement for as many miles as he could.

"Is it too late to put him back in that thing?" Blancanales asked.

"We should have brought it with us," Lyons grumbled.

"We could turn around," said Blancanales. "We could seriously just go back, pick it up. It's not that far out of the way."

"I think I saw that building on that show," said Lyons, pointing. "You know, they said it was the CDC?"

"That's not the CDC, Ironman," Blancanales said.

"I know that," Lyons said, driving skillfully through

the busy Atlanta traffic. "I'm saying that on that show they used that building to say it was the CDC because it looks like it could be."

"Which show?" Blancanales asked.

"You know," Lyons said. "The one with that guy."

"Oh, right," Schwarz said. He did not look up from his smartphone. "That guy. The one with the shirt. Who was always going places and doing things."

"Yeah," Lyons said. "That's the one."

The building to which they were traveling had been isolated by the Farm and determined to be Rhemsen's likely fallback headquarters. According to Kurtzman, the trail of financial transactions that formed the maze of Harold Rhemsen's banking activity ultimately led to this location in Atlanta. It would have taken weeks' more sleuthing to determine this if they'd had to find it on their own, but with the city of Atlanta as the starting point, it had been much easier to nail down that part of the operation.

Kurtzman and his team had also used the trap set at Hilton Head to identify the data cut-outs and other masking elements Rhemsen had used to set up Able Team the first time. They had compared this data to that set and determined that this time their intelligence was genuine. Kurtzman himself had personally verified it, spending a long night with a pot of his industrial-strength coffee and his bank of computers, cross-checking every piece of data, following it back to its source to make sure it wasn't some manufactured piece of misdirection.

Lyons tried to play it off as if it was all in a day's business, but he was furious. Not only had Rhemsen been dirty from the get-go, validating his urge to walk onto the man's property and immediately begin taking names, but multiple times now the forces of RhemCorp had deliberately targeted both Able Team and Phoenix Force. During their drive to Atlanta, Lyons had conferred with the Farm, bringing Price up to date on everything that had happened. The news from Phoenix Force's portion of the mission showed that Rhemsen and his people were as aggressive as ever. This was not just a mission, as far as Lyons was concerned. This was personal. Rhemsen had chosen to go to war with Able Team and Phoenix Force directly.

Carl Lyons was going to give him that war.

What was eating at him most was the feeling of utter helplessness he had confronted while staring down at Schwarz trapped in that murderous device. Yes, it had worked out. And, yes, thanks to the Farm they had been able to determine what to do to disengage it, but if both Lyons and Blancanales hadn't been there, if the Farm hadn't been able to relay them the information they'd needed, if the wires Schwarz had worried might be detonator lines had actually triggered explosives when Lyons blew them with his shotgun… There were so many ways that everything could have gone wrong, and Schwarz would have been killed in the nastiest way possible.

There was the question of whether this headquarters to which they now were headed would boast any civilian workers. That seemed likely, even if it was a secret facility. So just razing the entire building was out. Lyons vowed to himself that if it were within his power to do so without endangering possible innocents, he would call in an air strike and be done with it. To hell with Harold Rhemsen, whoever he really was, whatever he was really trying to do. To hell with Blackstar. To hell with Jason Fitzpatrick. He was going to keep his promise to that big bastard. Oh, yes, he was.

According to the GPS in the Suburban, they were nearing the target address. Lyons slowed the truck as they approached what looked like a ten-foot-high stone wall.

Unless he missed his guess, it was reinforced concrete faced with fake rock to make it look less like a prison and more like an upscale gated community.

"If I was trying to keep an entire manufacturing facility secret," Schwarz mused, peering out the windshield, "so that I could manufacture weapons that I intended to sell on the international market to contraindicated buyers, I think I would put my factory building behind a big wall."

"Yeah," Lyons said. "That's what I was thinking."

"When you weren't thinking about how much you would miss me if I got killed," Schwarz said. He batted his eyelashes at Lyons for comic effect.

"Gadgets?"

"Yes, Carl?"

"Shut up."

Lyons parked the Suburban across the street from the main gate to the RhemCorp facility. The gate was a steel-strut affair complete with an outside guardhouse. There was movement in the guardhouse, which itself was little more than a wood-and-glass structure that resembled a phone booth. As Lyons watched, a pair of silver SUVs bearing the Blackstar logo pulled up and into position. The men were carrying AR-pattern rifles and wore load-bearing vests full of gear. There were half a dozen security guards.

"Well," Lyons said, "looks like they're not going to come quietly. Hand me the bullhorn."

From the back of the truck, Blancanales found the bullhorn in the supplies organizer. He handed it to Lyons as he stepped out of the Suburban.

The big former cop put the device to his face, switched it on and flinched as a squeal of feedback cut through the air.

"That's telling them, Carl," Schwarz said.

Lyons shot him a vicious look but made no comment.

Into the bullhorn, he said, "You there. We're with the Justice Department. And you goons are working my last nerve. Lie down on the ground with your hands on your head or I swear to God I'm going to just blow you all up."

The Blackstar men exchanged glances. Then they took up positions behind their trucks, aimed their rifles and began to pop off rounds. Bullets struck the pavement and ricocheted from the dented metal skin of the Suburban.

Lyons, standing straight up and down, making no attempt to take cover, breathed a heavy sigh.

"Carl! Get down!" Schwarz called from inside the truck. Blancanales poked the barrel of his M-4 out the window, using the frame of the truck to brace it, and started to line up the shot.

"Ironman, they're shooting at us," Blancanales added.

Lyons turned without saying a word. He walked deliberately to the back of the truck, threw open the tailgate and opened the concealed ordnance drawer in the back. From it he took a collapsible LAWS rocket. The light antitank weapon snapped open when he pulled its pin and yanked on the halves of the tube. Sights snapped open as he did so.

"I," Lyons said, punctuating his words with his steps as he started to walk toward the street and away from the truck, "am…so…very…sick…of all of you!" He snapped the LAWS to his shoulder and pressed the top-mounted switch. A plume of smoke marked the progress of the explosive rocket as it hurtled across the street, caught the first of the silver SUVs and blew it apart. A secondary explosion enveloped the neighboring vehicle as its gas tank was punctured by flaming shrapnel.

Most of the enemy Blackstar gunners were killed in the explosion. A single man, on fire and screaming as he died slowly on his feet, ran from the truck, moving blindly down the street. Blancanales said, "Want me to pop him?"

"No," said Lyons. He dropped the empty LAWS tube, drew his Python and thumbed the hammer back. Then he carefully lined up his shot and pulled the trigger. The burning man's head snapped back and he dropped. The smell of burning flesh was awful.

"Wow," Schwarz said.

Lyons climbed back into the Suburban. "Put on your seat belts," he said.

"I hate it when he gets like this," Blancanales said.

"I love it when he gets like this," Schwarz said. The two Able Team members secured their shoulder belts as Lyon did the same.

Lyons slammed his foot down on the gas pedal and threw the truck into Drive. The massive Suburban very nearly burned rubber as its powerful engine shot them forward with all the low-end torque the truck could offer. They picked up speed as they crossed the street, bounced over the curb and knocked the corner of one of the burning SUVs out of the way. Metal shrieked on metal.

The nose of the Suburban met the gate.

The three Able Team members were jerked in their seats as their forward progress was stopped. Lyons grunted as his seat belt dug into his chest. The engine was racing, the Suburban struggling to keep pushing. But the gate, instead of falling, had simply bent.

"That hurt," Blancanales said. "What now, Ironman?"

"Lather," Carl Lyons said. He threw the Suburban into Reverse and stomped the gas pedal to the floor. The truck howled in protest and began to rocket back. Then Lyons slammed his foot on the brake, shifted again and said, "Rinse." Then once more his foot held the pedal to the metal. "Repeat!" he shouted.

This time, when the nose of the Suburban met the tortured, twisted metal gate, it ripped the gate from its hinges. The truck bounced and jostled over the remains of the fallen barrier, its tires slipping. Lyons jammed on the brakes again and switched to four-wheel drive. Then he was shoving the truck forward again, abusing the hell out of it, venting his rage and frustration at everything that had happened to Able Team during this mission.

Through the open window of the Suburban, the barrel of a rifle came poking in. A Blackstar guard had walked up to the truck while they were temporarily stalled and was now holding the barrel of his gun at Lyons's temple.

"All of you freeze!" the guard shouted. "Get out of the vehicle now!"

Lyons ducked forward, snaking his one arm up under his other arm. Flattening his stomach against the steering wheel, he leaned as far over as he could and pulled the trigger of the Colt Python still in its shoulder holster. The round blew a hole through the back of his bomber jacket, through the door of the Suburban, and into the Blackstar guard. He fell, gurgling, choking on his own blood, his look one of utter disbelief. He never managed to pull the trigger of his AR.

Lyons tossed the weapon out onto the pavement.

"You're a little on edge, aren't you, Carl?" Schwarz asked, pretending to sound casual. "You know, relaxing with a video game might—"

"Gadgets," Lyons said. "I will pistol-whip you. As God is my witness, I will pistol-whip you."

Schwarz stared at the roof of the truck and started whistling.

With the Suburban in four-wheel drive, Lyons hauled up the winding road that led to the RhemCorp building. He drove like a man possessed, not caring how it looked, not caring if either of his partners thought he was mad. He was mad. He was furious. He was ready to explode.

It was time to get the payback that RhemCorp, Rhemsen and Fitzpatrick so richly deserved.

"Please," Lyons said, "let him be here. Let him be waiting here. I said I would put him down with my boot on his neck, and I meant it. Please, let him be here."

"Ironman, are you praying?" Schwarz said.

"Not as such," Lyons said. "Just hoping the forces of irony and Murphy's Law are with us instead of against us."

The road wound through a stand of trees, most of them dogwoods and Southern pines. Blackstar goons began coming out of hiding. They were using the trees to hide themselves. One of them made the mistake of coming too close to the road, trying to line up a good shot through the windshield. Lyons poured on the speed, spun the wheel left and smashed him down with the gnarled sheet metal of the forward bumper. The man's cracking body snapped and crunched under the big Suburban's wheels. The doomed man never even had time to scream.

Schwarz and Blancanales exchanged glances.

Finally, the main facility came into view. Sandbag emplacements had been set up and behind the sandbags there were fire teams with machine guns. The second the Suburban was visible, the men behind the sandbags began shooting. Trace fire drew Technicolor lines across the property and ripped apart the trees screening the building.

Lyons looked to Schwarz. "Blow out the front windshield," he said.

"Ironman?"

"Do it!" Lyons said. Schwarz nodded and ripped his 93-R from its shoulder holster. Switching the weapon to 3-round burst, Schwarz pumped several trios of shots through the windshield. Lyons slowed their momentum long enough to recline his seat, throw his legs up over the dash and put the soles of his boots on the damaged safety glass. Schwarz did the same without prompting. Together, they kicked out what was left of the pane, leaving a few pebbles of safety glass in the interior of the truck.

Lyons pulled his seat back into driving position and slammed his foot down on the gas once more. "Pol," he said, "get that Milkor. Let's make it rain."

Blancanales didn't need to be told twice. With the rotary grenade launcher in his fists, he positioned himself between the front two seats. Then Lyons floored the accelerator once more. The transmission was making an alarming grinding noise.

"That doesn't sound good," Schwarz said.

"She'll hold together," Lyons said. "Pol, wait for it."

Machine-gun fire began to stitch the hood of the vehicle. Steam rose from the Suburban as they picked up velocity. Then black smoke started to pour out of the howling engine. A bullet blew apart the top of the seat just to the right of Lyons's shoulder. Lyons spat foam.

"Now, Pol! Fire!" Lyons shouted.

Blancanales began shooting, punching high-explosive grenades among the sandbag lines. The rounds had their intended effect. The enemy fortifications were blown to pieces, together with the Blackstar gunmen behind them. Lyons pushed the smoking, spewing and dying truck through the sandbag lines and gunned it as they headed up the ramp that was the front steps of the building.

Double doors, reinforced with metal bars, awaited.

The Suburban smashed through.

CHAPTER TWENTY-THREE

The members of Phoenix Force moved in formation to the nearest of the hatches that led inside the oil rig. Behind them, bodies and flaming debris littered the deck. There was still moaning and screaming audible as they closed the hatch behind them. There were a lot of wounded men out there who would not live to see the morning. Whether pirate or mercenary, there wasn't a man among the dying who was any concern to Phoenix Force.

McCarter wished for a can of Coke and wondered how he had gone this long without. The hatchway in which they stood led down a short corridor with no other doors except the exit. That hatch was locked down. Fortunately they had come equipped with explosives and something specifically for an oil rig environment: a portable torch.

Manning, who was good with explosives and demolitions in general, had opted to carry the torch as part of his kit. He fired up the little unit. The torch consisted of a trigger-equipped nozzle, a flow regulator and an arm's length of compressed gas tube. Its ignition was electric and, while it was a significant amount of additional weight, it was not so heavy that it would slow a big man like Gary Manning. The Canadian took a pair of industrial shades from his gear, put them over his eyes and went to work on the hatch wheel.

McCarter glanced at his chronograph, peeling back the black ballistic fabric cover that enclosed the watch face. They were vulnerable whenever they encountered a barrier such as this. He did not want them out here, rear ends swinging in the wind, any longer than was necessary. Phoenix Force bottled up, as it were, could not effectively fight. But these types of bottlenecks had to be fought through if they were to reach their goal.

Manning finished his work on the hatch and pulled it open. The rest of Phoenix Force was already in formation, with McCarter and Encizo kneeling, James and Hawkins standing behind them. Manning threw himself to the deck and protected his face with his arms.

The shooters who had been waiting on the other side, all wearing Blackstar uniforms, managed to get off a few wild shots, but nothing that came close to hurting the men of Phoenix Force. The coordinated bursts from their Tavor assault rifles mowed the thugs down, dropping their bodies in clumps that lined the floor of the platform corridor beyond. Blood began to well in large, spreading pools.

McCarter gave Manning a hand up. Loading a shotgun round in his Tavor's grenade launcher, Manning led the way, with the rest of Phoenix Force backing him up. They came to a split in the corridor. Signs posted for the oil rig workers indicated that to the left was a machine shop, while to the right were medical facilities.

"Machine shop or sick bay?" Manning asked.

"Go left," McCarter said. "I'm not in the mood for any of us to need medical, and if there are any wounded stragglers there, I'd rather consider them neutralized than have to put the poor buggers out of their misery for good."

They made their way down the path provided. They had not gone far, checking adjoining hatches as they went, when they found a wounded man lying in the corridor. He was wearing the overalls of an oil rig worker. A nasty, bloody stain spread across his abdomen. He appeared to be holding his guts in. Encizo and Hawkins knelt to check him over, while Manning took up station with his Tavor and its 40 mm grenade launcher, watching their backs.

"Easy, lad," McCarter said. "Do you speak English?"

"Yes," said the wounded man. He was Filipino, with a tattoo of a spider on his neck. He had the look of a manual laborer, the type of fellow you would expect to find on a rig such as this.

"What happened?" McCarter asked.

"Pirates," the man replied. "Pirates and soldiers. They had so much guns. So much guns. We tried to fight. We fight, and we fight. But they take the rig. Most workers escape. They go in boat. I am hurt and can't leave. I think I dying."

McCarter looked at Encizo, who turned from the wounded man and shook his head. "Machete wound, looks like," Encizo said quietly. "David, he's been gutted. I'm surprised he's stayed alive this long."

McCarter put his chin on his chest for a moment. When he made eye contact again with the wounded man, there was a pleading expression on the Filipino's face.

"I dying," the Filipino repeated.

"You are, mate," McCarter said. "I'm sorry. There's nothing I can do."

"There is," the wounded man said. "You can use your gun. I want go. I don't want stay. It hurts. It hurts too much. Please. Please help me go."

McCarter felt his face burning. It was what he'd feared the man would ask. He eased his Hi-Power out of its holster, made sure the suppressor was firmly attached, and placed its muzzle over the man's forehead.

"You're sure?" he asked softly.

"I sure," said the man. "Please. You number one. You help me. Thank you. Thank you."

McCarter looked the man in the eye and pulled the trigger.

The Briton stood. "Come on. Let's get out of here."

They made the machine shop. Here their progress was arrested by a group of pirates firing Kalashnikovs. The hollow clatter of the familiar weapons was deafening in the enclosed space. Empty shells bounced and jingled against the heavy machinery of the tool stations. All those motors and metal made for excellent cover from direct gunfire, but any oblique shots immediately ricocheted in every direction.

McCarter had to back off several steps and hunker down on one knee to lower his target profile as stray bullets buzzed and zinged over his head.

Unclipping a pair of grenades from his web gear, McCarter nodded to the others. "Grenades, lads," he said. "Unlimber them and prime them. On my three. One… Two…" He waited while his teammates readied their handheld bombs. Then he pulled the pins on first one grenade, then the other. "Three!"

Phoenix Force tossed their grenades into the machine shop. Then McCarter pulled the hatchway shot. There was a brief moment of silence when all the enemy guns stopped. Through the sealed hatch, they could hear frantic screaming.

The entire section of the oil rig vibrated with the strength of multiple explosions layered on one another. Just when the men of Phoenix Force thought the worst must be over, another rolling thunderhead of explosions shook the rig. It hammered the door that McCarter held, threatening to rip it from the hinges. This time, the explosions were accompanied by significant heat. McCarter was forced to release the hatch. He shook his hand in the air.

"Damn, that smarts," he said. "Gave me a good burn, that did."

Manning slid past his team leader and opened the hatch. He stepped inside. The others followed.

McCarter was amazed at what he saw. "Now that," he said, "is a well-shaken group of enemy gunmen."

"That's one way to put it," Manning said, sounding grim.

They walked through what had once been the machine shop, this time unopposed. The explosions had turned the space into a charnel house. There were bodies and pieces of bodies. Many of the corpses were charred and black, blown apart, unrecognizable as human. Weapons, both whole and broken, were everywhere. Metal shrapnel had torn the place to ribbons, smashing the machines, scattering their components across the space and embedding them in the walls and ceiling. Many of the pieces of metal were smoking. The stench of burning, scorched flesh was nauseating.

"Careful not to touch anything you don't have to," Manning warned. "This is all still hot. And there's no telling what other surprises there might be."

"You're thinking booby traps," James said.

"Got to be," Manning said. "That's the only thing I can think of that could have set everything off so badly in here. The grenades were designed to kill. But there was nothing in them that could have done this. There simply wasn't that kind of payload. This was other explosives, maybe satchel charges, maybe even explosive vests for use taking hostages or securing an exit. The grenades tore everything apart here, yes, but that was a precursor blast only. The explosives were set off by the grenades or by dying men in here. That's what did the majority of the damage we're seeing."

Encizo consulted his smartphone. He was checking the deck plan, and McCarter looked on over the Cuban-born guerilla fighter's shoulder. "That access hatchway at the other end," Encizo said, pointing, "will take us to one of the storage holds. Beyond that is a set of steps. That leads to a catwalk that connects one part of this section of the L to another part of the opposite section. The elevated walk has access points here and here." He indicated glowing icons on the phone's screen. "We're going to need to watch for a crossfire coming through there. It could get hairy."

"Understood," McCarter said. "All right. Let's move out."

They hit the hatchway and threw it open. The storage area beyond was fairly typical of such enclosures, although something about it struck McCarter as odd. He realized, at the last minute, what it was that was bothering him. The crates had been arrayed in a wedge formation, the very kind of formation you would use if you were going to defend the space from hostile attack—

"Down!" Manning roared. The big Canadian had noticed it, too, and he flattened himself against the deck while his teammates joined him. The Blackstar goons hidden behind those crates rose and began chattering away with Uzi submachine guns and a collection of automatic pistols and AR-patterned rifles. Their own barriers got in their way; the crates were broad enough across that they could not get an angle of fire low enough to take out Phoenix Force.

Gary Manning rolled himself up against the base of the wedge of crates.

McCarter tossed him a pair of door poppers.

Manning pressed the buttons on the mounds of plastic explosives and tossed them over the barrier.

The poppers, without a resisting surface to direct their

explosion, tore apart the gunmen on the other side of the crates. As the explosions were ripping them to pieces, Manning rolled up and leaped over the barrier. From that vantage, he aimed the mouth of his 40 mm launcher down the line of squirming, writhing Blackstar men and pulled the launcher's trigger. His shotgun round made ground meat of anyone still moving and of several bodies that were already on their way to assuming room temperature. When he was certain of his handiwork, Manning rolled off the barrier wedge and to the other side. There he stood among the blood and the bodies, his Tavor ready, his finger on the modular assault weapon's trigger.

"Clear," he said calmly.

The big Canadian helped his teammates over the barrier. Once there, they stalked on, through the opposite hatchway and to the entrance of the catwalk. Out there, the flames and smoke were thick. Dead bodies, the results of the initial run on the rig, were everywhere. From their position they could see the power-generation pod. It was intact, as it was supposed to be.

"Thank heaven for small favors," McCarter muttered. "Come on. Let's rush that catwalk. The faster we're across it, the safer we are. If we get hung up, they'll pick us off."

"I'll take the lead," Manning said. He shucked open his launcher and loaded another shotgun round. "Anything gets in our way, I'll play battering ram with this." He hefted the Tavor and launcher combination.

"Right, lads," McCarter said. "Go!"

They hit the catwalk with their boots pumping and the metal walkway clattering under their feet. "Watch those access points," Encizo warned. "Left and right. Watch them, watch them!"

His warning was either well timed or simply prescient. Pirates with machetes and pistols began to boil up over the walkway ladders. They were followed by black-uniformed mercenaries with AR rifles. The Phoenix Force commandos flattened themselves against the catwalk and began hosing the ladders down from above, walking their Tavors left and right. Men died. Other men fell, screaming, to the churning, bloody waters of the South China Sea below. At least one man lost his hands to a spray of bullets and screamed as he dropped down each rung of the ladder, trying and failing to grab on with the stumps of his forearms.

"We can't stay here!" McCarter called out. "They'll swamp us if we let them bog us down on the catwalk."

"Grab on to me!" Manning said. "Grab my belt!"

McCarter immediately saw what the big Canadian was after. He reached out, holding and firing his Tavor with one hand while hooking his hand in Manning's belt with the other. His teammates did the same, forming a human chain, staying flat against the catwalk so the enemy's guns couldn't effectively target the commandos. Encizo grabbed one of McCarter's boots. James took hold of Encizo's ankle. Hawkins grabbed on to both of James's feet.

Gary Manning began to pull.

Staying as low as he could, grabbing hold of the metal grate that was the walkway, the giant Canadian strained against their combined weight. The veins in his forehead and neck stood out. His face turned beet red. Holding his Tavor in front of his body like a spear, he dragged himself for all he was worth, switching the rifle from hand to hand as his fingers got tired, resting each side in turn.

Slowly, so slowly, Phoenix Force was being dragged across the catwalk.

His teammates had Manning's back, firing their weapons over the edge of the catwalk, keeping the approaching enemy at bay and thinning the numbers of the attacking herd in the process.

Manning reached the other end of the catwalk. Once he was over the lip of the railing, he was reasonably safe from enemy fire that came from below. He began grabbing each teammate in turn, hauling them bodily off the catwalk, throwing them past him and to safety from the opposition's bullets. When the last member of Phoenix Force had been thrown free, Manning took out his portable torch. He looked at McCarter for confirmation.

"Go ahead," the Briton said. "We won't be going back that way and, if we have to, we can have Jack ferry us over once the landing zone is clear."

Manning nodded. Several of the enemy fighters were now climbing up onto the catwalk from the access ladders. The Canadian ignited his torch and began melting the two points of connection holding the catwalk in place. The welds were thick and heavy. It was taking a lot of time to cut through them.

McCarter stepped up and started shooting. He brought down the nearest of the approaching gunmen, spilling them over the catwalk with his rounds.

"It's going," Manning said. "It's going!"

The catwalk unmoored from the section of oil rig on which Phoenix Force crouched.

One of the Blackstar men who had climbed up to the top of the walkway had time to reach out with one hand and scream. "No!"

"Yes," Gary Manning said, giving the entire catwalk a shove. Metal bent. The massive walkway, with nothing to hold it in place, started to collapse under its own weight, taking the men on its ladders and the hapless Blackstar mercenary with it. The screaming mass of humanity and metal landed in the South China Sea below.

The Stony Man Farm commandos entered the nearest access hatch and worked their way into this new section of the rig. According to the deck plan, they were three levels above the main control room. McCarter was willing to bet that it was there—where he had the most ability to monitor the rest of the rig—that Wijeya would be holed up. And if they were going to beard the dragon in its lair, they were going to need something working to their advantage. They needed Wijeya off balance, angry, ready to make a mistake.

McCarter opened his transceiver connection and switched the frequency of his radio to the band on which they had communicated with the pirate previously.

"Wijeya," said McCarter. "This is the man who killed your first mate. I just wanted you to know that he died badly. I have to admit I kind of shined you on a little before. I did put a bullet into him. But that was just to finish it."

"I love it when he starts telling stories," James said quietly.

"My men took turns torturing him," McCarter lied. "They get so bored, the lads. It seemed a shame to deny them some entertainment. So I let them go to work on him. It took a while. And the whole time, poor, loyal sod, he was calling your name. 'Wijeya! Wijeya! Why have you abandoned me?' he kept saying. I tell you, old chap, I finally put a bullet through his brain just because I couldn't take the wailing any longer."

McCarter waited. Finally he was rewarded. Wijeya's voice came on the line. "I am going to cut you apart, 'David.' I am going to make you pay for Mhusa. I am going to make your men watch while you die, and then I am going to torture each one of them so badly that death will not be a punishment, but a release about which they can only dream. When your men are lying, quivering, like sacks of deformed meat, and wishing they had never followed you, I will cut out your eyes and cut off your tongue and throw your body to the sea. And then I will force what I have taken from you down the throats of your men until they choke."

Once more, the line went dead.

"Well," James said, "I'd say you probably annoyed him a little."

"Just a little," Encizo agreed.

CHAPTER TWENTY-FOUR

The Suburban blasted through the entrance to the Rhem-Corp building, crushing Blackstar personnel under its wheels, scattering armed resistance with the force and the speed of its entry into the lobby. Carl Lyons threw the truck into Park and stepped down from the vehicle. He let his shotgun lie on its sling and drew his Colt Python. With the big pistol, he began firing mercy rounds into the heads of the struggling Blackstar men lying on the floor. Several of them had broken, twisted limbs hanging at odd angles. As Blancanales and Schwarz joined him, the gunshots silenced their screams and moans.

"Well, well," said the voice of Harold Rhemsen.

Lyons looked up. There were a pair of speakers set high on the wall, near the ceiling, and between them was a closed-circuit television camera. The light on the camera was blinking. As Lyons watched, the lens of the camera extended as the device zoomed in on him.

"Yeah," Lyons said. "Well, well. You're under arrest, Rhemsen. Call off your goons." He looked around the lobby. One of the entrances had been blown using grenades or some other kind of explosive. It was completely collapsed. There was another doorway, though, leading into the rest of the building. Obviously, Rhemsen was hoping his enemies would take this route. Lyons thought about the man-trap device that had nearly killed Schwarz. Not only did it stoke the fires of his anger, but it made him that much more determined not to play Rhemsen's game.

"I have money," Rhemsen said. "More money than you'll make in ten lifetimes as a paid assassin."

"We're not assassins," Lyons countered. "We're garbage men. Our job is to sweep up trash like you and make sure it gets where it belongs."

"That's very poetic," Rhemsen said. "And quite irrelevant. I know where I belong. It isn't here. It was never here."

"Cry me a river," said Lyons. "We know you've got a small army of goons in there. I will personally see to it that every last one of them dies on this property, today, along with you, if you don't surrender right now. I'm at the end of my patience with you, Rhemsen. This game is over. You lost. Now get with the program or get dead. Choice is yours."

"First," Rhemsen said, "we're going to play a little game. This building has been specially designed with defense in mind. You know that it is my fallback location. You wouldn't be here if you did not. If you thought the traps waiting for you in Hilton Head were bad, you haven't even begun to imagine what I'm going to put you through now."

"What are you getting out of this, Rhemsen?" Lyons demanded. "Money? Do you think you're going to have any financial assets in the United States that aren't frozen once the US government gets through with you? Your empire is over. Your reputation is destroyed. When this is done you'll be lucky if you're not flushed into some black-ops prison somewhere."

"Isn't that the American way," Rhemsen said.

There was a weird tinge to his voice now, an accent that Lyons could not place. He looked at his partners curiously. Schwarz shrugged. Blancanales shook his head. Neither of them knew what to make of it, either.

"Last I knew, *you* were American," Lyons said. "You're the kind of corrupt fat cat that's built the worst of our financial problems, Rhemsen. You think you won't be held accountable for everything you've done? The national security you've endangered? Hell, they might just charge you with treason. And the penalty for *that* is death. Think you're going to be chuckling so loud when they strap you into the gas chamber, or put you on a gurney for a final nap to Hell with a needle in your arm?"

"Tough talk, American," Rhemsen said. "But you still have to find me. And I think perhaps you'll be killed before you get this far. As for me, don't worry about what I get out of this. My future is planned. I know where I am headed, and I will be better off for it. I have stayed one step ahead of you and your pathetic government all the while. Nothing will change. Before this is over, the United States will experience the humiliation it so richly deserves."

"Stuff it, you plastic-faced freak," Lyons said. When Rhemsen did not immediately reply, Lyons piled it on. "That's right. You didn't think all that plastic surgery actually made you look *better*, did you? You could stop a clock from across a room and have enough ugly left over for seconds."

Lyons looked at Schwarz, who held his palm out, flat, parallel to the floor, and waggled it back and forth. "Meh," he said.

"Fine," Lyons said under his breath. To Rhemsen, he said, "So you want me to enter your little funhouse of horrors, right, Harry?" He thumbed back the hammer on his Colt Python. "I bet you'd really like that. I bet you're just salivating at the thought of me walking a death-trap-strewed path that leads straight to your door by way of some horror-movie, clockwork bear-trap thing. Well, I got news for you, you dumb bastard. I'm coming up. And I'm doing it my way."

Lyons raised his pistol and pulled the trigger. The remote camera exploded. For good measure, Lyons pumped a couple of bullets each into the speakers. The sound that came after that was scratchy and tinny, barely audible.

"Then come up here and catch me if you can," Rhemsen challenged. There was a final burst of static and the transmission stopped.

"That's our Ironman," Blancanales said. "Master of winning hearts and minds."

"My hero," Schwarz quipped.

"Now what?" Blancanales asked. "We still have to make our way up to wherever he's holed up."

"They always pull this video-game strategy," Schwarz said. "I guarantee you he's in some kind of office at the top level. Like the main boss at the end of a video game. And we've got to fight our way through the sublevel bosses to get to him. What do you want to bet that Fitzpatrick is lurking around here somewhere?"

"I should get so lucky," Lyons said. He examined the one doorway that they could use, the one that had not been collapsed by Rhemsen's trigger men. "I can tell you this. There's no way any of us is going through that door."

"How else?" Blancanales said. He examined the wrecked entrance. "We could try blowing this, but it looks bad. I don't think we're going to do anything but make the blockage worse."

"You guys," Lyons said. "You never have any faith in me." He walked to the Suburban and retrieved his war bag. Slinging it over his shoulder, he took out a drum that was specially tagged with a paint marker. This was how Cowboy Kissinger preferred to designate magazines. Every one of the loaded mags he provided to the Stony Man teams had a number. You never knew when you might discover a magazine had gotten bent during combat and become unusable, and if you didn't label them, how could you tell one from another?

This magazine was labeled with something more than a number: SO. That was Kissinger's designation for "slugs only." As Schwarz and Blancanales watched, Lyons began humming a song to himself.

"Is…is that…?" Schwarz said.

"No way," Blancanales said.

"You can't hum 'Soul Finger,'" Schwarz said. "It just… it just isn't right. Some things are just wrong, Ironman!"

But Lyons wasn't listening. He was too focused on how good what he was about to do was going to feel. The big former cop loaded the drum magazine into his automatic shotgun, jacked in the first round and began firing from the hip only six feet from the door. His target, however, was not the doorway from the lobby. He was shooting into the wall adjacent to that door.

It didn't take long to empty the drum. Still humming, he dropped the empty and loaded a fresh one. Again, he fired away, blazing with the deafening weapon, firing from the hip as the shotgun rested against its sling. When he had emptied a third drum, he was finally satisfied. He reloaded once again, stepped closer, raised his combat boot and kicked out with all his might.

The hole he had just carved in the wall broke open as he smashed through the piece of drywall he had just sectioned out. He used the force of his body like a battering ram, lowering his shoulder to shove through the rest of it. Once on the other side, covered in pieces of insulation and drywall dust, he gestured for Blancanales and Schwarz to follow.

"Well?" he said. "Don't just stand there staring with your mouths open. Let's get the hell going."

They stepped through the gap in the wall to follow their team leader. Lyons gestured to the other side of the door leading from the lobby. There were enough plastic explosives wired to that door to wipe out much of the lower floor of the building.

"I'd like to say that's a surprise," Schwarz said. "But it's really not. Not after everything we've seen from this guy so far."

"I really, really do not like Harold Rhemsen," Blancanales declared.

"Can you do anything about that, Gadgets?" Lyons said. "I'm not exactly comfortable leaving that behind us."

"Sure thing," Schwarz said. "I can work wonders when I don't have a slowly retracting un-fun box o' death clamped on my noggin." He began yanking detonator sticks out of the blocks of plastic explosives.

"Wait," Lyons said. "That's it? You're just pulling out the detonators? You don't want to cut any wires or do anything tricky?"

"I can cut wires if it makes you feel better," Schwarz said. "But this isn't exactly a tamper-proof circuit. It's designed to blow people up when they open the door. It doesn't need to be very tricky to do that." He finished. "All set. Let's go see what other fun things Rhemsen has waiting."

"Joy," Lyons growled.

What had once been an office cubicle farm had been torn apart. Wooden beams and plywood had been used to create a maze, similar to the one they had faced in Hilton Head. At first, Lyons had led the three men as they carefully crept through the path that was laid out, but by the time they discovered and circumvented their fourth tripwire, it was obvious that following the path Rhemsen had created was going to get them killed sooner rather than later.

"Give me all the door poppers," Lyons said.

Schwarz and Blancanales formed a relay team. Blancanales would dig through the duffel bag of goodies from the Farm, handing off the explosives to Schwarz. The electronics genius would then dole out the explosives one at a time to Lyons, who would use the bombs to blow hole after hole in Rhemsen's wooden maze. Soon, a trail of ragged, splintered craters led from one end of the room to other.

Once on the other side, the Able Team commandos looked over their handiwork. It was Blancanales who said what they were all thinking.

"We have to come through here in a hurry, especially under fire, we might blunder into something."

"Nah," Lyons said. "I don't think so. Give me the grens."

Once more they formed their little relay line, but this time, Blancanales would hand Schwarz grenades, Schwarz would pop the pins and Lyons would throw them. Lyons had a good, strong pitching arm. They worked their way from the back of the room to as close to their current position as they dared. It wouldn't do to nail themselves with one of their own explosive surprises.

At the end of the cubicle farm was an elevator shaft and a stairwell. The stairwell was blocked off with boards nailed to the wall. The elevator stood open, waiting. A piece of duct tape had been used to block the electric eye, which held the doors open.

"Wow," Schwarz said.

"I know, right?" Blancanales said. "Talk about considerate."

Lyons walked over and ripped the duct tape from the door before retreating to stand next to his teammates. He hunkered down and covered his head with his arms.

"Uh," Blancanales said.

"Right," Schwarz said. The two teammates joined their leader crouching on the floor. It was a good thing they did, too.

The moment the elevator doors closed, some kind of relay was triggered. The explosion that sounded from within the elevator dropped the metal box into the basement, from the sounds of things. The vibration of the blast shook this part of the building. Somewhere, a fire alarm started to go off. Sprinklers above them began to douse them with water.

Lyons stood. "That's much better," he sighed.

"Come on, guys," Schwarz said. "Let's see what's on the stairs. Oh, wait. We used all the door poppers."

"Popped door," Lyons said, "coming up." He brought up his shotgun and began mercilessly spraying the fire door to the stairs, splitting the wooden beams that had been nailed across it. When he had spent another two drums and exhausted his supply of shotgun ammunition, he placed the USAS-12 quietly on the floor, pulled the last of the wooden beams away and yanked the door open.

"Nothing went boom," Schwarz said.

"Yeah," Lyons said. "Let's get the hell up there. I'm tired of playing these games."

"You keep saying that," Schwarz said. "I have to admit, I'm kind of tired of playing my game, too. I'm stuck on Level 99 and I can't seem to get any farther."

They climbed the stairs, taking them one at a time, going slow to check for pressure plates and tripwires. This, unfortunately for Lyons, gave Schwarz entirely too much time to talk. "The real problem with the game," he said, "is the halo system."

"Stop talking, Gadgets," Lyons ordered as they climbed.

"See, if you complete level without using too much of your mana score," Schwarz went on, "you get a halo. And if you can do it within a time limit specified by each level, you get a second halo. But to get a perfect three-halo score on the level, you've got to find a way to complete the level in less than the recommended threshold times. It's a real bear, I can tell you. I got stuck on that level and—"

"I'm going to put you back in that bear-trap thing," Lyons rumbled. "I swear I will."

They reached the top. The fire door here was propped open. Beyond it was a series of darkened hallways. When Lyons's boot hit the floor, the floorboard creaked.

The sound of a rifle bolt being pulled back was all Lyons needed to tip him off.

There wasn't even time to shout an alarm. Lyons fell backward, throwing out his arms, knocking both of his team members to the floor with him. The gunfire that followed ripped apart the walls above them and coated them in Sheetrock fragments. Lyons, Schwarz and Blancanales returned fire. They emptied their guns, reloaded and emptied them again. The shooting went on and they started running low, finally, on ammunition. Blancanales tossed his Beretta 92-F to Lyons when he ran out of speedloaders for his Python. Lyons started burning through magazines of 9 mm bullets.

As bad as the odds were, Able Team was making a dent. The legions of Blackstar soldiers who came up against them fell, one after another. Soon the bodies were two and three deep. This was no longer an office, no longer a manufacturing facility. It was a slaughterhouse.

"I'm empty!" Schwarz shouted.

"Me, too," Blancanales said.

"Crap," Lyons swore. "Dry here, too."

But the shooting from the outer rooms had stopped. Lyons stood and, careful lest he take a bullet through the face for his trouble, poked one eye around the corner. All he saw were corpses.

"Carl?" Schwarz said. "What do you see?"

"The way out," Lyons answered. "Come on. The door past this section is clear."

Moving cautiously, the members of Able Team made it past the death-house floor. They cleared the final doorway. Beyond it was some kind of vast training area, the kind of modular conference room that had walls that could be extended from side to side to chop up the space and make for multiple sub-rooms. Everything had been cleared out to make the space as large as possible. The floor was completely bare except for the institutional carpeting.

Jason Fitzpatrick stood there.

"I gotta say," Fitzpatrick said, "I don't normally go in for this kind of thing. But you three? You've cost me a hell of a lot of time and aggravation. And I'm in a pretty good mood. See, I came into some money. So I thought to myself, 'Jason, you handsome devil, how are you going to reward yourself for all your hard work?' And I finally figured it out. I know what I deserve."

"You really need to stop talking now," Lyons said.

"I'm calling you out, boys," Fitzpatrick said. "It's the end of the line for you. It's time for Jay Fitzpatrick to teach you all a very valuable lesson."

"Oh, yeah?" Lyons taunted. "You and what army?"

"This one," Fitzpatrick said. From alcoves in the wall, concealed from view, emerged a large force of Blackstar men. They all held collapsible batons.

"I don't like where this is going," Schwarz muttered.

"I figured," Fitzpatrick said, "that my friends here and I would just beat you to death."

"Then come on if you're coming," Carl Lyons said.

CHAPTER TWENTY-FIVE

A maze of corridors separated Phoenix Force from the control deck level. Any of the compartments could house pirates, Blackstar forces or both. Just thinking about the unholy alliance made McCarter's skin crawl. And that's when he had an idea.

"Rafe," he said as the Phoenix Force commandos waited in a relatively safe corner of the deck they currently occupied. Manning was scouting ahead, trying to find the route most clear of enemies, but they were going to have to check compartment by compartment as they went unless they wanted to risk getting caught in a crossfire and cut apart.

But there might be a better way. There might be a way to do this that protected their own lives while also thinning the ranks of the enemy.

"The Sikorsky," McCarter said. "It's got an advanced communications package, doesn't it? To let us talk to the Farm?"

"Yes," Encizo said. "Of course. Why?"

"The same equipment that we use for transmitting can be used for jamming, yes?" the Briton continued. "The RF that we used to speak to Wijeya on his frequency. The scanning equipment we used to locate it is the same equipment we used to contact him. I'm correct, aren't I?"

"Where in the heck are you going with this, David?" Hawkins asked.

"Jack," McCarter said as he touched his transceiver. "G-Force, do you read? What is your status?"

"Overwatch," Grimaldi said. "I'm keeping a close eye on things up here, but staying far enough out that they can't light me up with rockets. How are things going with you?"

"We've got a lot of bad guys between us and Wijeya," McCarter explained. "Think you can help us out?"

"Can't fit the Sikorsky down there or I would," Grimaldi said. "You need an extra gun? I've got a trusty MAC-10 I never go anywhere without. Be happy to join you down there."

"No," McCarter said. "Not what I had in mind, mate. But I wonder. Think you can fire up the commo gear and step on Wijeya's frequency for me?"

"What's the matter, you can't get that pirate bastard on the horn?"

"No," McCarter said. "I want to talk over him, not talk to him. I want override on his frequency. I figure he must have walkie-talkies sprinkled among the ranks of the gunners here. It's the only way they would be able to communicate effectively. That means his line is a party line, and I want to be able to talk to everyone on the other end."

"I can do that," Grimaldi said. "But the kind of power drain it's going to take…I can't sustain that sort of thing for long or I'll drain the bird's batteries and then it's only a matter of time before I'm swimming."

"That's a problem?" McCarter asked.

"Only if you want to try to stop Captain Blackbeard down there from hearing what you say. I don't have that kind of juice."

"No," McCarter said. "It doesn't matter if Wijeya overhears. By the time I'm through talking, the damage will be done."

"You got it," Grimaldi said. "Give me a minute."

"Hurry, Jack," McCarter urged. "I have a feeling the hammer is about to come down on us."

No sooner had McCarter said that than the sound of gunfire began to sound farther down the corridor. A figure, moving at a full run, was approaching. The silhouette it made was far too large to be anyone but Gary Manning. The members of Phoenix Force took up a supporting fire position and waited as Manning cleared their location. Once he was safely back behind their lines, from their vantage in the hatchways at their end of the corridor, they braced their weapons and prepared to fire.

"Were you followed?" McCarter said.

"Wait for it," Gary Manning warned. He held up three fingers. Then he held up two. Then he held up just one.

Gunfire from the other end of the corridor began to ricochet through the space. The pursuing shooters were uniformed, firing high-tech AR weapons. That would be the Blackstar goons again. McCarter drew a bead on one of them in the red-dot scope of his Tavor, dragged in a breath and let out half of it. Holding what was left, he let his finger squeeze the trigger until the shot broke by surprise.

The man in McCarter's sights fell dead.

There were more. They fired, and they continued firing, until the sheer metal din of rounds striking the bulkheads around Phoenix Force was deafening and painful. The Stony Man Farm commandos returned fire, but they were now very much outgunned. The team at the end of the hall was made up of only Blackstar, with no pirate crew members in sight. That was bad, because while the Blackstar men weren't the most experienced soldiers in the world, they certainly had more discipline than pirate hirelings.

Of course, that was the root of the idea McCarter had, and that idea might just save them.

"Come on, Jack," he said quietly. "Don't let us down. Patch me through to Wijeya's men."

The intense gunfire continued. If they had to keep up this pace for too much longer, he had serious doubts about their ability to break through. There was a lot more rig between them and Wijeya. The goal was to neutralize the enemy force holding the oil rig. Their secondary purpose—to determine if China was behind the attacks—seemed pretty much moot at this point. These men were no more in league with China than Phoenix Force was, unless the Chinese had begun hiring American security contractors and castoff pirate crews to achieve their ill-conceived military goals.

The whole thing was just crazy. He was tired of thinking about it. He was tired of debating it. He wanted something simple. Just give him an enemy to shoot at. Just give him something direct.

"You're good," Grimaldi's voice said over the radio. "I repeat, David, you're good. Give me the word and I will step on them like a giant ant at a picnic."

"I'm not sure what the hell that means," McCarter said, "but I do thank you, G-Force. Transmit now."

Something in the tonal quality of the transmission changed. McCarter realized what that was. It was power.

"Attention," McCarter said. He imagined he could hear his voice echoing throughout the oil rig, but that was not likely. It was only in his head, what he expected to be happening. "Attention, all crewmen of Yanuar Wijeya. You don't know me. I represent the authorities. And I am here to tell you that if you continue fighting alongside the Blackstar men, you will be killed. Blackstar is a criminal organization. They are wanted men, desperate men. In every operation that Blackstar has conducted on foreign soil, they always murder their foreign allies."

Manning looked at his teammates, then to McCarter. The Briton shrugged. He was making all this up as he went along.

"I want you to know," he said, continuing, hoping Grimaldi's power levels would hold out long enough for him do what he had to do, "that we don't want you. We aren't interested in pirates. We are here to arrest Blackstar. And even better, there is a reward. For every Blackstar man who is captured or killed, there is a reward of… five hundred American dollars."

"You don't think that's overplaying it?" James whispered.

"A man with a gun who knows how to take care of himself…" McCarter paused. "Well, that chap could make himself a small fortune, hunting enemies like the Blackstar men. All you have to do is kill them and bring proof that you've killed them. You'll be handsomely paid. And then you will be allowed to board your boat and leave. This I promise you, lads. You'll know where to find me when the Navy arrives here in force. We've, uh, we've invited the Chinese to come here and board the rig. They're eager to prove they weren't involved in the attack. I can imagine that once they do get here with one of…with one of their aircraft carriers, anyone aboard who hasn't proved he's on the right side by taking down some Blackstar mercenary bounties will probably be horribly killed, instead of allowed to get on his launch and return to his life on the seas. Well, that's all, chaps. Good day…and good luck."

"Transmission cut," Grimaldi reported.

"Well, then," McCarter said. "Let's see what sort of mischief that's caused for us, shall we?"

"David…" James said. "What have you done?"

"If we're lucky," said McCarter, "I've just put the two groups we're trying to clear off this rig at each other's throats."

"Wait for it," Encizo said.

"Anybody notice something?" James said. They all looked at each other and the realization was simultaneous: the gunfire from the enemy had stopped. The Blackstar men had withdrawn.

"All right," McCarter said. "On me. We do this by the book, in twos, with me at the point. Gary, you bring up the rear with another of those shotgun busters loaded. We're going to check, compartment by compartment, until we reach the control deck level. And when we find Wijeya, we're going to put him out of his misery once and for all so we can all go home. Sound good?"

There was yet another chorus of assent from Phoenix Force. McCarter shouldered his Tavor, checked it out of ritual habit to make sure a round was chambered, and led the way, ready for whatever threat might present itself.

They had not gotten very far when they started to find dead Blackstar men. In the distance, they could hear explosions and gunfire. There were screams, too. The Blackstar mercenaries and the pirates were fighting each other. Every gunman on either side who was taken out was one less that Phoenix Force would have to deal with.

"Look at these poor buggers," McCarter said. "They're all missing ears."

"The pirates are taking proof," said James. "They think they're going to use it to rack up those imaginary bounties."

"Pity for the Blackstar goons, then," said the Briton. "That's life in the big city, isn't it?"

"Yeah," Manning said. "I guess it is." His tone was dark, but he did not sound critical. Every member of the team was tired of Blackstar and the harm the agency had caused. It was time to take them down, and if McCarter's ruse did some of the heavy lifting for them, that was all right. Only pragmatic dedication to the efficient completion of the mission had utility value here. None of the men of Phoenix Force would ever compromise their moral values, nor step one inch out of frame where justice was concerned…but when it came to taking down a vicious, murdering enemy, they would quickly embrace whatever method proved out their goals.

Which was a very long-winded way of saying, "Whatever got the job done," McCarter reflected.

"David," Grimaldi said in his ear. "I've got everybody's favorite pirate captain trying to perform spin control over the RF."

"Patch him in so we can listen, G-Force."

"You got it," the Stony Man pilot said.

"No bounties. Repeat, no bounties," Wijeya was saying. He sounded hysterical. "The only way we get paid is if you follow the plan I laid out! Our benefactor…the man funding our operation—the mercenaries in the black uniforms are his men! You fools, you fools, you must listen to me! There is a helicopter flying above us. The helicopter is obviously an asset of the Central Intelligence Agency. I will make contact with it. I will convince the CIA killers to give us safe passage off this oil rig…"

"Switch him off, Jack," McCarter said. The pilot did so. The Briton shook his head.

"Lonely at the top," he said quietly. "Let's keep on, lads. I think we've made sufficient trouble for that bastard that we can focus on moving to find him."

James moved into position to take point as McCarter examined bodies. The group of commandos continued down the corridor. Encizo checked the deck plan on his smartphone every few corridor junctions.

"This place is a lot larger on the inside than it seemed on the outside," Hawkins said.

"That's because the rig extends underground below the water," James said. "It's a drill rig, man. That's how these things work."

"Right," Hawkins drawled. "I'll try to wrap my head around that." Hawkins threw up his hand and James slapped it with a high-five.

"My man," James said, "that's all any of us can hope to do in this crazy world."

"Live man!" James shouted suddenly. "Guys, I've got a live one over here." He bent to inspect the Blackstar thug who was lying on the deck in front of him. Someone had tried to separate the man's ear and done a poor job of it. He had been gut shot and left to bleed out.

"Pick him up," McCarter directed. "Rafe, check that compartment. Gary, back him up."

Encizo spun the wheel on the compartment indicated and opened the hatch, being careful in case there were armed enemies inside. There was no one, only a bunk that had seen better days and a few sailors' trunks stacked haphazardly next to it. The Phoenix Force men dropped their recovered enemy onto the bunk. McCarter knelt beside the man.

"Medical kit," Manning said, handing the one he carried to McCarter. The Briton nodded and took it. He took out a bandage and pressed it against the ruin of the Blackstar man's ear.

"You son of a…" the man tried to say. "It was you. Your voice. On the radios."

"I'm afraid so," McCarter said. "And unless you'd like us to throw you back out into the corridor where we found you, so some other pirate can come along and scalp you, I suggest you tell me what I want to know."

"Ask your questions," the mercenary said sullenly.

"Your name, and who you work for," McCarter said.

"Burke," the man said. "Steven Burke. I'm an employee of Blackstar corporation."

"And Blackstar is more or less comfortable with breaking the law, yes?" McCarter said. "Black operations around the world. Murder for fun and profit. A few international incidents, a few laws broken. What's a bit of anarchy among friends, eh?"

"I don't run the company," Burke said. "I just follow orders. I just do what I'm told."

"And that includes conducting false flag operations that implicate China in this region?"

"We had nothing to do with that," Burke said. "Management sent us out here to back up the pirates. Said we had no choice but to cooperate with that scum. Said they were running some kind of covert op and we should just turn a blind eye to anything they did that seemed odd. Nobody mentioned that they'd turn on us the first chance they got. The first chance *you* gave them. Is there even any bounty?"

"I think that's the last of your concerns right now," McCarter said. He began examining the man's torso, probing with his hands. "Are you aware that your breathing is labored?"

"What? Yeah… Got a…got a weight in my chest. It'll pass. Just the stress of the op."

Manning came to kneel beside McCarter. "David," he said, "he sweating badly." To Burke, the Canadian said, "Are you feeling any shooting pains in your arm?"

"Yeah," Burke said. "Think I pulled something. I'll be okay. I just need to rest. Leave me alone, you bastards. I told you everything…everything…" His voice trailed off. Suddenly he clutched his chest and his eyes squeezed shut.

"He's having a heart attack," Manning said. "Here, help me with…" Now it was Manning's turn to trail off. Burke was staring at the ceiling, seeing nothing. A death rattle escaped his lungs.

"Poor blighter," McCarter said. "Nobody deserves to go out that way. Even murderous mercenary trash. Better a quick end than that."

"Well," Encizo said, "not our problem now." He shook his head. McCarter was inclined to agree with the sentiment. It sure was a bloody business, this war in which they were engaged.

"Onward," McCarter said.

Encizo checked his deck plan once more. He showed it to McCarter. "We just need to continue to the end, here." He pointed at the diagram. "Then down the manway. The control level is there. And it's a good bet Wijeya is there, too."

"Let's go find the bastard," McCarter said. "I'm ready to put a stop to all this."

The commandos of Phoenix Force walked on. They encountered little resistance. As they traveled, the screaming and gunfire faded. Either the fighting was diminishing or the enemy was withdrawing to the upper decks, leaving the interior of the rig.

"G-Force," Calvin James said. "What's happening up there?"

"Funny you should ask," Grimaldi answered. "Because I've got what looks like a party forming on the deck…and I like my chances of cleaning house."

"Go to work, Jack," McCarter said. "Go to work."

CHAPTER TWENTY-SIX

"Roger that," the ace Stony Man pilot acknowledged.

Grimaldi flipped the switches that would allow him to control the Sikorsky's weapons systems automatically. It wasn't nearly as accurate as having gunners on board. Without a crew, he could only angle the guns on either side in the general direction of the enemy by using the chopper itself. The same was true of the grenade launcher. This meant that, without people to man the guns and launcher, precision strikes were out of the question. But flying high above the oil rig platform, passing over the relatively untouched power-generation station and scoping the gathering beneath him, Grimaldi figured that precision was not going to be what was called for. Not for the next few minutes, anyway.

A group of the nastiest, most rag-tag, hopeless-looking pirates you could ever want to see was flooding out of the rig. Some of them were carrying dead bodies. That was a new one. The bodies all wore black uniforms. A few of the pirates were waving black pieces of fabric, some of which looked like the top half of BDU fatigues. That was McCarter's work, right there. The pirates had turned on their Blackstar helpers and were now looking to collect.

A delightful lack of gunfire was now directed his way. As a pilot who had spent more hours flying combat missions than he cared to admit, Grimaldi was necessarily allergic to taking small-arms fire from the ground. He was positively opposed to fielding anything heavier. The rockets and EMP weapons they had seen thus far were the stuff of nightmares for a man like Jack Grimaldi. He was grateful for the pirates' mistaken idea that he was somebody who could bestow money on them. Whatever delusion got you through the day, right?

The pirates were waving him down now, trying to get him to land so they could, as they mistakenly believed, collect their reward. Grimaldi started moving in tighter and tighter circles, getting closer to the rig each time. His purpose was twofold. First, he wanted to make sure he could spot an antiair weapon if this was all an elaborate ruse. The pirates were probably fairly uneducated, for the most part, but there were some among them who were very smart, as they had already seen. He didn't want to let them draw him into a trap. He was damned if he was going to let a bunch of second-rate pirates or mercenary hire-ons knock him out of the sky. He had been shot at by far worse.

The thought brought back memories for Jack Grimaldi. He couldn't really remember, sometimes, just how long he had been at this. His teammates never gave him any grief about it, but it was a fact that in his younger days, he had worked for the mafia. Eventually, with the help of the Big Guy, he had seen the error of his ways, first working as a mole, then coming aboard with the organization that would eventually become the Farm. In all the years since he had been warring with the predators who sought to destroy freedom and liberty around the globe. It was, he thought, a pretty damned good way to go through life. There was plenty of action, plenty of adventure. There was never a dull moment. And in between missions, there were pretty ladies to entertain.

Yeah, if he had it to do over again, he would, and he'd choose the same things.

His second purpose, in flying increasingly small arcs around the oil rig, was to herd the pirates. They were following him, fixed on him. He was no longer a Sikorsky helicopter to them. He was now, thanks to David Mc-Carter's trick, a great big flying piggy bank in the sky.

Time to give these bastards the surprise of their lives.

He opened up the external speakers. Once more, Wagner's "Ride of the Valkyries" began to play. That was when Grimaldi's radio lit up. The frequency was low-band RF. That was the one on which Wijeya broadcast. Interesting.

Grimaldi reached out and flicked the switch to answer the transmission.

"You, up there," Wijeya's voice called out. "You are a CIA pilot, yes?"

"This is G-Force," Grimaldi said. "We are not CIA. All we are is just another brick in the wall. I'm coming for you, Wijeya."

"Do not be a fool, American," Wijeya said. "I will make you a rich man. Bring your chopper down. Let me board it. Carry me from this place. I will give you money. I will make you wealthy. I have many resources. My benefactor can give you even more. Help us accomplish our goals."

"We don't need no money," Grimaldi said. "We don't need no education, and we don't need no thought control."

"I have heard this," Wijeya said. "You are quoting a song. You are trying to make me feel foolish."

"Pink Floyd is never foolish," Grimaldi said. "Now, if you'll excuse me, Blackbeard, I have some serious killing of your pirate scum crew to do."

"Wait," Wijeya said. "I will tell your government everything you want to know."

"Don't know what government that is," Grimaldi said.

"Stop playing games with me!" Wijeya demanded. "It was my benefactor who directed me to attack the targets we have chosen. He provided the money. He provided the weapons. He told us when and where to attack, and he told us to wear Chinese uniforms or fly Chinese flags or make other gestures to implicate the Chinese. This is information you want, yes?"

"You haven't really told me anything I don't know," Grimaldi said.

"I have told you that the Chinese are not behind these attacks," Wijeya countered. "Is this not what you want to know?"

"Give me the name of the person who hired you," Grimaldi said. "Do that, and maybe you even leave here alive, Wijeya."

There was a very pregnant pause. Finally, when Wijeya came back on the line, he sounded sheepish. "I...I do not know his name," Wijeya said.

"Then give me a description," Grimaldi said. "Something we can use to identify him."

"I do not know that, either," Wijeya said. "We never met. We only spoke by satellite phone."

"Not very helpful, are you?" Grimaldi said.

"Wait!"

Grimaldi cut the connection. He made one more tight arc, the closest yet, and when he was satisfied that all the pirates were in the kill zone, he brought the Sikorsky down to hover over the deck of the oil rig. He didn't dare use the grenade launcher, given the damage that might do and his inability to target more specifically, so he simply didn't switch it on. The 7.62 mm guns, though...they were all he would need, and he switched his fire control to "live."

"This is G-Force," he said into the radio for Phoenix Force's benefit. "I am commencing my attack run...now."

He pulled the trigger.

The guns on either side of the Sikorsky began belching

deadly lead. The pirates below were scythed like wheat. Grimaldi walked the chopper back and forth, making tight semicircles with the nose depressed. His rounds tore through the ranks of the pirates, blowing them open, ripping them to pieces. The deck of the oil rig was suddenly awash in blood and body parts.

When Grimaldi was satisfied that the majority of the pirates had been wiped out, he started to make wider circles around the rig. Now he was looking for stragglers. Phoenix Force was below. That meant the decks, which had been controlled by the enemy, were a free-fire zone. He roamed the air above the rig, picking off any Blackstar goon or pirate crew member he saw.

His "target rich environment" eventually became very sparse.

The Stony Man pilot completed several more sweeps of the rig. Finally, when he was satisfied, he prepared to contact the Farm. The commo gear on his chopper had been recording since the start of the mission. It was standard procedure to make a mission log. He opened the scrambler and placed a call by satellite relay to the Farm.

"Jack," Price said. "What have you got?"

"The decks of the rig are clean," Grimaldi said. "Phoenix successfully got most of the pirates belowdecks to come up for air. I've made sure that's the last air they'll draw. And it looks like those pirates managed to take out most of the Blackstar forces aboard the rig, as well."

"You've been busy," Price said. "That's fine work, Jack. Why are you calling, though? Normally David calls in with mission updates, unless he can't."

"My own initiative," Grimaldi confirmed. "I've just had an interesting conversation with Yanuar Wijeya, the pirate captain. He claims that the operations implicating the Chinese are all the actions of a mysterious benefactor who financed the ops and directed all of his activities. Unfortunately, if he's telling the truth, his employer used cut-outs and never dealt with him directly except through sat phone."

"Which we can't trace," Price speculated.

"I figured it wouldn't be a lot of help," Grimaldi said. "But every little bit…well, helps. I guess that's silly."

"No, Jack," Price said. "You did fine. Relay me through to David, will you?"

"Relaying," Grimaldi said. "David and company, I have Barb on the line. I think she's inquiring as to your general well-being."

"We have cleared out all resistance," McCarter said. "Wijeya and a small reserve force, we believe, have taken refuge on the control deck. They've barricaded the hatches. We're going to have to get creative to get in there. Once we do, though…well, once we do, I have reason to think this end of the operation is finished. The intel we've received has these folks as puppets, and I think it's most likely that Rhemsen is pulling the strings."

"Yes," Price said. "That squares with what Able has been able to tell us. And what Jack got out of Wijeya just now."

"Oh?" McCarter said. "I hadn't heard about that."

"He made me a better offer," Grimaldi said. "I'm going to hire on as a pirate pilot. Not a lot of pirates have their own air force."

"That sounds like a great career move, Jack," McCarter said. "That and junk bonds."

"I was thinking of investing in some internet startups, too," Grimaldi said. "Crowd-funding and all. Wave of the future. I'm bringing her in, David. Barb, I've got to let you go. I'm heading into the thick of it down there and I need to make sure nobody ganks me."

"Understood," Price said. "Good hunting. Farm, out."

Grimaldi set the chopper down on the oil rig's bloody, scorched landing pad. With his trusty MAC-10 submachine gun at the ready, he climbed out of the Sikorsky. As he always did, he felt naked, walking around without the big helicopter around him. He wondered if other pilots felt separation anxiety when they were outside their craft for some reason while still on a mission. It felt weird not to be in the seat of the chopper, not to have the stick in his hands. But he was no stranger to firing the occasional shot in anger from the ground, either.

He began checking the bodies on the deck. Most of them were obviously gone, but there were a few who warranted checking. He toed these with his boot. Smoke rose, spun in wild eddies by the still-moving blades of his chopper. It took a while to spin down the engine and bring those blades to a stop. Grimaldi also didn't intend to stray far from the whirlybird. It was, after all, their ticket off this rig, once all the enemy was neutralized.

He had a feeling they had come pretty close, even if there were a few enemies still moving under their own power. The pile of corpses in front of him was worse than anything in any war movie. But then, having fought this endless war, first against the mafia, then against terrorism, Grimaldi didn't understand why anyone watched war movies. Either they were so unrealistic they were laughable, or they were so real they brought back too many bad memories. Either way, there was no reason he could see to watch one.

The pirate near his right boot began to moan.

Grimaldi leaned down. He took the canteen from his belt and offered the dying man a drink. The pirate spoke no English, or was so far gone he did not try to speak even when Grimaldi prompted him several times.

The pilot supposed that seeing a man treat with compassion a former enemy, an enemy that the pilot himself had ripped apart with machine guns, might seem strange to an outsider. But once a man was down, once he was no longer a threat to you, even if he was an enemy…you could be compassionate to a fallen foe. No less than the Big Guy himself, had taught Grimaldi that.

The pirate he was examining quietly died. Grimaldi eased the man gently back down to the deck.

Standing, the pilot walked a long, slow death watch across the deck of the oil rig. He found nobody else still alive. Finally he climbed back into the Sikorsky, checked the status of the various gauges and readouts, and activated his communications system.

"David, this is G-Force," he said. "All clear up here. I repeat, all clear up here. To the best that I can assess, the rig is clear topside. What's your status below?"

"We're preparing for the final assault on the control deck," said McCarter. "Return to overwatch, Jack, and we'll be up to catch our ride out of town soon. Also, let me know if Wijeya tries to offer you any more side income. I'm happy to match his offer, mate."

"No need," Grimaldi said. "I was thinking of getting a paper route."

"It's all about income streams," McCarter said. "Phoenix, out."

"G-Force, out." Grimaldi spun up the Sikorsky, made sure everything was in the green, and took the big helicopter back into the sky.

This was where he belonged. Above it all, in the night, in the blue sky, in the space above. He couldn't imagine another life. He couldn't imagine being anything other than what he was: a Stony Man Farm pilot, standing on the front lines of the war between the predators and the forces of justice. He would do this job for as long as they let him. He would fly this chopper, and a hundred others, and anything else that had wings or rotors, until he couldn't wrap his fingers around the controls anymore. Plenty of men kept right on flying well into old age. Grimaldi didn't feel old. In his heart, he knew he was a long way from being forced to retire.

Jack Grimaldi smiled. He dipped and banked the chopper, bringing it around for a patrol pass. The oil rig was smoking. He checked his fuel levels. Everything was holding. He had plenty in the reserve tanks to keep him aloft and watching over his boys.

There were few flying machines that Grimaldi hadn't operated. There was just one quality that all of them had in common. That quality was freedom, the feeling of being unfettered, of leaving the Earth behind. Even when enemies were shooting at him, he felt the pull of freedom.

That was why they fought. That was the mission of Phoenix Force, of Able Team, of Stony Man Farm. They stood on the battle lines, on the ground, in the water, up here in the beautiful liberty of the skies, because freedom was the right of all human beings. They fought to make others free. They fought to preserve others' freedom.

They fought, and would keep on fighting.

Yeah.

CHAPTER TWENTY-SEVEN

Carl Lyons threw himself into the ranks of the enemy. He grabbed the nearest Blackstar goon, snapped his wrist and took his collapsible baton away. This he smashed across the face of the next man. Behind him he could hear Schwarz and Blancanales fighting, as well, backing him up, watching out for him.

He lost himself in the battle. There was nothing outside him now. There was no worrying about the mission, no anxiety for success or failure. There was no outrage at the ignominious fate Schwarz almost suffered. There was no emotion at all. Lyons was a creature very much driven by rage at times, he knew, but there was a point beyond rage, a point at which he stopped feeling anger and just felt…cold, numb, ready to take on the enemy and fight his way through no matter what.

He brought his borrowed baton down on the face of another man, then smashed it across the man's knees and then drove his foot into the man's gut. He plucked a second baton from this fallen Blackstar thug's nerveless fingers, stood and roared in defiance. Now he had a baton in each hand.

"Come on!" he bellowed. "Come on if you're coming!" The whirling, vicious cyclone of doom that was Carl Lyons with a blunt weapon in both fists started smashing, striking and slashing its way into the ranks of the Blackstar men. The mercenaries had seemed arrogant at first, confident in their greater numbers, but now, with Carl Lyons ruthlessly smashing them down, they were starting to flee.

Always, as he fought, Lyons was aware of Fitzpatrick. The coward was hanging back, hoping his goons would be able to do the job, maybe thinking that once the members of Able Team had been sufficiently beaten down, he would step in to finish the job. That squared with what they had seen of this prick's character up to now. How someone as venal and cowardly as Fitzpatrick reached a position of authority, even in a corrupt mercenary outfit, Lyons didn't know. Could the world of soldiering really have gone that far downhill?

He knew it hadn't, of course. Cowardice and self-service had always been qualities found in certain stripes in the military, just as in every other walk of life. People were people. Many of them were vile and there wasn't anything you could do about them.

Except smash them and break all the bones in their faces.

Lyons whipped his batons into the cheekbones of the man in front of him, feeling and hearing the crunch of bone fragments being smashed free. He followed up his attack by hammering down with the batons, alternating his strikes, beating and smashing and whipping.

At his flanks, his teammates had acquired batons of their own. Schwarz was alternating baton strikes with acrobatic kicks, doing a fair amount of damage in the process. Blancanales fought as he lived, with a kind of quiet dignity, striking targets of opportunity with his own baton and making quick work of the less-experienced Blackstar troops.

Finally they had smashed and beaten as many men as there were enemies willing to advance. Lyons broke his left-hand baton across the face of one of the last remaining goons. The Blackstar man went down like a steer with a bolt through its head. Lyons wheeled on Fitzpatrick then.

Blancanales and Schwarz finished their own batch of enemies. The big training hall was now filled with unconscious, dazed and dead men, their bodies askew at Able Team's feet.

Lyons looked down at his remaining baton. It was bent. That was the problem with those collapsible jobs. If you hit too hard with them, they couldn't stand up to it. Give him a good, old-fashioned hardwood baton any day. Something modern like a PR-24 side-handle. Or even an ancient Japanese *tonfa*. He liked a weapon you could really lean into, something that shattered bone and ruptured organs. He had done enough of that here today.

Well. Almost enough. There was still Fitzpatrick.

"Come on, you son of a bitch," Lyons said. "Let's do this." He cracked his knuckles, flexing his big, powerful fists.

"Oh, you just don't know when to quit," Fitzpatrick said. He talked tough, but Lyons could see it in the man's eyes: he was scared, and trying to cover it. Lyons charged, lowering his head and coming at Fitzpatrick like a bull, slamming into the man's chest and driving him back and to the floor.

To his credit, Fitzpatrick fought back hard. He hammered away with his fists and his knees, trying to get off low-line kicks that would have shattered Lyons's knees or ankles had any of the strikes connected. Lyons hammered away with strikes of his own. He had more training than Fitzpatrick. He had more experience than Fitzpatrick. He had dealt out more pain in the course of his career than Fitzpatrick could even dream about.

But he wanted to make sure Fitzpatrick felt this defeat. The bastard had it coming.

Lyons stood toe-to-toe with the big Blackstar commander. He started throwing shovel hooks, chipping away with tight arcs that landed with the force of jackhammers. Several times, the body blows rocked Fitzpatrick, driving him back, making him retreat.

The concept was called dominating space. All proper combative systems were forward systems. The fighter who won was the fighter who gained and kept the initiative. To do that against an aggressive enemy like Fitzpatrick, you had to put him back on his heels, make him feel as if he was trying and failing to recover. You had to come at him and overwhelm him, make him feel like a rag doll in a pit bull's mouth. He had to feel shaken, worried, slammed this way and that, and just when he tried to recover you had to be a step ahead of him and hit him some more.

At close range now, Lyons changed his tactics. He started throwing elbow strikes and edge-of-hand blows. The elbow and the edge of the hand were two of the body's natural weapons. Strikes such as this enabled a man to hit and hit hard, trusting his body to do the work. Lyons started hacking away at Fitzpatrick as if he were trying to sculpt a new human being from the clay of the old one. He just hammered and battered Fitzpatrick with every bit of his strength until crimson flowed freely.

Fitzpatrick spit blood. He was huffing and puffing now, completely out of breath, gassed out and almost unable to lift his arms.

"That's the problem with you arrogant pricks," Lyons said. "All mouth, no brains." He punched Fitzpatrick in the ribs, throwing his strikes at forty-five-degree angles, coming in from the sides to do maximum destruction. He was rewarded by the sound of ribs cracking. Fitzpatrick moaned again, struggling to breathe. Lyons's strikes had crushed his nose. Blood bubbled and flowed down his face and into his mouth. He coughed and wheezed, holding his ribs.

"What's the matter, Jay-to-your-friends?" Lyons said. Schwarz and Blancanales were simply watching now, making sure Lyons would not be interrupted in his work by the approach of some hidden Blackstar goon. As for Fitzpatrick, he might have weapons hidden on him. A miserable jerk like that was always willing to switch to an unfair fight if he couldn't win a fair one. Lyons kept a close eye on his prey as a result. He was not going to be tricked. They had all had enough of being tricked for one mission.

"Nobody is better," Fitzpatrick blubbered. "Nobody beats me."

Lyons punched him in the face.

He heard the nose break a second time, and this time Lyons pressed his advantage. He hammered away at Fitzpatrick's skull, using his fists to break the man's cheekbones. He thought he heard an orbital bone go, too, but that didn't matter. You weren't supposed to target a man's head for a closed-fist punch because of the danger of striking teeth or the top of the skull. Fitzpatrick was too far gone to avail himself of any tricks, though. Lyons could see the fog in the man's eyes, could see it in the way Fitzpatrick swayed and tried to keep his feet. He was nearly done.

But Carl Lyons wasn't.

"I made you a promise," Lyons said. "I wonder if you remember what that was."

Something about being challenged gave Fitzpatrick new energy. He dropped to one knee, but when he brought his hand up, there was an out-the-front switchblade in his right hand. The blade snapped open.

"Scared, hero?" Fitzpatrick said. "Well, you should be. Because I'm going to carve you like a Thanksgiving turkey."

Lyons punched him in the face again. Fitzpatrick swore, but he did not drop his knife. He poked at his flattened, misshaped nose with his free hand while swinging the knife in tight circles in front of his body.

"I'm in a generous mood," Lyons said. "Now that I've put you in your place, I think I can afford to be generous. You put that knife down, get on your knees, put your hands behind your head and interlace your fingers. You do all that and let me strap your wrists together with one of my zip ties, and we'll just take you in. I won't actually beat you to death. Remember, Jason. Remember what I promised you when you were beating my men. When you were laughing at inflicting pain on someone who couldn't stop you."

"To hell with you," Fitzpatrick raged through a mouthful of blood. "Who the hell do you think you are? I'm Jason Damned Fitzpatrick, you government monkey! I'm a rich man! I've finally made it in the world…and nobody is going to take that away from me!"

Using his anger to give him strength, Fitzpatrick lunged forward. He drove with the knife, trying to get it deep into Lyons's guts, probably picturing what it would feel like to stick it in there and twist it around. He was neither as fast nor as strong as he thought he was. Lyons was able to avoid the attack easily.

The former cop put his hands down at his sides. A lot of people thought you were supposed to get your hands up in a knife fight. What they didn't realize that there was no such thing as blocking a knife attack with your flesh without ending up bleeding all over the freaking place. He didn't want to see his own arms carved down to the bone. So he concentrated on his footwork, keeping his boots moving, watching the imaginary "barrel" in front of Fitzpatrick's body.

The knife in Jason Fitzpatrick's hand described a curve at the length of the Blackstar commander's arm. That was the barrel, the zone into which Lyons could not go if he wanted to stay alive. He danced aside, using male and female triangles—a footwork pattern that referred to forward and reverse steps at forty-five-degree angles. Fitzpatrick had never seen that before or, if he had, he hadn't understood it.

"You know," Lyons said, "there's not a lot to be said for getting all your combat training through online videos."

Fitzpatrick snarled. It was the reaction that Lyons wanted. He wanted to provoke the Blackstar man, keep him emotionally disrupted, prevent him from achieving the calm that Lyons himself possessed. When he progressed through rage to that icy center at his core, there was nothing he could not do, efficiently and methodically. Beating Jason Fitzpatrick to death with a kind of professional detachment... Well, that was actually pretty easy. He had plenty of practice in that department.

"Come on, Jay-to-your-friends," Lyons said. "What's the matter with you, Tinkerbell? You're letting me down. You're not the young, dumb, full-of-himself son of a whore that I thought you were. No, now you're just dumb. You figure the beating I put on your nose is going to change your luck with the ladies? But what am I saying. Somebody like you is a date rapist waiting on his next shipment of horse tranquilizer."

Fitzpatrick looked confused, so Lyons punched him in the eye. He did it again, and again, and again, battering away on Fitzpatrick's left eye until the man was so swollen and bloody he couldn't see through either side. When he went down, hitting the floor with a rib-cracking thud, Lyons put the boots to him. The Able Team leader's combat boots left deep imprints as Lyons stomped the casually sadistic Fitzpatrick.

"This is the part I really like, Fitzpatrick," Lyons said. "This is the part where you get payback for everything you've done to now. I'm sure your list of crimes goes back farther than anybody here realizes. I'm sure all your life you've been the sort of douche who sabotages his every effort to get ahead in life. Well, Jay-to-your-friends, I'm here to tell you that life as you know it is over. Your days of preying on others, of beating helpless prisoners, of arranging for murder and sending your goon squad all over the world to bolster illegal causes…all of that is over. It ends today. It ends now."

"I'm…worth ten of you…" Fitzpatrick wheezed. He was unable to open his eyes. He had rolled into a fetal position, clutching at his chest and abdomen, probably feeling the effects of multiple internal injuries. Left alone, he would die, and there was actually a chance that even with medical treatment, he might not survive the night. But guessing wasn't good enough for Lyons. He was not willing to leave this man behind to his fate. He thought again of Schwarz and Blancanales, and of the feeling of helplessness while shackled and watching his teammates tortured.

Lyons stopped attacking his enemy. He knelt by Fitzpatrick's bloody face. "Tell me where Rhemsen is," he said. "Is he here? Is he in the building?"

"He's…in his office…on the…top floor," Fitzpatrick said, breathing with difficulty. "I have money. I can pay. Let me go. Get me a doctor."

"You have nothing," Lyons said, "because I'm about to take away everything you have. You can't pay, because dead men don't pay bills. I'm not letting you go. And I'll be damned if I get the likes of you medical attention."

Lyons stood at full height. He was taking a risk, he knew. If Fitzpatrick was shamming, then getting this close to him, indulging himself in a moment like this, could lead to losing the fight. All it would take would be one good move on Fitzpatrick's part. Lyons only had to experience a moment's inattention for everything to change.

But he put his boot on Fitzpatrick's neck anyway.

"You son of a—" Fitzpatrick tried to say. Lyons applied pressure, cutting the Blackstar man off, choking him. When the Able Team leader let up a little Fitzpatrick once again tried to speak. "I was only following orders," he rasped quietly.

Schwarz and Blancanales looked on, content to let Lyons have this moment. Lyons looked at them, nodded and turned back to regard Fitzpatrick.

"Out of chances," Lyons said. "Out of excuses. Out of time."

"Please," Fitzpatrick begged. "I didn't mean it. I didn't mean any of it."

"Yeah," Lyons said. "You did."

"Please—"

Lyons drove his boot down with all his weight behind it. Then he snapped his foot inward. The loud crack he heard next was Fitzpatrick's neck breaking.

"Told you," said Carl Lyons.

CHAPTER TWENTY-EIGHT

The grenade round from Gary Manning's 40 mm launcher blew the hatch off its hinges. Using the round was a risk, but at this point in the operation, it was a risk McCarter was willing to take. Once the way was clear, and using the shockwave and surprise of the explosion to their advantage, Phoenix Force poured through the hatch and arrayed themselves in combat formation on the other side.

Although dazed, the reserve force of Blackstar security men whom Wijeya had held back tried to return fire. Phoenix Force cut them down, blazing away with deadly accuracy and in short, efficient bursts. The guards fell, lying in pools of their own blood, some of them discharging their weapons with their dying spasms. The battle was over before it could begin. And the only man left standing was Wijeya.

The pirate captain stepped forward. He looked utterly defeated. Perhaps it was dawning on him that everything he had attempted, everything he had hoped to accomplish, could only end in his capture. But just as the hopeless expression threatened to swamp him, he looked up, locked eyes with McCarter and smiled.

"You," he said. "You are the one. The British. You need not speak for me to recognize you. I see it in your eyes. I see the spirit of the warrior in you."

"I see a coward," McCarter said. "A pathetic little coward, hiding under his bed. Well, Mommy and Daddy are home, little Wijeya, and it's time to pay for the mess you've made."

"You do me a disservice, speaking to me so," Wijeya said.

"And you've killed a lot of good people," McCarter said. "Not to mention this trash all around you. How many have died because you took money to play political games you didn't understand? How many people have you murdered simply because a voice on the phone told you to do it? You make me sick, mate. And I think I'm going to enjoy putting you down like a dog."

"I have removed my weapons," Wijeya said. "I have only these." He drew the pair of *kerambits* from his waistband. The curved blades made his hands look like velociraptor claws. He spun the blades by their finger rings, twirling them on his index fingers.

McCarter pointed his Hi-Power and thumbed back the hammer. "Say good-night to Mhusa when you see him," he said.

"Come, British," Wijeya said. "You wish to test me? You wish to show me what a bad man I am? Take one of my knives. Face me as a man. You have honor. I can see it. You have the countenance of a warrior, despite whatever disrespect you hurl at me. Come. Fight me. Show me the warrior in you."

McCarter stood very still for a long moment. Finally he eased down the hammer of his pistol and put the weapon back in his waistband. He was wearing his Tavor on its sling. With a shrug of his shoulder, he dropped the weapon to the deck.

"David," Manning said, "are you sure about this?"

"He's got a point," James said.

"Trust me, lads," McCarter said. "Some things, I just have to do my way."

Wijeya smiled again. He took the knife from his left hand and placed it on the deck. Then he stepped back several paces. McCarter leaned down, picked it up and gave it an experimental twirl with his index finger. The Briton was not a complete stranger to the *kerambit*, but such a close-range blade had never been his preferred kit when conducting the kinds of missions that Phoenix Force did. Military ops required a bit more versatility, and that generally demanded a fixed blade of more conventional dimensions and blade style.

Still, he knew how deadly the Indonesian blade could be. The Indonesians taught martial arts like Silat, and Silat practitioners delighted in standing chest to chest with each other. A man like that could climb you like a circus monkey and stab you the whole way up and back. Wijeya obviously knew the methods. He began to run through a series of *djuru*, Indonesian patterns that combined several discrete movements into a fluid pattern of martial movements.

"Will you tell me the story of you and your men, British?" Wijeya asked. "Who are you? Where do you come from? Which government sent you?"

"That's none of your concern," McCarter said. "These are things you don't need to worry about at all, friend. Where you're going, there won't be any need to trouble yourself over the exact why and how of what put you there."

Wijeya slashed. He twirled his knife, obviously feeling the maneuver was impressive. "I will enjoy killing you, British," he said. "When a warrior kills another warrior, the dead man's spirit travels into the one who is still alive. The living man becomes stronger. This is why a warrior who has vanquished many is so powerful. His spirit is energized by the lives he takes."

"You don't believe that," McCarter said.

"But that is where you are wrong, British," Wijeya said. "You understand that I have education, yes? Such is the way of learning. We must all learn either from another or by experience. I choose to learn by experience. I fight to stay alive. I fight to put money in my pocket, too, but it is all survival. I need money. We all do. And if you believe you do not, you are a liar."

"That's pretty philosophical from somebody who captains a pirate ship."

"I am not some dumb brute, not some thug," Wijeya said.

"You take money to kill people," McCarter countered. "That's a thug in my book."

"I do not understand why you keep insulting me," Wijeya said. He was circling now. "We are not so different. We both will do whatever is required to reach our goals. I simply took a shorter path."

"Don't flatter yourself, mate," McCarter said. "I wish I had a pound note for every one of you blackguards who thinks he's the equal of the people hunting him. You're not a warrior, Wijeya. You're just a predator. Predators can be cunning, sure. They can also be intelligent. But they're never more than predators. Never more than scum. Because when the willingness to victimize others is rotting your soul, it touches everything you do and everything you are."

"I hate you," Wijeya said.

"Good," McCarter said. "Feeling's mutual, mate."

Wijeya howled in anger. Redoubling the elaborate patterns his blade was describing in the air, Wijeya danced in, slashing, and McCarter was forced to duck away. Then the smaller man was pressing his advantage, slashing at the air, cutting where McCarter's face and neck had been only fractions of a second before.

McCarter fought him off, at first with difficulty and then with increasing confidence. When he realized what was happening, he was actually kind of surprised. He wouldn't have thought it likely, although, of course, it was probably. He was a highly trained special operations commando, but he always assumed, when he came up against a man who favored a specific weapon, that the man in question would have pretty well-developed skills. In this case, Wijeya favored a highly specialized blade with a long martial history behind it. It stood to reason that the pirate captain would be exceptionally deadly with it. And, in Wijeya's defense, he was very good. There weren't many men in the world who would consider dealing with an armed Captain Yanuar Wijeya a walk in the park.

As McCarter fought, however, as he moved in small circles with his borrowed knife, looking to see which pieces of Wijeya he could snip off, he realized something.

He was better.

He was also faster. Some things couldn't be taught. Speed was a tricky one. You could learn to be smooth, and smooth had a confidence all its own. Smooth was fast and fast was smooth, or so the saying went. But if you rushed things you got nowhere.

Wijeya considered himself a warrior, but his skills were rudimentary at best. He was better at looking as though he could fight than he was at actually fighting.

McCarter scored a deep cut in Wijeya's cheek, then another along the pirate captain's forearm. Blood flowed freely.

"You're looking a little pale, mate," McCarter said. "Starting to feel a chill in the air? That's your body running out of blood. Look down at the floor, Wijeya. There's an awful lot of you down there. And it's only going to keep running."

Wijeya flailed, desperate now. The combination of the wounds he was taking and McCarter's relentless verbal manipulations was becoming too much for him. He started rushing, and in rushing, he made a mistake. McCarter came past him dragging the blade behind, and the curved edge took Wijeya in the guts. He screamed and fell to his knees, holding his insides. The expression on his face, when he looked once more at McCarter, was pale and indignant, shocked and surprised.

"You…" huffed Wijeya. "You should not have been able to beat me." He dropped his *kerambit*, as it was interfering with the ongoing task of holding his intestines in his body. "It isn't fair. I worked so hard. My parents…"

"Nobody cares, mate," McCarter said. He looked around the control console until he found the portable microphone attached to the PA system. This he put in front of Wijeya's face as the pirate captain swayed on his knees. McCarter switched the microphone on but then put his thumb on the mute button.

"You're going to make an announcement, Captain Wijeya," McCarter said. "You're going to tell the remainder of your forces, if there are any left alive, that you're surrendering. I want them to know that they are fighting alone now. That there's nobody left to serve. Do it."

"I cannot control my crew," Wijeya said. "They have… lost respect in me." He began to sway on his knees.

"Just make the announcement," McCarter said.

The pirate captain leaned toward the microphone. McCarter took his thumb off the mute button. Wijeya looked up at the ceiling, then down at his entrails spilling out of his body. "This…is Captain Wijeya," he rasped. His voice echoed throughout the oil rig platform. "I am announcing…my unconditional surrender. All forces, all of my crew, any security men who can still hear my voice, I surrender. They are taking me into custody. If you fight on, know that you fight for nothing and no one. Know that it is over. Know that I am over. Goodbye. This is Wijeya. I go to be with the gods. I go at the hands of a warrior. And I am sorry to my family for hurting them."

Wijeya seemed ready to collapse. He looked up at McCarter. "I thought you would shoot me," he said. "I thought you would tell me you had no patience for honor. That you were—what is the word?—practical. A practical man would take my knife and pretend to duel me, but then simply shoot me anyway."

"It has been done," McCarter said. "By others and by me."

"I do not wish to linger here," Wijeya said. "I can feel the life slowly ebbing out of me. This is…not dignified. I want you to give me the gift."

"You're asking a lot, friend, given that just a little while ago you were trying to kill me and every member of my squad."

"This is what is done among warriors, yes?"

"You're not a warrior," McCarter argued.

"Then…please," the pirate said. "An act of kindness for a foolish man. A man who now sees that he should have died long ago. Free me, British."

"Well," McCarter said. "If you're going to ask nicely." The Briton removed his Hi-Power from his belt, cocked the hammer and put the barrel of the gun up to Wijeya's temple. Wijeya bowed his head. His skin was ashen. Blood continue to gush from the wound in his abdomen.

"I was not a good man," Wijeya said quietly.

"No," McCarter said. "But I can help."

CHAPTER TWENTY-NINE

Carl Lyons smashed in the door to Rhemsen's office with his shoulder. It was a big, heavy door, and it made a big, heavy crash when it landed. The ghastly plastic face of Harold Rhemsen was waiting to meet Able Team from behind the corrupt businessman's desk.

"Gentlemen," he said, smiling. "Come in. Have a seat." He gestured to the chairs in front of him. "I think you'll find me hospitable. I'm ready to cooperate. I hereby renounce violence and apologize sincerely for my involvement in the events you have been investigating. May I get you some coffee? Please, please, sit. There's no need for any further rancor among us."

"No, thanks," Lyons said. "We'll stand. Been that kind of day. Now, Rhemsen, you get up from behind that desk. Any funny business, any bombs strapped to your chest, any self-destruct codes or dead man's switches or freaking bear-trap masks, and I promise you, as all that is good and pure in the world is my witness, I will beat you so hard your unborn children will feel it, and I will not stop until every inch of your body is a giant, aching bruise."

"How delightfully graphic," Rhemsen said. "But as I said, there's no need for that. I'm a businessman. This is a business transaction. I would like very much if you and I could come to some sort of mutually beneficial arrangement. And I think you'll find that I can be very generous with my money if the right opportunity presents itself.

"Gentlemen," Rhemsen said again, "I assure you that it was all, every bit of it, just business. Maybe not *good* business. Maybe not even advisable business. But everything I did, I did for money. The profit motive is my only god."

"Who, exactly, are you trying to convince?" Lyons said. "This speech sounds a little too rehearsed to me."

"Please, gentlemen," Rhemsen said. "You've caught me. I wish only to surrender. To confess. And I wish to do so on camera."

"Can't help you there," Lyons said.

"Oh, but you don't have to," Rhemsen said. "This entire office is wired for sound and video. I have activated the digital recording device. I am ready to give my statement."

"I'm listening," Lyons said.

"I am Harold Rhemsen," he said. "I wish to state, for the record, my unequivocal confession. I have conspired with forces hired by me, including the Blackstar security corporation, to implicate the People's Republic of China in schemes that were the result of my own doing in the South China Sea. I have arranged to have armed men conduct terrorist and pirate raids on assets in the region. I have done this all in the hope of discrediting China—"

"Rhemsen," Lyons said, moving quickly to stand over the businessman behind his desk, "I am really tired of your crap." Lyons's hand shot out and he grabbed Rhemsen's right wrist. The RhemCorp founder had been reaching for a revolver in his desk drawer.

"I...I..." Rhemsen stammered.

"Oh, I know," Lyons said, still applying a death grip to Rhemsen's wrist. "You figured you'd keep us busy with a confession while you worked your way around to gunning us down. That's just great, man. That's just the perfect cap to a lousy couple of days. Shut off the recording."

With difficulty because of the pain in his gun-hand

wrist, Rhemsen shut off the device. "I…I wasn't going to try to shoot you," he lied. Lyons could read the lie in the man's frozen mask of a face. "I was going to make my confession and then take my own life. I don't think you realize the kind of pressure a man in my position is in. The danger of suicide is ever-present. So many men like me take their own lives at moments of adversity."

"Well, great," Lyons said.

Rhemsen's eyes widened. "What do you mean?"

"Just what I said," Lyons said. "I think that's a fine idea. Because, Harold, as long as you're alive, people's lives are in danger. You'll find some way to set off a bomb, or you'll clamp another death trap over one of my buddies, or you'll pull a lever and drop us all into your pit of alligators and lawyers, or whatever it is a guy like you would keep in a secret pit under his office. And, really, the only thing that's going to put a stop to that is if you *do* commit suicide. Plus, I like the postscript that puts on your story. Wraps it up nice and neat."

"You are mad," Rhemsen said.

"Oh, I'm mad, all right," Lyons said, now gripping Rhemsen's arm tight enough to make the bones of Rhemsen's wrist grate together. "I'm furious, in fact. And I'm also completely serious."

Lyons started moving Rhemsen's gun arm. The barrel of the .38 revolver Rhemsen held started to move, inexorably, toward Rhemsen's face.

"You cannot do this!" Rhemsen shouted. "I have rights! I have rights!"

"You just don't get it, do you?" Lyons said. "This isn't about your rights, Harold. This is about payback for repeated attempts to murder us. And, even though the people I answer to could and would never give me this order, I happen to think that all the trouble you've caused justifies helping you wrap things up a little more neatly now that we're at the end of it. So, you killing yourself? Best idea you've had yet, and by a big margin. Now hold still."

"No! Stop! Stop!" Rhemsen cried.

Lyons folded Rhemsen's arm. The smaller man screamed in pain. Lyons jammed the barrel of the .38, with Rhemsen's hand wrapped around it and enveloped by Lyons's own huge mitt, up under Rhemsen's chin.

"Hey, what's that?" Lyons said, looking into the open desk drawer. "That looks like a diary. I'll bet there's some juicy stuff in there. Don't worry. We won't read through it. Not while you're alive, anyway."

"I beg you!" Rhemsen screamed. "Spare my life! I meant no harm! I only wanted to...wanted to..."

"Make money, blah, blah, blah, evils of capitalism, yadda, yadda," Lyons said, his tone mocking. "Yeah. We got that much. And I've got to tell you, Harold, I'm not buying it. Now, if you'll excuse me, I'd like to not talk to you for the rest of your life."

"Hey," Schwarz said, lifting Rhemsen's briefcase off the floor. "This has, like, a ballistic panel in it," he said. "Nothing else could make it this heavy."

"Check it for tons of money," Blancanales said.

"Nope," Schwarz said. "Just a ballistic panel, as I said."

"Bet that would have come in handy," Lyons said, "if we'd come in here shooting."

"Yeah," Schwarz said, suddenly excited. "Like, he would have dove for the floor with it, absorbing our gunfire, and then somehow gotten off a shot that let him escape."

"I guess bad guys can dream," Lyons said. He started to close his hand over Rhemsen's. "Dogs do it, and I like dogs a hell of a lot more than people."

"Anything you want!" Rhemsen pleaded. "I will give

you anything you want! Spare my life! I will give you intelligence, money. I will reveal my worst secrets!"

"Looks like we've already got those," Lyons said. "And I thought I told you to keep your mouth shut forever."

Rhemsen let out one last, blood-curdling scream.

Lyons made a fist. The gun went off, spraying Harold Rhemsen's brains all over the wall behind his desk.

EPILOGUE

Stony Man Farm, Virginia

Hal Brognola's image filled the flat-screen monitor on one wall of the briefing room. Seated at the conference table, the men of Able Team sat drinking coffee. Phoenix Force was once more using a satellite connection to join the meeting remotely, but this time they were transmitting from a Ford-class supercarrier leaving the area of the South China Sea. Kurtzman noted that as he watched the smaller screens and other displays in the high-tech briefing room, adjusting the gain on the various feeds as required.

"Go ahead, Hal," Price said. "What have we learned?"

"China has declared 'Harold Rhemsen,' born one Cheung Yeong, a rogue agent. Likewise a character officially identified as Feng "Simon" Lao, whom we know to be a black-ops veteran instrumental in their most covert intelligence operations for the past ten years. The Chinese government has disclaimed any involvement in, or knowledge of, Rhemsen's plot—first, to make it look as though China was behind the attacks in the South China Sea, and then to discredit those attacks as fabricated. The idea, as explained in the journal we found on Rhemsen's body, was to make critics of China look foolish and help deflect very real concern over Chinese grabs for territory."

"Rhemsen's journal, which Able Team recovered, is the

reason the Chinese have backed off so quickly," Price put in. "Apparently every facet of the Chinese black-ops plan, sponsored by Lao and coordinated by Rhemsen, was detailed in the journal, right down to how a Chinese sleeper agent named Cheung Yeong killed the real Rhemsen and assumed his identity."

"So the guy was never an American at all," said Lyons. "He was a Chinese-born spook?"

"Evidently," Brognola returned. "If you hadn't found the journal, it's possible his manufactured identity might have held. We had to dig pretty deep to verify the details 'Rhemsen' hinted at in his journal. And it was the second of two journals recovered."

"The other one was in Jason Fitzpatrick's possession," Price explained. "After Able Team took down Fitzpatrick, Justice got a warrant to search his apartment. He had hidden a briefcase there filled with a million dollars in counterfeit US currency. An equally fake journal, which we believe was also written by Cheung Yeong, was inside the briefcase, as well. As confirmed by the real journal, the fake journal details a nefarious plot by an American businessman, namely Rhemsen, to profit by making China look bad and stirring fear against it."

"So he was a double reverse backhand agent," Schwarz said. "This is getting complicated."

"We think his last-minute confession to Able Team was an attempt to preserve his cover and the operation," Price continued. "Maybe he even feared reprisals to his family back home for his failure, if he still has family. We don't really know. Getting caught wasn't part of his plan, but he obviously thought that playing the role of corrupt capitalist would benefit him in the long run once you had his back against the wall. Maybe, with the right lawyer, he could even have wrangled some kind of sweet plea or immunity deal. Stranger things have happened. And if he ever did make his way back to Beijing, he would have been able to say, with video evidence, that he rode the operation down to the last, trying like hell to make it work. But his unscheduled suicide—" she looked at Lyons, who nodded "—makes things that much more difficult for the Chinese. Rhemsen isn't here to stir up trouble by adding to his lies. We have his body, and we control the narrative now."

"Obviously the nation that stood to benefit from all this was China itself," Brognola said. "Had Cheung Yeong and Lao succeeded in first framing, then discrediting China, the nation's further territorial advancements could have enjoyed more freedom of movement. You know how politically correct bureaucrats tend to be. Everybody would be afraid to look like they were jumping on the bash-China train. And the engines of China's political propaganda would have plenty of fodder, with yet another corrupt American war profiteer as the star of the narrative."

"Where does that leave us with regard to our relations with China?" Encizo asked through the video link.

"It's about where it was," Brognola said. "They're pretending they don't know anything about it, we know they do, they also know we know they do, and we're pretending we don't know that they know that we know."

"Wow," Schwarz said. "Just…wow."

Brognola shot the electronics expert a sour look. "At any rate, our government and those of our allied nations will be looking at China pretty hard in the coming months. The incident has heightened suspicion about their activities, which is the opposite of what they wanted. And thanks to both of you, Able Team and Phoenix Force, both this group of Chinese sleeper agents and a mercenary force that was supporting them have been eliminated."

"Blackstar has been officially designated *corporation non grata* with the Department of Defense," Price said. "Justice is having their assets seized. It's going to take a few years to wind its way through the courts, but chances are good that most of the people involved in the company will be swept up in the endless investigation that follows. Thanks to you all, most of Blackstar's combat operatives are already dead. We've tracked down a few that managed to survive and make it to area hospitals near the zones of engagement. They'll end up in prison before it's over, and that's if they're lucky."

"If they're not," Brognola said, "they'll end up in a black-site prison without possibility of appeal, and disappear accordingly." He massaged the bridge of his nose with two thick fingers. "China's government is scrambling to contain the political fallout. I've got meetings all afternoon with politicians who, in turn, have meetings with the Chinese. It's going to be a long night. Communist China remains hungry to expand. That threat was dealt a setback today, but the danger is no less than it was before. It may even be greater, as you know how the Chinese get when they feel their national honor has been affronted."

"The Farm will closely monitor the territories in and around China, and especially these zones of expansion on which Beijing has been focusing," Price said. "We'll respond accordingly as circumstances dictate."

"All right, then," Brognola concluded. "Wish me luck. And, team? Good work out there, as always."

"Thanks, Hal," Price said. "Farm, out."

Brognola's image disappeared. "We'll be seeing you soon," McCarter said. "It's going to be good to grab a little rest."

"Don't count on getting much," Price said. "You know how it goes."

"Do I ever, Barb," McCarter said. "Do I ever. Phoenix, out." His image, too, disappeared.

"Able," Price said. "I assume you'll be taking your downtime here at the Farm. You'll find your accounts flush with combat pay."

"Then I'm off to the nearest diner to spend it," Lyons said. "I'm starved." He rose and walked out of the room. Blancanales followed. Schwarz, however, lingered.

"Uh," the electronics expert said. "About that. I can't seem to find my smartphone."

"Oh, that..." Kurtzman said. He produced a satellite smartphone from a pocket of his chair and passed it across the table to Schwarz. "You dropped it in the armory when you checked in your gear. Cowboy was kind enough to pass it along."

"I don't remember dropping it," Schwarz said.

"Kissinger might have taken it from your gear when you weren't looking," Kurtzman said.

"Why would he do that?"

"Because I asked him to," Kurtzman replied. "You'll need to log into your online bank account to acknowledge your payment and access your funds," he told Schwarz. "But before you can do that, you've got to play your game."

"What?" Schwarz asked. He switched on the phone. The candy monster game immediately loaded. "To tell you the truth, Bear, I'm kind of sick of playing it."

"Oh, I figured you would be," Kurtzman said. "That's why I rewrote the application. You'll need to complete all one hundred levels with a perfect three-halo score for each level before the phone unlocks."

"But...Bear," Schwarz complained. "That's just...that's just..."

"Cruel?" Kurtzman asked. "Swift and terrible, like my revenge?"

Schwarz slumped in his chair. He was silent for a moment. "Yeah," he finally said. "Something like that."

"Have fun," Kurtzman said, wheeling his way out of the conference room. Price followed him, leaving Schwarz to his electronic fate. Once more, she had to try not to laugh until she was out of earshot. She caught up to Kurtzman farther down the corridor.

"Back to work for you, Bear?" she asked.

"And for you," Kurtzman said. "Don't try to make me believe you're spending the night out on the town."

"No," she said. "Probably not. There's too much work to do. Too many security threats to catalog. Too many international threats to stare down."

"I'll put on a fresh pot of coffee," Kurtzman offered.

"Bear?" Price asked. "Do you ever wonder if it's worth it?"

Kurtzman stopped rolling and looked up at her. "The day I start second-guessing it," he told her, "is the day I retire. Until then, I'm on the job. It's who we are. It's what we do. For as long as it takes."

Price smiled and nodded. "For as long as it takes."

"Come on," Kurtzman said. "Play your cards right and I'll buy you a microwave pizza from the vending machine. You know, for, uh, America."

"Right," Price said. "Lead the way."

Laughing softly to herself, Barbara Price followed Kurtzman. There was work to be done. There would always be work to be done. Even if, one day, the powers that were wrote them off, told them to stand down, she couldn't imagine any of the members of her team complying with that order. There would always be danger to fight.

And there would always be Stony Man Farm to fight it.

* * * * *

"The second their weapons come up, take them down as
quickly as you can."

"Will they not have us in a cross fire?" Azmeh asked.

"That's their first mistake," Bolan replied and smiled.

At thirty yards, the gunmen started fanning out, but
not enough to matter. They were trying to intimidate
Bolan and Azmeh.

They were in for a surprise.

At fifteen yards, still smiling, Bolan asked the shooters
on his side of the Ranchero, "What's up, guys?"

One replied in Arabic, and Bolan nodded in phony
understanding. He heard the click of a safety as Azmeh
said something to the men on his side of the car. Go time.

Bolan hit the one who'd spoken to him with a three-
round burst and blew him back into the sand.

And then all hell broke loose.

Azmeh fired from his window, short bursts, while
his targets tried to scramble. Bolan focused on his own
remaining adversaries, who were ducking, dodging, not
as ready for resistance as they'd thought they were.

He caught the second shooter raising his Kalashnikov

and stitched him with a burst around belt level, gutting him. The guy collapsed but still managed to fire a few rounds skyward as he died.

Two left, and they were both diving for cover, counting on their SUV to shield them from incoming fire. It might have worked, if Bolan was intent on blowing past their roadblock in a cloud of dust, but he'd already shifted the Ranchero into Park and had his door open, pursuing them.

When one of them peeked up to find out what was happening, Bolan obliged him with a round between the shiny lenses of his shades. The fourth man saw his partner die, and he lunged forward, firing aimlessly. A double-tap smashed through his snarling face and finished him.

Bolan reversed direction, just in time to see Azmeh's last adversary fall. Bolan checked the SUVs, deciding that the Niva was their best bet for continuing their journey over rugged ground. They quickly transferred their gear from the Ranchero and discarded the dead men's personal effects.

"Ready?" Bolan asked Azmeh when they were settled in the Niva.

The smaller man nodded, then asked Bolan, "Do you ever weary of it?"

"What?"

"The killing."

Bolan didn't have to think about his answer. "Weary or not, it's part of the job."

Don't miss
SYRIAN RESCUE by Don Pendleton,
available September 2015 wherever
Gold Eagle® books and ebooks are sold.

THE EXECUTIONER
DON PENDLETON'S

A missing Chinese defector threatens global security...

Check out this sneak preview of
LETHAL RISK
by *Don Pendleton!*

The truck lurched forward along the side of the hill, and for a heart-stopping moment Bolan thought it was going to roll. Then he got it straightened and drove down to the road again. He hit the gas, heading straight toward the larger truck.

Seeing the oncoming vehicle, the bigger vehicle honked its horn, but Bolan didn't stop. When the two trucks were a hundred yards apart, he opened the door and dived onto the ground, rolling hard with the impact.

At that speed, the big truck couldn't turn aside fast enough. The front crashed into the smaller truck on the passenger side, crumpling the hood and engine compartment and sending the Italian truck flying through the air.

The large cargo truck hit its brakes after the impact, shuddering to a stop. Bolan didn't wait around to find out what they were doing. The moment he stopped rolling, he got up and bolted back to the truck, ignoring the steady stabs of pain from his left leg every time it hit the ground. He reached the vehicle, which Liao had thoughtfully backed up for him. Diving into the back, he banged his knee painfully on the machine gun on the floor as he yelled, "Go, go, go!"

Liao hit it and the truck sped away. "They'll never catch us now!" he shouted, pounding the roof with his fist. "We did it!"

"We aren't in Mongolia yet!" Bolan slumped against the tailgate, breathing heavily. His leg twitched, and he noticed his phone was vibrating.

He dug it out and answered. "We're—"

Akira Tokaido's voice screamed in his ear. "Missile! Evacuate the vehicle—they've locked-on an antitank missile!"

"Stop now! Right now!" Bolan yelled to Liao as he shoved the phone into his pocket and grabbed the machine gun with his other hand.

The truck skidded to a halt, and as the other man turned to him, Bolan yelled, "Incoming missile. Get out now!"

Liao scrabbled at the door handle and got it open as Bolan hit the ground on the other side of the rear door. He made sure Liao was scrambling away from the truck before running himself.

As he did, he saw the bright flash of a missile launch about a kilometer away, and shouted, "Hit the dirt!" as he dived to the ground.

Two seconds later the world exploded.

Don't miss
LETHAL RISK by Don Pendleton,
available September 2015 wherever
Gold Eagle® books and ebooks are sold.

Wow...Meow!

Tom turned to see if Charley was there. What he saw was the leg of the largest human he had ever seen, a boy who towered so high into the room, Tom could not see his head.

Confused, Tom called, "Charley?"

"Right here," came a voice from the huge boy.

A shock ran through Tom from the tip of his nose leather to the tip of his tail. He understood: He had a tail because he'd become a cat. A cat that looked exactly like Charley, even as Charley now looked exactly like Tom.

They had exchanged bodies.

Tom lifted a hand in front of his face. It was a paw covered with black-and-gray fur. "Cool," he said. "I've become a cat."

STRANGE

HAPPENINGS

Five Tales
of
Transformation

AVI

MAGIC CARPET BOOKS
HARCOURT, INC.
Orlando   Austin   New York   San Diego   London

www.HarcourtBooks.com

First Magic Carpet Books edition 2008

Magic Carpet Books and its logo are trademarks of Harcourt, Inc., registered
in the United States of America and/or other jurisdictions.

The Library of Congress has cataloged the hardcover edition as follows:
Avi, 1937–
Strange happenings: five tales of transformation/Avi.
p. cm.
Summary: Five original stories where strange changes occur,
from a boy and a cat changing places and a young man learning
the price of selfishness to an invisible princess finding herself.
1. Children's stories, American. 2. Metamorphosis—Juvenile fiction.
[1. Metamorphosis—Fiction. 2. Short stories.] I. Title.
PZ7.A953Str 2006
[Fic]—dc22 2004029579
ISBN 978-0-15-205790-9
ISBN 978-0-15-206461-7 pb

Text set in Bembo
Designed by April Ward

C E G H F D

Printed in the United States of America

For Carolyn Shute

STRANGE HAPPENINGS

BORED TOM

AT THE AGE OF TWELVE, Thomas Osborn Pitzhugh—better known as Tom—had few interests, little desire, and almost no energy. This was so despite a family—mother, father, older brother, and sister—that loved him. As for school, his teachers treated him fairly; he did what he was supposed to do and received passable grades. But if you were to ask Tom what the future held for him, he would have replied that, other than getting older, and hopefully taller, he expected no change. In short, Thomas Osborn Pitzhugh—better known as Tom—found life *boring*.

One day Tom was sitting on the front steps of his city house doing what he usually did: nothing. As he sat there a short-haired, black-and-gray cat with gray eyes approached and sat down in front of him. For a while the two—boy and cat—stared at each other.

The cat spoke first. "What's happening?" he asked.

"Not much," Tom replied.

"Doing anything?" the cat asked.

"Nope."

"Just hanging out?"

"I guess."

"That something you do often?"

"Yeah."

"How come?" the cat inquired.

"I'm bored."

The cat considered this remark and then said, "You look like my kind of friend. How about adopting me?"

"Why should I?"

"Got anything better to do?"

"I don't know."

"Well then?"

Tom asked, "What's your name?"

"Charley."

"Okay."

It was not long before Charley the cat became part of Tom's household. So familiar did he become that when Tom went to sleep, Charley slept next to his head on an extra pillow.

For a brief time, Tom—having a new friend—was almost not bored. After a while, however, his life settled back into its old, boring routine.

"Hey, man," Tom said to Charley one afternoon two months after the cat had moved in. "It's not fair! You get to sleep all day, but I have to go to school." Disgusted, he flung his schoolbooks onto his bed.

It was the statement more than the *thump* of books that awoke Charley from a sound nap. He studied Tom, and then stretched his back to curve like a McDonald's arch. "I am a cat," he said. "You are a boy. Some would say you had it better."

Tom sighed. "If you had to go to school every day like I do, you wouldn't say that."

"Don't you like school?" Charley asked.

"Oh, I like it all right," Tom replied. "The kids are okay. The teachers are all right. Once in a while it almost gets interesting. Mostly, though, it's just boring. I'd rather do nothing. Like you."

"What about after school?"

"*Bor*ing," Tom insisted.

"Doesn't *anything* interest you?"

Tom considered the question. "Television," he said at last. "On TV there's something happening. It's my life that's dull."

"A cat's life," said Charley, "can be dull, too."

"Your life is supposed to be dull," Tom said. "See, people are *always* telling me that I should get up and *do* something. Boy, wish I had permission to sleep all day the way you do."

To which Charley said, "How about you becoming me, a cat, while I become you, a boy?"

Tom sighed with regret. "Not possible," he said.

"Don't be so sure," said Charley. "Most people wouldn't believe that you and I could hold a conversation, but here we are doing just that."

"Actually," said Tom, "it's not that interesting a conversation."

"Whatever you say," Charley replied as he curled himself into a ball, closed his eyes, and went back to sleep. Tom did pretty much the same: He watched television.

The next day Tom, as usual, went to school. In most ways school was ordinary. Although Mr. Oliver called upon him once and Tom gave a reasonable response, he never raised his hand. Most of the time he doodled, stared out the window, or daydreamed, but about what he could not have said.

At the end of that day, Mr. Oliver announced a special homework assignment. He asked each student to write an essay titled "The Most Exciting Thing That Ever Happened to Me." It was due in one week's time.

Tom was worried. He could not think of anything in his life that had been exciting. He did remember a family trip when they'd had a flat tire on the highway. That was not so much exciting as it was nerve-racking.

Then there was the time he was taken to a base-ball game, but no one even got a hit until the bottom of the ninth inning.

Tom also recalled the time his mother had thought she might lose her job. That was scary, not exciting.

"You ever do anything exciting in your life?" Tom asked Charley when he got home.

Charley, who, as usual, had been sleeping on Tom's bed, stretched, yawned, and said, "As a cat?"

"Of course as a cat."

Charley said, "I caught a mouse once."

"Was that exciting?"

"It was just a small mouse. My first ever."

"What did you do with it?"

"Let it go."

"Anything else?"

"Since I've moved in here, I've caught a whiff of another cat passing through your backyard. I believe it's a cat of my acquaintance—her name is Maggie. She's in search of a home of her own."

"Is *that* exciting?"

"For a cat it can be hard," said Charley. "Why all these questions?"

Tom told Charley about the essay he had to write. "But," he complained, "nothing exciting has *ever* happened to me."

Charley thought for a while. "Tom," he said after a while, "do you remember what I told you—that you could become me and I could become you?"

"Yeah."

"You might find *that* exciting."

Tom smiled. "Sleeping all day with no one objecting sounds cool to me. Could it be done?"

"We can give it a shot," said Charley. "A few blocks from here there's a neighborhood wizard-cat. It's that Maggie I just mentioned. We could ask her."

"Just remember," Tom warned, "if we make the change, you'll have to write that essay. It's due next week."

"I know. And you'll get to sleep all day."

"Sounds good to me," Tom said. "Anyway, we could do it just long enough for you to write my essay."

Charley, ignoring *that* remark, said, "Let's make the change now."

"*Now?*" said Tom. He was not given to making quick decisions.

"Any reason not to?"

"Maybe my parents—"

"I'll handle them."

With Charlie leading the way, they left immediately.

It was dusk. A thin haze filled the air. Streetlamps began to flicker on. As it grew darker, people hurried to get home. Soon the streets were quite deserted. Tom was glad Charley knew the way.

They went two blocks to the right, one to the left, and then walked through a back alley Tom had never wanted to walk through. Finally they cut through a weed-and-bedspring-infested yard and approached what looked to Tom to be an abandoned building. Its windows were boarded. Tom hoped they would not be going there. But Charley, without a pause, padded into the building's basement and down a long empty corridor.

Tom, feeling nervous, said, "Do we have far to go?"

"Not too long," said Charley as he headed up a rickety flight of steps.

They reached the first floor. When Tom's eyes grew accustomed to the gloom, he realized that the building was full of cats. Some were sleeping. Others sat with tails curled about their feet, staring into the distance. A few prowled restlessly. Charley nodded— as if they were acquaintances.

With Charley leading the way, Tom entered a long, dimly lit hallway. Green paint peeled from the walls. The ceiling looked like it might collapse any moment. There were more cats. Some glanced at Tom, but most paid no attention.

At the end of the hallway was a door. In front of this door sat a large cat, the largest cat Tom had ever seen. He looked like a miniature tiger.

Charley approached this large cat with great respect. For a few moments the two cats stared at each other, their tails moving restlessly.

"What can we do for you?" said the large cat.

"A transformation," Charley said.

Tom saw the large cat's eyes shift to him, then turn back to Charley. "What's the reason?" the large cat asked.

"He's bored," Charley said. "And he has to write a school essay, 'The Most Exciting Thing That Ever Happened to Me.'"

"Ah! One of *those*," the large cat said as if he had heard it before. "You can enter."

"Watch your head," Charley cautioned Tom.

Tom was just about to ask Charley if this kind of transformation was common, when they stepped into a small, dim room. The floor was so carpeted with cats, it was hard to move about. Some cats were big, others small. Some were perched on ledges. Others sat on shelves like books in a library. The whole room throbbed with such a steady purring, it was as if one low note on a bass guitar were being continually thrummed.

No matter where the cats sat or lay, all eyes were fixed upon a raised platform at the far end of the room. The platform was dimly lit by dusty light that drifted through a broken piece of window boarding.

On the platform, on a purple pillow, a gray cat lay stretched out, one cheek resting on an extended front paw. Her long fur made it appear as if she were dressed in silk lounging pajamas. Her eyes were closed to narrow slits. Now and again the tip of her tail shivered delicately.

"Who's that?" Tom asked Charley.

"Maggie," Charley whispered. "The local wizard-cat. Most neighborhoods have them. On the street she leads a normal life. Here, she's a wizard. Stay close and don't say anything unless you're asked a direct question."

Charley padded his way to the platform. Once there he lay down and tucked his front paws under his chest. "Kneel," he whispered.

Tom knelt.

"Now, be patient."

Tom, curious how a cat could have become a wizard, gazed at Maggie.

The gray cat finally looked up. "What's happening?" she asked. Her voice was small, delicate.

"Maggie," said Charley, "we're requesting a transformation. This boy—his name is Tom—and myself."

"Wants to be a regular *tom*cat, I suppose," Maggie said. Her silky sides heaved slightly as she enjoyed her joke.

"Actually," Charley explained, "he's bored. Wants to sleep all day, the way I do."

"Lucky you," Maggie murmured to Charley. With a sidelong glance at Tom, she asked, "*Do* you really want to sleep all day?"

It took a moment for Tom to realize he had been asked a question. "Absolutely," he replied. "I love to sleep."

Maggie sighed. "I'd settle for a decent home off the streets."

"I've got that," Tom said.

"Whatever," Maggie mumbled. Then she said, "Bow down. You need to have your heads close together."

Tom and Charley put their heads side by side.

Tom was not sure what happened next. He sensed that Maggie's tail curled around and batted him on the forehead. He supposed the same thing had happened to Charley.

The next moment he heard Maggie say, "Charley, enjoy that home of yours."

"Let's go," said Charley. Tom turned and sensed the room had grown much larger. What's more, he was staring—nose to nose—into the face of a large calico cat with curled whiskers. "Beg pardon," said Tom, as he sidestepped the cat.

He turned to see if Charley was there. What he saw was the leg of the largest human he had ever seen, a boy who towered so high into the room, Tom could not see his head.

Confused, Tom called, "Charley?"

"Right here," came a voice from the huge boy.

A shock ran through Tom from the tip of his nose leather to the tip of his tail. He understood: He had a tail because he'd become a cat. A cat that looked exactly like Charley, even as Charley now looked exactly like Tom.

They had exchanged bodies.

Tom lifted a hand in front of his face. It was a paw covered with black-and-gray fur. "Cool," he said. "I've become a cat."

"Let's go," Charley urged, and gave Tom a gentle spank on his rump to get him out the door.

Though Tom had spent his whole life in that neighborhood, going home was like traveling through a foreign county. Everything was gigantic. Even things he could recognize—like mailboxes—appeared to be twisted into odd shapes. What's more, he seemed to be at the bottom of a sea of smells. One moment he sensed something delicious to eat. The next moment he had a trembling awareness of danger that was almost instantly followed by a whiff of calm. That in turn was taken over by the delicate scent of friendship. Tom, who had never been aware of such smells, was astonished he could identify them so clearly.

Even more amazing was that his body felt so different. He had never thought much about having hands and feet, or a head, for that matter, unless he bumped himself. Now he felt loose and jangly, as though he were not tied together tightly. He was also very aware of his skin. Some spots felt so dirty he had a desire to lick them clean. Other places itched and were in need of scratching. He even had a desire to stretch out and flex his nails into something deep and soft, like a nice stuffed chair.

The only reason he didn't do all these things was because he was having trouble keeping up with Charley, who was striding along on long human legs.

"Come on, now. Don't dawdle," Charley kept saying. Tom, fearing he would not be able to get back home on his own, hurried.

They reached the house. Tom was about to open the door when he realized he could not do it. Charley did.

"Oh, there you are," came the familiar voice of Tom's father. "I was getting worried about where you were."

Tom answered. He said, "Charley and I went for a walk," but the only sound he heard was a meow.

"That cat seems to know," Tom's father said with a good-natured laugh. "Where were you?"

"Just hanging around the neighborhood," said Charley vaguely.

"Don't you have homework to do?"

"No problem. I just have to start writing an essay called 'The Most Exciting Thing That Ever Happened to Me.'"

"Interesting. What are you going to write about?"

"Don't know. But I'm really looking forward to it."

"Hey," said Tom's father, "I love to hear that enthusiasm for a change."

Tom, curling about Charley's feet, felt contented. "I'm going off to sleep," he announced. Charley reached down and gave Tom a reassuring scratch behind the ear.

Tom strolled over to his own bed, leaped up, found the cat's pillow, and closed his eyes. In moments he was asleep, purring gently.

Charley sat down to compose the essay.

———

During the next few days, all went well. Tom enjoyed doing nothing, sleeping all day on his own bed. Occasionally he slept in a different place. Once, he went for a stroll in the backyard.

Meanwhile, Charley lived Tom's life. He went to school. He played with Tom's friends. He enjoyed Tom's family.

On the fifth day Tom began to get restless. He was bored with just sleeping. He would have watched television, but he had to wait for others to turn the TV on, and they didn't always choose his favorite programs.

Twice, Tom started to read the daily newspapers only to be picked up and placed firmly in the litter box. He was not being understood.

Frustrated, Tom ventured onto the streets. Once there he narrowly avoided being hit by a car, had his tail pulled by an infant, was teased by an older child, and then was chased by a dog. By then he'd begun to think he'd had enough of being a cat. He took a nap.

That afternoon, when he got home from school, Charley put his schoolbooks down and said, "Today was not a good day!"

Tom awoke, yawned, stretched, and looked around. "What's the matter?"

"Remember that essay?"

"'The Most Exciting Thing That Ever Happened to Me'?"

"Exactly," Charley said. "You know how hard I worked on it. It was due today. When we got to the moment to share papers, I volunteered to read mine."

"Mr. Oliver must have been surprised."

"He sure was. I guess you never volunteered for anything."

"No way," Tom agreed.

"Anyway, he called on me and I read."

"What happened?"

Charley held up the pages he had written. "He said my work was a fine piece of writing, but he didn't want fiction. He wanted something *real*."

"What did you write about?"

"Transformation: 'How I, Once a Boy, Became a Cat.' Though the whole class liked it and Mr. Oliver admitted it was fun, he said I have to do the whole thing again. Make it real. But every word of it was true!" Disgusted, Charley threw his paper onto his desk.

Tom scratched himself beneath the chin. "You could write about that time you caught a mouse."

"Oh sure. As if he'd believe that," said Charley, and he went off in a huff.

Tom, reminding himself that he wanted to talk to Charley about going through the transformation process again, was just about to slip back into a nap when something Charley had said floated through his mind. What was it? Oh yes . . . did Charley say that the subject he had written about was, "*How I, Once a Boy, Became a Cat*"?

Surely what Charley meant to say was the other way around—that is, "How I, Once a Cat, Became a Boy." Or was he writing about how *he,* Tom, became a cat?

It was too confusing. Tom yawned and shut his eyes again. But he could not sleep. What Charley had said bothered him.

At last he got up and looked around for Charley, but the boy had gone out. Back in his room, Tom noticed that the paper Charley had written was lying on the desk.

He read it. It was just what Charley had said: a report about a boy who had turned into a cat. This boy, so Charley had written, wished to become a cat and sleep all the time. That was familiar enough. In fact, as Tom went through it, the whole story was his *own* experience. However, in Charley's story, the boy's name was Charley and the cat's name was Felix.

Why, Tom wondered, *would Charley have every-thing the same,* except *the names?*

"Hey, Charley," Tom said that night as Charley sat at the desk working on his new essay. "I read your essay."

Charley glanced around. He seemed surprised. "That's not like you."

"You left it out."

"Whatever. Did you . . . like it?"

"It was fine," said Tom. "It was pretty accurate, too. Except for two things."

"What's that?"

"You changed the names around. You called the boy Charley and the cat Felix."

"Oh, right," said Charley, turning back to his work.

"How come you did that?" Tom asked.

"It was supposed to be true," Charley muttered.

Tom frowned. "I don't follow."

Charley turned around to gaze at Tom evenly. "I guess there's no harm in telling you *now.*"

"Telling what *now*?"

"Well, before I introduced myself to you and you took me in, I was once a boy, and my name was Charles."

"You *were*?"

"See, I was bored with my life—so bored, I began thinking that things would be better if I were a cat. As it turned out, I met a cat. Or rather, this cat introduced himself to me. His name was Felix. Felix knew about one of these neighborhood wizard-cats. Sound familiar? You can guess the rest."

As Charley was telling this story, Tom felt increasingly troubled. "Charley," he said, "are you telling me—as you sit at *my* desk, wearing *my* clothes, doing *my* homework, looking like *me*—that at one time *you* were a boy and *then* became a cat? But then you decided you didn't want to be a cat and so became me instead?"

"You've got it."

"But . . . but why didn't you and that Felix just change back to what you were?"

"Felix didn't want to be a cat again."

"He didn't?"

"Nope."

"Charley, are you saying you found me and tricked me into—"

Tom interrupted, "It was what you wanted, too."

"But that's outrageous!" cried Tom. "Anyway," he said, "I've had enough of sleeping. I want to change back."

"Sorry," Charley said. "Too late for that."

Tom, who was becoming increasingly upset, stared at Charley. "What do you mean?"

"I prefer being a boy again. This is a great place and your family is nice." So saying, he left the room, shutting the door behind him.

At first Tom was too astounded to do anything. Then he leaped off the bed and headed right for the door, only to remember that he had to get a person to open it for him. He called to Charley, but it was not Charley who came. It was his mother.

"Want to go out?" she asked, reaching down and chucking Tom under the chin.

"Of course I want to go out," Tom said in a rather irritated way. But when he spoke, all his mother heard was caterwauling.

"Isn't it cute the way cats talk," she said as she scooped him up and set him gently but firmly out the front door. "Now go play."

An indignant Tom looked up and down the street. It was all very different since he had become a cat. He closed his eyes and breathed deeply, trying to sort out the many scents. Then he began to go toward what he hoped would be an audience with Maggie.

It took a while, but at last Tom found the abandoned building. Once again he went into the basement, then to the long, dimly lit hallway, passing through the multitude of cats. The large tiger cat sat in front of the doorway at the end of the hall.

"What can we do for you?" asked the large cat.

Tom said, "A transformation."

"With whom?"

"With the one I was transformed from."

"Is he here?"

"Well, no."

"Then forget it. Anyway, Maggie's out."

"Where?"

"Hey, pal, she has her own life."

"But . . ."

"Beat it, tomcat," snarled the large cat, and he hissed. Tom backed away and made his way home.

That night Tom had it out with Charley.

"The point is," Tom said hotly, "you weren't

being honest with me. In your paper you said you were a boy."

"I was."

"Then you became a cat, and now you're a boy again."

"All true."

"Now you say you have no desire to change back."

"I'm being honest, dude," said Charley. "Come on, you *wanted* to sleep all day, didn't you? Just lay about."

"I know. But that's more boring than staying awake."

"Hey, Tom, you made a deal. If you don't like it, go find another kid who is as bored with things as you were. Believe me, there are plenty of them. A lot of the cats at Maggie's used to be kids who were bored with their lives."

"Is that true?"

"Half the kids in your class used to be cats!"

Tom was shocked. "They were?"

"Trust me," said Charley. "You know the story:

Kids get bored. Want to sleep all day instead of going to school. Bingo! Kids become cats. Cats become kids. They're the lively ones, always raising their hands."

"But I want to be a *human,*" Tom cried. "Not some cat!"

"Go find a kid to exchange with you. Now please, leave me in peace. I have to write this essay."

"But . . ."

Suddenly, Charley picked Tom up, and despite Tom's howl of protest, put him out of the room.

Tom slipped from the house through an open window. It was quite late, and the moon was large in the sky. He went around to the backyard, climbed the fence, and sniffed. The air was full of pungent smells. The only one he found interesting was the scent of his own home. It made his heart ache. Lifting his head, he let out a long piercing howl of misery. Then another.

A window opened. A voice growled, "Shut up, cat! I'm trying to sleep!"

A mournful Tom slunk out of the yard and onto

the street. A thousand distinct odors wafted through the air, a tapestry of smells too complex for Tom to untangle.

He wandered on, paying little attention to where he was going, up and down streets, through alleys, along back fences.

Tom had been walking for about an hour when he heard spitting and hissing. He stopped and listened. It was a catfight. He looked to see where it was coming from, spied an alley, and trotted over.

At the far end of the alley were two cats. One was a sleek brown Siamese, the other a gray cat. The gray one had been forced back against the fence by the Siamese.

"Help!" cried the gray cat. "Help!"

Hardly thinking of what he was doing, Tom let out a howl and dashed down the alley. The Siamese turned to confront him. Tom leaped over him and came down beside the gray cat. Tom hissed, showed his fangs, and raised a claw-extended paw.

The Siamese, confronted by two cats, backed off, turned, and fled.

"He's gone," Tom said, panting to catch his breath.

"Thank you," the gray cat replied.

Tom turned and looked at this other cat for the first time. "Hey, you're Maggie, the wizard-cat!" he cried.

"Do I know you?" said Maggie.

"My name is Tom. You transformed me from a boy. The cat was named Charley."

"I'm sorry. I can't remember. These transformations come by the litter. After a while all you people look alike."

"We do?"

"A certain blandness. No show of emotion. As if you can't bother. So, sorry, I don't remember you. But I'm ever so grateful. If I can return the favor . . ."

"Oh, but you can," Tom said eagerly.

"How's that?"

"Transform me back."

"To what you were?"

"Right."

"How does the other one—the one I transformed you with—feel?"

"I don't think he wants to switch."

"I'm afraid that's what usually happens. It makes retransformation nearly impossible."

"But you *can* do it, can't you?"

"Oh sure, but the point is, you have to get the two heads side by side. If one doesn't want to, and that one is a human, it isn't easy."

"I can arrange it!" Tom cried.

"How?"

"Follow me."

Tom led the way back to his own house. They reached it by two in the morning. Finding the window through which Tom had got out still open, they crawled inside.

Maggie looked about. "Nice place you got here," she muttered.

"*Shh,*" Tom whispered. He led the way to his room, and by standing up on his hind legs—Maggie helped—they were able to push the door open.

Charley, head upon a pillow, lay fast asleep on the bed.

"Now listen carefully," Tom said to Maggie, "I'll get on the pillow right next to him and put my head near his. Give me a minute. Then, you jump on and do what you normally do. Just make the transformation."

Maggie giggled. "Someone's going to be surprised."

"That's Charley's problem. He tricked me into this."

"That's what you all say," said Maggie.

Tom leaped onto the bed and padded to his own pillow. Once there he lay down, tucked his paws under his chest, and nestled his head right next to Charley's.

Within moments Maggie followed. "Ready?" she whispered.

"Ready," Tom replied.

"Here goes," Maggie warned.

Tom closed his eyes and waited for the tap on

his forehead. When nothing happened he opened his eyes and found himself staring right into the face of a gray cat.

Puzzled, Tom called, "Maggie?"

"The name's Charley," the cat said.

"*Charley?*" Tom cried, and looked down at himself. He was just the way he had been moments before—a cat. In a panic he turned. There, asleep, was a person who looked exactly like he had looked. As for the second cat, it looked just like Maggie.

"Hey," Charley—now Maggie—growled, "what's going on? How come I'm a cat again?"

"I'm afraid . . . Maggie did it," said Tom.

"Maggie? The wizard-cat?"

"I think so. She did the transformation on herself and you. She's become . . . *us.*"

One week later, Tom—who had spent all his time prowling the streets—suddenly stopped. He was in a park not far from a bench. Sitting on the bench was a girl. She was not doing anything in particular, just sitting. Now and again she swung a leg back and forth. Then she yawned, looked at her watch, and yawned again.

Tom watched her for about fifteen minutes. In all that time the girl continued to just sit there, a slight frown on her face. She looked bored.

Tom went forward and sat down in front of the girl.

"What's happening?" he said.

The girl looked down at him. After a moment she said, "Nothing."

"Doing anything?" asked Tom.

"Nothing *to* do," the girl replied.

"Bored?"

"Always."

Tom got up, stretched, and then rubbed himself against the girl's leg. "You sound like my kind of friend," he said.

BABETTE THE BEAUTIFUL

IN THE LAND OF SOLANDIA, it was a queen, not a king, who ruled. Some years ago it was Queen Isabelle—*not* King Alfredo—who was the reigning monarch. Hardly a surprise then that Isabelle wished to give birth to a girl so that her daughter might become the next queen. That said, the queen felt strongly that any daughter of hers *must* be very beautiful because she believed only beautiful girls could be happy.

The truth is, Queen Isabelle thought about having a beautiful daughter *all* the time. If you asked—and even if you did not ask—the queen could—and would—tell you what this hoped-for daughter would look like. What's more, the queen could—and would—describe this daughter's beauty in great detail for hours at a time. She even knew her name: Babette. The queen chose the name because she wanted her daughter—when she became queen—to be known as—Babette the Beautiful.

Unfortunately, there was no child. And time was passing.

One day a lady-in-waiting told Queen Isabelle about an old woman who had recently arrived in the city. The woman's name was Esmeralda. Esmeralda—so the lady-in-waiting claimed—had powers to enable women to bear *exactly* the kind of child they desired.

When the queen expressed interest in this Esmeralda, the lady-in-waiting told the queen where the old woman lived.

Disguising herself—and telling no one where she was going—Queen Isabelle made her way to a dark alley in the oldest part of the old city. There she knocked on an ancient door. The door was opened by a little old woman with a twisted body. Her face was ugly, her hair sparse and gray. Her hands were gnarled, and ribboned with veins. Upon her frail shoulders lay a tattered blue-and-green shawl.

The queen, shocked by the woman's appearance, stepped back from the door. "I think I have made a mistake," she said, and turned to leave.

Before the queen could go three steps, the old woman cried: "Stay, Queen! I am Esmeralda, the only person who can help you to have the beautiful daughter you desire!"

The queen looked back at the woman. "How do you know who I am and what I wish?" she said.

"Because," said Esmeralda, "my powers are mirrors that reflect your desires."

"But how can you, who are so ugly," said the queen, "help me to have a beautiful daughter?"

Though she heard the insult, Esmeralda said only, "You must trust me."

Queen Isabelle laughed. "Do you really expect me to trust someone who is as hideous as you?"

Esmeralda's eyes gleamed with anger. "My queen,

I have a large mirror which I will place between us. You can talk to me but only look upon yourself."

Though the queen was torn between wanting the daughter of her dreams and being revolted by Esmeralda's appearance, her desire proved stronger. "Very well," she said. "I shall allow you to help me." She stepped inside the hovel.

Esmeralda placed a large mirror in the center of her small jumbled room. This mirror was door-like—taller than it was wide. With a surface that fairly sparkled, it was framed by intricately carved wood—carvings of animals, birds, and flowers, crafted so well they seemed to be alive.

Esmeralda sat on one side of this mirror; Isabelle sat on the other, so that the queen gazed only at her own image. Though she had always thought herself beautiful, the mirror's image made her a picture of perfection. This pleased her greatly and she began to relax.

"Very well, my queen," Esmeralda called out from behind the mirror. "Tell me about this daughter you desire."

"My daughter Babette," began Isabelle, "must be the most beautiful girl in Solandia. She must be a child without so much as one blemish or irregularity."

"Why must she be so beautiful?"

"Why," said the queen, "the whole world knows that only the beautiful are happy."

"Ah then," said Esmeralda, "you wish her to be . . . what is the word?"

"*Flawless,*" the queen said.

"Very well," said Esmeralda. "My powers can reflect that."

"Then use them," Queen Isabelle commanded.

"So be it!" cried Esmeralda. Then the old hag placed one hand on the top of the mirror, and the other hand on the bottom. She began to squeeze. Instead of shattering, the mirror collapsed into a glassy lump. Esmeralda compressed this lump until it became smaller and smaller. When it became perfectly round, and no bigger than the tip of her small finger, she turned it inside out with her thumbs until it became invisible. She then placed this invisible pill in Queen Isabelle's hands.

"Swallow that," said Esmeralda, "and you shall have a daughter who will appear flawless."

Queen Isabelle hesitated. But when she recalled that the invisible pill was made from the mirror—which had made *her* look so beautiful—she swallowed it down. She waited for something to happen. When nothing did, she became annoyed. "I suppose you now wish me to pay you for something I cannot see?"

"My queen," Esmeralda replied with a bow deep enough to hide the glint in her eye, "who am I to ask anything from such a beautiful and gracious queen? Let me be content in thinking that I've been able to make you happy by helping you have a . . . flawless daughter."

Pleased by such a show of humility, Queen Isabelle flung a halfpenny at the woman's feet and hastened away.

But as the queen went on, she grew uneasy about this Esmeralda and what had transpired. Perhaps the ugly woman had been insincere in her parting words. Perhaps she would talk about the queen's secret visit. Perhaps she would mock her. Who knew what claims the woman might make?

By the time the queen had returned to her palace, she had decided it would be better to banish Esmeralda to the far reaches of the country—the Northern Forest. It was done immediately, but secretly. Not even King Alfredo or the Prime Minister knew about it.

It was not very much later that, with great joy, Queen Isabelle announced she was going to have a baby. The baby was a girl. At least, Queen Isabelle had no doubt the baby was a girl. The moment the child was born, the hardworking and distracted midwife automatically wrapped the baby up in a sweet-smelling blanket, then handed the precious bundle to her mother, the queen. Eagerly wishing to look upon the infant's perfections, the queen pulled aside the blankets and peeked at the baby's face. For a brief moment—a very, *very* brief moment—Queen Isabelle saw *nothing.* However, it was impossible for the queen to believe she had given birth to an *invisible* child. After all, the bundle had a lusty voice. It smelled like a baby. It wiggled and wriggled *just* like a baby. Certainly she had the appetite of a baby. In addition—there could be no denying it—the child had not a single noticeable blemish!

After that one brief frightening moment—when Queen Isabelle had seen *nothing*—the *next* second she was convinced she was looking at the most beautiful baby girl in the world, the very child she had long imagined and always wanted. Of course, she named the child Babette.

With Babette secure in her mother's arms, the midwife stepped outside the delivery room, where King Alfredo was waiting anxiously.

"How is my wife?" he asked.

"Everything went splendidly," said the midwife.

"Wonderful! And the child?"

"A perfect girl."

"Better than wonderful! May I see them?"

The midwife led King Alfredo to the queen's

bedside. There Queen Isabelle said, "Here, husband of mine, is Babette, our new daughter, the future queen of Solandia. Isn't she every bit as beautiful as I desired?"

The king peeked inside the bundle. For just the very small part of a very small second, he saw . . . *nothing*.

"Not so much as one blemish, has she?" said Queen Isabelle.

The king hesitated. "What," he said, "do you like most about her?"

"Exactly what I expected to like," returned the queen. "Her clear blue eyes and blond hair. Just like her mother's."

King Alfredo looked again, and this time he saw the beautiful daughter his wife had so often and vividly described. So he said, "Yes indeed, her eyes *are* quite splendid."

Then he added, "But I confess, it's her delicate nose, and noble forehead—which she gets from *my* side of the family—that *I* admire!"

"You are as perceptive as ever," said the queen.

Because the birth of Princess Babette was important news in the queendom of Solandia, the king went to the Prime Minister and told that wise gentleman how well everything had gone.

The Prime Minister asked, "Is the princess as perfect as her Queen Mother desired?"

"The girl is truly flawless," said King Alfredo. "Just what was wanted." In great detail he described Babette.

The Prime Minister went to the Lord High Information Officer and told *him* the happy news.

"We must send out a proclamation at once," said the Lord High Information Officer. "With," he added, "an appropriate portrait of the princess!"

The Prime Minister agreed.

"Of course," said the Lord High Information Officer, "to do so I must know what Princess Babette looks like."

The Prime Minister provided him with the king's description, adding some details from what he recalled as to the way Queen Isabelle had spoken of her much-desired child.

The Lord High Information Officer went to the Royal Court Artist and asked him to do a portrait of the new princess so every citizen in Solandia would know her likeness.

"Can you describe her to me?" said the Royal Court Artist.

"Of course!" said the Lord High Information Officer, and he gave a fine verbal portrait of Babette—just as *he* had been told.

The Royal Court Artist—who was famous not just for his skill but even more for his ability to create art that satisfied his clients' high ideals—made the portrait. Because there was no one he wished to satisfy more than Queen Isabelle, he painted a stunning picture of the new princess.

When Queen Isabelle saw the portrait, she said, "That's her—exactly!"

Very soon thereafter, a royal proclamation— complete with a portrait of beautiful Princess

Babette—was distributed to every person in Solandia. The citizens, seeing the sweet face of the new princess, their future queen, were very proud. How satisfying that Solandia had a princess without so much as one blemish.

Long live Solandia! Long live Babette the Beautiful!

Of course, when the people actually *saw* Princess Babette, they did experience a brief and puzzling moment of confusion because nothing *seemed* to be there. Nothing to worry about! All they had to do was glance at the proclamation portrait to tell them *exactly* what Babette looked like. Besides, the image they saw was indeed *perfect*.

One other thing of importance happened: Shortly after Babette's birth, Queen Isabelle banished all mirrors from Solandia.

But alas, before Babette was one year old, Queen Isabelle and King Alfredo faded away.

The queen was the first to die. The cause—it was whispered—was madness. Isabelle's symptoms appeared when she took to avoiding all light. Next she bound up her eyes and walked about like a blind person. Her actual death came during the night, when she accidentally fell from the highest point of the castle. It was said she could not see where she was going.

A rumor spread throughout Solandia that the death was somehow connected with the new princess. The Lord High Information Officer, in haste, made it a crime to speak of such a thing. As he explained to the Prime Minister: "The country must protect its image."

As for King Alfredo's death, though the doctors gave medical reasons, it was commonly understood that he died of grief over the loss of his beloved wife. Indeed, his last words were, "*I can no longer see any reason to live.*"

When these sad events transpired, Princess Babette, not yet one year of age, was far too young to take the throne. A queen had to be at least sixteen. So Solandia was ruled—quite properly, it must be said—on her behalf by the Prime Minister.

Years passed. Although Babette remained invisible,

and despite the fact that all mirrors had been banned from the land, the young princess knew exactly what she looked like. She knew this by looking at portraits of herself—which were placed on every wall of every room—throughout the palace. Indeed, the Prime Minister had decreed that a portrait of the princess be placed in every home throughout the entire country of Solandia.

The artists of Solandia were only too happy to comply with the decree, for they loved to paint Babette's picture, readily confessing that the young princess was—after all—the perfect subject.

Did Babette look the same in every portrait? Of course not! Because the talents of the artists differed, so too did the images differ. Still, certain qualities were there. Babette never had a blemish. And—she was always beautiful.

More years passed. Babette's sixteenth birthday approached. In Solandia it was the custom that only after the heir apparent married could she claim the throne as the country's rightful ruler. Of course the choice of a spouse was Babette's, but a choice had to be made. This selection of a husband was to be the most important decision of her young life. Hardly a wonder that the question raging about Solandia was this: Whom among the many suitors would Princess Babette choose to marry?

The court became a beehive of curiosity. Every move Babette made, everything she said, every man she met, was watched and talked about. Only one thing was generally agreed upon: For a princess as beautiful as Babette, only the most handsome man would do.

Shortly before her birthday, the Prime Minister invited Babette's favored suitors—the short list numbered seven—to join her for a week of festivities. Wisely wanting to provide a place for her to make her crucial decision far from the distractions of a court caught up in the frenzy of speculation, the Prime Minister chose a far corner of Solandia— the Northern Forest.

Before Babette left the castle in her carriage, the Prime Minister spoke some words to her: "Choose well, my princess. I have so much faith in your judgment I see no need to come along. Just remember, the eyes of history will be watching you."

With that, Babette went in her carriage, her seven suitors following close behind.

Each day of the following week proved perfect. The weather was lovely. Skies were cobalt blue by day, star bright and crisp by night. "Like Babette," one of the handsome young men noted as he glanced lovingly (so all could see him do so) at the portrait of Babette with which each suitor had been provided.

Babette, meanwhile, met first with one young man and then another. She gossiped idly with one, talked philosophy with another. With a third she went walking. With yet another she went hunting. She did a little of each with each.

"I think I am ready to choose," said Babette to the Royal Trail Master. "I should like to do so dramatically. Have you any suggestions?"

The Royal Trail Master told the princess about a spectacular wild rose he had discovered in the most isolated part of the forest. "It is the most beautiful rose I have ever seen," he informed Babette.

"As pretty as me?"

"Almost."

"Then I will pluck it and present it to the one I have chosen for a husband," said Babette.

Therefore, it was agreed that the entire party would walk through the forest, and then return to waiting coaches. At that point Babette would announce her choice of a husband by giving him the rose. The lucky man would escort her home. All agreed it would be wonderfully romantic and very picturesque.

With soldiers to guard against any mishaps, the party worked its way deep into the forest. But no matter where they all looked, the rose could not be found.

"How annoying," said Babette. "Still, I must make my choice."

When the Royal Trail Master announced it was time to go back to the coaches, a tremor of excitement passed through the crowd. Babette was about to make her decision.

At that moment Babette, remembering the Prime Minister's stern admonition to make her choice with care, called the Royal Trail Master and said, "I need just a few more moments of privacy to make my decision. I shall go for a stroll. Perhaps I'll come upon that beautiful rose."

"Maybe it would be best for me to stay," said the Trail Master.

"No, no," Babette replied. "I require only a short time. I can catch up easily."

Accordingly, the Trail Master waved everybody on. Babette remained. Alone, she clasped her hands and closed her eyes, and began to think very hard about her crucial decision.

While meditating deeply, she heard someone's footsteps. An indignant Babette opened her eyes.

Staring fixedly at her was a twisted old woman. The woman's face was haggard. Her hair was sparse and gray. Her hands were gnarled, and ribboned with veins. Upon her frail shoulders lay a tattered blue-and-green shawl. Babette thought her very ugly.

After a moment of alarm, Babette regained her composure and said, "Who are you? And what are you doing here?"

To which the woman responded, "Who are you to speak so rudely to me?"

"I am Babette, Royal Princess of Solandia."

"Are you?"

"Can you not tell just by looking at me?" Babette returned, annoyed with the rudeness of the woman.

"Perhaps you are what you say," the old woman said, "but perhaps you are not. I cannot tell because I cannot *see* you."

"What nonsense!" Babette replied. "You are talking to *me*. I am talking to *you*."

"I certainly hear you," the woman said. "But all I see is a suit, gloves, a hat, and boots. I don't see a *person*."

"Are you so blind that you don't see my *face*?"

"Be assured I'm not blind, but I don't see your face."

"But it's right here!" Babette cried, pulling off one of her gloves and touching a finger to her own nose. "What do you think I'm touching?"

"I have no idea!" the old woman exclaimed. "What's more, you have no hand, either. Are you, perhaps, a ghost?"

"I am the Royal Princess of Solandia!" cried Babette, stamping her foot with vexation. "Who are you?"

"My name is Esmeralda."

At that moment, the Royal Trail Master, concerned that Babette was overdue, had come back with soldiers. When he saw the princess talking to someone, he stopped.

Though Babette saw the Trail Master and soldiers approach, she continued to give her attention to the woman. "Are you aware," Babette said to the old woman, "that you have insulted me?"

"I beg your pardon," said Esmeralda. "I can tell you only what I see or—in this case—do not see."

"I want this woman arrested!" Babette demanded. "She has offended me grossly!"

It was but a moment's work for the soldiers to take the old woman into custody.

"Bring her to the castle prison!" Babette commanded.

That, too, was done, and in moments the Royal Trail Master and Babette were alone.

"Did the old woman hurt you, Princess?"

Babette was about to say no. Instead she said, "Do I look as if I've been hurt?"

The Royal Trail Master studied her carefully.

"No," he said. "Not as far as I can see."

"What about my face?"

"To me," replied the Royal Trail Master, "you look just as you have always looked."

"And what way is that?"

"Without a blemish. Perfect."

"Fine," Babette said. "That proves the woman is mad. We've probably saved her from harming herself. I feel better already. Let's catch up with the others."

When Babette reached the carriage, her suitors

were all lined up, ready for her great decision. Babette, however, could not free her mind from what had just occurred.

"I need a little more time," she announced.

Babette went home, alone in her carriage. Instead of pondering who would be her spouse, she kept thinking about what had happened in the forest. She did not, of course, believe what the old woman had said. Still, she could not get the incident out of her mind.

When Babette arrived at the castle, the Prime Minister hurried to meet her. "Princess, I understand you met with some trouble in the forest."

"A hideous old woman named Esmeralda insulted me."

"Ah, Princess, the world is full of people who do not see things the way they should. Lacking insight, they are blind to the true beauties of the world."

"It was nothing," Babette assured the Prime Minister. Then she asked, "What happened to her?"

"She's in the palace prison awaiting her punishment, which will be set by the Royal High Judge."

"Good," Babette said.

"And you, have you made up your mind about your future husband?" the Prime Minister inquired anxiously.

Babette replied, "I was too distracted and couldn't see my way clear. I'll make my decision tonight."

That night as Babette was preparing for bed, she examined her face in one of the portraits she used as a mirror. Turning to a lady-in-waiting, she asked, "Tell me, what do I look like?"

To this the woman replied, "Why, Princess, you look exactly like your portrait."

"Which one?"

"Your favorite one. The one on your vanity table."

Babette stared at the portrait for a long time. When she got into bed she kept asking herself, "Do I *really* look like that?"

She slept restlessly.

In the morning the Prime Minister came to ask if Babette had chosen her husband.

"Never mind that," Babette replied. "Has that woman I met in the forest been punished yet?"

"The punishment will be announced today. I can assure you she will be banished. You'll never have to set eyes on her again. But you're not worried about her, are you?"

"No," said Babette. "Though she did insult me, perhaps she feels remorse. If she would apologize and admit her mistake, I'd be inclined to pardon her."

"How gracious of you," the Prime Minister said. "And the matter of your husband . . . ?"

"All in good time . . ."

That afternoon Babette was seated in her audience chamber when Esmeralda was ushered in between two soldiers. The old woman's feet were in chains. Her hands were tied. As she approached the throne, she lifted her eyes and gazed at Babette.

"Very well, Esmeralda," Babette said, "when you look upon me, what do you see now?"

"Your clothes," Esmeralda said.

"No more?"

"If I speak the truth you'll imprison me again."

"Take off her chains. Undo her hands," Babette commanded.

It was done.

"You are a free woman," Babette said to Esmeralda. "Tell me what you see."

"Chains do not change my eyes. I still see . . . *nothing*."

"Tell me the truth!" cried Babette.

"Princess," said the old woman, "I cannot see what I cannot see."

"Everybody else sees me!" cried Babette.

"Princess," said Esmeralda, "the truth is, you are invisible."

"Invisible! What nonsense!"

"What would you say if I could prove it to you?" Esmeralda asked.

"You can't!"

"Then request that a mirror be brought here."

"A what?" asked a puzzled Babette.

"A mirror."

"What is a mirror?"

"It's a device for seeing the truth about yourself."

"More nonsense!" Babette cried with indignation. "It's impossible to see oneself."

To which Esmeralda said only, "It may be difficult to see yourself, but how else can you know the person you truly are?"

Babette laughed at the old woman. "Look about the walls. What do you see?"

Esmeralda gazed at the portraits of Babette that hung everywhere. Then she said, "I see one false face in many different poses."

"You are mocking me!" cried Babette. "I need only look at my portraits to know what I look like. They are art, and the whole world knows art tells the truth. Those faces are *me.*"

Esmeralda looked from the portraits to Babette and back again. "That's as may be," she said, "but I can't see your real face—if you have one."

"Go back to jail!" Babette cried.

Esmeralda was led away.

Alone, Babette was greatly agitated. She paced and fretted, then sent for the Prime Minister.

"Your Highness," he said, "have you—"

Babette interrupted. "Are there such things called mirrors, devices by which one can see oneself?"

"My princess," the Prime Minister said soothingly, "a mirror is an ancient device. Mirrors distort life. Here in Solandia, we are civilized. Mirrors are . . . primitive. We live by the arts. It was your wise mother who banished them from the nation."

"Fetch me a mirror!" Babette demanded.

"Are you dissatisfied by your portraits?" said the Prime Minister. "Would you like a new one painted? We have some wonderful new young artists who can paint whatever you'd like. Besides, all of Solandia is waiting—"

"Fetch me a mirror!"

"I suppose," said the Prime Minister, "there is one in the attic of the Royal Museum, but—"

"Get it!"

After a long search, an old mirror—hardly bigger than her own hand, and covered by a cloth—was brought to Princess Babette.

Babette first gave the mirror to the Prime

Minister. "Look at it," she commanded, "and tell me what you see."

The nervous Prime Minister did as he'd been ordered to do.

"Well, what do you see?"

"A very old man."

Babette gave the mirror to a lady-in-waiting. "What do *you* see?"

"A very nervous woman."

She gave it to a guard. "And you?"

"A very frightened soldier."

"Leave me!" cried Babette. "All of you!"

It was done. Alone, Babette took the mirror and propped it before her on her vanity table. With very great care she combed her hair, patted her cheeks, pouted her lips, then lifted her chin ever so slightly. That was the way her favorite portrait showed her. Only then did Babette reach out and—heart pounding—look into the mirror.

Seeing *nothing,* Babette gave a shriek and collapsed upon the floor.

———

For the remainder of the day, Babette refused to see anyone. Nor would she let anyone see her. Instead she spent hours sitting before the small mirror, staring at her invisibility. How painful it was to admit that she was nothing. Not only did it mean that no one could truly see her, it meant that they had *never* seen her.

Babette tried to convince herself that she was dreaming, ill, going mad. Had not her mother gone mad?

Before Babette was willing to admit the truth—that the old woman was right, and she *was* invisible—she decided on another test. She took down all her portraits from the walls. Then she sent for the Prime Minister.

"Princess," he said, "the entire country is waiting for—"

"Prime Minister," she said, "look at me."

"With pleasure."

"What do you see?" she asked.

As he normally did, the Prime Minister stole a hasty glance at the walls where the portraits of

Princess Babette usually hung. When he saw that they were gone, he gasped, placed a hand over his eyes, and said, "Princess, I've a frightful headache."

"I insist!" Babette cried. "Tell me what I look like!"

"I don't know," he admitted.

"Go away from me," Babette cried. "Send that Esmeralda to me."

"She's gone."

"Gone!"

"For her unspeakable rudeness to you, dear princess, the Royal High Judge banished her."

"Banished? Where?"

"Where you found her. The remote Northern Forest."

"But . . . !"

"She did, however, leave you a note."

"Give it to me!"

The Prime Minister hurried away, and though he himself did not return, he had Esmeralda's note slipped underneath Babette's door. It read:

Babette: If you wish to become visible, first find yourself in a mirror, and then take what you want.

Esmeralda

Though Babette read the note three times, she could make little sense of it. Raging with frustration, she tore it into shreds. For a while she was too agitated to do anything but prowl about her room, pausing now and again to steal glances at the small mirror. Seeing nothing, she moaned and paced some more.

Now and again there was a knocking on the door. A lady-in-waiting or some other member of the court asking permission to enter, to help her, to feed her, to conduct some business—wondering if she had chosen a husband.

Babette ignored them all.

When she could no longer deny her hunger, she did request food, and also requested a box of paints and a paintbrush. When all was delivered, she forgot about eating. Instead she sat before her mirror and, with the brush, painted on her own face.

First she painted the outlines, then her eyes, nose, and mouth. She could see what she had painted in the mirror, but because Babette was no artist, the result was that she looked like a clown with bad makeup.

"I shall take art lessons," Babette told herself. "I'll pay artists to paint on my face every day."

The thought made her sad. The sadness brought tears that trickled down her cheeks, leaving tracks of emptiness through the paint she had just applied. She tried to smooth out the spots. Her face became a blur.

Babette picked up one of the portraits she had removed from the walls. With scissors she cut out the canvas face, punched out holes for her eyes, attached string to the mask she had made, and placed the image over her face.

When she looked in the mirror, she saw herself as she had always looked before. The canvas mask, however, was hot and sticky. What's more, with the mask in place she could not eat or scratch her nose. It was hard for her to breathe. Stymied to the point of fury, Babette tore off the mask and cut it up into tiny bits.

All that night Babette lay upon her bed, weeping. How she wished she had never met Esmeralda! That made her recall the message that had been left:

Babette: If you wish to become visible, first find yourself in a mirror, and then take what you want.

Esmeralda

"Ah," Babette said to herself with a sigh, "if only I knew how! If only I could talk to Esmeralda and ask her advice." She resolved to find the old woman.

It was about two in the morning when Princess Babette slipped down to the castle stables, saddled a fast horse, and set off at a gallop.

Dawn had arrived when Babette reached the Northern Forest, and the place where she had first met Esmeralda. All was still. Babette's horse blew a frosty breath and nervously pawed the ground.

In the not-too-far distance, Babette observed a glow. At first she thought it was the rising sun. When the glow did not move, however, Babette decided to investigate. She began to walk among the forest trees. A chill wind blew into her face. The only sound was her tread upon the ground. She walked on. The glow grew brighter. Now and again sparks of light exploded as if from a spinning diamond. A cool gray mist began to flow down among the tree roots. The mist seemed to be coming from the glow.

Babette stepped into the mist. It eddied about her ankles like flowing water. She walked through it, moving toward its glowing source. The glow grew brighter.

Babette saw the cause of the glow. Suspended between two great tree trunks was a gigantic mirror. The mirror was taller than it was wide—like a door—and was framed by wood that had been intricately carved. These carvings were of animals and birds, as well as flowers, crafted so well they seemed to be alive. The mirror's surface shimmered and sparkled even as it reflected the forest that surrounded it.

Though the mirror appeared to be solid, at the bottom a stream of gray mist flowed out. It was the same gray mist that ran through the trees, the mist Babette had followed.

Babette approached the mirror. She stood before it and looked at herself. What she saw was the clothing she wore, though as before, nothing showed of her face or hands. But the more she gazed at the mirror, the more she saw what appeared to be a multitude of shadowy faces *within* the mirror itself. There were hundreds, thousands of these faces, none very distinct, all drifting like feathers in a gentle wind.

Babette reached toward the mirror. Her fingers passed into the mirror itself. She pushed farther until her arm went in up to the elbow. It was as if the mirror—or what she thought was the mirror—was in fact a doorway.

She placed her other hand against the glass. It, too, went through. Babette stood there, arms extended into the mirror. Then—her heart pounding—she stepped inside.

Babette found herself in a large room suffused with dusty light. The room contained nothing but mirrored doors complete with hinges and handles. These doors were everywhere—on the walls, the ceiling, the floor—so many doors it was impossible to count them. None were marked, nor was there any indication of what lay behind them.

As Babette stood there, all her movements were reflected in the mirrored doors. It was as if she were in the middle of a kaleidoscope.

"Hello!" she cried.

No answer.

Feeling as though she had entered a trap, Babette reached toward the door she had used to enter the room. It swung open slowly.

Beyond was another room. Babette looked in. The room was full of eyes, millions and millions of them. Each one was a different color, a different shape. Some seemed sad. Others were bright and cheerful. A few blinked. Others stared brazenly.

Some appeared brave, some evasive. A few of the eyes gaped fixedly at her, while some, as if shy, shifted away.

Babette reached out and touched one of the eyes. It winked and fell into the palm of her hand. It lay there gazing up at her. Babette looked back. As she did so, she remembered the message from Esmeralda:

Babette: If you wish to become visible, first find yourself in a mirror, and then take what you want.
                                                    Esmeralda

Her hand trembling, Babette lifted the eye to her face and pressed it in. She took away her hand. The eye stayed.

Not sure what she was doing, Babette reached out for another eye, took it into her hand, and then pressed it, too, into her face.

Next she turned and stepped out of the room, back into the central hall. She gazed about into the mirrors. In countless images she saw her new eyes. But when she looked back at the doorway through which she had just come, the eye room behind it had vanished.

Babette went to another door and pulled it open. It was a roomful of thumbs. There were thumbs of all shapes, colors, and sizes. She reached for one and pulled it onto her right hand like the finger of a glove.

She held the thumb up before her eyes—and saw it. With growing excitement, Babette reached for another thumb—only to realize just in time that it was also for a right hand. She had to make sure to get a left one. She found one and slipped it on.

Babette went from room to room, finding that each contained something different: ears here, there elbows. Ankles in this one. Noses in another. Knees, wrists, and thighs—all had their own rooms.

When Babette had finished assembling herself, one door remained shut. What could she have forgotten?

She turned the knob. It was a room full of hearts. She picked a large, passionate one and pressed it into her chest.

Another door materialized. She opened it. Beyond was the forest. She stepped out, and then turned back toward the great mirror. For the first time Babette saw herself as she was—complete.

Of course, what she saw was not perfect. She had been in such a rush! Her left foot was slightly bigger than her right. One earlobe had a crease, the other did not. Her face was not quite symmetrical. What's more, she realized that in her haste she had selected one blue eye and one brown eye. But—she reminded herself—it did not matter. They were now *her* eyes and they could see themselves.

She turned toward her horse. The horse looked up, saw who it was, and nodded.

Babette galloped back home.

Did Babette marry? Did she become queen? Did she live happily ever after? None of that is known. What *is* known is that from that time on,

Babette not only could see herself but liked what she saw. Moreover, the world saw her—*truly* saw her—as she was, as she had made herself.

And from that day on she was called—Babette the Visible.

Curious

"Jeff Marley," a teacher said to him, "don't you *ever* mind your own business?"

Jeff said, "I'm just curious."

"But, do you have to know *everything*?" she asked.

"I thought," said Jeff, "that's what students are supposed to do."

"Curiosity killed the cat."

"Why?" asked Jeff. "What was that cat curious about?"

"Oh, Jeff," said the exasperated teacher, and walked away.

Jeff—twelve years old—lived in Rolerton,

Wisconsin, a town with a population of forty thousand. Locals said it was the perfect place to live. Every Fourth of July the town newspaper, the *Rolerton Observer,* ran an editorial stating that if you wanted to experience the real America, Rolerton was the town to visit.

The town was home to Bevlin Farm Machinery, Universe Plumbing Fixtures, the Duckworth Regional Medical Center, Luther Junior College, and the Rolerton Astros, a minor-league baseball team. The original team sponsors were the people who owned the Universe Plumbing Company. They picked the name *Astros* hoping folks would make a connection between *Universe Plumbing* and *Astros.* No one did.

The Astros played in the Midwestern League. Teams came from midsized towns in Illinois, Wisconsin, Minnesota, and Iowa. Most players were right out of college. The season began on Memorial Day. Labor Day saw its end.

The team played in Rolerton Park. It had a perfectly symmetrical field with emerald green grass that looked especially good at night when the arc lights came on. Owned by the town, which maintained it, the park had comfortable wooden seats in open stands. Dugouts were clean. There was a concrete field house, with locker rooms for the two teams and the umpires. The Astros uniforms were bright gray with purple trim, the numbers and the name *Astros* in old-timey letters. Most games started at 7:00 P.M. There were lots of special games, such as Fan Appreciation Night, Kids Night, and Helmet Night. The young ballplayers—if they weren't talking to the high school girls—were always willing to give autographs.

General admission was two bucks. Kids got in for one dollar, though some kids snuck in by way of the right-field bleachers. No one seemed to mind. Two more bucks got you a hot dog and a soda. The hot dogs were plump, the sauerkraut was sour, the mustard plentiful. Fifty cents for some pink cotton candy. Or, you could hang out behind the low center-field fence in hopes that someone would hit a home run. Shag a ball, and you kept it.

Though Jeff liked baseball—he played on a Little

League team—what he really loved about the Astros games was the team mascot. The mascot was known as the Alien.

This Alien was a bulbous bright green creature covered with red polka dots. He had a stubby spiked tail and huge claw-hands with ten fingers on *each* hand, which, being rubbery, bent in all different directions. His face—perhaps a third of his whole body length—was long and narrow, with two large, round blue eyes, which gave him a quizzical look. The creature also had a long pointy nose—carrot-like—the end of which lit up red when one of the Astros did something unusual, like make a good catch, a classy putout, or an error.

The Alien's mouth was purple, large, and perfectly round, giving him a perpetual look of surprise. Two red horns sprouted from his head. When his nose lit up, so did the horns.

Jeff was really curious about the Alien. There was nothing in Rolerton like him. He'd do things like follow behind players, imitating any quirky walks with mocking perfection. If the umpire called an out against an Astro, the Alien would call the player safe, his stubby arms spread wide, nose and horns flashing furiously. Sometimes he ran the bases backward or made fun of the umpires or coaches. Or he would pretend to faint—falling backward—at exciting moments. The Alien posed for pictures with anyone, hugging pretty girls, playfully kicking boys on their butts.

If, during a game, the crowd roared, Jeff was probably not paying attention: He'd have been watching the Alien do a somersault, horns and nose brightly lit. Jeff had seen plenty of mascots for professional teams on TV. Every team in America seemed to have one. But the Astros' Alien, according to Jeff, was the best. Of course, Jeff understood that the Alien was a *costume,* which he supposed was made from foam rubber. That meant *somebody* was *inside* the foam rubber. The more Jeff watched the Alien's funny, mocking ways, the more he wanted to know who the person was inside. As far as Jeff was concerned, it was as if the Alien was making fun of Rolerton. Rolerton people didn't usually act the way it did: mocking things. Of course, people accused Jeff of acting the same way. Maybe that's why he found the Alien so interesting.

Jeff asked his friends if they knew who the person inside the mascot costume was. Not only did they not know—they didn't care. That made Jeff want to know even more.

One night he hung around after a game, waiting at the gate for the players, umpires, and coaches to straggle out. The food vendors, ticket takers, and park staff also left. Since none emerged with horns or a nose that lit up, Jeff could only assume that the Alien was *one* of the people who had already come out. But *which* one? His curiosity grew.

The next day, after the game was over, Jeff waited till everybody had gone home. When the last person came out of the park—an old guy who started locking up the gates—Jeff went up to him.

"Excuse me, sir," he said.

The man looked around. "Hey, kid, it's late. Your parents know where you are?"

"Yes, sir, they do. I'm going home right now. But I was just wondering: Did the Alien come out yet?"

"*Who?*"

"You know, the mascot. The Alien."

"Oh, *him*. Everybody's gone. I suppose he has, too."

"Do you know who he is?"

The man thought a moment, and then shrugged. "Now that you mention it, I don't. Hey, my job is to make sure everyone is gone and things are locked tight. And they are. So I guess that guy is gone, too. Unless it's a different person each night."

"I don't think so," said Jeff. "He's always funny in the same way."

"Funny?" said the man. "Ask me, I think he's just rude. But no, I don't know who he is." That said, the old guy drove off in a pickup, calling, "Better get yourself home, boy!"

The following day, Jeff got to the ballpark early. The Astros, being the local team, arrived in ones and twos. The Iowa City Jayhawks came in an old school bus. Any number of other people arrived, too. Jeff studied them all but did not have a hint as to whom the Alien might be.

"Excuse me, please," he said to one guy who seemed the right size. "Are you the Alien?"

"Who?"

"You know, the mascot."

"Are you kidding?"

When a man in a suit arrived—he looked important—Jeff went up to him. "Excuse me, sir, do you know if the Alien has arrived?"

"Who?"

"The mascot. The guy in the green suit."

"Oh, him? Kid, to tell you the truth, I'm the general manager of the Astros. If it were up to me, I wouldn't have him around. Sort of offensive. But the town seems to enjoy him. Least, they pay his salary. So, no, I've got no idea who he is."

Jeff bought a ticket. Because he was so early, he wandered among the empty seats, and made his way down toward the field, where the Jayhawks were taking batting practice. The gate leading onto the field had been left open. After a moment of nervousness, Jeff went on through, half expecting to be shooed off. When no one paid him any mind, he looked around. The Alien was not there.

Moving along the edge of the playing area, Jeff went toward the field house, which was behind home plate. He kept his eye on the open door.

When he reached it, some of the Astros players were wandering out, carrying gloves and bats. They nodded to Jeff in a friendly way.

"Hey, is the Alien in there?" Jeff asked one of them.

"Nope. Least, not that I saw. You can go on in and look."

Excited, Jeff found himself in a corridor with gray concrete walls and three doors. HOME TEAM and VISITORS were lettered on the doors to the left and right. The middle one was marked OFFICIALS.

Jeff opened the HOME TEAM door into a large bare room with glaring lights. One wall was lined with steel lockers. A long bench sat before it. The floor was littered with clothing. At the far end was another room in which Jeff could see toilet stalls and showers. Nobody was there.

Jeff went to the OFFICIALS room and looked in. It was a smaller version of the HOME TEAM room. Two men in umpire uniforms were straddling a bench, playing cards.

"What's up, kid?"

"I'm looking for the Alien. The guy in the green costume."

"Not here, I'm glad to say," said one of the officials as he slapped down a card with gusto and cried, "Gin!"

"How come no one likes him?" Jeff asked.

The other umpire looked around. "'Cause he's always making fun of people. Like he was better or something."

"Do you know who he is?"

"Nope. Good thing, too. If I did I'd punch him in the nose."

Jeff tried the VISITORS locker room. It was exactly like the HOME TEAM room, even to the discarded clothing on the floor—but still no Alien.

Jeff went back to the playing field. To his surprise the mascot was already out there. Jeff tried to approach him a few times. The Alien kept his distance. Then a town policeman told Jeff to get off the field.

"Do you know who that guy is?" Jeff asked the cop, pointing.

"The mascot? Ask someone from the team. He works for them."

"I thought he worked for the town."

"No way."

During the game Jeff stayed on the third-base side of the field, paying almost no attention to baseball. He spent all his time watching the Alien. As the innings wound down, Jeff's tension mounted. At the top of the ninth, an easy fly ball to the Astros' center fielder provided the third out. The game was over. The Alien ran onto the field and gave the relief pitcher high fives. When the players from both teams lined up and shook hands, the Alien took his place at the end of the Astros' line and acted silly. The players seemed annoyed. Once the handshaking was done, and the players had run across the diamond toward the field house, the Alien went to the two umpires and offered to shake their hands, too. The umpires refused and hurried back to the field house.

The Alien was alone on the field. As Jeff studied him, the creature suddenly turned and stared at Jeff with its enormous eyes. This gave Jeff an odd sensation, as if the Alien was studying him. The next moment the mascot turned away and started toward the field house. Jeff ran after him.

"Hey, kid!"

Jeff stopped.

"No spectators down here." It was a groundskeeper.

"But . . . ," Jeff began. He swung back around to make sure the Alien was still in sight. He had vanished.

"Off the field, kid."

Jeff stared at where the mascot had been. "Where'd the Alien go?"

"Back to Mars, I hope," said the groundskeeper. "Now, beat it."

Jeff ran to the park entrance. He asked five different people if they had seen where the mascot had gone. No one knew.

How can he just disappear? Jeff wondered.

Jeff spent the whole next day trying to figure out a way to get to the Alien. By game time he had an idea. It required an assistant.

"I need some camera help," Jeff said to his friend Dave.

"Is it about the Alien?"

"Yeah."

"You are getting stupid about this," said his friend. "You know, nobody likes him but you. People think he's weird. Like you."

"Just help me," said Jeff as he handed over his cheap camera. "I'll pay your way into the game."

"It's your dime."

Jeff bought two tickets, and the boys went into the park. Game time was in half an hour. The mascot was already on the field, teasing the visiting team, the Duluth Diamondbacks, as they did infield warm-ups.

With Dave right behind, Jeff led the way. He waited till the Alien's back was turned. Then he crept quietly up and tapped him on the shoulder, which was soft and bouncy. "Excuse me," said Jeff.

The Alien spun about, his enormous eyes fixed on Jeff. He started to back away.

"Please!" cried Jeff. "Can I get my picture taken with you?" He gestured toward Dave, who held up the camera.

The Alien paused, then drew closer and threw his arms around Jeff, squeezing tightly. Very tightly.

Suddenly fighting for breath, Jeff pushed the arms off him. For a second the Alien squeezed some more, only to abruptly release the boy.

Gasping for breath, Jeff said, "Who . . . are you . . . *really*?"

Dave clicked the camera. The moment he did, the Alien shoved Jeff away and walked off in his funny fashion.

"Learn anything?" Dave asked.

"No," Jeff admitted. He rubbed his arms. They were sore. He looked at the retreating Alien. *Who is that guy?*

A week passed before Jeff went back to Rolerton Park because the Astros had gone off on a road trip. It was Labor Day weekend, and the last games of the season. If Jeff didn't find out about the Alien soon, he would have to wait until next year.

So he went to the game very early—but not in his usual way. Instead of taking a seat in the stands, he crept *under* the bleachers, which was hard to do. It took a while for Jeff's eyes to adjust to the murkiness of the area with its forest of metal stanchions holding up the seats. The place was littered with old paper cups, bottles—some broken—and discarded food. It stank, too. *It's like a rubbish dump,* Jeff thought. A part of Rolerton one did not see often.

Jeff looked through the bleacher seats onto the field. He was so early he could see a few of the players doing stretches. A groundskeeper was moving around the bases, anchoring bags to their proper places. Jeff read the sign on the low wooden fence that ringed the outfield: TO VISIT AMERICA—VISIT ROLERTON! The Alien wasn't in sight.

Because he was sure he could not be seen, Jeff decided his spot was perfect. The Alien would not know he was there, watching. Jeff kept scanning the field in hopes he would see the mascot emerge from his place—wherever it was.

As Jeff stood there, staring out to the bright field, he heard a soft scraping sound. At first he ignored it, but when it persisted, Jeff looked about, puzzled. With a start, he realized the sound was coming from a pile of discarded hot dog boxes. Or rather, from *under* the boxes.

Jeff watched. The boxes were moving, rising and falling as if something was pushing up from *below*. Then the top box slid to one side, revealing a dark spot beneath. Jeff—his heart beating fast—realized the spot was a *hole* in the ground.

The boxes continued to shift, revealing more of the hole.

In the gloom, Jeff began to see something pink move *within* the hole. He could not tell what it was, though it reminded him of cotton candy—soft, without any particular shape, a blob.

Jeff, realizing he was holding his breath, sucked in some air and stepped back. He told himself he should get out of there. *This is not right.* Even as he had the thought, the upper part of the pink blob began to shape itself into a thin tendril.

Jeff watched, transfixed. The tendril elongated and began to creep—still connected to the main blob—snakelike, over the ground, coiling itself around one of the bleacher stanchions. Having established a grip, the tendril began to ripple until the pink shape began to emerge from the hole—as if it were being pulled. It was only moments before an entire pink mass had emerged—looking, Jeff thought, like a compact, throbbing brain.

Too amazed to move, hardly daring to breathe, a mesmerized Jeff stared at the *thing,* as still another tendril emerged from the mass. That tendril crept down into the hole. Within moments it pulled up a lumpish green mass with red spots. It was, Jeff realized, the Alien *costume.*

Once the oufit was completely out of the ground, the pink tendril pulled down a zipper on the back. The costume fell open, exposing a dark interior. The next moment the whole pink mass slid inside.

Jeff watched as the zipper closed from within. After a moment's pause, the costume trembled, heaved, shook, stood up, and turned around.

"So you finally found me," the Alien said, looking right at Jeff. The voice was thick, clotted.

"Wh—what are you?" Jeff managed to ask.

"A student."

"A *student*? From . . . where?"

"Very far away. What you people call outer space." The Alien's nose and horns lit up.

"What are you . . . doing in that suit?" asked Jeff.

"I use it to study your world."

"*Study?*"

"To observe humans."

"What's that supposed to mean?"

"I'm here to learn about your natural habitat, your way of life. What you consume for food. Your social activities. That sort of thing."

"Why?"

"Curious."

"Are you the only . . . student?"

"The only one in Rolerton," said the Alien. "But

in other—what do you call them? . . . sport parks—there are lots of us."

"You mean," cried Jeff, "all those mascots at all those baseball and football games . . . they have . . . things . . . like you in them?"

"The perfect disguise," said the Alien as his nose lit up. "That way we get to see you at the activity and place that is most important to your lives—your fun and games."

"And you live right *here*?" asked Jeff. "All the time? Under the stands?"

"I don't think Rolerton would be pleased to know about me," said the Alien. "Too much the outsider. Too curious. So I stay. Everything I need is here."

"Everything? What about food? I mean, do you eat this junk?"

"I only eat once a year. Since I'm here just for the season, I'll be gone in a few days. Next season it'll be another student like me. Not that anyone will know about it—except you."

"But . . . what if I tell?" asked Jeff.

"You won't," said the Alien.

"Why?"

"Because," said the Alien, "it's time for my annual meal."

And before Jeff could react, the creature's twenty-fingered hands shot out and grabbed him. Jeff struggled, but the Alien's grip was too tight. The costume zipper opened. Pink tendrils whipped out and wrapped around the boy. In a matter of moments Jeff was pulled into the costume. The zipper slid shut.

The costume bulged here, there, here again, and then ceased to move. Then the Alien went out onto the field for the game.

The Astros won.

Jeff was lost.

Inquiries were made. Rolerton's police chief was puzzled. The town didn't lose too many kids, hardly more than one a year.

Usually it was right around the last day of Rolerton's baseball season. Curious.

THE SHOEMAKER AND OLD SCRATCH

THERE ONCE WAS A POOR SHOEMAKER who had little more than the tools of his trade. Not having a place to work, he searched everywhere until he found a very small and dilapidated house. But no sooner did he move in than he discovered the house was overrun with mice. They chewed holes in his leather, drank his glue, and made nests with his thread.

Frustrated, the shoemaker sat upon his front steps to ponder what he could do. After a while a black cat with lemon-colored eyes appeared.

Ah, thought the shoemaker, *the very creature to do the work.*

The shoemaker introduced himself to the cat, explaining that he was a poor maker of shoes who had recently moved into the house only to find it full of mice. "If you get rid of those mice," he said to the cat, "I'll pay you very well."

"How well?" asked the cat.

"Rid my house of mice," said the shoemaker, "and I'll share all my earnings with you."

"How about fifty-fifty?" asked the cat.

"Fifty-fifty," agreed the shoemaker.

"Forever and ever?"

"Forever and ever."

"Deal," said the cat, and she offered a paw, which the shoemaker shook with great solemnity.

The cat went to work. Within a week there was not one mouse to be found in the house.

"Wonderful!" said the shoemaker. "Now I can set down to do my work."

Not only did the shoemaker do that, he soon became quite successful. Each day, however, he waited until he was sure the black cat was sleeping, counted the money he had made, and hid it under the floorboards. He was quite certain the cat did not notice.

One year to the day from when the shoemaker and the cat had made their bargain, the cat announced it was time for her to receive what the shoemaker had promised—half of his earnings.

"Oh, don't be silly," the shoemaker said to the cat. "A cat has no need for money. Besides, you only worked a week. I've worked a whole year. You should be content with a sunny window and the saucer of milk I leave for you each day."

"What about 'forever and ever'?" said the cat.

"Things change," said the shoemaker.

"But a bargain is a bargain," the cat protested.

"Things change," repeated the shoemaker.

The black cat stared up at the shoemaker with her lemon-colored eyes, put up her tail, and went out for a walk. When she returned she did not speak of the matter. In fact, she never spoke to the shoemaker again—not once.

A few days later—it was evening—the shoemaker returned home after delivering some shoes he had made. All he wished to do was get inside his house, count the money he'd earned, hide it away, and then eat the splendid dinner he'd prepared for himself.

Much to his surprise the front door to his house would not open. He tried the rear door, as well as the windows. Nothing budged. He threw a rock at a window. The rock bounced away. Finally he called inside to the cat to open the door, but the cat did not come.

Frustrated, the shoemaker sat down on the front steps of his house and tried to think of what to do. As he sat there he heard sounds coming from inside. Putting his ear to the door, he listened. The shoemaker was sure *someone* was inside. He knocked on the door.

"Who's there?" came a voice from within. The shoemaker had never heard such a voice—it rumbled like a barn fire. All the same, he answered, "It's me, the shoemaker."

"What do you want?" the voice demanded.

"What do *I* want?" the shoemaker said. "Why, this is my house. I want to get in."

"You may do so."

"The door won't open."

"I have opened it," said the voice.

The shoemaker put his hand on the door, and this time he was able to unlatch it. He walked in.

Sitting at his table—the remains of the shoemaker's dinner before him—was the strangest person the shoemaker had ever seen. One moment the man was thin. The next moment he was fat. Then he became thin again. When first seen, the man seemed very tall, but within the space of an eyeblink he became quite short. One moment his hair was red, then gray, and then the man became bald. He had a beard. He had no beard. He had a stub nose. No, his nose was long! It was as if the man sitting behind the shoemaker's table was not one man but many men, yet in the end he was but one.

"Who are you?" the shoemaker demanded.

The man behind the table studied the shoemaker

as if to evaluate him. Even as he looked, he changed into a hundred different shapes. But at last he said, "I am the Devil. But if you prefer, you can call me by my more familiar name, 'Old Scratch.'"

"Why are you called Old Scratch?"

"Oh, it's nothing you need bother yourself about, that," said Old Scratch. "Not *now,* anyway."

"Then why do you take on such different shapes?"

"Things change."

"Well then, Old Scratch, why have you come here? And, by the way, where is my cat?"

Old Scratch offered thirteen kinds of smiles, and said, "I have just been playing with your black cat. Lovely creature. Beautiful eyes. We shared your supper. But then we are good friends."

The shoemaker looked about. The cat was asleep on the stranger's lap—or was it his knee, perhaps his shoulder?

"You had no right to do so," said the shoemaker. "That's my dinner, and my cat."

"But you see," said Old Scratch, "my occupation

is to go from house to house throughout the world and pick and choose as best I may."

"Why choose me?"

"Well now," Old Scratch said, "you're not a very important person. You can barely feed yourself and your cat. At least your cat told me you had no money. Is that true?"

"Absolutely."

"By the by, is this cat a partner of yours?"

"Nothing of the kind," said the shoemaker.

"I see," said Old Scratch, as he changed his shape, size, and look. "Well then, since you have nothing worth taking, I thought I should take your cat. Unless, of course, you want her. You could bargain with me. I'm always willing to bargain."

"I've already told you," said the shoemaker, "I've nothing to give. So if you must, take the cat."

"Ah, so that's how you care for old friends!" cried Old Scratch. "Consider my offer a test." As he spoke his head grew long, short, fat, and then thin. "And since you have failed that test, it's *you* I'll take."

The shoemaker became alarmed.

Old Scratch smiled—or was the smile a frown, or a grin, or a pout—and said, "Perhaps you would prefer some kind of bargain which will give you a chance to stay."

"Yes, a bargain!" cried the shoemaker, determined to outwit this changeable fellow.

"I'd like that," said Old Scratch. "You are a maker of shoes. From time to time—considering how much I travel—I need shoes. Would you be willing to try your skills on me?"

What a fool this fellow is, thought the shoemaker. *If there is one thing I can do, it's make shoes.* He said, "That sounds like an excellent idea."

"Here's my deal," said Old Scratch. "Things change, so I shall visit you three times. I shall visit you small. I shall visit you tall. I shall visit you one and all. Each time I come, if you can find a way to put shoes on my feet, I'll not take you. But if ever you can*not* shod me, it's you and your soul I'll take."

The shoemaker, quick as anything, said, "I accept."

The bargain made, Old Scratch vanished.

As for the black cat, she woke up, stretched, and then looked coolly at the shoemaker with her lemon-colored eyes.

Days, months, years passed. After the shoemaker made his bargain with Old Scratch, his fortunes changed much for the better. He began to greatly prosper. He married well. He and his wife had healthy, happy children.

During all this time the shoemaker was not visited by Old Scratch. In fact, so much time went by without his seeing or hearing from him, the shoemaker began to think his bargain was nothing more than a dream. *There's nothing to fear from him!*

As for the black cat—she remained.

One afternoon—it was a hot and lazy summer day—as the shoemaker worked at his bench, a fly began to buzz about his head. Finding it very annoying, the shoemaker tried to brush it away with his hand, but it didn't work. Finally the fly landed right before him on his workbench.

The shoemaker picked up a shoe. He was just about to bring it down on the fly when the insect called out: "Would you kill me, Shoemaker?"

The shoemaker was so startled, he could neither move nor speak.

"Why would you want to kill me?" asked the fly.

"Forgive me," said the shoemaker, thinking, *Where have I heard this voice before?* Then he said, "I didn't stop to consider you might have feelings on the subject."

"Things change," said the fly. "But no one likes to die."

"I apologize," said the shoemaker as he put the shoe he was working on aside.

The fly cocked his head and looked up at the shoemaker. "Does it mean nothing to you that I have no shoes and must go barefoot all the time?"

The shoemaker looked closely at the fly. It was true: The fly had no shoes. At that very moment he realized who the fly was: Old Scratch.

"Yes," said the fly with a chuckle, as if reading the shoemaker's thoughts, "this time, as promised, I am visiting you small. Can you make me shoes?"

The shoemaker remembered his bargain. Knowing he had no choice, he said, "Yes, I can make shoes for you."

"Then do so," said the fly. "And, as you can see, I require three pairs."

The shoemaker set to work. First he measured each of the fly's feet. They were so small he could hardly see what he was doing. Next he cut the necessary leather. What tiny bits they were!

The fly—promising to return when the shoes were done, *if* they were done—flew off.

The shoemaker worked with infinitesimal stitches to make the shoes. Three pairs. It took the shoemaker a year to make them. In addition, his eyes had become so sore as he made the shoes, he could no longer see: He had become blind.

However, no sooner were the shoes complete than the fly returned. "I'm back!" he announced.

The shoemaker fit the shoes to the fly. "There,"

he said with pride, for he had done what he was sure Old Scratch did not think he could do. "I've kept the bargain."

"Things change," said the fly. And he flew off.

As for the black cat, she with the lemon-colored eyes, she slept in a snug and sunny corner, purring blissfully.

Though the shoemaker did not regain his sight, his skills had grown so much while he made the tiny shoes that he no longer *needed* to see. So great was the dexterity and preciseness of his work, he became very famous for making the finest, most delicate of shoes. In addition, he grew quite rich.

More time passed, so much time that the shoemaker began to think his bargain with Old Scratch had been fulfilled.

But one fine fall day—when the air was crisp and cool—while the blind shoemaker was working on a pair of shoes for a duchess, he heard a sound he could not identify. The sound was heavy and rough. Every time it came, the workshop floor shook as if it were atop an earthquake.

Because the shoemaker was blind, he could not see who (or what) was causing such a commotion. "Who's there?" he called.

No reply.

The shoemaker went back to his work thinking that perhaps he had dozed off and had only imagined the sounds. The next moment more crashing and thrashing interrupted him. Now the shoemaker knew something (or someone) *was* there. "Tell me what you are!" he demanded.

Still, no answer.

The shoemaker became angry. He picked up one of his razor-sharp leather cutters, and was about to fling it in the direction from which the sound came, when a voice boomed, "Would you kill me?"

"Who are you?" demanded the shoemaker.

"I am," answered a great voice, "a creature of change. I thought you might know me."

The shoemaker instantly recognized the voice

of Old Scratch. "Forgive me," he said. "I didn't realize it was you."

"Forgive you?" said Old Scratch. "You might have killed me with that sharp cutter of yours. Think of all my friends who would have missed me."

"I'm truly sorry," said the shoemaker, wondering what part of the bargain he would have to fulfill now.

The great voice went on. "It is even worse for me when you consider the great distance I have to go, and yet I have no shoes upon my feet."

"What happened to the ones I made you?"

"Souls and soles both will wear."

"Would you like me to make you new shoes?" asked the shoemaker, knowing very well what the answer would be.

Sure enough the voice replied, "I have visited you small. Now I visit you tall. Yes, I'd like shoes upon my feet. Can you do it? Happily, today my feet number only four."

"I'm sure I can make them," said the shoemaker.

That said, he climbed off his workbench and groped his way to the sound of the voice, feeling for the feet. It was just as Old Scratch had said. He had four feet—but each foot was as big as a house!

When the shoemaker measured the huge feet—it took three days to do so—Old Scratch lumbered off, promising to return when the shoes were done, *if* they were done. The shoemaker purchased all the leather he could find, hundreds and hundreds of yards, and set to work.

As for the black cat, she merely watched.

So big, so heavy were the shoes that the shoemaker made, each took a year to construct. Still, at the end of those four years—working every day, some nights, plus holidays, election days, and one extra leap-year day—the shoemaker made the four shoes. Hardly had they been made when Old Scratch returned. The shoemaker fitted the shoes, and they fit wonderfully well.

Old Scratch thanked the shoemaker for his work. "Well done," he said. "I can almost forgive you for thinking of throwing that cutter at me." Then off he clumped, the ground trembling with every step he took.

Unfortunately, all the shoemaker's hard work making the huge shoes had crippled his hands. They had become so tired, so weak, during the four years, he could hardly cut a piece of paper, let alone leather. He could not even pick up a needle.

Unable to work for himself anymore, the shoemaker had to employ others. No great hardship there. His fame as a skilled shoemaker had spread so widely, he attracted many an apprentice, all of whom he instructed. He did it very well, too. He became richer than he had ever been before. The whole world seemed to desire shoes made under his direction.

So, though the shoemaker was blind and could no longer use his hands, he thought his bargain was not a bad one—and that he had fulfilled his promise. Had he not outdone Old Scratch?

As for the black cat, she with the lemon-colored eyes, she continued to doze her days away in a sunny window.

———

The shoemaker's life went on. As time passed he quite forgot that his bargain—like all good old bargains that had been bargained since time began—had *three* parts. That did not change.

One bitterly cold winter's day—when he was sitting in his warm shop, listening to the whistling wind outside and feeling quite content to be inside—the shoemaker heard a knock on his door.

"I'm sorry!" called the shoemaker. "I cannot open the door for you. My hands are too weak and I am blind. Please let yourself in."

The door opened. Bone-numbing cold filled the workroom.

"Be so good as to make yourself and your business known!" said the shoemaker.

"My voice should tell you all," came the reply.

In an instant the shoemaker knew then that it was Old Scratch. He knew, too, that Old Scratch had come to visit him for the third and final time. He was not afraid. Had he not outwitted Old Scratch each previous visit? He was sure he could do so again.

"Well then," he said, "what brings you to me this time?"

"No more than we bargained," returned Old Scratch. "Things change. The shoes I've been wearing have traveled so far they've dwindled to nothing."

"Have you thought of retiring?" asked the shoemaker. "That would certainly cheer up many."

"To tell the truth," said Old Scratch, "I'd like to. But I fear retirement would be dull. No, the work I do isn't pleasant, but . . . well, somebody has to do it. Fortunately, I make bargains such as I've made with you. They keep me amused. In fact, I really have no time to chat. I've come to make my last request."

"Request away," said the shoemaker.

"This time," said Old Scratch, "I must have shoes for me as I truly am."

"That's all very well for you to ask," returned the shoemaker. "But how do you expect me to make shoes for you when I can't see what you are?"

"No eye is so blind it cannot see the likes of *me*," said Old Scratch. "Look up!"

The shoemaker looked up. And he *saw* Old

Scratch just as he had been before, a constantly changing man. He was tall, he was short, he was thin and fat. All at once and all the time, he wore a thousand different fashions of every color and hue.

"Yes," the shoemaker said at last, "I can see you. But because of you, my hands have become quite useless. I can make nothing. That's *not* very fair, is it?"

"I suppose not," said Old Scratch. "But I assure you, no old hand is so old it can't feel my presence. Reach out. You'll be able to feel *me.*"

The shoemaker did as told. It was as Old Scratch said: He was there, and a very cold *there* at that. "Very well," said the shoemaker. "What must I do for you?"

"Only as you promised," said Old Scratch. "I have visited you small. I have visited you tall. Now I visit you as one and all." So saying, he held out one of his feet. The shoemaker took hold of it. Even as he did the foot changed. First it was wide, then narrow. Then it became short, only to become long. It had five toes. It had sixteen. It turned into a hoof. It had claws. It never stopped changing.

"Now then," said Old Scratch in his most pleasant voice. "Can you make a shoe that fits or not?"

"I think I can," said the shoemaker, trying to gain some time. "But I must work out a plan."

"I have waited long enough," said Old Scratch. His voice was not so pleasant as it had been.

"Three days," said the shoemaker.

"I can spare two," snapped Old Scratch. "I'll be back in forty-eight hours. If you do not have my shoes, then you must come with me." So saying, he went away.

Alone in his shop, the shoemaker thought and thought how he could make shoes for a foot that constantly changed. It seemed impossible. Oh, how he wished he had *not* made this bargain! But he had.

On the second day he began to have an idea, his sole idea. It would have to do.

Fortunately, Old Scratch had restored his vision and healed his hands. That night he labored on a pair of shoes for *himself*. The shoes fit so perfectly, so snugly, that there was *absolutely* no space between foot and leather. They were like a second skin, the best shoes he had ever made. When he had put them on, the exhausted shoemaker lay down to sleep.

As for the black cat, she with the lemon-colored eyes, she just waited, watched, and purred.

When the shoemaker awoke, there, standing before him, was Old Scratch. He was tall, he was short, he was thin and fat—all at once and all the time. "I hope you slept well," said Old Scratch. "You have a distance to go."

"I slept very well indeed, thank you," said the shoemaker. "But I don't plan on going anywhere."

"Do you have my shoes or not?" said Old Scratch. He had many expressions on his face. Not one of them included a smile.

"Almost," said the shoemaker.

"*Almost* is not good enough."

"That's to say," said the shoemaker, "the shoes are made. There is only the question of making them fit."

Old Scratch sneered. "I'm willing to try," he said.

The shoemaker reached down and took off one of his new shoes. He set it before Old Scratch.

"Do you mean to suggest that *this* shoe is for me?" growled Old Scratch.

"I do," said the shoemaker. "Of course, like all good shoes, they will take a little adjusting. Fortunately, you are of a type that can make these adjustments well."

"That's true," said Old Scratch, rather puzzled.

"Very well," said the shoemaker, "try it on."

Old Scratch took up the shoe. Even as he did, his foot grew as large as an elephant's. So though he attempted to put on the shoemaker's shoe, it did not fit. Old Scratch grinned. "I'm afraid you have failed at last. There is no way I can get my foot into this shoe of yours."

"Ah," said the shoemaker. "It must be something caught in the tip of the shoe that prevents you from getting all of your foot in. Try taking it out."

Old Scratch darted a quizzical look at the shoemaker, but nonetheless picked up the shoe and peered inside. "Nothing," he said.

"Search harder," said the shoemaker.

Old Scratch shook the shoe. Nothing fell out.

He reached in. He found nothing. "Empty," he proclaimed.

"You're not looking hard enough," insisted the shoemaker. "You know how skilled I am in my trade. That shoe will fit but only if you are willing to try."

"You're a stupid man after all," Old Scratch snapped. "There is nothing here!"

"Perhaps," said the shoemaker, "you are too big at the moment to reach in. I thought Old Scratch could go anywhere. I guess I was wrong."

Old Scratch was stung by these words. It must be said, he was nothing if not vain. "Of course I can go anywhere!" he cried. "No place is too big or too small for the likes of *me*!" So saying, he made himself small enough to jump into the shoe.

The second he did, the shoemaker grabbed the shoe, pulled it on, and laced it up, trapping Old Scratch against the bottom of the shoe. The shoe fit so tightly, so perfectly, not even Old Scratch could get free.

"Let me out!" he cried.

Instead of answering, the shoemaker opened the

door of his house and began to run as fast as he could. Every time he came down on that foot, he squashed Old Scratch against the bottom of the shoe. Each time he did, Old Scratch shouted, "Ouch! Free me!"

"Not until you release *me* from my bargain," replied the shoemaker.

"Never!" returned Old Scratch, who made up his mind to wait until the shoemaker became tired.

The shoemaker, however, had not run for years and years, so he had lots of energy and strength. Hour after hour, day after day, month after month, he ran.

Seriously pounded, Old Scratch began to think of what he might do to get out of his predicament. It took him a while, but at last he had an idea. He turned himself into an itch.

At first it was a very mild itch—a small, nibbling, wiggling, tickling, crawly sort of an itch. What's more, it settled itself right beneath the shoemaker's smallest toe. At first the shoemaker was not sure what had happened to Old Scratch. He began to

think that Old Scratch was gone, that he had outwitted him. That was good, because he had begun
to feel a tiny little itch right there beneath his little
toe, quite the hardest place of all to scratch.

The shoemaker tried to ignore the itch, hoping
it would go away. The itch persisted. It grew worse.
It began to crawl up and down along the sole of his
foot with a prickly, stickly, tickly, highly irritating
sensation that never ceased.

As the shoemaker ran, he tried to stamp his foot
down extra hard. The itch stayed. The shoemaker
rubbed his itching foot atop his other foot. The itch
stayed.

Finally the shoemaker sat down. Was the itch
gone? No! It was twice as bad as before. It was as if
twenty little fingers with cracked fingernails were
plucking, poking, picking, and tickling him.

Desperate, the shoemaker began to take off his
shoe. As he did he heard a laugh. As soon as the
shoemaker heard the laugh, he realized that the itch
was Old Scratch. The shoemaker began to run
again.

The itch would not go away. The more the shoemaker refused to scratch, the worse it got. It began to drive him crazy.

He tried to run faster. That did not help. He tried stopping. No better. He plunged his foot in cold water. Nothing. In hot water. Nothing. He ran on ice. He ran on hot coals. Nothing could get rid of the itch!

The shoemaker began to think that if only he could stop for *one* moment—just one small, tiny, infinitesimal moment—and get to that itch, all would be saved.

He had to try.

He stopped. He sat down. He set the foot with its itch before him. He bent over. He unlaced the shoe. He reached down. He counted to ten. One-two-three-four-five-six-seven-eight-nine-ten! Fast as anything, he tipped off his shoe and started to scratch that itch! *Ahhhhh!*

No sooner did the shoemaker do that than Old Scratch jumped out of the shoe, became full size, and dragged the shoemaker away.

"Now you know two things: why I'm called Old Scratch and that some things definitely *don't* change."

But what ever did happen to that black cat, she with the lemon-colored eyes? Why, she was back in the shoemaker's house. When she learned what had happened to the shoemaker—*how* she learned, I don't know—she took from beneath the floorboards one-half—not a penny more, not a penny less—of the money the shoemaker had made. For that was the exact bargain *they* had made so many years ago.

Then the black cat, she with the lemon-colored eyes, went away. Where she went, I don't know.

SIMON

AS AN ONLY CHILD, Simon was indulged by both his mother and father to such a degree that he grew up to be someone who always assumed he was the center of attention. As Simon grew older, he found that he could charm anyone with his bright looks and sharp wit. Though he always managed to avoid doing anything that might be of help or use to his parents, he was quite comfortable in demanding and taking food, clothing, or pleasure—as much as he wished. It didn't matter to him that his parents had little money: No wish or whim of Simon's went unanswered.

As Simon grew into manhood, his demands grew, too. Nothing but the finest would satisfy him. He constantly groomed himself. He dressed lavishly. No surprise that he came to believe people could do no better than admire him.

To the question "What do you want to do with your life?" he would say, "I intend to have the world gaze upon me with admiration and envy."

One of the things Simon had asked for and received was a rifle. From the moment he had the gun in his hands, Simon's chief desire was to become known as the best hunter in the land.

Such were Simon's demands that after a while his parents grew quite poor. When the time came that they could give him no more, Simon became angry. "You are unappreciative parents," he told them. "I must have only the best."

"Simon," said his poor father, "for all I know what you say may be true. But we have nothing left to give you."

To which his mother added: "Your wants and demands have quite ruined us. If you desire more, you must get it elsewhere—and you must get it for yourself."

At these words Simon picked up his rifle and left home without so much as a farewell. Though his mother and father wept to see him go, Simon did not even look back.

Simon journeyed to a village near a great forest. This forest was famous for its wild animals, so Simon decided to become a hunter. He was sure that by selling what he killed, he could earn enough money for his wants and needs.

All Simon's energies now turned to hunting. He was very good at it. It did not take long before the sound of him coming through the forest was enough to bring terror to all the creatures that lived there. They knew that Simon was an excellent shot, that he was greedy, and that he had no mercy.

One day when Simon brought his slaughter to the marketplace, a merchant said, "Simon, you do very well with what you bring me. But let me give you some advice: As great as is the demand for furs and hides, what the rich really want these days are *feathers.* Not *ordinary* feathers, but gloriously colored ones. The kind you can only find in the deepest parts of the forest. A good shot like you should have no trouble with that. Bring me such feathers, and you shall become truly rich!"

That was enough for Simon. Rifle in hand, he set off into the forest and began hunting birds. He shot hundreds of them, stripped them of their plumage, and left their carcasses to rot. As for the feathers, he sold them to the merchant.

As the merchant had promised, Simon soon grew not only rich but also quite famous in that part of the world. He was not satisfied. Wanting everyone to look upon him with awe, he hunted even more.

As Simon brought in more and more wonderful feathers, the demand for them actually grew. Not only were greater quantities in demand, but he was paid higher prices for the most unusual kinds.

One day Simon's merchant friend said, "Simon, it is believed that in the most remote part of the forest lives the Queen-of-All-the-Birds. Her feathers—

so the rumor goes—have the look, the feel of pure gold. She's known as the Golden Bird. Fetch me *her* feathers and you shall be the wealthiest of men. The entire world shall sit up and take notice of you."

His head bursting with visions of wealth and glory, Simon set off in pursuit of the Golden Bird. Though he traveled where few hunters had been, the Golden Bird never passed before his eyes. Simon kept searching.

One day he found himself in the most tangled part of the forest. As he stood looking about, his hunting bag full of feathers, he caught sight of what appeared to be like gold among the trees. Not sure at first that he was seeing correctly, he stealthily approached the glitter.

It *was* a bird but a bird such as he had never seen before. Her beak was blue, sharp, and precise. Her feet were crimson. On her head a jet black crown. But in the rays of light that filtered down among the many-fingered branches, her golden wings sparkled brighter than the sun itself.

The moment Simon saw this bird he was certain she was the Queen-of-All-the-Birds, the Golden Bird herself. Instantly his mind was filled with thoughts of the money and fame he was sure to get after he killed her and stripped her feathers.

Rifle in hand, Simon inched forward. The bird did not seem to notice. She even fluttered down to a closer branch.

Simon crept to within a few feet of the bird. Silently he lifted his rifle and took precise aim at her breast. Just as he was about to squeeze the trigger, the bird turned to him and quite calmly said, "Why do you want to shoot me, Simon?"

Simon, never taking the Golden Bird out of his gun sight, said, "Because I need your feathers."

"You don't *need* them," the bird replied. "In any case, they are not yours to have."

"The world is there for me to take," replied Simon. "When I take what I want, everybody shall take notice of me."

"*Everybody?*" the bird asked.

"*Everybody,*" Simon insisted.

"Then," the bird replied, "I shall help you achieve what you want." With a sudden flutter of her great wings, she sprang upon Simon.

Even as she did, Simon pulled the trigger. The gun fired. The bullet struck true, piercing the Golden Bird's heart. Still, she had sufficient strength to just reach Simon. As she fell, one wing brushed over his face and neck. Then she lay at his feet.

At the same moment, all the leaves from all the trees fell, too, cascading down like the sound of rain— or tears. The forest grew as silent as a cloudless sky.

Simon looked around. Hundreds of birds were sitting on the now leafless branches, gazing mutely at him and the Golden Bird, which lay on the ground before his feet.

Simon merely gazed back. When the birds did nothing, he shrugged, snatched up the dead Golden Bird by the neck, and stuffed her into his hunting bag. Turning his back on the silent, watching birds, Simon started off. His mind was already trying to calculate how much he would get for the golden feathers.

As Simon walked through the forest, he began to hear high-pitched sounds. He paid them no mind. But as the sounds continued, he realized that his name was being called. "Simon!" "Simon!" "Simon!"

Simon stopped. He looked about in search of the people who were calling his name. He saw no humans. It was the birds that were following him.

A little nervous now, Simon continued on.

"Simon!" "Simon!" This time the calls came from directly overhead.

Simon stopped and looked up. The birds he had seen before were gone. Now, barely four feet above him, three black ravens had come to rest upon the branches of a dead tree. Their bright beady eyes, like burning black candles with shiny black flames, were hard focused on Simon.

"Is it a bird or a man?" Simon heard one of the ravens whisper. The voice was high and shrill.

"Ask it," suggested the second raven. Its voice was smooth.

Simon, puzzled that he could understand what the birds were saying to one another, paused to listen.

The third raven hopped along the leafless branch until it dipped and, like an accusing finger, hung a few inches from Simon's face. Cocking its head now this way and now that, the third raven, in a low voice said, "What are you, Simon, bird or man?"

"I am a man, of course," Simon replied.

"And yet," said the first raven, "you speak to us."

To which the second raven added, "What is more, Simon, your neck is like the neck of a bird."

"For *that* matter," the third raven concluded, "so is your head."

Taken aback, Simon put a hand to his neck—to his face. It was just as the ravens had said: From his neck up he was all . . . feathers! What's more, that neck, which had grown to a considerable length, supported an oval-shaped head.

Simon felt his eyes. They were perfectly round and set on either side of his face. Where his nose and mouth had been, he felt a long pointed beak.

Still, when he looked down at himself, the rest of his body remained as it had been—human.

Frightened, Simon dropped his rifle and sack and tried to rub away the feathers.

"We say you are a bird," screamed the ravens. "You are no more a man than we. And you killed the Golden Bird!"

Screaming, the ravens fell upon Simon, pulling and clawing at him. So fierce was the attack that Simon ran off into the forest as fast as he could go. The ravens pursued him so until Simon had to force his way into thick thorny underbrush that was too tangled for them to follow.

The three ravens flew away. As they went, Simon heard them calling his name. "Simon—Simon—Simon." It sounded as if they were laughing.

When he was sure he was safe, Simon crawled out from his hiding place. Having no idea where he was, he began to search for a way out of the forest. All that day and night, he wandered.

At night, by the light of a full moon, he came

upon a pool of water. Thirsty, he paused and bent down. Reflected upon the surface of the pool, mirrorlike, he saw an image of himself. From his neck up—wherever the Golden Bird had touched him with her wing—he had turned into a bird.

Simon stared at his image. At first he tried to tell himself that it was all a dream, that he would wake up and be what he had always been. Even as he tried to convince himself of this, a pack of hunting dogs, howling and baying, leaped out of the bushes and attacked him.

To protect himself, Simon sprang onto a large boulder. The dogs—baying, snapping, and growling—could not reach him. But nonetheless, he was trapped.

Simon was still standing on the rock above the snarling dogs, trying to think how to make his escape, when a group of hunters appeared. They carried rifles and torches. When the hunters saw Simon atop the rock, they stopped short, amazed by his appearance.

After a moment one of the hunters lifted his gun, and was about to fire, when Simon called, "Don't shoot!"

If the hunters had been amazed at the *sight* of Simon, they were even more astonished that the strange creature could *talk*.

"Are you man or bird?" called one of the hunters.

"I am a man!" insisted Simon, relieved to know that though he had understood the talk of birds, he could still speak a human tongue.

"Friend or enemy?" called another hunter.

"Friend to all!" cried Simon.

From somewhere he thought he heard the laughter of the ravens.

"Lift your hands, or wings, or whatever they are!" one of the hunters shouted. "And come down here."

"Call off your dogs," said Simon.

When the dogs were pulled away, Simon climbed down from the rock and approached the hunters. Only then did he realize that one of them had a crown on his head. He was a prince.

"Who are you?" asked the prince, staring with amazement at Simon.

"I am Simon."

"Well then, *what* are you?"

"Through no fault of mine," said Simon, "magic has turned me into what you see."

"I know nothing of magic," said the prince. "But I do know you are the most curious spectacle I have ever seen! You must come with me. Others will enjoy the sight of you."

Simon objected, but the prince would hear no refusal.

Suddenly fearful of what might happen, Simon turned and tried to run away. Two hunters sprang after him, caught him with ease, and held him tightly. They tied Simon's hands behind his back and placed a rope around his neck. Holding this rope, they led him through the woods.

Simon, shocked and hurt to be so badly treated, demanded to be set free. The prince took no interest in what he said. Quite the contrary. Though the hunters kept gawking and talking about him, these men acted as if Simon were incapable of any understanding.

Once, twice, Simon tried to pull on the rope that held him. For his efforts he received a sharp, painful yank. He had to go along.

The hunters reached their camp. Many people were there, men and women of the court. Some were dressed in furs and feathers; Simon recognized these as adornments he had supplied.

Very excited, the courtiers gathered around Simon, looked at him, poked him, treating him as if—marvel though he might be—he were no more than a dumb beast.

Enraged, Simon cursed at them all. This made the people laugh and tease him more, for they found him to be very funny. At last, for the sake of his own pride, Simon decided to say nothing.

When it was time to eat, a great feast was served to all the court. Simon, tied up, could do nothing but watch. No one seemed to consider that he might like to join the festivities. True, from time to time people at the prince's table threw him bits of food. Simon, who was used to eating at a table, at first refused to eat from the ground. But when his hunger grew to be too much, he tried to pick up a few morsels when no one was looking. The rope, however, held him short. He had to stretch his neck forward and peck at the ground. When people noticed, they found his antics amusing, and laughed. Simon stopped eating.

At the feast the prince announced that because he was sure he would find nothing more wonderful than the half-man, half-bird he had caught, his hunt was over. He ordered a cage to be built. Simon was forced inside.

It was not a very big cage. Simon could only sit, and he had to hold the bars to keep his balance. Sometimes a fury took hold of Simon and he shook the bars, causing laughter that made him furious. But there was nothing he could do about it.

The next morning when the prince's party was ready to move on, the cage, with Simon in it, was loaded onto a cart and pulled along with all the other baggage. Simon, in his cage, was displayed as the supreme trophy.

For three days the prince and his party traveled. To Simon's great mortification, he was the center of attraction in every town through which they passed. Because they were going from the country to the city, they went through larger and larger towns. News of the bird-man had gone ahead. Larger and larger crowds came to stare, to cheer, to jeer and poke fun.

Simon glowered at his tormentors. Secretly, he plotted all the malevolent things he would do to them when he got free.

At last the traveling party came to a great city. The prince was led in triumph to his palace through large crowds.

In anticipation of Simon's arrival, an elaborate cage had been built. Simon was forced into it. Then the cage, with him inside, was hoisted into the air and hung like a chandelier in the very center of the court. That way he could be viewed by everyone at every hour.

Sometimes people prodded at him, or banged on the cage to get a reaction. Occasionally Simon would lose his temper. That made people laugh. He screamed insults at them. More laughter. Though people were at first amused, it did not take long for them to take offense—and then lose interest. His cage was placed in a corner by a window. He was ignored.

Days passed. Simon grew sullen. He would not talk or respond to anything or anybody.

Months went by. Simon had no view of the outside world except through a small window in the palace wall. This window looked out into the sky. The most Simon could see of the world was the changing weather.

One day a great banquet was held in the hall. In his cage Simon listened to the talk, the jokes, the songs. Growing restless, he turned to look through the window. Outside, a storm was raging. As Simon snapped at the occasional bit of food thrown to him, he thought that at least he was being fed, and he was dry and safe.

A small brown sparrow flew into the hall to take refuge from the storm. Exhausted, she rested on the window ledge. The sparrow fluffed out her feathers, shook her head dry, and began to preen her tail. Then she caught sight of Simon sitting in his cage.

Simon, though pretending not to, watched the sparrow eagerly.

The bird took a hop closer and studied Simon with great interest. "What ghastly weather!" she chirped.

Simon, grateful for a little friendly conversation, replied, "Yes, it looks it."

"Are you a bird?" the brown sparrow whispered.

Desperate for sympathy, Simon pressed against the bars of his cage, as close to the sparrow as possible. "I was a man," he replied. "But I was turned, partly, into a bird. Now I'm nothing but a creature in a cage for people to stare at and make fun of."

The sparrow settled down. "How did you come to be the way you are?" she asked

Simon told the sparrow how he had hunted

birds and sold their feathers. But then one day he had shot a most unusual bird and—

The sparrow rose up, her beak snapping with anger. "So *you* are the one who shot our Golden Queen!" she cried with fury. "You deserve all the punishment you have. I'd rather be out in the cold storm than warm inside with you." So saying, the sparrow turned and flew out the window.

Simon could only wish that he, too, could fly into the storm.

Two years went by. The prince, who had once prized Simon as his most curious possession, came to be interested in other things. The cage was moved from the central court to a distant room.

As much as Simon hated being looked upon and made fun of, he found his isolation worse. He had nothing to gaze upon but empty walls.

Occasionally the prince would come by and show Simon to a visitor. Desperate for company, Simon would snap his beak and do tricks, anything to keep the visitors a little longer.

The prince was not amused. He called Simon a vain creature and made a point of *not* staying long. His visits grew fewer, then stopped altogether.

Days went by without Simon seeing anyone.

At length the prince decided that keeping Simon was more trouble than it was worth. He came to Simon's cage and opened the door.

"Come out," said the prince. "No one is interested in looking at you anymore. You've become common. It's time for you to go."

An astonished Simon could hardly believe his ears. He thought the prince was simply playing a trick on him, and refused to leave. The prince had Simon yanked from the cage and unceremoniously thrown out of the palace—from the back door.

For the first time in two years, Simon was free. He was elated—at first. His moment of joy was brief. As he stood against the palace door, trying to think of what to do, a group of children found him. They made fun of him, called him names.

In a fury Simon bent down, picked up a stone, and threw it. His arm was weak. The stone fell short. The children laughed and mocked him all the more.

Simon ran away. As the day wore on, Simon began to feel a pain in his stomach that he knew was hunger. With anger and shock, he realized that the prince had put him out without food or money. He was homeless. With nothing to eat, he began to wish he were back in his safe cage.

As he walked along in search of food, he passed an open-air café. Stomach growling, he stopped and watched people eat.

Someone complained about his staring. The manager came out and tried to shoo him away.

"I only want something to eat," Simon begged.

"Do you think you get food for nothing?" replied the manager. "One has to work for it. Or is your brain as small as most birds'?"

"Please!" cried Simon. "It's just that I've not worked in an ordinary way. I've been on exhibition for the prince. I'm willing to do anything for food."

"Ah," said the manager. "You've led a soft life. But I have a kind heart. I'll make you an offer. With that long beak of yours, you should be good at picking up bits the way your fellow birds do. People are always leaving crumbs where they eat. Crumbs attract rats, and I hate rats. You can pick up the crumbs. My place will be clean, and you'll get something to eat."

Simon was revolted by the suggestion. He started to turn away.

"Where else are you going to get food?" asked the manager.

Simon, hearing his stomach growl, agreed to take the job.

The manager led Simon into the restaurant through the back way. He gave him a gray apron and placed a silly cap on his head. "You might as well amuse my patrons," he said. He pushed Simon out onto the floor and told him to get busy. "Don't assume you'll have this job forever," he warned. "If you don't work hard, you'll be gone!"

At first Simon hung back against the walls of the restaurant, pecking only at crumbs he found there. The bits of food whetted his appetite. He reached for more and more. The patrons were greatly amused. They began to throw food at him. Simon, unable to resist, gobbled greedily. People laughed.

Within a short time, Simon, in order to encourage the patrons and keep his job, began to perform tricks, jokes, and songs he had heard at the banquet tables of the prince.

This went over well—for a time. But before long the patrons, most of whom came to the café on a regular basis, grew annoyed. They grew tired of the same jokes, the same songs. They began to complain to the manager that the bird-man was a distraction. After a few complaints, Simon was told to leave.

In despair Simon left. Unable to think of any other place to go, he decided to return to his parents and beg for mercy.

For a week Simon traveled. He went through all the cities and towns he had passed on his way to the palace. He traveled by night so he would not be seen. Only when he grew hungry would he emerge into the light of day to do tricks on street corners for bits of bread.

When he came to the edge of his own village, he grew fearful. Ashamed to show himself, he waited until the day grew dark. When darkness came, he made his way through back alleys to his parents' house. He knocked on the door, timidly.

His mother opened the door. His father stood behind her. When they saw the strange creature, they were taken aback.

"May we help you?" his mother asked.

"I am your son, Simon."

The two old people looked at the creature on the doorstep with disbelief. Then they became angry.

"Our Simon," said his father, "was the most handsome of young men. He would dress in nothing but the best. But you, strange creature, your feathers are dirty, your clothing is ragged."

"Anyway," added his mother, "Simon would not come here. This house wasn't good enough for him. He went off to make his fortune, and no doubt has become rich and powerful. No, Simon wouldn't come back here."

"In fact," his father added, "I suspect that he sent you here to mock us!"

So saying, his parents slammed the door shut.

Heartbroken and exhausted, Simon made his way by cover of night into the forest. When he found a soft place beneath a tree, he lay down. He began to wish that he might never rise again.

Just as he was falling asleep, he heard the baying of hunting dogs. Instantly he remembered how he had been captured. He had not the slightest desire to be caught again.

To protect himself, he dashed deeper into the wood, running from the sound. Alas, no matter where he ran, the baying grew louder. First it was on one side of him, then on the other. He was surrounded.

Frantic, Simon plunged about in search of an escape. Suddenly he caught sight of a glimmer of gold springing among the leaves.

He ran forward. There, flitting from branch to branch, was the Golden Bird. In the moonlight he saw her just as he had seen her before—wings aglitter, black crown upon her head, red feet, blue beak sharp and precise.

Simon stood still, amazed to see the bird alive. Had he not killed her? As he was about to call out to her, he saw a hunter break from a thicket. The hunter raised his gun to his shoulder and aimed right at the Golden Bird.

Simon leaped forward. The bullet intended for the Golden Bird struck him. He fell.

The hunter, seeing a human form fall and fearing he had killed a man, turned and fled.

As Simon lay upon the ground dying, the forest became utterly still. He opened his eyes and looked up. The trees were covered with birds, all of which were staring at him. Among them was the Golden Bird. Simon gazed at her. "Is it really you?" he managed to ask. "The one I thought I killed?"

The Golden Bird fluttered down by his side. "Yes, it's me," she replied softly. "And you, are you the one whom all the world was to notice?"

"Yes," he whispered.

"And *did* the whole world take notice?"

After a moment Simon said, "Yes, but there was one who never noticed the world."

"Who was that?"

"Me," said Simon, and he closed his eyes.

In the forest nothing moved.

The Golden Bird swept her wings over Simon's body. As she did, Simon was again transformed. He became a bird—a complete bird—of great majesty. With another sweep of her wings, the Golden Bird brought Simon back to life.

The Golden Bird leaped into the air. And Simon followed, his great wings beating the dark night, flying by her side, free and whole at last.